HONEY IN LOUISIANA

HONEY IN LOUISIANA

TWO FULL NOVELS
HONEY AND *LOVE IN LOUISIANA*

JOHN B. THOMPSON & JACK WOODFORD

CUTTING EDGE

Paperback ISBN-13: 978-1-957868-15-8

Published by
Cutting Edge Books
PO Box 8212
Calabasas, CA 91372
www.cuttingedgebooks.com

HONEY

CHAPTER ONE

DOGWOOD CREEK, NAMED for the myriads of trees that blossom whitely along its banks in the spring, wanders carelessly through St. Louis Parish. A great deal of its wandering is quite senseless, with any number of double-back and blind crawlings.

On the Lock Ness Plantation, Dogwood runs through pasture-land and woods, always protected by at least a fringe of leafy trees which accounts for its extremely low temperature. It requires considerable nerve, of the sort small boys have in such quantity, to plunge into its cold depths even in summer.

The weather was hot and humid. Insects wandered lazily about and the birds were quiet. In the distance an ivory-billed woodpecker let go a volley of "wocks" and hammered out a message on the hollow gum snag where he perched in regal majesty. Beech trees, smothered in green foliage, told of the stillness of the air and even the stalwart magnolias whose leaves are nearly always noisy were silent and calm. Oak, pine, gum, and ironwood, dogwood and elm, all stood straight and still with not a twig betraying the passage of air. Through the shaded avenues among the trees trodden by the passage of cattle walked a slender slip of a girl. Her simple but clean cotton garment managed to acquire on her a look of magnificence, probably because it fitted well, and her slim but promising body filled it with a certain delicate sufficiency that was at the same time simple and delightful. Her loveliness was not of the sort that derives from garments or the application of false cosmetic outlines. She had the free, uninhibited stride of health. She walked down the trail cut by cattle hoofs to the creek, which was paralleled by a small beach of white clean sand.

With a sinuous motion she slipped out of her garment and, throwing it over an elderberry bush, walked with mincing theatrical steps to the edge of the water where she gingerly inserted a toe. She shivered a little and walked away to loll in the sand with the sun's fierce rays beating deliciously on her tan skin. She stretched with pagan freedom and breathed deeply the multitude of woodsy scents mingled with the odor of dank rotting wood. For a time she watched a lone kingfisher as he sat motionless on the branch of driftwood that lay across the stream.

With sudden resolution tightening her lips she leaped to her feet and dashed into the water. The kingfisher clattered with irritation and flew to another branch ten feet away where he eyed her for a moment then dozed again. She swam playfully about with strong graceful strokes, sending up showers of crystalline drops that glittered in the sun like sequins. She came out and sat in the sand, rubbing quantities of the abrasive on her thighs and stomach, her skin prickling from its rough bite.

A face appeared behind her above the fringe of elderberry bushes that screened the pool. It was a young, fat face with piggy eyes and thick sensuous lips. A red tongue licked the lips in anticipation while the face watched the lovely figure on the sand. The watcher tensed and leaped over the bushes to land in the sand only a few feet from her. She gasped with dismay and with a quick motion pulled her dress from the bush and slipped it over her head.

"Is this your idea of fun?"

He grinned. "Ain't you the biggety talkin' nigger. That's on account of all those good clothes Uncle Allen gives you to strut around in on Sunday."

She said nothing but flinched at the word "nigger."

"Uncle Allen ain't no fool," he went on. "He'll get it all back when you grow a little bigger. You're about fifteen, but in another year you'll be just right for him ..."

"Mr. Emil, I don't think Mr. Allen would like that."

"You don't?" He was sneering.

He stepped close and seized her in his arms. She was taut and hard but her eyes still blazed fearlessly into his.

"Turn me loose, Mr. Emil."

"I'll turn you loose when I want to." His right hand slipped in the neck of her dress and grabbed roughly. She froze for a second, then raked her sharp nails across his face, leaving four ragged parallel lines.

"Why, you ..." He threw her roughly to the sand. Fear flashed across her consciousness, cold weakening terror because she knew he was too much for her to handle. She screamed loud, long. He clapped a sweaty palm across her mouth and with one sweep of his hand ripped her dress from shoulder to hem. She bit him hard and let go another scream that was hoarser and weaker. Then they struggled silently.

A big Negro appeared on the bank above them, paused and sprang outward, landing in the sand with a thud. With a terrific, openhanded slap he knocked the man from her. Emil Brame tumbled across the sand, regaining his feet at the water's edge, but lost his balance again and fell in with a splash. He came up spitting curses. He stood in the shallow water for a second.

"You goddamn black son-of-a-bitch. I'm gonna kill you for that."

"I don't think so, Mr. Emil," said Jake quietly.

Emil rushed, only to be dumped back into the water again by a hard stiff arm.

His face flushed with rage, he came out slower this time, and in his hand was a long wicked pocketknife.

"This'll take care of you," he said between clenched teeth. "I'll carve you into ..." He rushed again and this time Jake side-stepped and shot a short right hook to the jaw. Emil, carried on by the impetus of his rush, landed in a deep bed of blackberry briars. He did not rise.

The girl, her face frozen with terror, merely looked at her savior.

Jake took off his shirt and handed it to her. "This here shirt'll do to cover you up, Moleen. You kin make a sorta diaper out of the rest of your dress."

As he helped her on the wagon, she spoke for the first time. "What about Mr. Emil?"

Jake shook his head again. "I ain't never tetched a white man before, but I couldn't let him do that to you and I couldn't let him cut me wid that knife."

Moleen held the shirt tightly about her, her eyes still wide and staring.

"What's Mr. Allen going to think?"

Jake nodded dolefully. "That's the thing. I got to tell him, though."

"You ... you think ... Jake, what'll he think ... about me, I mean?"

He smiled a little. "You oughtn't to worry about that. Mr. Allen wouldn't blame you for anything."

"He said some things about Mr. Allen, Jake ... some awful things."

"Whutever they was, it's a lie," said Jake tonelessly.

"Mr. Allen is the best white man I know."

"You said whut Gawd loves," agreed Jake fervently.

Old Allen Ogilvie MacReady Gordon had been a shrewd, austere man. Deadly either with his fists or in a trade, he had wrung more than a living from his broad acres. He thrived not because he was mean but because he was canny as sin where business was concerned. He never confused generosity with business, much to the depair and sometimes hatred of those who chose to tilt with him on his own terms.

His son had all the shrewdness of the father but this sub-tropical land had thawed the granite from his soul. Moreover, he did not have to begin from the beginning as had his father, and though he did business by instinct, he was not driven to it by necessity. Allen Gordon inherited from some line of forebears an outsized zest for living and a strange disease of the eye which made him see things as they are rather than as they should be.

A crusader or meddler usually sent him soaring into one of his infrequent but spectacular fits of fury, and people of this sort soon learned that to approach Allen with platitudinous suggestions that he support this or that movement for the salvation of his immortal soul, had upon occasion been known to earn for them contusions and purple eyes.

He was a large rangy man who strode about his domain like a conqueror, yet maintained an imperious calm and dignity found in men at peace with themselves, nature's really kindly gentlemen.

It was Monday and Allen, having eaten the noonday meal, felt at peace with the world.

Bonnie, his unlawfully attractive niece, sauntered into his den where he lay dozing. She was clad in shorts and halter which on a girl of her size and endowments seemed to reveal considerably more than they obscured. She tickled his nose with a straw for a while then stood up to watch.

His face worked involuntarily then he sneezed and sat up, eyeing her with disapproval that didn't quite make it. "Whatever it is, I don't want any, and what do you mean waking me up?"

"I thought you might like to see me in the new playsuit."

"I always like your playsuits with you in them, however I'd just as soon see you without them."

"I'll bet you would too. Some day I'll let you to see you fry and curl up like bacon." She took a cigarette from a bronze container and lit it.

"Hah ... me fry. To begin with, I don't have an ounce of lard on me. To end with, I've watched the best and maintained a cool, if not entirely undisturbed exterior."

"How did they stand it?"

"A good question but your uncle is the breath of honor and far be it..."

"Unk, do you sleep with Miss Billie?"

"Naturally—you curious nymph. Miss Billie is a master at her art."

"Mistress," corrected Bonnie, leaning back on a hide-covered lounge and breathing deeply, producing an effect which she knew well.

"All right, then, mistress, but I don't like the word. Neither does Billie. We are very fond of each other and she's very attractive. So am I, I might add. Neither of us feels that it's anybody's business and we like it. I needn't tell you, though, I don't care to have it bandied about as common gossip."

Bonnie sat up and a smile crept over her full damp lips. "You know, Unk, I never lived until we came to live with you. I guess I'm just a pagan at heart..."

"So's everyone else, but they aren't satisfied with being pagans; they have to build up a structure of false values so high that they can't see reality any more. Natural reaction reminds them that they're animals in the purest sense therefore they resent it. They've got to be something *higher* than that. Some of them even elevate themselves right into Jackson."

"Jackson?"

"Yeah... the bug house." He lit a long thin cigar and puffed it contentedly.

He continued to gaze out of the window where the heat waves marcelled the afternoon atmosphere.

"Your father was a good example. He was so bound up inside that he never really opened up."

Bonnie crushed out her cigarette. "You know, Unk, I don't remember much about father except that he was always mousy and afraid of mother, but he wasn't your real brother was he?"

"No. Pop raised him and he tagged everywhere I went for fifteen years. He was older and I should have been following him but it never worked out that way. He was a numb member but I always had a sneaking affection for him."

"I've always wondered why you took us in. It certainly hasn't been too happy for you—the way mother is and Emil and Jane."

He shrugged. "You and Hank more than make up for it. It was pretty lonely here."

She bent over impulsively and planted a moist kiss full on his lips. "That's for being the best Unk in the world."

"Do it again for the same reason and of course you're right."

She did, with considerably more vigor and artistry than the first time.

"Wow," he breathed. "Let me go, you tart, or I'll forget that I'm an uncle who is, of course, no relation to you whatever."

Bonnie sat back and veiled her blue eyes with long silky lashes. "I think that'd be nice."

"You probably do and I dare say it would but ... Go away and don't bother me. You upset me too soon after dinner."

Bonnie laughed a meaty guttural laugh. "Unk, I like the hell out of you. You're so ... so ... abandoned and on the surface. Mother'd simply have cats if she heard us talk."

"She would and I'd want them to come out clawing and fighting."

"What do you think of Hank?"

Allen laughed gently. "That little son-of-a-bitch if he doesn't get killed will make a whale of a man someday. Tell me, Bonnie, how the devil did your mother whelp such a garden of opposites?"

"The moon probably had something to do with it."

"Your mother didn't run around on Fred, did she?"

"Holy cats, no. As a matter of fact, as soon as the four of us arrived they had separate rooms and she kept her door locked."

He shook his head. "Poor Fred."

"Right, and poor Jane."

7

"Why poor Jane?"

"Mother could get to Jane whereas Hank and I always held her off. I'm natural and Jane is just a bundle of nerves and neuroses."

"She's nothing to look at, that's certain."

"She could be if she would only live a little, use some make up, wear a dress that fitted, and throw away those horrible glasses."

"Maybe she can't see without them."

"She can't see with them, so what's the difference. They make her look like the witch of Endor."

"Did she ever have any boy friends?"

"Sure. A couple of myopics like herself. The three of them would get together and discuss long-haired music, philately, Greek and Roman culture ... and drink tea."

"Phew," muttered Allen distastefully, "the combination makes me want to retch. Inhibited up to there, hunh?"

"Especially up there," said Bonnie crossing lavish legs.

Allen cocked an eye at her. "I suspect you of having a thoroughly dirty mind."

"A healthily dirty mind let us say."

"Well, at least you don't hug it to your breast and let it ferment."

"Not me. With your prize Hereford, Horton, performing, I get vicarious thrills even if his finesse is somewhat primeval."

"So you've been spying on Horton?"

"Yeah ... just like you last week, watching that big Hampshire boar and his girl friend cut paper dolls."

"Business ... purely. I'm a breeder you know."

"I don't care what you call it ... I'm just honest and admit I like to see the lower orders at work, and right now I'm stopping the gab and going swimming in Dogwood. In the raw I suppose."

"I think I'll creep down there and look at you."

"Come, come, Unk. We don't have to go to all that trouble, do we?"

"Go away, you lascivious trull, before, as I said, I forget ..."

A knock sounded on the door.

"Come in."

Jake stood on the threshold with his battered hat in his hand. "Can I see you, Mr. Allen."

Jake threw a quick glance at Bonnie and looked unhappy.

"Jake is a Puritan in some ways," said Allen to his niece. "Scram."

"Go on, Jake," said Bonnie, "I know where little calves come from and I also know that unless she's a lot luckier than about ten more I could name, Lotty'll turn up as big as the side of the smokehouse before too long."

The only thing that kept Jake from turning a bright scarlet was the fact that he was as black as three o'clock in the morning with a full overcast. As it was, he managed a sort of ashy maroon.

"Git, Bonnie. We don't wash our dirty laundry in public. I dare say I could snoop and catch you up to something."

"Wouldn't take a bit of snooping," she said casually, and walked from the room.

Jake pulled a faded bandanna from his hip pocket and mopped his perspiring face. "Do, Jesus," he breathed "That's one more gal, ain't she, Mr. Allen?"

"One more and none of us would live long," said his boss. "What's on your mind?"

Jake shuffled his big feet around and groped for words. He punished the hat in his hands and sweat broke out anew on his suffering face.

"Come on, Jake. We grew up together and fought every day until I found out I couldn't whip you. You know you can talk to me."

Jake gasped and swallowed. "Mr. Allen, I ain't never in my life struck a white man."

"Well, I recall some haymakers that didn't do anything but cross my eyes and buckle my knees, but I was just a lad then so that lets you out ... What the hell's the matter with you?"

"Mr. Allen, I done struck a white man."

Allen was silent a moment. "Well, so what? If you hit him, I know you had to. If you're afraid someone'll do something to you, forget it. No one bothers my people. You know that."

"Yes sir. I had to hit him. He pulled a knife on me."

"Good. You should have broken his neck. Who was it?"

"Mr. Emil."

"I don't give a damn … *EMIL*, holy Jesus! What the hell did he pull a knife on you for? I knew he was a nogood, but … Go on, what happened?"

"Mr. Allen, please sir, get a holt of yourself 'cause this is gonna throw you. Try to hold on to your temper, please sir …"

"Go on, Jake, talk."

Jake scuffed his feet on the carpet and looked even more miserable. "Mr. Allen … I was comin' through the woods down near the creek and I hyeerd somebody squall. I got down from the wagon, I was haulin' wood, and run over to the edge of the creek. Mr. Emil had her down on the sand …"

"*WHO*, Jake?" Allen Gordon's face grew purple and his nostrils flared like those of a mad stallion.

Jake looked about to drop then, with a despairing glance at the ceiling, said one word. "Moleen."

Allen got slowly to his feet, his breath whistling through his nose like escaping steam. With one sweep of his arm he tore a ten-foot black snake whip from the wall, knocking down spurs, ropes and a Mexican machete by the sheer fury of the motion.

Jake moved aside and Allen stalked out of the room and slammed the oak door with a shivering crash that shook the house. Jane poked her mousy head out of the living room, goggled briefly at the murderous ferocity on her uncle's face and fled.

Millie Brame accosted him as he crossed the back porch. "Why, Allen, dear, what on earth can be the matter? Where are you going with that whip?"

He stopped and faced her, his blue eyes now shaded to a deep violet, flecked with little points of yellow flame. His thick red hair stuck out like a gout of ragged fire. "I'm going to beat Emil to death." With that he walked stiffly down the porch steps and turned toward the barn. Millie screamed and looked about for someone in whose arms she could faint but no one being handy, she compromised and sank in a melodramatic heap on the floor. Jane rushed to her mother's side after making sure her uncle had gone.

Bonnie came out on the porch in a riding shirt and blue jeans, carrying a heavy shot-loaded quirt.

"What in the name of suffering ears is this all about?"

Jane's face, screwed up and wet with tears, looked like nothing as much as a long immersed rat.

She bleated, "Uncle Allen is going to beat Emil to death."

Bonnie eyed them for a moment in silence, then leaped from the porch.

Emil Brame, after washing his face free of blood and his eyes of sand, had made a slow way homeward, cursing bitterly while revenge filled his brain to the exclusion of everything else. He was in such a state of helpless rage that Allen's stentorian bellow rang out twice before Emil reacted. Immediately all thoughts of revenge were replaced by thoughts of escape because the look on Allen's face drained the hot blood from his head with such speed that he swayed and blinked stupidly. He was now in the middle of the pen and Allen was only a hundred feet away. It was a strong high board affair that had been built to restrain the frenzied efforts of wild steers and Emil doubted his ability to get over the top in time. He was too big to get under or to be very nimble at climbing, but he turned with a squeal and raced heavily for the nearest part of the fence with Allen bearing down on him from behind.

When Emil reached the fence he was surprised at his own lightness, and went to the top board with the ease of a acrobat. Feeling relatively safe, he paused and looked back and this was his downfall. He had forgotten the ten-foot whip in his pursuer's hand. The whip snaked out with the report of a rifle and a blaze of acid fire squirted over Emil's back like a flood. His back muscles contracted like strutted hawsers and he screamed and fell to the packed earth of the loading pen. He was on his feet immediately and now had his knife in his hand open and ready.

"I'll kill you," he yelled, nearly mad with pain, terror and the hopelessness of his position. The whip snaked out again and Emil's hand opened involuntarily, dropping the knife. Across the back of his hand was a ragged gash, ghastly blue from blood not yet flowing. Again the stunning report, and this time his legs felt severed at the knees. He screamed and fell to the ground and Allen went berserk. Back and forth in the terrible crisscross figure-eight manner the whip hissed and cracked. Emil groveled on his knees crying for mercy but the inexorable whip continued to thunder and hiss.

Bonnie flung herself on his arm. "For God's sake, Unk, that's enough. You'll kill him."

He flung her sliding in the dirt with a single powerful sweep of his arm. "I'm *trying* to kill him."

Emil had taken advantage of the respite to try to force his bulk under the fence where he became fastened. He struggled and squealed like a trapped shoat and the whip began its snarling song on his buttocks and legs. Sweat poured from Allen and his face turned beefy red under the fury of his anger and efforts.

Bonnie looked him over carefully; then, taking a firmer grip on her quirt, reversed it and approaching him from behind, struck him a sharp exact blow on the back of his head.

The whip fell from Allen's nerveless hands and he sank quietly to the ground.

Emil, seeing what had happened, extricated himself from the fence, picked up his knife and leaped toward the prone man, his eyes gleaming with a queer greenish light.

Bonnie stood astride her fallen uncle and swung the quirt again, its heavy half thudding solidly against her brother's head.

"I didn't stop him to let you murder him, you gutless swine," she blazed at the unconscious Emil and to emphasize the remark, she cracked him again for good measure.

"Jake, come over here and help me get Unk back to the house." But Unk didn't need help.

He sat up just as she called Jake.

"Who," he asked muzzily, "conked me?"

"I did," said Bonnie belligerently, her hands on her hips. "Not that I care two whoops in hell for that bag of crap at your feet, but I love my uncle too much to let him become a murderer."

Allen got unsteadily to his feet and looked down at Emil. "So the minute you conked me he comes after me with a knife and you have to drop one on him."

"I dropped two on him thought I doubt the last one was necessary."

Allen picked up the knife, broke the blade and flung it away from him with fierce force.

"Dirty meaty bastard laying his rotten hands on Honey, I still ought to ..."

"Come away, Unk. He isn't worth it. Let's go get a drink."

"Leave it to you to make the sensible suggestions and do the right thing." He grinned as he felt the rising lump on the back of his head.

"What's this about Emil and Honey?"

"He caught her down by the creek and tried to rape her ... and it's a goddam good thing he didn't succeed." He shuddered from a fresh wave of rage.

"Now, now…" Bonnie looked thoughtful. "Unk, I know you think the world of that little girl, but there's a lot I don't understand. She's Lucindy's daughter, isn't she?"

Allen nodded heavily, shaking his head which still rang like a belfry. "Yes, sort of. Want to hear the story?"

"Yes… wait, let me tell Jake… Jake, get a bucket of water and pour it over my precious kin there. He'll come to."

"Yes, Miss Bonnie, but what if he wants to fight me when he comes to."

"Kill the son-of-a-bitch," bellowed Allen, his eyes flashing blue fire. "Beat the hell out of him. In fact, if you don't I'll…"

"Yes sir," said Jake with alacrity. "Just like you say, sir."

In the office, Lucinda, in answer to a summons, brought ice, ginger ale, Coke and a bottle of bourbon so old that the worms and millers had all but eaten the label away.

"Yeow… what nectar," exclaimed Bonnie as she unsealed it and sniffed the aroma.

"That was another of Pop's American preferences. According to him, bourbon was the only liquor fit to drink. "I dinna ken why a' the blather aboot Scots whuskey. Nosty smoked-up bilge water. Gi' me the braw honey o' the grassy blue hills o' Kentucky, hoondred proof and wi' a flavor a mon can endure.' "

"A huzza to the tastes of your reverend sire. He must have been an individualist. He and Mr. Glencannon wouldn't have gotten along well."

"Indeed not. Mr. Glencannon likes oatmeal porridge, too, and the ole man wouldn't even have it in the house. He was a hog for grits and gravy, though."

He handed her a highball and took his own straight, chasing it with a sip of iced ginger ale.

"Now you were going to tell me about Honey—her real name is Moleen, isn't it?"

Allen leaned back on his lounge and sighed with contentment, wincing when his head touched.

"Yes. I hate it and just fell into calling her Honey. Don't even know when I started it. She's such an appealing and beautiful little thing."

"She certainly is that. I fear for my position when she gets to her full stature."

He grinned. "You should, and any other woman hereabouts. Come to think of it, why don't we …"

He punched a bell button at his elbow and in a few seconds Lucindy appeared. She was a large quiet-faced woman.

"Lucindy, Honey's your daughter, is she?"

The colored woman smiled, showing white perfect teeth. "No, sir … she goes for mine, but you know she ain't. Granny Denham give her to me when she was a baby. I lost Tassy, he was borned dead."

"Yes, I remember, but about Honey. Where'd Granny get her?"

"I sho' don't know, Mr. Allen. Granny was a granny, you know." She turned to Bonnie. "A granny, Miss Bonnie, is a woman that helps wimmens have babies."

Bonnie nodded. "Yes, they're called midwives."

"Yassum. Us calls 'em grannies. Well, sometimes Granny'd take a chile from some young gal and would try to find a home for it. I was glad to get Honey 'cause the doctor said I couldn't have no more children."

"Then you have no idea who Honey's parents are?"

"No, sir. Granny, she been dead four years, so we can't ax her."

He nodded. "All right, Lucindy. I just wanted Miss Bonnie to hear."

He lit a cigar and sighed. "Getting mad makes me sick, Bonnie. It ruins me for three days. That's why I try to keep from losing my temper, but today … that was the limit."

"What are you going to do with Emil?"

"Nothing."

"You mean you're going to let him stay?"

"Yes. Bonnie, I was wrong a while ago. It struck me just now that Emil is really a case of arrested mental development. He'll never make a go of it outside. I'm stuck with him."

"You still haven't told me about this attachment you have for Honey. I don't usually question motives, but people in this part of the world may misunderstand about colored girls no matter how cute they may be."

Allen poured himself another drink. "All things considered I see what you mean, but it came on so gradually that even I have to think hard to catch the exact mechanics of it."

"Start where she made the very first impression on you. The start of your first quiver."

CHAPTER TWO

Allen crushed out his cigar. "It was early one morning, and I was on my way toward the creek. Lucindy lives down there by the red gate and that morning I wasn't feeling up to snuff. So instead of leaning down from old Straw, I dismounted to open the gate. As I led him through, I saw her standing there looking interested and scared. I smiled at her.

"She wriggled and took a few steps closer. 'Mr. Allen, that sho' is a purty hoss.'

"I thanked her and gave her a nickel. From that day on, every time she saw me coming she was there to open the gate for me. Every time she had the same thing to say. 'Mr. Allen, that sho' is a purty hoss'. That went on till she was seven or eight years old. She'd open the gate, compliment the horse, and I'd give her the nickel. Finally, one day I noticed that she had a dirty paper bag in her hands and was trying to hide it behind herself as she opened the gate, so I asked her what it was. It embarrassed her to death but she finally rushed up, handed it to me, and dashed madly away, not even stopping for her nickel. It was a bag full of plums, and I found out later that she had walked two miles to get them and earned a switching from Lucinda for it. Lucinda, of course, didn't know what she intended to do with them and had switched her for straying that far from home."

"And you gave Lucinda hell for switching her."

Allen grinned. "I did that, and till this day Lucinda hasn't touched her again. Well, as she got older she'd come to the store and sometimes I'd be there piddling around. Usually I'd give her some candy or something. One day I gave her a box of firecrackers… it was near Christmas and some little colored boy tried to take them from her. She fought him like a tiger and wound up bouncing a brick off his head. Tinker had to take him to the doctor to get his head stitched up. The next day, she was back and as soon as I saw her, I came out to talk to her about it. She was crying her eyes out because she thought I'd be mad with her. I took her back into the feed room and gave her a good talking to. I told her that she had only been protecting her own property and was entirely right. Her relief sort of knotted up my throat. She laughed and cried at the same time. 'You ain't mad at me then, Mr. Allen?'

" 'No, Honey, I'm not mad at you.'

" 'And you still love me?'

"Well, that set me back on my heels for sure. I don't ever remember being taken so completely aback. There she was sitting on a sack of feed, her big brown eyes wet from her crying, and I think my hesitation must have begun to frighten her because her eyes grew sort of wide and hurt. And do you know what I did?"

Bonnie laughed sympathetically. "I do, but I'll let you tell it."

"I armed her up like a mother hugging a lost child and be damned if I didn't shed a few. She held onto me so tightly that it actually hurt. All this time she had been building me up as some genie who could do anything, who was the kindest person in the world, and it just appeared to her that I'd love her as a matter of course. If I hadn't, she reasoned, I'd never have done those little kindnesses for her and paid attention to her. I went into Lucindy's house one day to take a look at a leak in the roof she had been heckling me about, and right by Honey's bed was a terrible old magazine picture of me cut from the Hereford Journal. Lucindy said that in the spring and summer, Honey'd keep a little garland of wild flowers around it whenever she could find them. This was in the fall and there was a little sprig of red sumac leaves under it.

Flies had specked it and it was generally horrible, but it was her prized possession."

"Bet that gave you a charge, didn't it?"

"It did. Then I did something I had never done for any woman other than my mother. I made a special trip to Baton Rouge, had a big portrait made of me with a brand new white Stetson on my head. I bought a really nice ebony frame, and I must say that all in all it was quite a snazzy job. When it came, I started to walk over to Lucindy's house to take it. It was nearly dark, right after supper and I caught up with Honey walking home from the well carrying a pail of water not much smaller than she was. I took the water and gave her the picture to carry. When I told her it was hers, she let out a squeal and dashed for the house as hard as she could go. I took out after her because I didn't want to miss seeing her face when she opened it. I tripped and fell sprawling and the water bucket dumped the contents all over me. I left it there and got to the house just as she was getting the outside wrapper off. I had wrapped it well and there were several more layers, and I thought she'd have a fit getting them all off.

"Well, I had something of an inspiration then. I thought she'd be rather overcome and shy around Lucindy and Amos, so I motioned them out of the room and I'm glad I did. She was slugged, but good. When she finally got her breath, she looked at me, her big eyes shining with tears. She laid it reverently on the packing and crawled over and hugged my leg. 'It's all for me?' she asked.

"'It's all for you, Honey.' My throat felt like I had swallowed a whole potato and I think I felt a little guilty. What the hell is a portrait?"

Bonnie's eyes were shining. "Why, you modest dope. It was the very thing she wanted most in the world."

He smiled. "I guess it was, at that. Well, she cried a little, then crawled into my lap and gave me a salty kiss. From then on, I was a lost man. I made Lucindy send her to school and did she set it on fire! Blazed her way right on through, making seven grades in four years. She couldn't go any further than seven grades without going away. I asked her about that, and she didn't want to, so I didn't pressure her into it. I take all the best magazines for her … in her name, and you should see her haunt the post office when they are due. I have a good library here and she reads almost constantly. She could pin our ears back on anything from Shakespeare to Caldwell."

"Smokes, you let her read him?"

"Certainly … if she wants to. I must say, though, he doesn't impress her too greatly. Neither does Maugham, Steinbeck nor Farrell. Wolfe and Mann she adores, and how's that for a fifteen-year-old?"

Bonnie sighed. "I'm a little ashamed that I didn't know all this sooner. The child's a prodigy, Unk. I'm wondering if you are doing right letting her grow up this way."

He nodded. "I've thought I should give her every advantage and all that, but I want her to grow up as naturally as possible. If she wants to get away and soar, she knows she can do it."

The door flew open and Hank burst in excitedly, his blonde curly hair mussed and a streak of dirt across his freckled nose. "Hi, Unk. Hi, Sis. Gee, but Mom's sore … she's looking for you. Boy, did you give Emil a walloping. What'd he do … boy, is she burned up, and Emil's back and fanny look like somebody run him through a Cherokee rose thicket. What'd he do, Unk, huh?"

"Slow down, bub, and let me get a word in …" The door burst open and Millie swept in like the angel of wrath. She stood stiffly and pointed a plump finger at Allen.

"You … you …" She stopped and swallowed a mouthful of spit which was threatening to strangle her. "You … Allen Gordon. How *dare* you brutalize Emil the way you did … bleeding … suffering … all cut up with that whip. You monster … you sadistic fiend, you … I shall not stay another night in this terrible house."

Allen propped himself up on the couch and pared the end from a cheroot with great care and deliberation.

"We'll leave at once ... Bonnie ... Henry ... both of you come with me, at once." Hank looked sullen and didn't move. Bonnie emulated her uncle by preparing a cigarette with more than necessary care. Millie slowly began to purple.

"Did you two hear me? I said come and I mean it ... right now."

"I ain't goin'," growled Hank, sullenly.

Millie gasped. "You're ... whom do you think you're taking to, young man ... Bonnie ... come along. As for you, Henry, I shall have something to say to you in private."

"Mother, I wish you'd go ... er ... knit a sock or something. You are not even third rate with your histrionics. Pray tell me where you'd go and on what?"

It was a blow which for calculated shock was a honey. Millie had not a sou to her name except the little checking account which Allen had given her for spending money and gimcracks. She could not go a hundred miles, and Montgomery, Alabama was a lot farther than that. Their house had been seized and even if she got there she'd have no place to stay. She took it like a boxer takes the last blow before the long count. She sagged into a handy straight chair and proceeded to launch a shipload of hysterics. In the midst of them, Allen made a sign and they trooped silently out and left her. As a cure for hysterics, there is no equal to what he did.

In the waning sun of the calm clear afternoon, the three sat on the top board of the loading pen watching Mose deprive a young bull of his manhood.

"Seems a shame," murmured Bonnie, scratching her thigh through her jeans where a splinter had pricked her.

"You mean about your mother?" asked Allen.

"No, about the bull—oops, I mean the steer."

JOHN B. THOMPSON & JACK WOODFORD

"What we gonna do about Mom," asked Hank, his face going suddenly serious. "You won't let her take me away, will you, Unk?"

Allen shrugged. "I think it'd be sort of hard to take you, Hank, if you didn't want to go. Personally, I think if we ignore her she'll come around. We can't make her stay, but we certainly don't have to provide her a way to leave."

"What'd you wallop Emil for, Unk?" asked Hank.

"Son, your brother did the worst thing a man can do. He tried to rape Honey. If Bonnie there hadn't conked me on the head, I'd probably have killed him."

"Oh!" The exclamation slipped out spontaneously, but it was weak and quavery. Allen snapped a quick look at the boy and then looked away.

"Well, what say we go see what Lucindy has for supper, kids?"

Bonnie slipped from the fence with alacrity, but Hank didn't move. "I'll be along, Unk...I want to see Mose about tomorrow...where's he going..." His voice was thin and ragged, and again Allen glanced at him but said nothing. Hank's voice was betraying him occasionally. Mostly he kept it pretty coarse and manly, but now and again, like this afternoon, it played him false. He was just past seventeen and very conscious of his voice. Allen grinned as they walked away.

As usual Lucindy had weighted the table with succulent country food, practically all raised on the plantation. Meats and vegetables in plenty, home cured, cooked with Lucindy's own inimitable touch. Lucindy's mother before her had held sway over the kitchen until she was too old, but by then her daughter had learned all the old woman could teach her and had picked up much of her own.

Millie Brame sat stiffly and silently at the table, eating little. Jane sat by her side but ate very well, Allen noted. If she kept this up, she'd put some much-needed meat on her bones.

Bonnie ate like a healthy animal and Hank, usually a gorger, sat and toyed with his food, looking ill. He would grin fleetingly at some of the chatter between Allen and Bonnie, but then he'd go back to white-faced contemplation of his plate.

Bonnie eyed him, raised her eyebrows at Allen who had also noted the boy's preoccupation. He shrugged and shook his head at her. He looked at Jane. "Jane, if you keep up that appetite, you'll have enough meat on your bones to get ten whistles a block in town one of these days." Jane started guiltily, but recovered instantly and smiled at Allen. A wave of pink came up from her collar, improving her looks greatly.

"It is to be hoped," put in Millie bitterly, with a blistering glance divided equally between Allen and Jane, "that her ambition shall reach for higher things. It would seem that I cannot leave, Allen, because I'm a helpless widow living on your bounty, but in the name of charity I shall expect you not to make a scarlet woman of my daughter. You have beaten my son half to death. Leave me at least my daughter."

"What about Bonnie. Aren't you afraid I'll contaminate her, too?"

Millie glanced at Bonnie and he could see a flash of hatred in her eyes. "Bonnie has seen fit to throw off the parental yoke."

Bonnie eyed her mother levelly. "For once, Mom, you are dead right."

Millie signed and roled her eyes heavenward to indicate her earthly burden was almost too much to bear.

Poor Jane, finding herself the cause of it all, became so miserable that her supper threatened to come up and she had to leave the table. Allen leaped to his feet and followed her.

In the hall he caught her by the arm. She shrank back, possibly thinking that he was about to stroke her. His voice was low, caressing, and kind.

"Look, Janie. You've done nothing to be ashamed of. All you did was eat a good supper. The other was the fault the rest of us. I want you to feel free here in my house .. your house ... our house. I want you to come and go as you please, do as you please. You appear fearful of me, Janie, and I don't want that. I want you to be happy. I want you to effervesce like Hank and become a healthy animal like Bonnie. Can't you see what a change has occurred in them since they came?"

Jane's bosom heaved and tears came into her eyes, requiring that she take her glasses off to wipe them. Her eyes were not at all bad, Allen noted. She essayed a smile and her rabbit-like front teeth protruded. She covered them with a lip that was too short in the first place and the effort was what forced her face into such contortion. A pang struck him beneath the breast bone. Poor girl. What terrible things must be going on inside her, none of which were at all necessary.

He put a hand on her shoulder and patted it paternally. "We'll get all this fixed up, Janie."

With a sob, the frail, unattractive girl collapsed on his broad chest. He put his arms around her affectionately and held her close.

"Just like I told you, Janie, things are going to be different from now on."

She cried all the harder and he held her closer. A flood of incoherent pent-up speech poured from her muffled lips. Her hand clutched the flesh of his side with such strength that he almost gasped from the pain. He let her cry, holding her thin shoulders and patting her occasionally. Suddenly, he was aware of a strange motion of her hips.

A less experienced or a less wise man than Allen might have been disgusted or even horrified. A pitying smile crept across his face. Suddenly, with a furious lunge, she struck his leg with the mad strength of hysteria ... and fainted dead away.

Out of the gloom of the hall came Bonnie, her eyes wide from wonderment. "What in the world, Unk?"

He shushed her, gathered the slight body in his arms and carried her upstairs to the room she and her mother shared. He laid her tenderly on the bed. "Bonnie, go wet a rag and ... Bonnie, look at her face."

Bonnie drew in her breath with a sibilant hiss. "Unk it's almost beautiful, what in the world ..."

"Get the wash rag and bring it back wet."

Bonnie came back with the rag but hesitated. "Unk, if she sees you here, she'll be mortified."

"I doubt that she'll remember a thing." He took the rag and began to bathe the girl's face.

"How old is she, Bonnie?"

"Twenty-six, Unk, why?"

He sighed heavily. "Oh ... I was just wondering how much she had crammed inside of her, wanting out. That reveals much."

"Well, it doesn't to me, I ..."

"Scram, Bonnie. I'll do this alone. Go along now, she's coming to."

Jane opened her eyes and looked sleepily about. "Hello, Unk ... Uncle Allen," she amended hastily.

He grinned at her. "Unk ... and I won't have anything else. All my kids call me that."

"I'm sorry I passed out on you. I can't imagine ..."

"Nonsense. People do that all the time. You had a belly full of chow and with that scene at the table, it just sort of revolted on you."

"But I feel fine now. I feel ..." She bit her lip and her eyes roved about.

"Never mind that. You're all right now. Janie, how about you and me going to Baton Rouge tomorrow and seeing a dentist about your front teeth. If he can't straighten them, we'll get him to pull 'em and put in one of those bridges that no one can tell from the natural. What about it?"

Tears came to her eyes and she seized one of his hands and squeezed it. "I just knew mother was wrong about you."

"She doesn't think I'm much of a prize, does she?" He was smiling.

"No, and that's cruel and unjust because you are fine and generous and noble ..."

"Here, here," said Allen, in something like confusion. "No one is all that."

"You are, too," she maintained stoutly, "and I'm going to tell her so."

He shook his head. "Let it go, Janie. If she can't find out all by herself then all you'll do is start another argument and we've had enough of them. Now undress and go to bed, or shall I do it for you?"

Jane flinched and blushed a fiery red. "Oh ... no ... I ..."

His guffaw cut into her confusion like a kindly knife. He started for the door and turned. "Nite ... Cleopatra." He waved his hand and was gratified to see a small hesitant smile creep across her lips like a footsore caterpillar.

Bonnie collared him as soon as he closed the door. "Don't try to put me off, Unk. What the hell happend to Jane?"

He threw an arm across her shoulder as they walked back toward the big dining room. "Her long dammed-up nature caught her in a moment of weakness. She hadn't had any real affection in so long that for a moment she was bowled over by a little kindness. She melted and I put my arms around her. Then the dam cracked. I was startled at first but then I realized what was happening, so I just let her go ..."

"But, Unk, fainting like that ..."

"Listen to old and experienced. You, you unmoral trull, probably had your first such experience at the age of six. At twenty-six, it is something else again."

She stopped him. "Unk," she made him face her. "Unk, I just now realized what you were talking about. Dumb is the word for

Bonnie ... Poor Jane." She looked into his eyes for a long moment. "I still say you're the finest man in this wicked world. I mean that."

"Of course you do," he said, swinging his shoulders swaggeringly, "and of course you're right."

She hauled off and slapped his behind as hard as she could. "Why, you vain ..."

He leaped away laughing and went into the dining room where the others were drinking their after supper coffee. He sobered and walked over to Millie. His voice was quiet and level.

"Millie, as long as I have roof over my head, you're welcome to part of it. I have no intention of requiring you to do a thing for me. I shall, however, require that in the future you confine your poison to some other time of the day. The supper table is no place for it. In the future, you will be pleasant at meals or you will eat alone." With that, he sat down and rang for Lucindy.

Millie grew very white and stiff in her chair. Then she rose and walked haughtily from the room. Lucindy came in bringing a steaming cup of hot coffee.

He accepted it with thanks and said, "I wish you'd fix a tray and take it up to Emil, Lucindy."

Lucindy gasped and swallowed but did not reply. He looked up.

"Well?"

"I'll ... I'll ... fix the tray, Mr. Allen ..."

He frowned, "But you won't take it up to him, is that it?"

Lucindy shuffled from one foot to the other. Bonnie sat bolt upright in her chair and opened her mouth to speak but closed it again. Hank watched, hardly breathing.

"If you tells me to ..."

"I'm not going to tell you to, Lucindy. Fix the tray and someone else will take it. I don't blame you."

Lucindy was so relieved that tears came into her eyes. She threw her apron over her mouth and ran into the kitchen.

Hank stood up. His lips wore a white halo and his eyes glittered. "I'll take it, Unk."

Allen opened his eyes in surprise, but he just looked at the boy. What were his reasons? He didn't care for his brutish brother at all. Why? Allen shrugged. Later it would come out ... Later.

"Sure, if you want to ... go ahead."

After Hank had departed with the tray, Allen patted Bonnie's hand. "Hi, bulwark of strength, leaning post, old faithful and reliable."

Bonnie smiled mistily at her uncle. "Hi, god."

The next morning three of them sat at breakfast: Hank, Bonnie and Allen.

Bonnie spoke. "Er ... I looked at Jane before I came down this morning."

"Er ... you did?" mimicked Allen.

"Er ... yes, and she was sleeping like a log. Know what mother said ... said she bet you knocked her out with some powerful sedative or other."

He grinned. "Your mother doesn't know it, kitten, but she told the unvarnished truth."

The girl paused in mid-bite and eyed him. Then her eyes smiled. "Oh," she said and drank some coffee.

"What do you suppose she'd have if she knew that?" he asked.

Bonnie shrugged. "Thirty dozen swallow-tailed ring dang do's all whistling 'Dipsy Doodle'."

"Humm," grunted Allen. "That reminds me of a dirty verse I learned when I was in college."

"I was certain," she remarked pointedly, "that before the day was very old, you'd be reminded of something dirty. You must be desperate to rake up something that old."

"Hell," Hank grunted, his first offering of the morning. "It ain't that old. It goes ..."

"If you dare," said his sister warningly. "I'll murder you."

"Aww!"

"The breakfast table, Henry," said Allen, frowning ferociously, "is hardly the place for bawdy verse. However, behind the barn later on today, I should be delighted to renew my acquaintance with the fabulous doings of Ring Dang Do, probably with several newer versions."

"Yeah ... there's one about a '48 Ford. It ..."

"That," said Bonnie, "Is enough, Henry. And I do mean enough."

"Awww!"

CHAPTER THREE

J ANE WALKED BRISKLY into the dining room. "Good morning." Her voice had an oddly confident ring. All three looked up in something like surprise. She flushed and sat down and Allen used the instant to blister Hank and Bonnie with a glance.

"Looking chipper this morning, Janie. Sleep well?"

"Better than I can remember," she said, pinking afresh and attacking her cereal and cream. "I'm just about starved."

"After what you ate last night?" breathed Hank. "Geee."

"That," said Jane, pointedly but confidently, "was last night. Some twelve hours ago, I believe."

Hank sat back, words stricken from him while Allen and Bonnie traded delighted glances.

"What time can you leave this morning, Janie?" he asked.

She put her spoon down and looked gratefully across the table at him. "I'm ready right now, Unk."

"Good. I'll be busy for an hour, then we'll take off. Want to fly or go in the car?"

"Oh, let's fly."

"O.K., we'll fly. The plane had a flat yesterday but Jake can fix it in ten minutes."

Bonnie followed Allen out to the barn where the clink of trace chains and the creak of leather told of mules being readied for a day's plowing. "Now I've seen everything, Unk."

"What are you talking about?"

"Do you mean that ... something like that and a night's sleep can do all this?"

"Not by itself. Remember a dam broke last night. Much can happen in a little while, especially when a person actually hates the condition."

Allen gave his field hands orders for the day, changed to a pair of fawn-colored gabardine pants and shirt to match, and called Jane. Together they walked across the big yard with its camellias, live oaks and magnolia trees, out through the gate where they heard a shrill cry from the house.

"You, Jane…where are you going? Come back here this instant."

He sensed Jane's pause before it ever materialized and grabbing her by the arm, began to talk at a great rate, pointing out some fictitious sights as he talked.

"This is for you, Janie, and we can't let you stop now. You're on the way up and out. Go back now and you're lost."

Jane gulped noisily and straightened her shoulders. "You're right, Unk," She gave his hand an affectionate squeeze.

At the plane, she halted, her heart in her throat. She had never flown and had a deadly fear of planes, but this time she resolved to fly if it killed her. While Allen pulled the prop through several times, she climbed gingerly in, taut and white-faced but with teeth clamped hard with determination. Jake came along and helped push it from the small sheet iron hangar onto the green runway. Allen started the motor and Jake backed away from the slipstream, holding on to his hat. Jane buckled the belt around her slim waist with trembling hands.

As they left the ground, she clenched her teeth anew, shut her eyes tightly and fought back the leaden falling-elevator feeling in the pit of her stomach. Then all became smooth and she found the courage to open her eyes. The ground presented such an absorbing picture that she forgot her fear and began to feel exultant and stimulated. She took a deep breath and relaxed, smiling at Allen who tooled the plane along with a deft and practiced hand.

They cruised along at an easy hundred and twenty miles an hour at three thousand feet, Allen pointing out this and that point of attraction. Finally Harding Field crept under their left wing tip. He throttled back.

Dr. Tetlowe smiled sympathetically at Jane. "You'll like this," he said. "We won't have to pull your teeth. They aren't as bucked as they are crooked. We'll grind them down and put caps over them. I'll defy anyone to tell the difference at three feet. At six inches they might, but I have an idea when they get that close, they won't be thinking about teeth, if they're men."

Jane flushed happily but said nothing. In the outer office, Allen chuckled silently. Dr. Tetlowe had taken his coaching well.

"Of course, these caps will be temporary till the permanent ones are made."

It was nearly dark that night when the silver wings dipped and made the last turn into the wind. The wheels touched the ground gently and coasted smoothly up to the hangar. Jake had been waiting and came to the plane and opened the doors for them.

"Good god a'mighty, Mr. Allen—is that her?"

"That's her, Jake. A little transformed, eh?"

Jake shook his head. "The things peoples can do now. You want them boxes brung to the house?"

"Yes, Jake, bring them along if they aren't too much for you. That's Miss Jane's new wardrobe."

"'Scuse me, Miss Jane, but whut they done to your teeth … if you don't mind me askin'?"

"Ask me every day, Jake, every day," she was laughing and crying at the same time. "They cut the horrible things off and put caps on them. Now I can smile and not feel like sticking my head in the sand."

He abject gratitude and bursting happiness made Allen's heart swell mightily within him, and he threw an affectionate arm about her. "Come on, Sugar, and let's see how many of the others know you. Did they butcher you up at the beauty parlor?"

"They flayed me, and I hated every inch of that dowdy hide I lost, Unk."

As they walked in the gate, Allen, who had been walking behind, noticed that she even walked differently. Her creepy, frightened skulk had been replaced by a head-up, shoulders back stride that shoved her small busts out and trimmed her slight figure to a much better advantage. She turned around suddenly.

"Unk... this is silly, but I'm afraid."

"Of what?"

"I know it sounds crazy, but... mother."

He looked at her queerly. "I don't think it's so crazy, sugar... not at all, but don't let it get you. You've lived under her shadow too long as it is. There's too much of the world to confine yourself like that. Let her think what she wants... in other words, the hell with her."

Her hand flew to her mouth. "Oh..."

"Oh, my athletes foot. I could have put it another way, but that's the way I like it."

Slowly the hand came down from her face and a glimmer of comprehension of this big fierce red-headed man came to her. Her eyes softened. "Unk..."

"Shet up, wench, and let's go, and if I hear another word of gratitude out of you, I'll turn you over my lap and spank what I confidently predict will soon be as trim a fanny as ever strained an imagination."

She blushed furiously, but she was smiling.

"That's the way to take it. You know I'm talking sense. That blushing just makes you prettier."

Tears came again to her eyes. "Unk, if I can't thank you any more, can I say I love you very, very much and that I think you're the greatest guy in the world?"

He nodded and chuckled. "You can tell me that all you want to, but I'll have to warn you I can't give you much originality on it. It's been said before."

"I'll bet it has. I've heard you and Bonnie kidding like that and wished so hard that I could join you."

He clapped her smartly on the behind. "Well, that's your initiation, kid ... you're in."

She smote him back smartly in the same place, giggling like school girl. "Now, I do feel like one of you."

Arm in arm they strolled up to the porch where Millie, Hank and Bonnie sat. Millie sat at some distance from Hank, and Bonnie had sniffed indignantly at such carryings on in the front. She didn't recognize the girl, but that didn't make any difference. Furthermore, what had he done with Jane?

They walked proudly up the steps and bowed to the assembly. "Folks ... allow me to present Miss Richbitch."

Millie stiffened and looked down her nose with great disapproval, and Bonnie lazed to her feet and walked over. "How do you do," she said cordially. "You mustn't mind my uncle, he's just a superannuated wolf with no sense of propriety ... holy balls of atmosphere ... no ... I flat don't believe it. There's trickery afoot." Her eyes were glazed with astonishment.

Millie's face was puckered with anger. "What have you done to my Janie?"

Jane looked around, her face shining with happiness. "Can't you see, mother? He's made a person of me, that's all."

"He's made a street walker of you ... all painted up like a woman on the prowl."

"Who said she wasn't" said Hank from his chair where amazement had rooted him.

Jane looked at him with soft eyes. She loved him for that. She loved everybody.

"Oh, come, Millie. She's just come into her own. What about Bonnie? She dresses fit to kill and uses make-up."

Millie snorted loudly and whirled angrily away. "I shall never forgive you for this, Allen Gordon, and don't be throwing Bonnie at me as a model ... not a model lady, at any rate." She went in and slammed the door.

"For which let's all be properly thankful," retorted Bonnie at the retreating back.

Allen chided teasingly, "That is impertinence. How's to lope back to the kitchen and tell Lucindy to fetch a couple of rounds of set-ups and a deck of sandwiches. We need to celebrate and a full supper might slow it down."

Lucindy brought out a bottle, glasses, ice, ginger ale and Coke and set up a table on the porch.

Jane timidly tasted her first highball, looking at the others and laughing self-consciously. "I hope I don't get ... er ..."

"The word," put in Bonnie, "is crocked ... and I hope you do. God knows you've had little enough fun."

"Can I have a short one, Unk?"

Allen glared at Hank. "Of course, you can. You can have all you can carry, but woe betide you if you get more than that. That's one thing I can't take, a person getting sloppy drunk."

Jane put her glass down immediately. "Maybe I'd better ..."

"Nuts, eat a couple of these big sandwiches after your first, then to hell with the chips. You'll probably get tiddily and have a hell of a hangover in the morning, but you'll have a lot of fun doing it. After you find your drinking legs, you'll be able to gauge your amount better. This is your night and all rules are off."

"It's my first night, too, Unk," put in Hank, hopefully.

"Well, you can't learn any sooner. The rules are off for you, too."

Hank sat suddenly upright in his chair and emitted a loud "Haw." He startled no one more than himself and looked like a nice dark hole might be comforting.

"Exultant, hunh, bub?" asked Allen, laughing heartily.

"I don't know, sire," he admitted shamefacedly. "All of a-sudden I just sort of blew up with..." He stopped and looked ashamed again.

Allen dropped a paternal hand on his shoulder. "You can talk freely here, son. What did you sort of blow up with?"

Hank swallowed noisily but came out with it. "With happiness."

Allen grinned and hugged him. "That's the best compliment you can pay me, son. Thanks."

"The trouble with you, Unk," said Bonnie seriously, "is that you don't know how we were cooped up before we came here. Montgomery is a nice enough town, but it isn't Loch Ness."

"What's Loch Ness?" asked Jane, washing the last of her sandwich down with milk.

"Why, goose, that's the name of Unk's place here," snorted Hank, outraged at her ignorance.

Jane almost cringed from habit. "Well, I knew that was the name of the post office, but I didn't know it was the name of the place. Isn't Loch Ness supposed to have a monster?"

"Not this one," said Allen, "unless it's me. The one in Scotland has, according to Pop. Pop was a pretended believer in warlocks and such. He claimed he saw it. According to him, 'It wa' a vurutable monster wi' lang heer on its head like a woomun. Tushes lik' ma best Hompshire boar only mooch langer. It had twa tails and saven arms all clotching a buttle o' the best Kentucky bourbon whiskey.'"

"Awww... he was kidden yuh," scoffed Hank.

"He was, but it used to amuse him to tell the tale. The only consistent point was that of the bourbon whiskey. He insisted on that off note."

Jane made a sudden motion with her arm. "I'm going to start on another," she said. "Unk, I'm afraid I don't know how much... will you fix it for me?"

"That I will," he said, pouring her a generous portion, putting in ice and ginger ale. He fixed drinks all around, handing Hank a man-sized drink which made Bonnie frown.

"Isn't he sort of young..."

"Aww, you shut up, Bonnie," Hank was offended. "I guess Unk knows what to fix me."

Jane drained her glass and emitted a great whoosh and slid forward in her chair. "Unk, the Great Jane requires another drink, if you will be so kind."

"Unk will be so kind, and being even kinder, he'll suggest that you go upstairs and put on something more comfortable. That outfit you have on cost a hundred dollars."

Jane gasped and leaped to her feet. "Gosh, I had forgotten that." She whirled like a ballet dancer and whipped gracefully through the screen door, letting it slam with a bang.

"Or recently arrived member has just enough to make her very positive in her movements. Two more and they won't be nearly so positive."

To prove his uncle's assertion, Hank leaped to his feet and balanced himself precariously on the edge of the porch. Then he promptly fell with a thud into the yard.

"The capacity of women for alcohol," said Allen, gasping with mirth as Hank picked himself off the ground, "has been the fall of many a man better equipped than you, son. Sometimes they get stinking with ease and next time they'll drink three men under the table in relays."

"My foot slipped," said Hank ruefully.

Jane dashed through the door and sat down quickly. She had changed to a play suit of green and white polka dots, which fitted her well, and Allen let out a whistle. Her body, thought spare and knobby in places, showed promise and with a little more good food and peace of mind she stood a good chance of covering up the angles.

"Mother saw me," she gasped. "I'm afraid she's coming down to..."

"She'll raise hell, probably," said Allen easily. "I'll leave her to Bonnie."

"I'm no lady," said Bonnie with a noticeable lack of grief.

"That's why I'm leaving her to you," said Allen. "I'm too much of a gentleman ..."

Millie swept out on the porch with fire in her eye. "Well, Allen, was that your idea, getting that child a shocking playsuit like that ... sinful, that's what it is."

"Why, mother," put in Bonnie, "any of mine are much worse than that."

"I'm not speaking to you," snapped her mother. "What you choose to wear or not wear is no concern of mine. As for Jane ... Jane, I order you to return to the room at once and remove that disgraceful attire ... do you hear me, Jane?"

Jane looked at Allen miserably and appeared on the verge of obeying her mother.

Allen, watching her narrowy, saw her lack of determination and stepped into the breach. "Millie," he spoke blithely, "sit down and have a drink."

Millie flinched as though struck. "I will not and ... merciful heavens, are you actually feeding these children liquor?"

"Not actually," he said easily, "I build a drink for them but they manage to feed themselves quite well."

"Well ... I never! Jane ... inside at once."

Allen stood up. "Go on to bed, Millie. Jane isn't going anywhere and these clothes are perfectly respectable. If you want to starch your own drawers and wear ankle-length skirts as of 1910, help yourself. Now if you aren't going to join us, go to bed. We have more drinking to do." He sat down again tugging at his hair and struggling to hold his temper.

Millie fixed her cold eyes on Jane. "Will you come, or shall I be forced to slap you."

Jane shrank back and made an effort to get up. Allen came to his feet again with a bound.

"Go to your room," his voice had the quiet ring of gently stroked spring steel. Had he struck her, the effect couldn't have been more profound.

"You order *me* to ..."

"I do. I think your hearing is in perfect order, Millie."

She went, leaving Jane white-faced and scared. She put her drink down and swallowed hard. "I ... I ... don't think I'd better drink any more, Unk. Maybe I'd better go up now."

He sighed.

Jane went through the door again but this time her step was dead and without spirit.

"That," said Bonnie, "is a bloody shame."

"It's a goddam rotten shame," said Hank with a curious exultation as he downed the last of his drink and held the empty glass to his uncle.

"The shame has been taken care of rather well," said Allen breathing hard to keep his temper in leash. He fixed Hank another drink and handed it to him.

"What exactly do you make of mother, Unk?" asked Bonnie.

"An inhibited, bitter, thwarted woman who hated you as soon as you showed signs of being such a plush beauty, which was, I suspect, somewhere about the age of six and about the time you threw the first gauntlet in her face."

Bonnie smiled. "That proves it. You're psychic. When we left to come here, she had just made a whole flock of rules for me which I could either observe or leave home. I'll leave you to guess what I would have done."

Jane came dispiritedly through the door again and sat in her chair.

"She locked me out."

Bonnie grinned openly and Allen's face brightened. "Well, that's a break for you. You can have the room behind Bonnie's all for your own."

"She can sleep with me if she wants to," said Bonnie, patting her hand. "I'll need someone come winter."

"Gee, Bonnie, can I … I've wanted to sleep with you for so long and watch you fix your hair and do your face and nails and …"

"Then it's settled," said Allen. "Get your things tomorrow and move in."

"Whummmm," said Hank in a surprising bass. He looked at his glass and squinted. "Don't know as I ever felt this way before, Unk." Then his face fell and the band of white appeared about his lips. "I guess Honey is developing into a first-class whore."

"What makes you say that, son?" asked Allen softly.

"Well … I know you think a lot of her, Unk, and she is a good kid, but …"

"But what?"

"Well, when I took Emil's supper to his room last night, he said she tried to rape *him*. He said you cut him up with your whip on the say-so of two …"

"Just a minute. Have you ever known Emil to be particularly truthful, Hank?"

The boy shook his head. "No, sir. I've caught him in plenty of lies."

"Then, why did you happen to believe that?"

Hank squirmed uncomfortably. "I …"

"Precisely." Allen's voice was still and quiet, but it carried a sort of soft whip. "Now, Hank, you run along to bed and think that over. In the morning, I want you to hear the story first hand."

"Oh, that's all right, Unk, if you say …"

"And while you're thinking it over," the whip was no longer soft, "ask yourself how was it a girl … fifteen-year-old girl on the make, would try to rake half the face off the man she was trying to rape. Put your glass down and go give it a little thought."

Hank swallowed hard and put his glass down. "Yes sir." His voice broke and he walked stiffly through the door, letting it close softly.

Allen cursed heavily. "Now what in the hell's wrong with him? What ever interested him in the matter in the first place?"

"Now the great Bonnie steps into the breach and shows up her usually acute uncle. Remember out on the fence yesterday afternoon when you told him about it? Well, I was watching him. It almost knocked him from the fence. He didn't eat any supper and he wanted to take Emil's tray up to him. It ate on him all today in fits and starts."

Allen sat up and frowned at her. "What are you trying to tell me?"

Bonnie let go a tinkle of a laugh. "The neighbors are beginning to talk about your attachment to Honey, and now your nephew has a crush on her. If you didn't see that, then using some of your own famous psychology, you just didn't want to."

He lit a cheroot carefully. "Well, I'll be damned. I never really thought of it."

"Oh, rats," snorted Bonnie. "It isn't love, it's just a crush. He'll get over it."

He gazed out into the moon-splashed night and during the silence, the sawing of katydids and the chorus of toads sweetened the cool, still air.

"The noise you just heard," said Allen calmly, "was a premonition being born."

"Much pain with it?" asked Bonnie.

"Not right now," he said slowly, "but look at it. What situation was ever made for more downright explosiveness, more hell for leather hooraw. Lord, what a sensation that announcement would make...Mr. Allen O. Mac R. Gordon announces the marriage of his nephew Henry Maxwell Brame to Moleen Anderson, daughter of Amos and Lucindy Anderson, cook and field hand extraordinary."

"But..." stammered Jane aghast. "She's not really their daughter, is she...but she is Negro, isn't she?"

He sighed heavily. "She's not their daughter, but she might as well be."

"Hell, Unk, you're getting concerned over nothing. They're both kids and though I'll admit he has a crush on her ..."

"Oh ... the devil. He has a crush on her as many a white boy has had on some cute colored girl. I'm not bothered about that. It's just that the whole situation is made for a ... er ... situation. Well, thank goodness, we have some years ahead. I'm glad I don't have to face it tomorrow."

The party was a flop, so Jane went off to bed while Allen and Bonnie had a last snort. Bonnie wriggled luxuriously in her chair and gazed at Allen through dreamy eyes. "We are no relation at all, are we?"

He grinned. "No kin, but I'm occupied with my thoughts tonight."

"I could occupy you a lot better."

"I dare say, you shameless witch, but I have a few inhibitions myself."

"Expensive luxury, old boy. Too damned expensive for yours truly ... I'll get you though."

He shrugged. "Possibly, and I doubt that you'll have too much trouble. But doesn't it strike you as a trifle forward, even in these enlightened days for a twenty-three-year-old niece to go to bed with a forty-year-old uncle?"

Bonnie yawned outrageously. "She should be doing a good bit better, I'll admit, as regards the forty-year-old-man, but it still is a fact that, even though we are saddled with the uncle-niece handle, there's no relationship. However, if it were known just how many sister and brother relationships there are, there'd be just such a howl as arose when Kinsey showed that farm boys were not all choosey about their companions."

Allen Gordon eyed his shocking niece with speculative eyes. "I know now, you educated voluptuary, that I just thought I was an open-faced, on-the-surface person."

She nodded, yawning again. "Yeah … I *thought* you thought you were."

Allen honored her yawn with one of his own. "Sack time, niece. Let's hit it."

"Together or separately?"

"Separately. You have a sister to sleep with."

"Yeah … tough, ain't it? A good buzz on and a sister to sleep with."

"Well, it isn't too late. I think I'll ride over and see Miss Billie."

"That's just about what I'd expect you to do. I hate you."

He smiled and stretched. "See you at breakfast."

She snorted and turned away. "Not if I see you first."

Willi Del Marquot's house was very much like Willie Dell, or as she was known to most people in St. Louis Parish, Miss Billie. She had lived in the modern ranch type cottage long enough to give it some of her quietly restrained splendor and easy comfortable personality.

Allen reflected on this comfort as he walked up the flagstone path leading from the side gate, which he used because it was a better place to hitch his horse. She would be, he knew glad to see him. No matter when he called, or when he appeared Miss Billie was always glad to see him nor did she fail to show her pleasure.

He knocked on the little side door that was painted an orange yellow. Almost instantly it opened and she stood framed in the opening, the light shining as always on her silvery blonde hair.

"Come in, Allen." Her voice was soft and caressing as was the hand with which she touched his cheek. He closed the door behind him and gathered her into his arms fragrant, light, and warmly passionate.

"You'd welcome me at three in the morning, I believe," he said, his face alight with his appreciation of her. Her smile was slow and comfortable, making him delightfully uncomfortable.

"I have welcomed you at three o'clock."

"That's right isn't it?" He followed her into a cozy living room and sat on a low couch while she made him a drink.

"I'm always glad to see you, Allen. You know that."

"I know that and I appreciate it, but anyone like you who never complains and never raises hell, they're always the ones who get imposed on." She nestled closer to him, her hair tickling his chin and her small sigh warming his neck.

"Allen, too many people are always looking gift horses in the mouths. You come and when you come my world lights up. If I pulled the possessive female on you you'd perform in some fashion, but I only want you to perform in the fashion that suits you. I don't buy forced attention."

"If this bores you stop me, but you are an extraordinary woman."

"Why should that bore me?"

"Because I say it so much."

Her laugh was throaty and rich as she nestled her head on his chest and sighed.

"Allen, say it again." She got up and going to the small lamp on the blonde wood table turned it out leaving only a small light in the hallway to throw a dim illumination into the living room. She was, he knew readying herself for one of her symbolic rituals that always seemed to him just a little barbaric or unlady-like except that it was a little hard to think of Miss Billie as anything but lady-like. She was a quietly beautiful animal with silken smooth muscles that sometimes grew as hard as steel and as tough as whipcord. Miss Billie in daylight and Miss Billie in dim reflected light were two different persons, both delightful, each in her own way. Tonight she was dressed in some thin silky stuff that seemed to float about her like a nimbus of half light revealing suggestions of rounded limbs, of delightfully seductive depressions, fragrant limbs and skin of a petal like fragility, white and delightful to touch. When she came back to him she tripped lightly along as though in the first steps of some ritualistic dance the origin and achievement being wholly hers.

She slipped to her knees before him and extended a flame for his cheroot. He took it and puffed comfortably. "Why do you do things like that?"

"I've told you not to say things like that." She remained on her knees and, in the way that always intrigued him, her garment seemed to melt gradually away from her lovely shoulders with terrifying slowness and he could feel the tensing of his muscles. She smiled up at him and capturning his hands put them beside her face. It was warm and so smooth that he wanted to squeeze it hard to see if it wouldn't come off on his palms like a soft unguent, but he could never be rough with her. She was too gentle and small and appealing. Still she herself was anything but gentle under certain stimuli and he could feel the ripple that possessed her body as his hands slid down to her shoulders. She raised up and like a mountain shedding its blanket of morning mist she came toward him.

She was warm and tremulous in his arms and her mouth was sweetly eager, capturing his and playing upon it like some transfigured Aphrodite of old touched with the wand of life.

CHAPTER FOUR

AFTER BREAKFAST NEXT morning, Allen took Hank to the barn and calling Jake to them, he said, "Tell Hank here what you saw day before yesterday."

Jake did so without color or histrionics. He dismissed Jake and turning to Hank, said, "There you are, son. You'll have to learn one of these days the difference between fact and fiction, and learn to wait 'til the dope is all in before you go about calling people names. Honey is a colored girl, but she wouldn't like what you called her. In this country white people rarely apologize to colored people, but I'm leaving it up to you. Do whatever your manhood prompts."

Hank nodded dumbly and turning, walked away.

Allen mounted Straw, his big rangy roan gelding, and rode the mile to Lucindy's house. Amos was in the field and he could see Honey in the yard working in her flowers which she loved second only to Allen. He rode up and dismounted, and Honey ran to the gate to meet him.

She flung herself headlong into his arms. "Mr. Allen... I'm so glad you came. I wanted to come to the house, but... I was afraid."

He held her at arms length and looked into her damp eyes. "Afraid of what, Honey?"

She dropped her eyes and her sensitive lips quivered. "I was afraid you might be mad at me... I heard what you did to Mr. Emil."

He petted her soft black hair tenderly. "You know better than that, Honey. When have I ever been mad at you?"

She nodded happily. "Yes sir, I know...but...I was just afraid. I was...was sort of sick, too..."

Allen's deep blue eyes began to show golden flecks and his jaw tightened. "If you can, Honey, I'd like for you to forget that. I know it was bad but he's not right. I think he's a little off in the head, but I don't think he'll try such a thing again."

She shuddered and laid her head on his chest. "I sometimes try to think what I'd do without you," she said simply. "But my mind just shuts up on me."

"You won't have to do without me for a long time yet. You're growing up, you know, and one day you'll be married." He watched her narrowly as he spoke but she didn't react. In fact, she might even have not heard him at all. He felt strangely relieved. "You can come to the house whenever you want to," he said. "There'll never be a time when you can't. I have some new detective books I bought in Baton Rouge the other day."

She smiled and reached up and kissed him with simple childish directness. "I'll come, Mr. Allen, and I'm glad you're not mad at me. I feel sorry for Mr. Emil, though. I'm sorry I'm the cause of him getting that whipping."

"That whipping was brought on by himself alone, Honey. Don't worry about it. It does show what a big heart you have that you can feel sorry for him."

She frowned slightly. "It isn't because of Mr. Emil just by himself. I hate to see anything hurt."

He drew her close and squeezed her. "Yes, Honey, I know."

He looked toward the house and saw Hank on the paint riding at a dead run toward the red gate. He was a good quarter of a mile away yet. He patted the girl on a bare satiny shoulder. "Have to get on out to the field, Honey. Come to the house whenever you feel like it."

She watched him with dark, gravely beautiful eyes. "Yes, Mr. Allen, I'll come."

He whipped old Straw into a racing gallop and put the house between them so Hank wouldn't see him. Once hidden, he rode swiftly toward a clump of fig trees close behind the house, dismounted and hitched the big horse to a branch. In a fast walk, he approached the house from the rear just as Hank rode up to the front. Walking quietly, he approached the corner of the house where a trellis of rose bushes would make an effective point of vantage affording him protection.

Hank looked at Honey self-consciously. "Good morning," he said.

"Good morning, Mr. Henry."

"Why can't you call me Hank like everybody else does?"

"Do you want me to call you Hank ... and not say mister?"

Hank seemed at a loss. All Negroes called white Mister and he wasn't sure upon what he could base such a departure from the accepted code. "Well ..." He stopped and squirmed. He covered his discomfiture by sliding from the horse and throwing the reins over one of the pickets of the fence. He opened the gate and walked in.

"Honey, come over here and sit down with me. I want to talk to you."

She obeyed docilely and they sat on Amos' fish pond made of bricks in which there was neither water nor fish.

"Honey, I've just come to this country and where I came from it was a town and I don't know a lot of things about this place yet. I know I don't like to hear you call me mister. I'd rather you called me Hank. Maybe it isn't right for you to, but we could let you do it when no one is around, sort of. Then, when you were at the house or around people, you could call me mister if you want to.

Honey nodded seriously. "Yes sir. That would be the best way."

"And don't be saying yes sir. That's one thing you don't have to do."

She smiled, showing her white perfect teeth. "O.K., Hank."

He beamed. "Say that again," he begged. She obliged and they both laughed.

Hank grew serious. "Honey ... I'm sorry about the other day."

She placed a soft hand on his in a companionable way. "That's all right. It wasn't your fault."

"Yes, I know that," he said bitterly. "It was my brother's fault, but something else is my fault. I listened to him and thought some bad things about you when I oughtn't to have done it."

"What did you think?"

Hank paled, then flushed. "Gosh, Honey, I hate to tell you what I said. Couldn't I just say I'm awfully sorry and then it would be all right, wouldn't it?"

She regarded him steadily, but his eyes couldn't stand the impact, and he looked miserably away.

"If that's the way you want it, then it's all right with me."

Hank gripped the bricks with such strength that his finger-tips grew white.

"Now I gotta tell you, but please, it was because I was mad at everybody and I ... well, I guess I didn't have my right mind. I was a little drunk, too." He seemed to have the hope that the last remark would remove some of the stain.

"Amos says people don't know what they're doing when they're drunk."

Hank gasped gratefully. "Amos is plumb right. I just know I'd a never said what I said if Unk hadn't of give me those drinks."

"What did you say Mr .... Hank?"

Hank gripped his hands together and his eyes roved around while he strove to think of a soft way to express it. His mind grew a little muddled, however, and he had to blurt out. "Honey, I called you a whore." His voice squeaked alarmingly.

She regarded him silently for a long while. "Mr. Henry," he winced because he knew she said it deliberately. "Why did you say that about me?"

"Good God, Honey, Emil said you tried … wanted him to."

"He couldn't have said that."

"He *did* say it. I know I was wrong to believe him and I really didn't … it was the drinking that did it."

She sighed and from his hiding place, Allen saw her head tilt forward and he knew she was crying.

Hank put an arm gingerly about her shoulders. "Gee, Honey, I'm sorry. I didn't mean to make you cry. I didn't really believe him. I was crazy for saying such a thing." There was genuine heartbreak in the lad's voice and Allen swallowed a lump in his throat. Honey knew it, too, because she raised her head and dried her eyes on the hem of her dress, unconsciously baring some length of a softly rounded thigh.

She looked at the boy. "It's all right, Mr. Henry. I know you didn't really mean it."

Hank gulped and sniffed. "Gee, Honey, you're swell. Please, couldn't you call me Hank?"

She smiled softly and patted his hand again. "All right … Hank."

Hank was so relieved that he leaped to his feet beaming. "Gosh, Honey, it's good to get that off my mind. You've really been swell about it."

"Hank, you know you didn't have to tell me. You could have kept it to yourself and I never would have known."

Henry sat down again and shook his head. "No, I couldn't. Not the way Unk put it up to me."

"What did he say?"

"He said that people in this part of the country don't apologize to colored people, but for me to let my manhood be my guide." He shook his head. "You know, Honey, I guess I'm sort of dumb. And I don't understand people very well."

"I don't either...sometimes. Not even myself. I remember the time I thought Mr. Allen was mad at me, the time I cut Toome's head with a brick. I thought I'd die. When he saw me crying, he took me into the feed room and talked to me like a father, and before I knew it he was holding me in his arms, and I was asking him if he still loved me and he said he did. I've often wondered what made me have the nerve to do that. Colored girls just *don't* talk to white folks like that. Still, if I hadn't, I guess things wouldn't be so nice now. I don't guess anyone could love anybody like I do Mr. Allen."

"I guess so," agreed Hank, a trifle hazily. "I wouldn't leave here for a million dollars...well, I gotta go. Mose and I gotta look over the herd again for screw worms."

He got up and started for the gate with Honey walking beside him. He opened the gate and turned about. "Thanks again for...well, for being nice, Honey."

Her smile was all he needed. They stood facing each other just a foot apart, looking into each other's eyes and it happened. No one could say just how, but suddenly Hank put his hands on her shoulders, bent forward and kissed her softly on the lips. Then he leaped on his horse and was gone. Honey stood there for a long time, then she touched her lips gently as if afraid she might drive the sensation away, yet wanting to explore the region of such a wonderful happening. She turned around and, walking back to the fish pond, sat with languorous grace, her eyes opaque and her mind miles away. Allen Gordon swallowed hard and walked quietly away.

After a hot morning in the fields doing battle with Bermuda grass and the boll weevil, using his willing field hands and lead arsenate as weapons, Allen returned to the house to find two oddly contrasted characters sitting on the porch. One swilled a gargantuan highball while the other sipped austerely at a glass of lemonade. The first visitor was Dr. Alcide Fontenot, a retired man of medicine, who was little bigger than the drink he was treating so manfully. He sported a full head of heavy, curly black hair, spade beard and goatee and had never been seen wearing a hat. His wise, slightly cynical eyes had seen, as he put it, too much pain. Being the only Franco-American in St. Louis Parish he was looked upon with a variety of reactions, spanning generous limits.

The Reverend Charles Packenham Rathbone was cut from an entirely different cloth. He was tall, grave-faced, and carried God's word about like a sword with the air of being sorry it wasn't of a more destructive, if less divine, metal. He was against sin and man's weaknesses, professing to have overcome both in his early youth, which remark Dr. Fontenot considered obvious to anyone with any training in the medical profession. Allen made a grimace that had to do battle with a smile as he recognized his guests. He touched Straw with a light spur and cantered briskly up to the front gate. Hooking the reins over the saddle horn, he smote the big horse briskly on the rump and allowed hunger to direct him to his stable. He swung open the hoary old picket gate and walked briskly up the brick walk.

"Hi, Doc. You old reprobate. Since when have you been keeping company with the cloth?"

The little man bounced to his feet with remarkable suppleness. "The cloth was preceded by me," he announced managing to imply that the idea was first his. The Rev. Rathbone rose stiffly to his feet.

"Good morning, Allen."

Allen shook hands with them and took a handy chair with the boneless abandon of a juvenile. "What brings you two around today unless it was the smells coming from my kitchen?"

"The smells were enough for me," said the doctor, eying his drink speculatively. They and your cellar. Solomon couldn't decide the better."

"I should like to think that Solomon would have had something better to do," said the Reverend sourly.

Dr. Fontenot waved an airily expressive hand. "Think what you please, but should you ever really want to know what Solomon was like, I suggest you resort to your Bible. I hear that it is accepted as something of an authority on the subject."

Reverend's eyebrows knitted savagely and his thin lips became thinner. "Allen, there are some things that I'd like to say to you in private."

"Okay, Reverend. Doc, take that faltering highball back to the kitchen and let Lucindy give it a transfusion ... we won't be long, I hope."

The little man got to his feet, allowing a devilish glance to sweep the other two. "Hope," he quoted breezily, "springs eternal in the human breast."

Rathbone's smoking glance followed the doctor to the door. "A man," he declared in the tone of a judge passing sentence, "who shall roast in Hell."

"You're free to entertain your choice of opinions," said Allen with a touch of irritation. "Now what was it you wanted to talk about?"

"Allen, I was your father's best friend and counselor ..."

"That," said the other woodenly, "Is a fabrication. My father's best friend was Mancel O'Reilly. He happened to be a man who was in need of no earthly counselor."

"Possibly," said the other in no way discomfited. "I was not speaking of earthly counsel. The fact is, Allen, since I held your father in high esteem, I feel that I would be remiss in my duty if I did not hold out my hand to you."

"What the devil are you talking about? If it's about coming to church, you're wasting your time. I think we had that out when I was seventeen. I haven't changed."

Rathbone sighed and looked above to let all see his burden. "I was not about to broach that subject. The truth is, people are beginning to talk."

"Yes, I know," said Allen crisply. "As near as can be ascertained, it happened about fifteen thousand years ago. Do you have a theory on how to stop it?"

The older man flushed. "I'll thank you not to be facetious when I'm only trying to help you."

"I gathered that was your personal conviction, but you haven't made the nature of your help apparent."

"I told you people were beginning to talk."

"And I answered that. If I do say so myself, it was a dilly of a crack."

Rathbone frowned. "Is it possible that you don't know what I'm talking about?"

"That would seem the obvious conclusion."

"I mean, Allen, that this carrying on openly with that nigger girl will have to cease."

Allen Gordon gripped the arms of his chair and fought silently the lurid spray of red rage that flamed up inside him. For a full moment he fought half blind, choked and stunned by the fury of his emotion. He faced the minister, his hot eyes flecked with little pots of molten gold.

"It is common talk that you are grooming her to be your mistress and certain quarters have it that you have already…taken her…er, aside." The man was singularly dense. "And," he continued, "the fact that you horse-whipped your own nephew because of his intentions concerning her seems to confirm what is being said."

When Allen finally got his breath under control, he said in deadly calm, "Your granddaughter is about sixteen, isn't she?"

"Yes…er, I think, on the twentieth of August…why?"

"Then since you seem to think so little of rape, suppose you bring her around. I can assure her of some rousing fun with my half-witted nephew."

If Rathbone had suddenly been garroted, his reaction could not have been more dramatic. Blood rushed to his face and he stood up. "I did not come here to be…"

Allen also stood and lashed the older man across the face with his eyes. "And I didn't ask you to come for any reason at all, much less to air your opinions on tawdry gossip. You are old enough to be my father or I'd break your sanctimonious neck. What I choose to do on my plantation neither you nor any other man shall presume to dictate…" He grasped the front of the man's dark suit and twisted it cruelly, forcing him back against the wall. "Who," he spat the word out like a bullet, "told you all this crap?"

Rathbone gasped and paled from fright. He could see now what his acuteness had failed to reveal earlier in the discussion, and his voice was flat and emotionless, and for that reason all the more terrible. "I … I … It … was Sam Tanken."

Allen released him and stood back watching him with eyes that glowed as hard as diamonds. "Tanken … Christ, what a laugh. I could tell you a few things about him. One has to do with chasing him off my place two weeks ago for disturbing one of Jake's little Saturday night parties. What a gold fish you chose as your informant. Now! Get the hell off this place and if I *ever* see you here again, you won't get a chance to open your mouth. You'll go out on your pious ear."

The Reverend Rathbone practically fell from the porch in his haste and Allen stood watching him with one hand on his hip while the other absently mussed his thick flaming hair until it stood up like the hackles of a game cock.

Dr. Fontenot chuckled as he sidled out on the porch with a fresh drink. "Now a man overburdened with honor might have remained discreetly out of earshot. Unfortunately, my profession endowed me with a flagellating curiosity that shoves such halting and unedifying matters as honor completely in the background."

"From that verbiage, I glean that you heard all," Allen relaxed into a tight bitter grin.

"All and more. I say more because I know a great deal more than the good brother was allowed to tell. Tanken has been plying the poisoned tongue where it would do the most good ... er harm. Oddly enough, I came to tell you about it, but he beat me to it."

"You probably could have gone about it a little differently, Doctor."

"Not being an ass, I should have taken exquisite pains to do so." He sipped a little of his drink with the relish of an epicure. "Just what Tanken's idea is remains a mystery. Is it the snapping back of a jackal that has been sprinkled with bird shot, or is the man merely a constitutional malice monger?"

"Some of both, I'd say," said Allen, heavily taking his seat again.

"Just the same, it is taking root all over the parish, and I hate to see it. You told me about the girl, and I've seen her. Oh, I've been raised here in the South and I know that people just don't publicly love little Negro girls, no matter how cute and smart they are, yet you are a bachelor and you were lonely. The girl was obviously crazy about you in a perfectly harmless, daughter-to-father way. Still ..." he stopped and smiled. Allen's face had darkened, but the little man seemed to know what was coming.

"As you well know, Doc, whites have always been much *better* than the Negro, whatever that means. So much better that he had to set up a system in which hate and retaliation came out whenever he couldn't justify himself any other way, *yet how many pure Negroes can you find in the South today as compared to those with white blood in them?* In other words, a white man won't eat at the same table with a Negro, but he'll *sleep* with his daughter, sister, wife or ... hell, maybe grandmother. What sort of sense does that make to you?"

The little man laughed delightedly. "Your father caused consternation hereabouts as a man of uncanny business instincts. He left you well enough fixed so that you have time to repeat his performance in another field."

Allen made a forceful gesture with his left hand. "Hell, I know I've got a lot of that same thing in me. If a Negro came up and said to me, 'Come on, Allen, let's eat,' I'd probably throw him off the place, because the way the set up is, it wouldn't be just ordinary familiarity and a request to have dinner with me, it would be the height of insolence. That I take from no man, whatever color of the spectrum fate handed him as pigment."

"Um … yes. I fancy I just saw a good example of that not more than ten minutes ago. You are in the position of being pilloried for being right."

"A lousy state, isn't it?"

"Oh, come now. You know you don't care a hoot what people think."

The other nodded stiffly. "True, but I have a family now and rather than cause any of these kids pain and embarrassment, I'll take a lot. They are not to be harpooned because of me. I'll see Tanken soon and I think he will be sorry he spread tales."

"I somehow share that belief, since I worked on a man once whom your father had taken to task for beating a horse that was too poor to pull a wagon. I think I took some seventy stitches in him in sundry places. Your father also had a way with a bull whip."

Lucindy called them to dinner and Allen said, "Come on and taste the fruits of your nose for food. I still think that's why you came really."

They walked through the long hall and while passing the stairway saw Emil coming down. He stopped abruptly as he saw Allen and seemed about to retreat in haste. "Come on down, Emil," said Allen conversationally. "Time for dinner." The tenseness vanished, and with a look of great relief, Emil came on down the steps and followed the others into the dining room.

"Where's your mother, Emil?" asked Allen conversationally as he spooned his soup.

"She's in her room."

"Does she know dinner's ready?"

"Yessir, she says she ain't hungry."

Dr. Fontenot glanced at Emil, then at Allen, then back to his soup. There was an undercurrent that he could feel but couldn't identify. Hank stormed into the dining room and seeing company at the table, he calmed down immediately and walked sedately to his chair.

"Hi, Doctor."

"Good noon, Henry…where's your…Ah, there you are my dear. I was wondering where you were."

Bonnie came in dressed in a pair of well fitting jeans and a khaki shirt. She went behind the little man and playfully pulled his ear. "Plotting your latest medical murder," she teased. "I can tell by the color of your neck…and while you're eating, too. You'd make an excellent mad doctor for the movies."

Fontenot chuckled. "All my murders are legal, my dear. I shall be called on to visit you some day, so you'd better stay in my good graces."

"I thought you had retired."

"Would retirement or anything less than a fractured spine or death keep me from you if you even had indigestion?"

"Gallantry is not dead." She took her seat and attacked her soup with gusto. The khaki shirt was well fitting, which meant that just two buttons down it began to strain and the third buttonhole seemed to be in torture, the fourth little better. From there on, the buttons appeared smug and self-satisfied. After dinner, Bonnie, the doctor, and Allen sat on the porch.

"Sam could cause you some trouble you know…or should we discuss that before Bonnie?"

Allen waved a careless hand. "Don't mind her. She could take anything and toast it if there was any good liquor about."

Fontenot glanced at her quickly. "She could do a little toasting speaking in terms of thermal units, if I'm any judge…and it has been said that in my day, I was quite a judge."

Bonnie grinned and stretched like a healthy animal. "If your present tastes are any standard, I'd say you're still doing all right, but in your day the torso must have been a complete mystery and therefore sometimes a disappointment."

"Sometimes," admitted the little man. "However, you must remember that they revealed certain salient points even in those days."

"What do you mean he could cause me some trouble … Sam, I mean."

"Well, you have a terrible temper, Allen, and it gets the best of you sometimes. You might kill him, which in itself wouldn't be too bad, but it would be said that you did it because he told the truth on you. Truth, so far as people hereabouts are concerned."

Allen nodded, then sat erect. "You have seen Honey probably, but have you seen her lately?"

"Not since she was about ten … why?"

"Take a look out there about fifty feet from the front gate."

The doctor followed the pointing finger with his eyes and saw her coming up the path with a free springy stride. There was a marvelous grace to her bearing, and a kind of super awareness that almost shone from her bright alert eyes. "Shades of my ancestors, is that she?"

"That's her," said Bonnie. "Say what you please … I'm excepted company."

"Comparison is not necessary. The child's physical endowments are more than sufficient, but look at the unspoiled grace of her. Look at her attitude, her walk. She has all of what models go to charm school to learn and she has it by right of birth."

Honey opened the front gate and closed it behind her carefully. She walked lithely up the walk and stopped respectfully near the steps. "Good evening, Mr. Allen … Doctor … Miss Bonnie."

After they had all spoken, Allen said, "Come on up and sit with us, Honey."

She looked embarrassed. "Mr. Allen, I've heard what people have been saying. Maybe I'd better not."

He stood up suddenly. His bushy brows contracted till they almost met. His red hair seemed to stiffen and spark. "I said come on and sit with us, Honey." He didn't raise his voice, but the authority rang from it like the resonance of a powerful bridge to a passing vehicle.

Now, thought the doctor, I'll see... He saw. The commanding mien didn't even touch the girl.

She smiled sweetly, affectionately and came on up the steps. Allen met her and throwing an arm about her shoulders, squeezed her gently. She gave him a quick convulsive clutch and turned away and took a rocker.

"I wouldn't mention it, Honey," said Bonnie kindly, "but we three are your friends... I'm sorry about the other day..."

Honey interrupted her. "I know you are, Miss Bonnie, but it's done now and I know you just wanted me to know how you felt. I knew how you felt, Miss Bonnie, because I know you. You wouldn't hurt anyone and you don't like to see anyone else hurt."

The little Frenchman leaned forward, his black eyes sparkling. "How did you know that, my dear?"

Honey smiled. "Doctor, you could tell how it works maybe, but all I know is that I know it. Miss Bonnie saw me at the store not long after she came. She came up, asked my name and chatted with me for a while. Right then I knew she was a good person."

Fontenot leaned back and cackled rustily. "Woman's intuition, Allen. It can be explained but why do it." He turned again to Honey. "With what you have, my dear, you do not need wisdom. You will accumulate that in time, but the other you were born with."

"Thank you, sir."

Dr. Fontenot rose to his feet. "Have to go, Allen. I promised Maud I'd bring a fish home for supper. Mind if I cast a while on the lake as I go out?"

"Go ahead. I wish you'd catch all those big ones. The county agent tells me that they eat up so many smaller ones that they're a hazard and ought to be seined out."

"I'll take care of them," bragged the doctor.

The big bell rang in the back yard announcing that it was half past one and time to go to the fields. A big red setter howled dismally as the sound of the bell smote his ears, and was joined later by a yellow and black Belgian shepherd who was more dignified and reserved in his protests.

Allen rose to his feet. "Well, gals, I think I'll take a short nap. Keeps the mind clean."

"You ought to sleep all the time then," jibed Bonnie.

"Listen to who's talking. Did you want to see me about anything in particular, Honey?"

"No sir. I just wanted to get some books."

"O.K. Help yourself. You know where they are."

"Yes sir."

"See you later." He waved his hand and disappeared through the front door.

Honey's eyes followed him eagerly, then she went in to the library.

Jane came out on the porch taking her glasses off and putting them on again. "Bonnie, I think I can see as well with them off as ... Bonnie, what's the matter?"

Bonnie looked up at her sister. "Some day I'll tell you all about it, and I think you'll understand. You look swell, sister of mine. Another fifteen pounds and you'll be a distinct hazard to the male population of St. Louis Parish."

Jane blushed but held up her head. "You really think so?"

"Certainly ... wait a minute, I hear voices."

Honey sat on the floor reading the teaser on a book called "Treasure of the Dead" by Afton St. Clair. She smiled at a passage and picked up another. Hearing a slight noise behind her, she turned. Millie Brame stood in the doorway, her white hair in disarray, her eyes gleaming feverishly.

"What are you doing in here?" Her voice was trembling with rage, harsh and forbidding.

Honey eyed her steadily. "I'm getting a book."

Millie walked over till she towered over the girl. "How dare you show your face in this house after what you did to my son. *How dare you.*"

"Mr. Allen said I could."

"Mr. Allen …" Millie spat the words out like they were offal. Her breath came in hoarse gasping gulps, her face flushed and her eyes gleaming madly. With a cry like that of some beast of prey, Millie picked up a heavy book end and raised it high over her head. "I'll *kill* you, you …" The book end fell from her fingers to the floor and she was jerked around with a force that wrenched her neck. A hard forearm rammed itself into her throat and would have knocked her to the floor had she not fallen across a couch.

Bonnie breathed hard. "Have you lost your mind, or do you think Unk might let you off because you're a woman? Unless you learn to control yourself, I'm afraid we'll have to slip you into a padded cell."

Millie's face had gone white as chalk. She struggled into sitting position. She pointed a quavering finger at Honey. "Get her out of here."

"Go to your room, or shall I summon Unk? This is Unk's house and if he decided to stable a couple of steers in your room, you'd have to take it."

"Who's calling Unk?" Allen appeared at the door and stood taking in the little tableau.

"Mother seems to resent your letting Honey in the parlor," said Bonnie coolly. "She was about to get vehement."

"Get up, Millie."

She cowered back on the divan watching him with wide fearful eyes.

"I said get up, Millie."

A loose window vibrated lightly from the muted thunder of his voice. She got up without volition or direction. He caught her by the arm and led her to the door.

"Go upstairs to your room and remain there 'til I tell you to come down. I should hate to use harsh methods on you, but just let this be repeated once more and you'll be sorry."

She walked vacantly away, rubbing her arm where his hard fingers had bruised it.

He turned back to the two girls. Honey was standing white and still at the end of the table. He drew her close to his chest. "Everyone wants to pick on you, and all you've done has been to be good and lovely and a joy to a lonely bachelor."

Honey buried her face in his shirt and sobbed. "Mr. Allen, I don't want to make you get in trouble with your own folks. I don't have to come to the house."

"Honey, look at me." He put a hand under her chin. Her big eyes glistened with tears. The long lashes were jeweled with crystalline drops. "You know I love you, don't you?"

"Yes sir. That's why I don't want to cause you any trouble. Please, Mr. Allen..."

"You love me, too, don't you?"

She gasped deeply and shuddered. "So much I can't even talk about it."

"O.K. That's the situation. If I can't have the people I love in my house, then... then *I'll burn the goddamned place down and everything in it.*"

Bonnie caught a glimpse of his eyes and felt a little scared. She also felt as though she ought to do something. She sat beside them and placed a hand on the girl's shoulder. "Honey'll come here whenever she wants, Unk. Just like she did. I'll make it my business to be with her whenever she's here. You'll have nothing to worry about."

"You're a good egg, Bonnie. I guess it's a good thing. I don't know what I'd do without you."

"I don't know what either of us would do without you."

Honey rose from the lounge and picked up the books. "I'm taking two of them, Mr. Allen. Miss Bonnie, I left your Nero Wolfe book on the table… Miss Bonnie?"

"What is it, Honey?"

The girl looked at her a moment, then seized her hand, held it to her cheek for a second, then almost ran from the room.

"What are we going to do about Mother and Emil, Unk? We've got to do something. Since we've been here, there's been nothing but ups and downs for you. You've lost your temper several times in the last few days and don't think I don't know what it's doing to you. You look older and I don't like that."

He smiled wearily. "I can't think of anything, Bonnie. I know one thing, if this keeps up, something is going to happen and it won't be good."

Jane came in white-faced and frightened but with a certain air of determination.

"I want to make a confession."

Allen grinned at her. "Shoot. We'll listen."

"I've been listening to everything that went on. I saw it all. I've been thinking. I never fully understood 'til just now what I really have for a mother. Now it seems incredible that I didn't see it before."

Bonnie said, "Janie, you were so entirely in her clutches all your life that you couldn't know anything but what she told you. She didn't ever let you think."

"That is becoming evident," she said, sitting in a chair, folding her hands loosely in her lap. "All those terrible things she told me that men do to women … I fooled her there, though. I read books and I found out it wasn't so terrible … could be wonderful."

She stopped and colored at the temerity of her speech. "All about the cross that women bore because God intended that they bear it. That all men were animals, full of lust, greed and cruelty. I used to wonder how she could think father cruel, I even asked her once. She rolled her eyes and hinted darkly that things went on in the bedroom that made ravening maniacs out of the meekest men ... fool that I was, I believed it."

"Now, we'll have to watch her, Unk. A man won't be safe with her any more."

"What do you mean any more?" said Jane, flushed but spirited. "I've never had the first chance."

Later that afternoon, Dr. Fontenot returned to the house bearing eleven large bass. He bore them to the front porch with all the pride of a buck private bearing a captured flag. "Hah," he barked to Allen, Jane and Bonnie as they sat on the porch. "There are some big ones that'll never eat any more little fish. Call Lucindy, Bonnie, and give her some to cook for you all. Let her take three or four home. Two are plenty for my wife and I ... no, better take four. Albert is coming home from Tulane this week. I'll put one in the deep freeze for him."

"Albert Telesphore Aniset Fontenot. What a handle you and Maud tacked onto that suffering boy."

"*Mon Dieu,*" chuckled the little man. "Don't ever mention it. He despises those names."

"I know how he feels," sympathized Allen. "I recall the day I had to give my full name to my school teacher. I was mortified for a week. Bring him over some night. If he likes to fish, tell him the lake is his."

"Sure do thank you for them fish, Doctor," said Lucindy, her eyes shining as she looked at the bass.

"Tut, tut ... nothing to it, Lucindy. Probably catch some more tomorrow."

"I seem to recall a number of times when all you caught was a pair of muddy shoes and a cold."

"Pouf on your wet blankets, Allen. I have no such memories. This day will keep them back in my unconscious for a long time."

"I didn't know you old medics knew anything about psychiatry, Doctor," put in Bonnie. "You used that word like you were familiar with it."

"All old people are not fools, my dear. Right after I retired I took a course in it at Tulane. Led the class, by the way. Put in four days a week at Camp Shelby in that capacity all during the war, plus two a week at Harding Field. You are not very up-to-date on the Great Fontenot yourself. I retired because I was killing myself, and I can see no difference between that sort of death and cyanide except the latter is probably the more sensible of the two, being swifter and less painful. About Albert, I don't think you'll have any trouble getting him over here. Trouble running him off, I'd say. I meant to tell you, Jane. When you came to dinner today, I picked you for a stranger and almost leaped to my feet to throw you a bow. I recognized you just in time." He closed one eye and ogled her with the other. "Your beauteous sister will have to look to her laurels now."

Jane swept him a curtsey and thanked him prettily. She didn't blush and Bonnie felt a touch of pride.

"Well, good evening all. See you soon." He threw them a parting gesture with his free hand and strode down the walk, swinging his fish in the other.

They watched him climb into his little coupe and dash madly down the drive.

"Nice old man," commented Jane.

"Very nice," agreed Allen. "People have given up their last mystery to him. I wonder if there's anything he doesn't know about us."

"There's plenty he doesn't know about me," put in Bonnie with a half smile on her lips. "It hasn't happened yet."

Allen pinched her and she squealed and backed away. "He's probably hanging around so he can see it first hand, you terrible creature."

"Nothing has happened to me, either," said Jane dreamily, with a tinge of regret detectable in her voice.

"All in good time," said Allen easily. "You're young yet."

"But I don't have a lot of time, Unk," she protested. "Look how much has been wasted."

He nodded sympathetically. "I know, but hasty hand catches perch for pickerel or some such."

CHAPTER FIVE

THE MEETING WITH Sam Tanken didn't occur until a month later under circumstances that chance arranged. Allen had taken the Ford and gone to town for a haircut and to listen in on any gossip to see if it concerned him. He winced a little as the thought struck him that he was deliberately planning to listen to gossip. Hunting for personal tidbits was something else, he told himself and felt better about it. Kenton was a small town of some two thousand inhabitants with more than the usual sprinkling of small town drunks, dead beats and nosey, clatter-tongued old maids and widows. When he made his monthly visits to Police Jury meetings, he stayed only as long as was necessary. These meetings were a bore, but the people in his ward had elected his father so many times that people lost count and when he died, they insisted over Allen's protests that he run also. Though he had not electioneered, he won handily several times and it seemed that he would equal his father's record. The elder Gordon had made enemies at these meetings because of his ready tongue and steel trap mind, neither of which he chose to put under wraps. Allen was even more vocal and many had been the times that he won his point by sheer superiority of reason and the weight of his logic. As Allen neared the town through a little valley made by two creeks, he breathed deeply of the damp, cool sweetness of the air. He drove past the Court House Square, which contained historic twin-domed court house, in back of which was the squat ugly little jail with its barred windows, rusty and void like empty eyesockets. Past the little red brick bank with its ridiculous gargoyles flanking the door, the drug-store with its enticing smells, as varied as the pedigree of a back yard tomcat. The barber shop occupied a single frame building with a false front and inside sat the usual complement of gossips who smoked, chewed, whittled or gabbed as the taste and mood moved them. He parked the Ford close to the barber shop, and shoving back his cream Stetson, stepped out. He peeled off his doeskin riding gloves without which he never felt the house, and tossed them to the seat of the car. As he stepped into the shop, he noticed an empty chair and an atmosphere that had suddenly quieted. A man lay back in the other chair, his face thick with fragrant lather. The barber stood frozen in the attitude of the first shaving stroke. The man in the chair must have been singularly dense because in spite of the abrupt cessation of talk, he contin-ued flipping a pudgy hand in restrained gestures to punctuate his remarks. The hand had a thick growth of golden red hair that seemed to be polished, so brightly did it shine.

"Yeah, boys, I always say, when a man eddicates a nigger an' buys clothes fer her and keeps all the nigger boys away, that don't mean but one thing." He laughed gutturally. "And don't none of y'all need tellin' what it is. Yes sir. You know, sorta like Jason there when he grooms Maude S. fer the races at the fair." He guf-fawed and still did not notice the intense silence nor the sud-den rigidity of the barber with one hand on his forehead and the other with the razor poised in mid air.

Allen's eyes sparked in the subdued light of the shop, and men edged away from him. He hung up his hat carefully and began to rumple his hair unconsciously until it stood on end like the bristles of a mad bear.

"*Sit up, Sam!*" The voice sounded like a high speed saw in an oak knot. Men winced and edged still farther away. It cut through the thickness of Sam's wits like a cheese knife, and he sat up so abruptly that he almost cut himself on the razor that Price Boggs held nervelessly in his right hand. Sam Tanken was thick-bodied and fat. Pulpy flesh fell in folds from his chin to his breast and his tiny ears sat at right angles from his head. His hair was reddish gold on his head as on his hands, except that there was less of it. His skin had the intense pinkness often seen in Albinos. Right now it was the color of watermelon juice on white sand, sort of marbled in pink and white. His piggy pale blue eyes popped as he looked at Allen standing feet spread apart in the doorway.

"Get out of the chair, Sam," he said. "Out here in this vacant lot."

Sam did not move. It seemed that he did not breathe.

"What you gonna do, Allen?" quavered Price, his razor still poised in the air.

"I'm going to kill Sam Tanken."

"Ain't nobody goin' to kill nobody," Morris Bodine stalked importantly through the door, and put a hand on Allen's shoulder. "Come on, son. Can't be havin' no killings 'round here."

Allen ignored the sheriff with such complete indifference that the little short, bowlegged man took a couple of backward steps, removed his black hat and swept an unconscious hand over his bald head. His cigar butt hung damp, dead and limp in the corner of his mouth. He took another step to the rear and almost sat in Jim Stanncell's lap.

"I said get up, Sam. If I have to come to you, you'll wish I hadn't."

Sam found his voice. "Now look here, Allen, I ain't said ..."

"I heard what you said, and I talked to Rathbone so I know who you were talking about."

"I didn't mean no harm, Allen, I was just talkin' ..."

"You talked too much, Sam ... *get up!*"

"What you gonna do?"

"I'm going to stomp the ass off you. I'll teach you to spread your goddam dirty gossip around, using my name."

"Now, here ... you boys," the sheriff's voice had lost its authority and this time he could hardly hear himself. Sweat began to pop out in little scattered patches on his white head. He forgot to brush them off.

"I ain't gonna do no fightin'," Sam managed to choke out. "I ain't feelin' well. I ..."

"You'll feel a hell of a lot worse when I'm through with you."

"I tell you, I'm a sick man," he cried desperately. "I can prove it ... Ain't I a sick man, Elly?"

A small, desiccated man with mousy hair and a sardonic face in the corner of the room nodded. "Sure, he's sick, Allen," he said quietly. "Look at him. He et a full dinner an hour ago and five bottles of beer, but anybody can see he's sick."

A relieved snicker ran over the crowd. The sheriff took heart and drew his gun. "In the name of the law," he began, but Elly Walters tugged at his sleeve.

"Got the sight filed offen that there gun, Sheriff?"

"Why'n hell would I file the sight offa my gun?" he fumed, peeved because Elly had ruined his opening speech.

"You stand a good chanct of gettin' it rammed up your ass ... that's why."

The sheriff snorted and looked at Allen, startled to find the fierce eyes staring at him. "Put up that gun, Sheriff."

The old man winced and retreated again. "Sure, Allen, I was, just ..."

Allen walked over to the barber chair and tore the towel from Sam's chest and flung it into a corner. Grasping the fat man in the shirt front, he lifted him from the chair. Then he tensed and almost hurled the man into the street where he stumbled and fell flat.

He stood over him, waiting till he would rise, but Sam wouldn't get up. He came to his hands and knees and scuttled back into the barber shop. The sight was so ludicrous that the sheriff burst into a bellow of laughter which was echoed by the rest of the onlookers. Once inside, Sam straightened up and ran through the back door and disappeared.

A tiny muscle in Allen's sharply sculptured cheek twitched gently, and he raised his hand to still it. Then he reached inside and got his hat. "Don't you want a trim, Allen. You're next."

"I'll be back, Price, after I've walked my mad off."

As he started up the street, he heard rapid steps as Elly came alongside. "Come on and let's git a drink." Elly spat with distaste. "Been listenin' to that son of a bitch for half an hour and they's a bad taste in my mouth."

"Talked a lot, did he?"

"Don't never do nuthin' but talk. Never seen his beat. I knowed one o' these days he was gonna overtalk hisself."

"What was your reaction to what he said, Elly?"

They turned into a bar, and Allen ordered a double straight and Elly followed suit. "What I think or don't think don't make no difference. I keeps it to myself mostly. A man can do whatever he's a mind to, long as he don't step on me none. If you want to groom you a good lookin' nigger gal, then that's your business, and it sure ain't none o' mine to be sellin' on the streets."

Allen downed his drink while Elly sipped his with old maidish care. Then he told him about Honey from beginning to end, omitting not a single detail.

Elly nodded his small head wisely. "Tain't bein' done hereabouts, but fur as I know they ain't no law says you can't. I can't see as Sam's talkin' and your actin' is made him a better man or you a wuss one. You too much like your daddy 'cept I spec the old man woulda stomped the guts out of Sam, or whupped him half to death like he did 'Lisha Simms fer beatin' that pore old hoss be uster drive. Still and all, what you done is a lot wuss in some ways. You made him look ridickerlis and we all laughed at him. That'll burn a long time after a whip woulda stopped burnin'. Better keep a eye on him."

Allen nodded and ordered another round of drinks. "I'm glad you came along, Elly. I enjoyed talking to you."

Elly almost blushed. "Shucks. Why shouldn't I talk to you. Knowed your daddy when you couldn't understand a word he said. He talked that thick. I wasn't nuthin' but a kid then, and the old man uster have some of the best lookin' white faces in the country. When I was twenty, he give me a bull and a heifer." Elly chuckled. "Guess he knowed I'd never amount to nuthin' what took too much brainwork, so he give me a start in the beef business. Outa that start, I now got money in the bank, a daughter goin' to L.S.U., a son finished and a thousand head of as good beef as you'll find in a day's ridin'. The old man give me the dangdest beatin' two years 'fore he died I ever took in a trade. That was the old man. If he give you somethin', it was somethin' good and no strings, but if you tied into him in business, you was good to git skinned. You got too kind a heart. It's good in a way, but it's liable to git you in trouble some day."

Summer passed, hot, humid, and enervating. September's end was at hand and the fall round-up. Hank begged off from school for a week to help and Allen allowed it because the lad was so set on helping. The family sat at the dinner table chattering affably, all except Millie. She still maintained her stiff, offended air, from which none tried to pry her. She sat silently and picked at her food, answering what few questions were put to her but offering nothing. Allen had worked on Emil, giving him a horse and saddle and letting him help with the round-up. He entered it with enthusiasm and worked hard, seeming to forget the terrible whipping he had received.

The visit of Albert promised by Dr. Fontenot had not materialized as Albert had to return to the Charity Hospital where he was interning, but now he was through and going into general practice in Kenton. Allen made a mental note to invite him over for supper some night.

"I am going swimming this afternoon," announced Bonnie. "I'm going in a little private hole I found on Dogwood and I'm going in raw. Want to come, Janie?"

Janie looked up and threw her sister a sparkling smile. "Try and keep me away. We won't have much longer to swim this summer."

"What the hell," said Hank loudly. "Unk and I are going to swim all winter, ain't we, Unk?"

"I'll back you all out on a swim Christmas day," boasted Allen. He could feel a cold disapproving look of Millie's, but he ignored it. It seemed the best thing to do.

"I'll take that dare, you loud-mouthed braggart," retorted Jane.

"I'll make that two," said Bonnie.

"Me three," yelled Hank. "S'matter, Emil ... scared?"

Emil looked up from his plate and grinned slowly. "No. I just don't like cold water."

"What say we all go in Christmas day. Me, Jane, Unk, Bonnie, and ..." Hank shut his mouth with a snap and devoted too much attention to his steak.

"What were you saying, Hank?" asked Jane. Hank glowered at his plate.

"I was just talkin'. I didn't say nuthin' at all."

Allen glanced at the boy. He had grown half a foot it seemed since he came last May. He wondered what had dampened his enthusiasm about the swim, then he knew. He had automatically wanted to include Honey and had caught himself just in time to keep from mentioning her name. He sighed. He began to feel that he didn't have as many years as he had thought free of complications involving Honey and Hank.

He glanced at Jane as she ate her dinner with the gusto of active youth. She had spent most of the summer in the sun and her skin was the color of a ripe peach. She had gained not fifteen, but twenty pounds, and her figure had increased in attractiveness, had developed to an exciting degree and she dressed to show it off. Millie detested the new Jane with all the hammer-headed narrowness that she had shown toward Bonnie and for the same reason. Jane had been a case of delayed ripening, and now she had grabbed her freedom and held on. So far she had not had any social life but that would come in time. Allen, remembering his first affectionate gesture toward the girl and her frantic hysterical response, wondered if her arrested development might not make her a little too avid for pleasures of the senses. He could hardly blame her if it did. There was danger, though, and a plan was being born in his mind.

CHAPTER SIX

"So you see why I'm talking to you this way, Albert? That's why I want you to be the first to take her out. You understand people and you have your training."

Albert Fontenot had the black hair of his father and the good-natured regular features of his mother. He was medium in size but his body had the husky, compact frame of an athlete.

He grinned at Allen engagingly. "Let's don't misunderstand each other, Mr. Gordon. I'm afraid I'm not a very noble person. If she's all you say in looks, then I'd better keep myself fur, fur away."

Allen snorted. "If you were anything else you wouldn't be your father's son. I'm not asking that. You're a man and that covers a lot of territory, nor do I expect you to be anything else. I'm just pointing out that being a more acute person, you are better able to handle whatever comes up. If you are well versed in the ways of women, and I dare say you are, then you're still my man. Were you ever in a jam?"

"No sir. I've been too smart for that."

"Well, that's all I ask of you. Don't go rooting up the landscape like a razor-back hog and ruin things. If I didn't think you were the man for the job, I'd never have mentioned it. If it was Bonnie you were going out with, I'd say *you* might be in a position to learn something, but Jane is different. She's twenty-six years old, and as far as I know she's never had a date. It's time she had one."

"I see what you're driving at, Mr. Gordon…"

"Stop calling me Mr. Gordon! Call me Allen!"

Albert grinned. "O.K., Allen. When shall I call?"

Allen shrugged. "Make it light on yourself. The sooner the better."

"Sooner," agreed Albert. "When I get started in practice I won't have much time. My equipment is slow coming in."

When Albert Fontenot came tearing up the drive in his little convertible, Jane suddenly lost her nerve and dashed back into the house with Bonnie in hot pursuit. Allen shook with mirth and rocked comfortably in his chair. The sun was just going down, throwing showers of fiery lances through the branches of the live oaks, splashing the white walls of the old house with gold. It was getting cooler but not chilly. Albert skidded the car to a stop and bounded out with Gallic enthusiasm.

"Hi, Allen," he yelled as he opened the gate. Allen stood and walked to the steps.

Albert whizzed up the steps and grasped the older man by the hand. "The old place is as grand as ever, I see."

Allen nodded. "Come on over and take a chair. The fairy princess was seized with a fit of shyness when she saw you coming, but Bonnie will fetch her soon."

"This Bonnie you speak of, she must be some gal."

"That is an understatement, the extent of which you will not be able to realize till you know Bonnie. That woman, Albert, would rattle the teeth of the most blasé man I know."

"A loose woman?"

"No. Just a blunt spoken realist. Loose women usually are the worst ones for propriety. Bonnie spits on propriety."

"Hooray for Bonnie. Say I forgot. I'm supposed to be a dignified medico."

Allen chuckled. "Don't know where you'd get it. The old man has about as much dignity as me."

Albert took a cigarette from his pocket, thumped it on his thumb nail and lighted it. "The old man was born with a sort of dignity but he sure never put any on. Never seemed to hurt his bedside manner any."

"The old man is some relief to be around," said Allen. "He epitomizes Kipling's remark in "IF" of keeping one's virtue 'nor look too good or seem too wise.' If you're wise like he is, then there's no need to look that way. He made a remark to me once that sort of crystallized my own philosophy for me. He said that it appeared that in order to face a fact or admit a truth, one had to become immoral. He also wondered why the best things in life were considered sinful."

Albert considered his shoe laces with quiet seriousness. "The medical game strips away a lot of tinsel of false values," he said. "But, I'm glad I had the background I did. Pop grounded me in concrete before I even knew what he was doing. I started out with a free mind, but you should see some of them who have to start from scratch. It's pitiful."

Lucindy served them two mighty highballs and quietly withdrew. Albert smacked his lips and his dark eyes twinkled. "Pop told me that one of the most attractive points in this place is the cellar."

"Your pop is a discerning man. He has mentioned other qualities which you will no doubt get around to sooner or later," Allen said in a bantering tone, but Albert did not join him. Instead, he looked Allen in the eyes and said, "Yes. I was going to add…a man whose own convictions dictate his actions even in an environment which is inimical to them."

"You've heard, then, that I have an abnormal affection for a little colored girl?"

"Yes, I've heard it, but I do not consider it abnormal. Many things produce abnormality. Nothing whatever has been shown to be wrong with one person's affection toward another. The barriers between races are something which we acquire. We weren't born with them."

"Careful," said Allen jokingly, "you're a Southerner."

"By an accident of geography. I was in the war, and I found out how small the difference is between people, no matter where they come from. They have the same basic qualities and bad points. Some of my buddies couldn't quite understand why being a Southerner I didn't hate Negroes. I don't hate anyone. It is the most ignoble emotion ever to rise in the breast of man."

"Well spoken, but there are too few like that, Albert. I'm glad to say that things are getting better. Just how it is managed I don't know because all the facts are against it, but we are looked on as the only section of the United States that practices discrimination."

Albert nodded vigorously. "The war years surely threw a wrench into that little bit of nonsense. I think the best way I ever heard the race question described was by a student, Northwestern, I believe. A colored boy. Let's see… I read it not too long ago… oh, yes. 'If I'm dirty, I can cleanse myself. If I'm ignorant, I can better myself, but if you deny me justice because of the color of my skin, I can only refer you to God who made me that way.'"

"Wow," breathed Allen. "He really laid it on the line, didn't he?"

"Exactly. Well…" He took a long drink. "I have to get along with people and to some extent I have to concede to their idiotic social decisions, but I'll be damned if I have to think the way they do. If I thought so, I'd go back to Samoa where people are people. Here they seem to be a raving bunch of maniacs giving the knee to the almighty dollar and using their leisure time to persecute their less fortunate neighbors. They don't shoot or put them to the stake, but there are different kinds of persecution."

"I want you to see Honey, Albert," said Allen gravely. "You might then have some small idea why I love the child."

Lucindy came out bringing fresh drinks and the girls came out behind her. Albert leaped to his feet and was introduced. Jane was flushed and pretty, dressed in a cool green and white seersucker outfit that amounted to a skirt and bolero jacket leaving several inches of well-upholstered tan skin visible to the eye. Bonnie was just as resplendent in a pair of Arabian jersey pajamas that clung to her generous proportions with affectionate closeness.

Allen whistled at them in the approved style and they bowed politely. "Thanks for them kind noises, Unk," said Bonnie. "Say, Albert, is there a scarcity of men around these parts?"

"Oh, no," said Albert quickly. "There are several in Kenton ..."

She held up her hand. "Spare me if you have in mind such characters as Bennie Kinsmore, Jerry Albright or Manny Kurts. I've had all I want of them. They're the type who'll show you all the courtesies, faint if you offer to pay for a drink and try to demolish you before it is dark good with about as much finesse as ... as ..."

"Horton," supplied Allen.

"Who's Horton?" Albert wanted to know.

"My prize Hereford bull. Which, of course, is libel, because Horton's technique is flawless. He never misses."

"Horton and I," said Bonnie coolly stroking the glass in her hand with long fingers, "strive for one and the same thing but the end results are different."

Albert laughed delightedly. "I think now I know what you meant in your description of Bonnie. Seriously, Bonnie, although I sympathize with you regarding the men, there are none that I could very well guarantee ..."

"Never mind the guarantees. Just find me a man with a brain and I'll take care of the way he wears. If there's a flaw in the workmanship, I'll find it out before he has gone twenty-five thousand miles."

Lucindy came to announce supper and they all went in to the dining room. Hank was sitting at the table, his hair all slicked down, face washed, nails clean and looking like he had places to go. Emil sat quietly at his place and nodded as Albert was introduced. Millie gave him a frozen nod which earned her a quick searching glance from Albert. Lucindy came in with a covered plate which she put by Albert's place. He glanced at her questioningly and raised the cover. In the dish lay a hot golden brown blackberry fritter.

"Cat and dogs, Lucindy, how did you know I liked blackberry fritters?"

"Ain't I made enough of 'em for you when you was a little boy? I made the first one you ate and you made your momma find out how I made 'em."

"Well, I sure do appreciate this. I haven't had one in years. Thanks a lot, Lucindy."

"That's all right, Mr. Albert. Your daddy come to see me and Amos many a time in the middle of the night, rain or shine."

After dinner Hank, Bonnie, Allen, Jane and Albert sat on the porch in the cool breeze that had sprung up after the sun went down.

"Where are you going, Hank?" asked Allen. "I haven't seen you that clean all summer."

Hank, grateful for the dark, said in a gruff, well-controlled voice, "Don't know that I'll go anywhere. Just thought I'd clean up a bit. Been riding hard all day, you know."

"Age," said Bonnie critically, "is working some wonders. I expect any day now to see an honest hair sprouting on his lip."

"They don't start there first," retorted Hank pungently. "And you know I been shavin' a year."

The resultant laugh was at Bonnie's expense. "I think it's high time someone took you down a peg," said Allen, coughing from his laugh. "You usually ride high and now you see how it feels."

"I accept my chastisement with the fortitude for which the Brames have been famous for years," orated Bonnie, getting up from her chair. "I'm going for a drink. Whom shall I include?"

Everyone wanted a drink it seemed except Hank. "What's the matter with you?" queried Bonnie. "Unk emancipated you as regards the bottle months ago."

"The last time I drank … which was the first, I made a fool of myself," said Hank moodily. "Besides, I had a hell of a headache the next morning."

Bonnie and Lucindy came back bringing an oak bridge table, ice mixers and a quart bottle.

"Yummy," gloated Albert. "After all the potato whiskey that I went through school on, I can see where I'm going to make a hog of myself."

"Hogs have a very short distance to fall," said Jane crisply, "therefore, I shan't hold you up. If you stumble, you fall, so there."

Hank rose to his feet and stretched prodigiously … too much so. "Think I'll hit the hay. Got a hard day tomorrow. Unk, that blazed face steer … the crippled one, died. We missed him this summer and I guess the screw worms got him. I found his bones this morning. I could tell by that twisted horn."

"That was your steer, you know," Allen reminded him.

"Yes sir. I was hoping maybe you'd give me that calf I nursed …"

"O.K., you can have him, but you'd better watch him better than you did that steer."

"Yes sir." Hank departed with a light step.

"Methinks," said Bonnie watching her brother as he went through the door, "a man has been born here of late. His voice seems to have decided what register it likes best and he's losing his Afro-American pidgin. I do not for a moment believe he has gone to bed."

"You," her uncle pointed out carefully, "are a suspicious and evil woman."

"To prove the strength of my suspicion I require one and all to follow me stealthily to the end of the verandah and to peer cautiously across the moonlit sward."

They followed her after a wait of a couple of minutes and peered over her shoulder.

"As I said," she pointed a casual forefinger, "there goes Lothario whistling tunelessly."

They could see him walking with the quick spring stride of carefree youth whistling "Buttons and Bows" hideously off key.

"There's another complication in the making, Albert," said Allen turning away and draining the last of his drink. "Ten to one he's headed for Honey's house right now."

"Not jealous, are you?"

"Now you're talking like everybody else. No, I'm not, but I don't want to see something bloom here that will only succeed in making them unhappy. Unhappiness is the mortal sin as far as I'm concerned."

"Ditto here," returned Albert as they sat down, "but aren't you getting ahead of things a little? It seems to me that they are both too young to have any serious ideas."

"Yes … I keep telling myself that. However, I always remember one thing. Of course, I'm a bachelor and will probably always be one, so maybe my reactions aren't right, but I'll be damned if I ever felt any difference between my boyhood crushes and that so-called more mature feeling. I felt one as keenly as the other."

"I think I felt mine keener," put in Bonnie building herself and Jane another drink.

"I can see no way around that sort of unhappiness," offered Albert. "In matters of the heart, people are in for a good deal of aches and pains. The main thing is to try to avoid any lasting scar.

Youth generally takes care of that. Heartbreak in my language is nothing more than a bad case of a crushed ingrown ego. Hurt of the romantic sort when you come down to it, is nothing more than a wild cry in the night of 'You just can't do that to me.' "

"It would seem to me," said Allen showing his glass suggestively toward Bonnie, "that you two would want to take a ride or a walk or something. All this philosophy is well enough but in my day…"

"I can take a hint as well as the next one," said Albert getting to his feet. "Come along, Jane, we're not wanted."

"You gentlemen saved me from making a forward woman out of myself," said Jane as she rose. "I was about to call a halt to all this."

They walked out to the car, sniffing the cool night air with appreciation. "What shall we do, Jane, ride or walk?"

"Walk," said Jane. "The night is too beautiful to soil with gasoline fumes."

There was not a cloud in the sky and few stars as the moon with its intense flood of light had chased its less brilliant kinsmen into obscurity. They walked down the slope of the back pasture toward Dogwood, the grass soft and fragrant under their feet. Further down the creek where the woods grew thick, came the mournful hoot of an owl and Jane shivered a little and her arm brushed Albert's arm. "That noise always gives me the creeps."

"I prefer it to those little screech owls," Albert said. "The Negroes say that when they make that noise someone is dying."

"Gruesome," murmured Jane. She stumbled on a tuft of grass and Albert quickly caught her beneath her arms and righted her.

"Careful or your nylons will be a memory."

"Don't have any on," she said gaily, striving to still the tumult the touch of his hands on her bare skin had started. Her head swam and she breathed deeply several times. She put a hand up to her face and saw that it was trembling. On my first date, she thought, I get tossed for a loop the minute the man touches me. It must be all those years ...

"I seem to remember a thin ribbon of very clean sandy beach over toward the left near the bridge."

She nodded. "It's still there. I have a private little beach at one end of it where I get my tan. I found it one day by accident. I had loosened the bra to my bathing suit and a puff of wind blew it off. I almost fainted because that part of the beach is pretty much exposed, and I didn't know who might be looking. I scuttled after it and kept on going down where a patch of vines and briars offered something I could sort of hide in. They extended right down to the water's edge. While I adjusted my bra, I could see this little place ... just a tiny little beach, almost entirely screened. I waded around the briars and now I can sun all I want without worrying about who's peeping."

"And I'll bet you don't have any bathing suit marks on you now."

She flushed so deeply that he could see it easily in the moonlight. She overcame it bravely and looked at him still laughing shyly. "I hate myself for blushing so much. It seems to be a habit. You're right, of course. I was belted like one of Unk's pigs, but I'm solid now."

They were now at the edge of the creek and could hear the batrachian symphony being sent up from hundreds of amphibian throats all around them. A snake slithered away through the grass making Jane gasp and grab Albert by the arm. Katydids kept up their incessant arguments in the trees, and a bass splashed not far away. Across the creek a frog set up a choked pleading protest as a snake fanged him deeply. "What is that?" whispered Jane, fearfully.

"Frog. They never sound like that unless caught by a snake. It's their special snake cry. I've often wondered about that. Most other animals cry because they are hurt or because they hope to summon aid. A frog does neither. I can't imagine a frog going to another's rescue or doing anything once he got there. They're helpless animals."

Jane shuddered. "Seems cruel."

"To us, possibly, but the frogs win in the end by outbreeding the snakes."

"Albert, you seem to have the answer to everything."

He smiled but felt a slight qualm. "That's because you haven't known me long. There's plenty of things I can't answer. Maybe I've just made some attractive explanations. They might not be on the ball, you know."

She sighed. "Let's cross on the bridge or we'll have to wade."

"Wasn't for these new shoes, I wouldn't even mind that," he said.

"Wouldn't it be nice to swim on a night like this?" she said enthusiastically. "Why didn't we think to bring suits?"

He grinned devilishly. "Do we gotta have suits? You still haven't proved to me that you're the same color all over."

Her hands flew to her face. "I am now I bet ... the devil ... every time you open your mouth I get hot all over. Must be my retarded development. Come on let's get through that fence, the wire gap is tricky."

He followed her through the fence and they walked out on the graveled road. They crossed the bridge, climbed through the fence again and walked back toward the creek.

"It should be over there," she pointed. "We'll have to wade to get to my private beach or would you just as soon use the big one?"

"Me for privacy every time because I have a feeling that I might want to kiss you and I wouldn't want witnesses ... except us two."

Her mouth flew open and she stopped and held her breath. "There—did you see it?"

"Oh, a little one, and I must say that you were awfully pretty there in the moonlight holding your breath."

Jane turned away and started walking. "You're the only man that ever told me that, Albert." There was something like a sob in her voice. He caught up and caught her by the hand.

"Maybe the first but not the last, I'll bet. Just wait, Jane, you've got a lot of living ahead of you."

They walked out on the soft sand, brilliant in the bright light of the moon. "I've seen Waikiki Beach, but it wasn't like this. When I saw it, it was full of barbed wire and men."

They walked downstream for a hundred yards, and Jane sat suddenly in the sand. "Off with the shoes. Better roll up your pant legs, too. The water is a couple of feet deep here."

Albert thrilled to the cold water and the itchy feeling of the gravel on his shoe-tender feet. He made a great to-do of the wade, splashing and throwing water on Jane who squealed and ran out on the sand of the little enclosed beach.

"Better stay in close," she called out. "There's a drop-off about ten feet out there and no bottom."

The little beach was a gem. About thirty feet wide and not more than twice that long. The sand was clean and grated audibly as they walked about on it. Elder and blackberry bushes hung over it, making an impenetrable screen of brambles and leaves on three sides, leaving only the creek side open. On the other side of the stream was a dense growth of sumac, its lacquered leaves glinting in the moonlight like little knives of silver. It also provided excellent cover. Jane started toward the bushes and halted. "You have a cigarette lighter?"

"Sure. Want a smoke?"

"No. Come over here, I don't want to find a snake coiled up in my blanket."

He struck a light and Jane pulled a bundle from the leaves. "I keep this here so I won't have to bring it with me every time I want to soak up the sun."

She took off several layers of heavy paper and disclosed a tremendous beach blanket gaudily decorated with fish, crab, storks and other such aquatic fauna.

Her eyes softened as she spread the blanket. "Just another of the dozens of reasons why I love Unk so. This blanket…I came home one day from a sun bath griping that I had sand all over me. I had stayed in the water till I didn't want to stay in any longer, then I came out and sunned for a while. I had sand all over me and didn't want to go in again." Jane sat on the blanket and fell back propped up by her arms. Albert flopped on his belly. "So, I slipped my dress on over my swim suit and walked home with the sand grinding me at every step. He heard me fussing and the next day this turns up, all wrapped like a gift. The card said, 'Save your skin, sugar. It can be put to better use.' How about that for an uncle who is no kin at all—just a thoughtful man."

"I salute your uncle's perception," said Albert. "He must have had something like this in mind." He turned his head and kissed the hollow of her elbow. Blood thundered in Jane's head and again she had to take recourse to her deep breathing exercise.

She placed a soft hand on his thick black hair. A spasm shook her and her hand closed convulsively, causing Albert to wince.

"It must be my lack of experience, but…or do you shake all women like that by merely touching them?"

Albert grinned and rolled over on his back. "My fatal charm does it. They swoon in droves."

"Then I'm just falling in line with the crowd."

He sat up. "Oscar Wilde made a remark that suits the occasion very well. 'True love comes once to every man. Therefore, it is his duty to repeat that delightful occasion as many times as possible.' That's a literal translation. Love, Jane, is a much used word, but it means so many things that it isn't a good term. In Europe love means close relationship between sexes. Sleeping together, to be blunt. Of course, it has other uses, but love, like lover, as it is generally used, means quite a different thing than it does here.

Pop has the best definition of love I ever heard and in its abstruseness lies its excellence. He says that love is nothing more than a coincidence of affinities and truly, that's about all one can say about it. I have seen people who were so 'spiritually' in love that they breathed air much too rare for other people. They married. Now somewhere between the wedding day and ten years, that love came down to earth and some of the glitter came off. Their love seemed more like other people's and the man at least wasn't averse to picking up a little love on the side. Given the opportunity and security from the eyes of friends who were shrewder and uncaught at the time, the woman would have probably done so, too. Now... where did that triple distilled love go and why? All this stuff about loving only one is poetic rot. Hell, I'm strung out again and that was one reason why we left the house."

"No.... No!" said Jane earnestly. "Please go on, Albert, you make such wonderful sense and ... I'm, well, not very well up on such things."

He smiled. "I'm not going to sit here and stuff you full of Fontainisms all night."

They were silent for a while. Jane nibbled abstractedly at a succulent willow twig and Albert eyed the moon as though trying to stare it down.

"Then you feel," said Jane smiling, "that if, due to my narrowed youth, I fell in love with you..." She halted and took a deep breath, "I might still go on living?"

He nodded. "Living and thriving. Broken hearts are the playthings of poets and writers of fiction."

Albert possessed himself of one of her hands and kissed it slowly from wrist to fingertips.

She gave way to a series of restrained muscular motions that seemed to spring from her very depths. "Albert... Albert..."

She caught and held his eyes, her own glowing from some inner fire like little golden lamps reflecting the moon. The hand he had released clutched his arm tightly.

"Are you afraid, Jane?"

She shook her head. "Not really … only, I mean, the strangeness of it all and …"

He covered her lips with his fingers and sat erect drawing her into the cradle of his arms, brushing tendrils of hair gently away from her temples. She bit her lip and her body tensed, rock hard, stiff, and fearful. He passed a hand across her cheek and bringing her face closer, kissed her gently on the lips. She gave a frightened gasp and urged herself into a closer embrace. Her mouth opened and she bruised her lips against his teeth in the frenzied hunger of the emotionally starved. His hands kneaded her back muscles and traced the cleft from shoulders to waist. Her body erupted into a convulsive heave and her breathing was harsh, gasping and rapid. He touched her, and she tensed anew at the touch and a cry escaped her lips. The motion of her body became a frenzy, her arms clutched him like bands of steel and her lips roved over his face like live things.

He laid her gently back on the blanket and his hand touched the taut hard tendon under her knee.

Some time later she gave a little ragged sigh.

"Albert?"

"Yes, Janie."

"Albert, you're wonderful."

He rolled over and kissed her calm brow. "Thank you. You're better than that. You're scrumptious."

"Albert, can I say I love you?"

He grinned. "Sure. As a matter of fact, you do love me and I love you. It's inevitable."

He gathered her in his arms and kissed her lingeringly and when he released her, she was breathing hard. "Albert, I'm afraid of myself."

"Why, Sugar?"

A ripple possessed her body for a fleeting second. "Because…Albert, maybe it's because I haven't ever had any affection, love. No one ever petted me…do you suppose that could have given me…made me…" She stopped, unable to frame the words to convey her meaning.

He nibbled her small pink ear, causing her to shiver and cling to him. "You mean you think you have a sort of overblown appetite?"

"Yes, that's it."

"There could be a number of reasons. Maybe your repressions have something to do with it. Maybe it goes deeper than that. Time will tell."

"Albert, will you help me? I mean, if it's something bad…I…"

"Sure. I'm a doctor, remember? Of course, I started my treatments in an unorthodox manner, but don't you worry. We'll whip it, whatever it is. I'm with you all the way."

"Please, Albert, will you tell me…I mean, if it's something…something bad…will you tell me?"

He frowned at her severely. "As your physician, I shall tell you what I think. It is best that you know. A patient has a doctor to do his worrying. Worry ruined more humans and enriched more quacks than any one malady in existence. You'll have to trust me to do what I think is best."

She snuggled close to him and buried her face in the curve of his neck. He took the lobe of her ear in his mouth and worried it gently. She lifted her face and kissed him hungrily with the same heady passion and demand. Her beauty in the white moonlight struck him an actual physical blow. He lowered his face and kissed her gently. She pulled him forcibly to her, breathing hard.

The moon had fallen away to the West and now the sumac bushes cast little scimitars of shadow all over the sand.

"Sleep, Janie?"

"I slept a little." She rolled over and sat up, her dress high, showing a smooth gently rounded thigh crisscrossed with shadows.

Her hand dropped to his head and crept through his hair.

"May I say that I love you very much, Janie?"

"Oh, Albert. Say it any time you wish ... often ... often."

"You won't misunderstand?"

"No, Albert. Love me when you can and I will appreciate it. I won't hang about your neck or heckle you over the phone or make you wish I'd go drown myself."

"Janie, you're an immensely sensible girl in spite of your lack of experience."

"All my sense came at once. Even now I often feel like I'm existing in someone else's body."

"You certainly borrowed a fine body. You could drive a man mad."

She smiled ruefully. "I think I'd like that. Six months ago a man wouldn't have looked at me." She leaned back on her elbows again and breathed a long breath which she let go gustily.

"Albert ..." Her hand sought his face.

He pulled her fiercely to him, his hand caressing the skin of her side and back, coming to rest now and again.

"Albert ..."

"Janie ..."

An hour later they walked hand in hand across the pasture which was only dimly aglow from the moon which was dying in the West.

Jane turned her smooth sated face toward his. "Thanks for tonight, Albert. It seems that anything Unk does springs from immortal genius."

"You know then?"

"Certainly. Who in his right mind would have chosen me in place of Bonnie?"

"The night is almost over, Janie, and tomorrow is another day. Although I will not deny that Allen asked if I'd take you out and that I accepted because he requested it, I can say that tomorrow I'd be free to see Bonnie. Now it so happens that while I admire Bonnie and admit that she is a disturbing female, pretty, witty, smart and all that, when I come back to Loch Ness, it will be to see Janie."

Jane turned her face away and squeezed his hand. "Thanks a lot, Albert."

"Nuts," he retorted.

"I'm wondering," she said in a small voice, "how you can still be so kind to me. After all, I was pretty terrible." She started to cry. "But I couldn't help it, Albert. Not if it would have killed me."

He stopped her and took her in his arms. "Listen, cut that out. I don't admire you any the less. I actually admire you a hell of a lot more, because you have a certain fearless honesty about you that is hard to find. The only thing that seems to bother you is what I might think. Well, you can forget that. You and Bonnie both are my kind of people, and Allen, too. I'm struck, too, that you and Bonnie are a great deal alike. She just had more of whatever you call that belligerent push that kept her from conforming early in life whereas you took a lot longer. Now you even look alike."

Jane laid her cheek against his and sighed, a tattered little burbling noise that ended half a sob and half a laugh. He lifted her face with a forefinger and kissed her. She drew back and looked full in his face. His hand moved bringing a gasp from her. "Please don't, Albert. I can't stand it … not even now."

His hand moved again, his eyes holding hers steadily.

"Oh, Albert, what you must think … of … me …"

"I love you," he said huskily. "That's what I think of you." The soft grass received them gently.

Bonnie woke from a deep sleep. For a moment she stared about in the darkness, then she realized it was the thread of light coming from the bathroom that had awakened her. That

JOHN B. THOMPSON & JACK WOODFORD

and a rather inexperienced but mellow voice singing "Roses of Picardy," with some gusto.

She turned on the bedlight and saw it was four thirty. She swore aloud. "What in the billy hell?"

Finally the bathroom door opened and Jane came through with a towel cast negligently over her left shoulder. Her skin was pink and damp from the cold shower but this was the first time Jane had ever emerged from the bath without her robe tied firmly about her middle.

"Hi," she said languorously as she whipped the towel from her shoulder and sat in front of the huge dressing mirror. She considered herself critically for a moment and then began to wipe about the corners of her hair where the bathing cap had leaked. She fluffed out her hair and uttered a word that sounded suspiciously cussy.

"What did you say?" asked Bonnie hardly believing her ears.

"Oh ... I got my head full of sand and I didn't wash it. Well, I'll brush it out and wash it tomorrow."

"Unless this clock is unworthy of its name, tomorrow is already here and I note that you haven't been to bed."

Jane bent forward and considered her face at close range. "Unh, hunh," she agreed absently and began counting the strokes in a stage whisper. She finished and fished for stray grains with a fingernail, then stood up, walked to a closet. She whipped out a set of sleeping rompers and slipped them on.

Approaching the bed, she reached out for the light but Bonnie stopped her.

"Hold it. Stand there a moment, I want to look at you."

Jane's eyes were cool and placid. Their lids were relaxed and her face reposed and as smooth as a new pearl.

"Ooooooo what you did," accused Bonnie incredulously.

Instead of blushing, Jane grinned from ear to ear. "Wonderful man. Gorgeous moon. What else can you ask? Now, push over. I feel like sleeping a week."

Bonnie shrugged helplessly and moved over. Jane plumped into bed and was asleep almost instantly...

Christmas arrived in Louisiana in weather that might have been mistaken for spring. The nights were cold and clear but the days were calm, warm, and sunny. In the big living room stood a fancily decorated cedar tree, its tip almost brushing the ceiling. Standing about in a circle, packed as tightly as sardines stood every Negro on the plantation. Some had overflowed into the hall where they stood grinning and craning their necks.

It was an unspoken rule at Loch Ness that all the colored folk received their presents first. Then they trooped down into the cellar where Jake gave each family a gallon of wine to take home.

Bonnie was busy under the tree calling names. Then she'd hand the packages to Hank or Emil who would in turn hand them to the recipients. Allen Gordon walked about among them as much as the press would allow, making cracks and reaping gales of happy laughter from his retainers. After all the tenants had been served and some of the excitement had subsided the family began to open their own presents.

Hank received three pairs of Levis and a pair of hand made Justin boots that made him yell with joy, his voice cracking on him for the first time in months. "How'd you know my size, Unk? They fit like a glove."

"Us tuck hit offen yo' feets one night after you wuz sleep," said Mose in his habitually caustic tones. "Us coulda tuck de feets and you wouldn'ta knowed de differunce."

Emil had also drawn a pair of Justins and a pair of gray leather chaps and a horsehair band for the ten gallon hat that his uncle had given him with the horse and saddle. He was almost overcome by the gift. "Gee... Uncle Allen... I..."

Allen patted him on the back. " 'S'all right, Em. You've been a big help to Mose and me this fall. Hasn't he, Mose?"

Mose nodded. "Good hand wid hosses and cows, too."

For Jane there was a silver dresser set and half a dozen pairs of hose. In the first pair there were three twenty dollar bills tucked in neatly. "Oh … Unk … you …"

"Shaddap," he scolded. "What the hell do I know about buying things for women. Buy 'em yourself."

Bonnie reaped half a dozen pairs of hose and a cigarette case of severely simple design, beautifully done in stainless steel and gold. In it were three twenties. She leaped up and smacked him heartily on the mouth. "Wait and see what I have for you." She thrust a package at him.

He tore off the wrappers and there lay four Thorne Smith books that he had moved heaven and earth to locate but always failed. He whooped and descended on Bonnie and returned her kiss with a smack that could be heard out in the hall.

Jane shyly thrust out her package to him and sat quickly on the floor.

He opened it slowly and as it came out of the package, Allen's throat suddenly contracted on him and tears stung his eyes. He turned and walked rapidly toward the door. He stopped and said in a low voice, "Come with me, Janie."

Jane followed him as the others looked on in wonderment. Allen walked rapidly back to his office with Jane at his heels. He closed the door and turned to her. "Janie, I think that made me happier than I have ever been in my life. It would take a fine mind like yours to think of it."

Jane's eyes flooded and she ran into his arms. "I couldn't think of a thing to give you," she said in a choked voice. "I used to paint and letter a little and that's all I could think of."

"It's the most wonderful present I ever had. Now, let's both of us cut out this sniveling and hang it right here … that damned old diploma has been there much too long anyhow. It can go into a closet somewhere." He took the diploma down and put it on the couch. In its place he hung Jane's gift. It was in a simple blond wood frame covered by glass. Under the glass was a piece of mellow old parchment upon which Jane had painted the Gordon coat of arms complete in the colors of the tartan of the clan. The work was fine and wonderfully detailed while the most beautiful thing of all was the inscription in the lower right hand corner in the shaded Spencerian of old England with royal purple ink. It read, "What can one give to another in return for a life? Your Jane."

He maneuvered it perfectly level and straight. Then he turned and kissed her with infinite gentleness and held her to his breast for a moment. "I didn't really do it, Jane. It was in you all the time. No one ever makes a person, they merely avail themselves of the opportunity to be an instrument for the operation."

"And if no one cares enough to be the instrument..." Her big damp eyes held his steadily.

He smiled and kissed her again. "You won't be done out of it, will you?"

"No," she said.

"Now let's get back to the others. By the way, when's Albert coming?"

"He'll be here this afternoon. He'll eat at home, then come over."

"Sort of a steady, isn't he?"

She smiled delightedly. "Yes... I'm glad to say he's been pretty steady since the first night. Thanks again to you."

Back in the living room, he was surprised to see Millie standing under the tree with a strange look in her eyes. He had given her an exquisite negligee of the finest silk chiffon with real lace as well as a pair of sheep-lined casual slippers. She looked alone and miserable. The others ignored her completely.

As Allen came in, they trooped out as though by order.

"I'm glad you decided to come down, Millie."

She nodded. "I had to come, Allen. I want to beg your forgiveness for the way I've acted since I've been here."

"Sit down, Millie," he said in a kindly voice.

She made a sharp little sound in her throat, shoved the fingers of one hand forcibly against her eyes and sat with a thud on the couch. "Don't be kind to me, Allen. Curse me ... slap me ... take a whip to me." Her voice was rising and heavy tearing sobs welled from deep within her. "You've never been anything but kind to me and I ... God Almighty, forgive me. What have I done?"

"You have been narrow, Millie, and you have been malicious, but I guess you acted by your own lights. Please believe me, I didn't do to you what I did out of a sense of hatred or revenge, but to give the children a chance. You've seen them this morning and you don't need me to tell you whether my efforts have been a success ... Wait here a moment. I have something I want to show you." He walked swiftly back to his office and took down the coat of arms and brought it back to the parlor.

"Here's what Janie gave me for Christmas." Millie looked at it for a long time, then handed it back.

"Allen, can you understand a mother's feeling who has done what I have and lives to see the love she craves transferred to someone else because the children have no alternative?"

"I think I do," he replied gravely. "But you must not think that all is lost. Your children will still love you if you treat them in terms of individuals, mature people of these times and do not try to interpret them in terms of 1900. That was your trouble with Bonnie and Hank. Children don't hate parents unless the parents have failed along the line somewhere."

She nodded a tired head. "I know. I was sitting in my room this morning ... Emil brought my presents ... I had sneaked a look under the tree and saw it ... thinking of some good way to throw them in your face and stalk from the room. I must have shown what was on my face because Emil asked me in his blunt illiterate sort of way, 'Mom, when are you going to quit being a damned fool and wise up?'

"'You can say that?' I asked in amazement, 'After that awful whipping?'

"For a moment I thought he was going to say, 'What whipping.' He has forgotten it that completely. Then he sneered a little at me.

"'If a man can't take what's coming to him, then he's a pretty weak sister.' He walked out on me then and I think he hated me... there was loathing in his eyes. Then there was a sermon over my radio ... 'Peace on earth, good will toward men.' I began to think." Tears poured from her eyes but she tried neither to hide nor check them. They were the rent veil of repentance and they were there for all to see.

"There's one thing I will not have in this house," he said with mock severity, "and that is useless recriminations. There is nothing you can tell us that we don't know. It took courage to do what you just did, Millie. I admire that in you and so will your children. That, I guarantee."

She took in a shuddering sigh and a little mouse of a smile crept over her mouth as though half afraid. "You have been so good to all of us. If you can do that, then..." she sighed sobbingly. "If you wish, I'll go to my knees before that little girl I treated so shamefully once. I ..."

"You'll do no such thing. There isn't a mean or vengeful bone in Honey's body and you'd only embarrass her. She has already forgiven you. She felt sorry for Emil the day after their fracas." He rose to his feet. "Leave it to me, Millie. I'll take care of it." He walked rapidly from the room. He went out on the porch.

"All of you go into the living room. Your mother wants to see you. She asks your forgiveness for her actions and only wants to be treated decently. I'll expect each of you to try to understand. Now go on in." He left them with varied looks on their faces, amazement being the common denominator.

He hurried to the kitchen. "Lucindy, where's Honey?"

"I s'pose she's at home, Mr. Allen. She wasn't at the tree."

"No, and dammit, I didn't think of her till Millie mentioned her a while ago. Where's Amos?"

"He jes' went out to get a load of wood ... there he is now."

Amos, big black and muscular, came in with a load of wood that would have broken the back of an ordinary man. He dumped it noisily back of the stove and said, "Chrissmus gif,' Mr. Allen."

"Got no time for games, Amos. Honey wasn't at the tree and I forgot her. Go tell her to come on over ... never mind. I'll go myself. Lucindy, all the kids gave her presents and they're still under the tree. I'll take mine myself. You and Amos take the others when you go home."

Without waiting for an answer, he wheeled and stalked out cursing under his breath. The very one he had wanted to enjoy the tree he had forgotten. He was furious with himself and took it out on the Jeep which stood in front of the house, left there by Emil after an errand. He tore across the pasture and was almost thrown out as a wheel fell in a stump hole. This calmed him and he drove more sedately the rest of the way. The red gate stood open and he cursed the offender roundly as he sped through. People didn't leave gates open on Loch Ness.

He slithered to a stop in front of the house and leaped out with the spring of a youth. Package under his arm, he strode up the walk. Suddenly he stopped ... frozen in the icy grip of fear. The package dropped from his nerveless fingers and thudded to the ground. In front of the closed door was Tickles, a lively little Boston Bull he had given Honey the Christmas before. His head was a pulpy mass of blood and brains. His mouth was open and a snarl of rage still on his blood-smeared lips. Something snapped within him and back from long dead ages there sprang into his blood stream the berserker vapors of his savage forebears. Honey's absence from the Christmas tree, the broken body of the dog, told a story all too easy to read. With a bellow that seemed torn from his pain-knotted intestines, he rammed headlong into the obstructing portal which caved in like a door of glass. He swept on and finding Honey's door closed, he smashed it flat with one bull-like rush. As he had feared, she was there. Lying across the bed, a small round hole beneath her left breast telling the story. He fell to his knees racked and torn by hideous sobs like the last throes of a dying animal. Through a mist of blinding tears, he looked at her lying so calm, cold ... He touched her. She was not cold. The fact sleeted over him like a douche of icy water. He caught a wrist and detected a pulse beat. Whirling about, he dashed outside and began to roar at the top of his voice. Mighty brass-lunged bellows that stunned the air and tore at his throat like steel rakes. His eyes protruded from the force of those terrible cries. At the house, Lucindy dropped a huge platter which she was preparing for the turkey and looked fearfully at Amos.

"Jesus ... did you hear that? That's Mr. Allen." She turned and fled from the kitchen as fast as she could go. Emil came tearing down the stairs as fast as he could with Hank close behind him.

Jane and Bonnie were in the living room playing records but the mighty brazen cries came in over the music like the trampet of an elephant over the cheep of a frog. Bonnie turned white and sprang to her feet. "My God ..."

Jane came up from the floor with a bound. "That's Unk. Something awful must have happened."

Together they raced out of the front door and down the steps to see Lucindy, Amos, Emil and Hank all strung out across the pasture, running as though all the imps of hell were after them.

Allen lay bonelessly in his chair on the front porch. His face was white and his lips forced into a straight line. Jane came softly on the porch. "Unk?"

He might not have heard her. She spoke again. This time he answered but didn't open his eyes. "Albert says she'll be all right."

He nodded but said nothing. Hot tears forced themselves from under his closed lids and burned pathways down his cheeks. Jane knelt by him and sobbed softly on his shoulder in sympathy. Some ten minutes later, Bonnie came out bearing half a water glass of neat whiskey and a little ginger ale. "O.K. Break it up. All's well that ends well. She'll pull through. Take this little token of the glad news and pull yourself together. With a quart of my blood, how can she miss?"

Allen sat up and opened his eyes. He reached out and took the drink. It burned his raw throat and made him cough. "Damn, that stuff's strong," he said hardly above a whisper. He coughed again but finished the drink.

"Not all that strong, you just about tore your throat out yelling. Ye gods, I haven't heard such a noise since the L.S.U.-Tulane game. That came from fifty thousand people."

"Had a reason," he rasped. "Some son-of-a-bitch ... Bonnie, go get the sheriff on the phone. Tell him to round up all the deputies that are still sober and come out here. Tell Hank and Emil to come here."

Hank came but Emil couldn't be found, so Allen told him what he wanted. "Go saddle Straw. Get my rifle from the closet with a box of cartridges ... where's Emil?"

"I don't know, sir. I came out behind him. He had your automatic with him, but after we got to the house, I didn't see him again." Hank's eyes burned feverishly in their sockets and his mouth was rimmed in white.

Mose came around the corner of the house. "I seen Mr. Emil ridin' off right after y'all come back from Amos' house. He had yo' shotgun."

Allen swore hoarsely. "Now where in hell can he be? Mose, I want a bunch of horses saddled ... no, just have them ready. I don't know how many men the sheriff is bringing. Wait till they get here. We're going to comb this place from end to end. All I want before I die is to get my hands on that ... whoever it was."

Sheriff Bodine put the friction heavy on his bald pate. "We combed that house like a monkey lookin' for fleas, Allen. We didn't find a thing. They just ain't nothin' there."

Allen nodded tiredly. "I didn't expect you to find anything. A man that'll do a thing like that in broad daylight will certainly take care that he leaves nothing around. You did get the bullet, didn't you?"

The sheriff nodded. "Yeah. It was layin' right there on the bed. Went plumb through the kid. How's she doin'?"

"Very well, I think… Let's go in and see. I haven't seen her yet myself."

They walked upstairs to Bonnie's room and tapped gently on the door. Albert opened it and raised his finger to his lips. "Come in, but don't make any noise. That transfusion did the job. Made my own tests right here, too." he added proudly. "Saves time. Bonnie took it like a trooper. Said she heard people were given a stiff drink after they gave blood and she insisted on it. Said she was a sick woman and demanded her treatment."

Allen walked softly in, followed by the sheriff who was walking like the villain in a ghost picture. They walked over and looked down on the quiet composed face. The sheriff sucked his teeth noisily. "That a nigger gal?" he asked.

Allen nodded absently.

The sheriff shook his head. "Can't believe it. Her nails ain't got them blue moons."

Allen was about to snort some remark, but he looked at her nails involuntarily. He drew in his breath so sharply that Albert, standing ten feet away, started. Allen bent over and picked something from the girl's finger. He strode rapidly to the window. He held his hand in a ray of sunlight and the object glinted like red gold. His left hand began to tear and rumple his thick hair, his nostrils flaring like those of a horse. "Sheriff…"

The Sheriff walked over to him.

"Have you ever seen a hair like that?"

The other bent over and looked at it carefully. He straightened up slowly and looked Allen in the eyes. "Yeah… I've seen hair like that and I know right where I can find some more… come on out in the hall."

Allen almost ran over the sheriff in his haste to leave the room but once outside the older man whirled and placed a palm on his breast. "Now, son, hold ... hold on here a while. I know jes' how you feel, but it ain't no good. I'm the law and I'll take care of it ... Now don't go to raisin' ..."

Allen's breath came in labored gasps, he tore savagely at his hair and ground his teeth like a mad man. "Sheriff, I've known you since I was a kid. You're an old man, but if you don't get out of my way, so help me, I'm going to break you in half."

There was a sharp crack of leather on bone and Allen sank in a heap on the floor just as Bonnie came out of her mother's room a little pale and a little drunk. "Nice rap, Sheriff."

"So help me, Miss Bonnie, I tried to talk to him. I tried to argue him out of goin', but he wouldn't lissen ..."

"Out of going where?"

"He found one of Sam Tanken's hairs under the little gal's fingernails."

"Uh oh." Bonnie reeled a little and sat down in a handy chair. "That does it. You stopped him the only way you could have managed it. Now what you'll have to do is to beat him to Sam. Don't wait around, get the hell goin'."

The sheriff got and Bonnie, after calling Albert to the door and telling him what had happened, followed the sheriff down the stairs. At the front door she thrust a bottle of fine old bourbon in his hand. "This'll take some of the sting out of whatever happens to you, Sheriff. Better take it along."

He nodded and clutching the bottle lunged down the steps, howling for his deputy.

A sharp urgent voice stopped him. "Hold it, Sheriff," yelled Bonnie. "Come back up here."

Breathlessly the sheriff ran back to the porch. Bonnie pointed an unsteady finger. "That's Emil's horse but Emil isn't on him. It's a Negro. We'd better see what's happened before you leave."

Across the back pasture came the little red horse, belly almost to the ground, in a dead run. On his back was a long, skinny, very black Negro. He wore no hat, his clothes billowed with the wind and his long legs almost met beneath the horse's stomach with every bound. At the first fence, he left the horse in a flying leap and came on afoot with speed scarcely diminished.

He came straight to the porch, gasping out his news while he was still a hundred feet away. "Mr. Emil... Mr. Tanken... Miss Billie... dead... Gawd a'mighty... all bloody... dead..."

"Hold it, Sheriff," said Bonnie. "This is one thing Unk can be in on. He ought to be coming around by now."

Miss Billie was as beautiful in death as she had been in life. She sat on her living room sofa slumped a little, her head resting back like she was tired. Her eyes were still half open and only the trickle of blood that ran down her breast from the small hole in her neck was the jarring note. Sam Tanken lay against the far wall in a smother of his own blood. His throat had been torn completely away by a blast from the shotgun. One arm hung by a shred of skin, a wide bloody hole showed in the exact center of his chest and his face was a pulverized scramble of blood, brains and cartilage. Almost in the doorway, Emil lay across the barrel of the shotgun. The sheriff motioned to Albert. "See if we can move him, Doc."

Albert bent over and maneuvered a flat stethoscope beneath Emil's chest. He shook his head. "Can't get any heart beat but... Here, help me turn him over."

They turned the boy over on his back. He had been shot three times, twice in the abdomen and once in the right chest high up. A faint gasp came from between his lips. Albert leaped erect. "Allen, did you ever land the plane over here?"

Allen nodded numbly. "Yes, back there in that old oat field. It's pretty smooth."

"Go get it. He'll have to be operated on, so he'll have to be taken to a hospital. The bullets are still in him. He's in shock and that'll kill him pretty quick. Get it here as fast as you can. I'll call Harding Field from here and have an ambulance waiting when we get there. He'll make it, I think, if I can give him some blood before we leave here. Bonnie, send one of the men after my bag."

Allen strode rapidly from the room and they could hear the Jeep tear away from the drive.

"What about Miss Billie, Doc?" The sheriff's face was white and drawn.

"There's nothing we can do there, Morris. She's dead."

Nevertheless he examined her carefully, but the spark had gone out.

Her hair, fine and ash golden, spread behind her well-shaped head as though someone had arranged it. Her hands lay crossed in her lap. On her lips was the tiniest suggestion of a smile.

"See that, Doc?" said Morris pointing.

Albert nodded. "Yes, looks like she was smiling."

The sheriff nodded. "That's what I was talkin' about. I'll bet she saw Emil kill him. That's what I'll always believe anyhow." He turned away, shaking his head, his nose wrinkling against the sickly thick smell of fresh blood.

Bonnie burst into the living room with his bag and Albert bent over the wounded boy and went to work.

CHAPTER SEVEN

S PRING ARRIVED WITH a rush and bluster to calm down immediately and start about its business of putting life into all plants and creatures. Warm rains alternated with brilliant sunny days and nature turned over and came awake. Oak, poplar, beech, gum and uncounted other species were covered with a frosty froth of green mist while evergreens began to look less winter beaten with the arrival of new foliage.

On the porch of the big house at Loch Ness sat Bonnie, Allen, and Emil.

Allen was saying, "Looks like you'll be riding again pretty soon, Emil." The boy nodded. "Sure will be glad too, Unk., I haven't even tried out those boots and chaps." Emil had lost thirty pounds and his skin looked wan and unhealthy.

"No need to rush it." Allen lit a long cheroot. "What you need is some long walks and a lot of sun."

"What he needs is to get his appetite back," said Bonnie tapping a long ash from her cigarette.

"I still don't see how you managed to spot that red hair," said Allen, "when it took the rest of us an hour. I haven't talked about it because I didn't know but maybe you didn't want to."

"I just saw it the first thing," said Emil. "I don't know how. I just looked at her ... her nails always sort of scared me after ..." He flushed red. "I always looked at them. I saw it and I remembered the car that passed about half an hour before you yelled. It was the same car Sam Tanken was in the night you run him away from Jake's. I just took out after it. I didn't know which way it had went so I just followed the freshest tracks. They led straight to Miss Billie's. When I stepped in, he had just shot her. I guess I sort of went crazy 'cause I tried to shoot him and he beat me to it. He shot me three times … like hitting me with an axe, but I didn't go down 'til I had emptied the gun. The last shot went through the window." He looked away as though ashamed of the shot he had missed. "Why do you suppose he wanted to kill Miss Billie and Honey?"

"He wanted to kill everything I loved," said Allen in a tired voice. "I wonder that he didn't try to kill me."

Emil grinned. "I know why that was."

Bonnie and Allen looked at him questioningly.

"That little guy what come to see me at the hospital … named Elly something. He said he told Sam you was packin' a gun and just wanted him to blink his eye and you'd blast him."

"Well, I'll be damned. Good old Elly. The little bastard probably saved my life."

"Who's he?" asked Bonnie.

"Oh, he's a wizened little man that lives about three miles east of Kenton. Pop gave him a bull and a heifer when he was just out of high school and Elly claims his prosperity started then."

"That was bread cast on the waters," mused Bonnie smiling. "Even if it did take a long time to come home tenfold. That is, if you consider yourself ten times as important as a heifer and a bull."

"I ignore that sally with the richest and most piquant contempt."

"I love heckling you, Unk, but there's something else on my mind. It looks like Albert and Jane will make it, doesn't it?"

He nodded. "Yep. Think they will. I wish all my experiments turned out that way."

"Maybe you should try more of them," she suggested. Her tone might have meant anything.

He looked at her sharply. "And what might that mean?"

She grinned at him devilishly. "Make it as easy on your scrambled faculties as you can."

"Never try to understand women, Emil."

"No sir," said Emil obediently.

Bonnie leaped to her feet with a burst of animal exuberance. "I think I'll go stun my tail in Dogwood and break the ice."

Emil shuddered. "Go ahead. I hope you freeze."

Bonnie danced through the door and disappeared.

Allen looked for a long time at Emil. He had matured the hard way and his attitude had changed from the time of his terrible whipping till the day he nearly died on Miss Billie's living room floor. Now no one could say Emil was not a man. Perhaps not too quick mentally but solid and dependable. Of his courage there could be no question.

"Emil, did you ever think of finishing school?"

The boy flushed. "No sir. I stayed in the eighth grade two years. I just couldn't get a hold of them school subjects 'cause I wasn't interested in 'em."

"What about a couple of special courses at L.S.U. on animal husbandry or something like that."

His face brightened. "You think I could pass them?"

"Wouldn't make any difference whether you did or not. Just so you learned something. There was a time, Emil, when I considered you worthless. I won't deny it, but that was a blot on my own intelligence, not yours. You're a grown man now, and you're worth a lot more than your spending money. As of today I'm giving you a hundred head of cattle and the old O'Fallon place. You can do whatever you want with them. It'll be a good way to start yourself a herd. Also beginning the day you start riding again, you'll get a hundred dollars a month."

Emil sat very still for a few moments and Allen could see that he was struggling with some inner conflict. Finally he stood up and approached the older man. "I ain't much at talkin', Uncle Allen, but all I can say is you won't ever want to run me off no more. After you whipped me and I saw you wasn't mad at me no more, I sort of woke up then. I been woke ever since."

Allen rose and took the boy by the hand. "And the day you stood in Miss Billie's living room and blasted a son-of-a-bitch and risked your life to do it, wiped everything as clean as a new bed sheet. From now on, we'll sort of say we're partners. O.K. by you?"

"O.K. by me, sir." His voice was husky and his eyes moist.

"Go on now and knit a sock some place. Is Hank around?"

"No sir, he's at school."

"That's right. I forgot. I have a little proposition I want to make him, too."

After supper that night, Allen cornered Hank. "Graduate this year, don't you?"

"Yes, sir ... if I don't fail my algebra."

"You'd better not. What do you intend to do?"

A look of surprise spread over the boy's face. "Why ... I guess ... well, hell, you need me here."

Obviously he had never thought of doing anything else.

"That's right, I do, but I don't want to keep you from doing something you'd like better."

"Well, gosh ... what ... there ain't anything better. You think I'd leave here and just ... Awww." He sat down abruptly. It was a shock that his uncle had even considered that he do anything else.

"What about college, Hank?"

The boy looked up belligerently. "Well, what about it? I'm no fancy dan college man. All I want to know you can teach me right here."

"If you go to L.S.U., you'd learn a lot more about cattle and the farm than I could ever teach you."

"Yes, sir, but I'll never pass that damn mathematics. The stuff kills me. I don't even know enough to tell the teacher what I don't understand."

"Well, it's up to you. Want to give it a go?"

Hank thought a long time. "If I fail, couldn't I take a lot of special courses and learn all that?"

"You could... *if* you didn't pass."

"I'll try it, sir. I guess I could get a job in the dairy or around the barns..."

"Not on your life. I don't want you to go there for books alone and work yourself to death. Some of the best things in college aren't found in books."

"Well, if you're talking about women, I don't want any," said Hank positively.

Allen bent over and said in a quiet voice, "Hank, you're in love with Honey."

He sighed heavily. "God," he said bitterly. "What does a man do in a case like this?"

Allen sighed with him and sat down. "Son, you're much too young to let it make you unhappy. It has happened before and generally there was always a way around it. I don't know but one white man, maybe two or three, that could ever admit that he loved a Negro girl. Yet there have been any number of men shot over colored girls. Something that rarely happens over a white girl. There *are* ways..."

"Sure..." Hank stiffened in his chair and glared at his uncle. "Sure, there are ways. Take her off in the bushes or build her a little house back in the woods and marry a white wife to raise children and spend half my time back in the woods raising another family. No thanks. Of all the stinking dirty deals I ever heard of that's the limit, and I must say that I'm surprised that you'd suggest it."

Allen almost reeled from the impact of the boy's impassioned outburst. This, he thought, is bad, really bad. "You asked me what a man did under these circumstances and I told you the only thing I could think of. They gossip behind my back because I have a father's love for the girl. What chance do you think you'd have if you married her and tried to live in this country?"

The boy's lips had a bitter twist. He cursed low and hard ending up finally in an explosive sob. He looked about distractedly, then leaped to his feet and disappeared through the door. Allen could hear his feet pounding up the stairs.

"Mr. Allen." The voice came from near the steps.

"That you, Honey?"

"Yes, sir."

"Come on in. You feeling all right?"

She ran lightly up the steps. She was thin but otherwise she showed no effects of her wound. "Yes, sir, I feel fine. You know something, I just found your Christmas present. Someone had kicked it under the house. I suppose when the sheriff was at the house."

He pulled her over on his lap and hugged her tightly. "I'm glad you did. I couldn't remember a thing after seeing Tickles there with his head split open. I sort of blacked out then. I just knew something was wrong."

She kissed him as softly as the touch of a butterfly's wing and nestled her face in the curve of his neck. "Mr. Allen, I'm so glad everything came out all right. I'm glad you didn't have to kill him."

Allen compressed his lips. "Emil did a rather good job of that, but God, it was messy." A quiver went through her frame and he patted her shoulder. "I won't mention it again, Honey."

She raised her head. "I haven't thanked you for the robe. It's getting too warm for it, but it surely will come in handy next winter, and it fits like a glove. I don't know how you got my size."

"Blame Bonnie. I snitched the measurements from her. Remember she measured you for that dress?"

"Oh... I had forgotten that." She was silent for a while. "Mr. Allen?"

"Yes, Honey."

"I guess it isn't very nice, but I overheard you and Mr. Henry talking. You see, I walked up and didn't want to interrupt. It was dark there and I heard ..."

"You knew anyway, didn't you, Honey?"

"Yes, sir. I've known for a long time and, really, you were telling him the only way it can ever be."

"Yes, but young love, Honey, is a very noble emotion. He can't see it that way."

"No, sir, and I can't see it any other way."

"I can't either and it gets next to him and you can't blame him. I've laid awake nights trying to figure some way out of it, and I get nowhere. This just isn't the locality for such a thing."

"That's right, it isn't," she said looking at the fireflies play in the darkness. "There's only one way and that was the way you suggested."

"A puzzle conceived in the mind of man may be unraveled by the same instrument."

She smiled one of her slow comprehending smiles. "Yes, sir, but you didn't have it just right. Emanuel Kant said that."

He looked at her in blank amazement. "Hell's fire, you don't mean to tell me that you've read him, too?"

"I didn't understand all of it," she admitted, "but I tried."

"Well, strike me pink," he breathed. "I read snatches of it and threw it down because I got bored. What are you reading now?"

"That book Dr. Fontenot loaned Miss Jane, 'Principles of Psychiatry.' Do we have a medical dictionary in the library?"

"No, but you shall have one as soon as I can get it. Good God, what'll you be reading next?"

"It won't be a best seller," she said positively. "I'm fed right up to the teeth with them. They're all alike."

"Now you're getting wise. I dropped 'em fifteen years ago with a few solid exceptions. But we got off the subject, Honey. You speak as if you'd be willing to have it the way we see as the only way ... with Hank, I mean."

"Mr. Allen … I … I'm just a child, I know, but I've read a lot and I believe I can think. I don't think anyone in the world has the right to stand between people who are in love. It isn't my fault that I'm not white and it isn't Mr. Henry's fault that he's not colored. But people don't see things that way. Mr. Henry won't be able to marry me. I won't be happy unless I have him, so I'm willing to have him any way I can. If he can't take me like a man is supposed to take a woman, under his own roof to raise his own children, then he'll have to take me the best way he can."

"But, Honey, it won't work. Hank won't have it that way."

She smiled and he was struck with the aura of wisdom that lighted her face. "Mr. Allen, when the time comes, he won't have a chance. I'm not worried about that."

Allen looked at her for a long time. "You know, Honey, damned if I don't think you're right. To hear you tell it, I can't help but believe … Now sit on this other leg, that one is tired."

"Let me sit at your feet, Mr. Allen, so I can put my face on your knee." She sat on the floor and laid her head against his hard leg. He stroked her glossy hair and the soft classic curve of her jaw and cheek. How smooth and delightful her skin was to touch. "Honey, you're seventeen and Hank is only nineteen. How can you both be so sure?"

She let a little sigh escape her. "I don't know, sir. The first day I saw Mr. Henry I felt funny … sort of. He looked at me and I looked at him. Neither of us spoke but right then I knew it. I could have been wrong and so could he, but we weren't. That's what we have to deal with now. We were *right*."

"This is pretty personal and you don't have to answer it if you don't want to … Have you ever felt sexually attracted to Hank?"

She caught his lean hand and pressed it to her cheek. "Mr. Allen, you can ask me anything you want. You know that. I can't answer it very well because I'm afraid I don't know what it is yet. I know from reading that it is a powerful thing. It can be beautiful … it seems the most wonderful thing in the world when people are in the right sort of … I don't know very well how to say it … I mean when it is *right* not just something for an idle pastime. Mr. Henry has kissed me several times, but he was always afraid and bashful with it. I know I wanted him to take me and hold me close to his stomach and just hold me and hold me and kiss me hard … hard … to hurt me kissing me. When I'd think like that I'd feel strange and I couldn't breathe very well and I could feel it down here." She made a simple, naive gesture.

Allen bent over and kissed her tenderly. "That's what it is. You've felt it, and I'd give a mint to be able to remember your description word for word."

She hugged his hand. "You're so sweet to me."

"Of the few times in my life when I've really felt that Allen Ogilvie MacReady Gordon was a passable man, one is every time I remember that I had the courage to be sweet to you. It's the best thing that ever happened to me. Certainly the return has been big."

She clung to his hand and kissed each knuckle separately and he could feel a suspicious wetness of her cheeks. "It hasn't been easy," she said softly. "Don't think I don't know what it took for you to love me. The danger of setting your own people, even your own family against you, but you never failed me. Look at me now. I'm well read, I can speak well, I have more clothes than I can wear, but I'm a nobody. Just an orphan that an old Negro woman took from some poor frightened single girl, probably, and gave to Lucindy and Amos because they wanted a child."

He cupped his hand about her neck. "An orphan, yes … once, not now. Now you're mine. A nobody you never were. That was obvious the first time I saw you. Honey, I want you to move up here to the house. You can have that room back of my office and you and Bonnie and Jane can decorate it just like you want it. There's a bath adjoining and it'll be just right. I want you near me because when I get old, I'll always look back and curse myself for the years I missed having you here."

Honey wept silently for a few minutes. "I ... I ... hardly know what to say, and I know you want me ... but .. She rose to her knees and buried her face in his lap. Finally she looked up, her face wet but composed. "You may not believe me, Mr. Allen, but I always knew you'd ask me."

"I'm beginning to believe practically anything you say, Honey. You'll come?"

"No, sir."

"What? You just said you've always thought about it ..."

"Yes, sir, I'll come, but not now. Some day, I'll come but not now. It is too soon after your trouble and all. I've got to think about it and make it right in my mind."

He smoothed her wet cheeks and nodded. "You come whenever you feel it's right, Honey."

"In a way, it won't ever be right, sir ... right, the way people think. I meant I had to make it right with *me*. If you order me to come I couldn't refuse you because I can't ever refuse you anything, but I'd rather come in my own time ... just sort of get it fixed in my mind."

"Very well. Whenever you get it set in your mind, come on. It'll be there waiting for you."

After she left, he sat on his porch and breathed deeply of the fragrant spring air. It seemed refreshed, washed and all the winter staleness filtered out. It was this time of year that life swelled within him to the bursting.

Bonnie came quietly out on the porch and sat where Honey had been. "I heard you and Honey talking, so I didn't come out."

He patted her shoulder. "You always know the right thing to do, don't you? All the way from leaving a man his privacy to conking him on the head when he's lost his mind."

"That's Bonnie. Anything to be right ... anything for a laugh." She bit him on the leg.

"Ow!" He rubbed the spot and cracked her on the head with a huge signet ring.

"That was a dirty blow. My back was turned."

"I fairly wallow in dirt," he assured her. "Dirty stories, dirty blows ... what have you. Go fetch us a set-up and let's get drunk."

"A noble thought. I shall be back in a flash with the mash."

She came back in ten minutes loaded with drinking equipment. Allen took his straight with a chaser and she watched him drink it.

"There must be a trick to that. I want to learn it."

"Why?"

"For the same reason you do it. You have to drink too much in a highball to get the result. You know me, I've always been one for results."

"Or the lack of them."

"I sense a Scotch crack in that."

"Hurrah for your senses. Well, here's the trick. You take a sip of whiskey and hold it in the front part of your mouth. Then you bring the chaser up and it follows the drink right on down and you never taste it. Here, take mine and try it."

She tried it and her face beamed. "I should knife you for not showing me this long ago. Now I can be a right smart drinkin' woman." She tried it again with equal success, and sat back to enjoy the heady burn of the whiskey.

They sat silently for some minutes. Then Bonnie said, "Unk, you never mentioned it, but I think Miss Billie's death got you where you live."

He nodded gravely. "Yes, it did and there is still an empty spot there. I don't hug grief to my breast, however. Pop said it was a silly thing to do. He said it 'Dinna make sense and the guid book is dead against it.' He didn't have time for anything that didn't make sense. He was a lot stronger than me in that respect."

Bonnie sat on the edge of his chair. "I don't care what you say, you're just like him. If you thought it would make anyone else unhappy you'd never mention it."

"It isn't all that, sugar. Billie loved life and it banged her about some but she was a trooper. Her husband blew his brains all over his office, in her presence. Some women would have cracked a rocker but not Billie. We talked a lot about life, death and kindred subjects. Her belief in higher rewards was not sufficient to prevent her enjoying things in this life."

"Few people ever get that deep into anything," said Bonnie sipping her drink.

Allen fixed another drink and took half of it at a gulp. "Another thing, Billie was the beautiful and artistic provider of biological necessity. I do not mean that disrespectfully and if I did I wouldn't have said it. I'm a rake all right but I don't play a wide field and haven't since I was twenty-five. Since her death I've been sort of up against it because she was not only a highly satisfactory partner but also the most handy."

"That," said Bonnie casually, applying a light to her cigarette, "Is a matter of opinion."

"The moment I said that I knew I shouldn't."

"Old age's getting you ... say, by the way, you come from a long line of long livers. I was looking at that old Bible in the library the other day. Your great granddaddy Jock Mac Duff was a hundred and two when he died. There were half a dozen that lived into their nineties."

"Mom was seventy-six and Pop was eighty. What killed him was a bout with a bad bull."

"There ... you're barely a boy in that family."

He grinned. "Honestly, I feel just like I did when I used to run the two-twenty. Bet I could do it in respectable time now."

"Whatever it had to do with respectability, you couldn't do it. If you did then, it was before you learned your evil ways."

"I have learned much since you've been here."

"Not enough ... Here drink up. I'm one up on you." She poured him a hefty slug and took one herself.

"When you said get drunk you weren't kidding, were you?"

"I never kid," she said. "Especially when I talk about you and me."

"Ummm...you sound like someone working up to something."

"All in good time, Jackson...all in good time. Didn't I see Albert and Jane darting about here before supper looking for a spot of privacy?"

"You saw them. What they were looking for, I can't say."

"It was a red letter day in her life when he took her down on that little beach. What a rolling good time they must have had."

"What a thing to say."

"Aw...you and your propriety...as though you didn't arrange the whole thing."

"Well, it looks like it'll come out all right."

"Naturally, although I don't know how they stand it. Every moment he's away from the office, he's here and the moment he gets here they duck off some place."

Bonnie was sitting much too close for comfort. Her shoulder was pressing against his cheek and her body emanated the fresh cool smell of cleanliness. He turned his cheek slightly and the solid resiliency of it made his blood race.

"Here, sit some place else," he snapped. "You're driving me dizzy."

"That was the idea...get it?"

"I get it, but you get going."

She pouted and sat in another rocker. He began to feel powerful and exultant as the whiskey began to tingle in his body. He stretched his legs in front of him and heaved a deep satisfied sigh. "Life is good, life is gay. I must be on my merry way."

"That was a fairly silly remark."

"Yeah...I know that's the way I feel tonight."

"Me, too. That makes two of us."

"Which makes two of us," added Allen complacently.

"That's what I said."

"You said what?"

"I said that makes two of us."

"Well, that's what I said."

"Wait ... oh, hell, you're just trying to confuse me."

"That would be the day. Speaking of my biological needs, what about yours?"

"Now, that's what I wanted you to become concerned about."

"The devil ... I merely asked you a question."

"The answer is you're a long time getting curious. How's that for evasion, Unkie Wunkie."

"Dammit, don't talk baby talk."

"Well, you get embarrassed every time I talk grown-up talk."

Allen shivered a little. "It's getting chilly out here."

"O.K., sissy, let's go back to your office. You bring the ice, I'll take the bottle and the glasses."

In the office, he turned on a butane heater and closed the one window. Bonnie switched on the small reading lamp on the desk and turned it so the glare wouldn't shine in their eyes.

He dropped to full length on the couch and kicked off his boots and socks while Bonnie arranged the drinking material on a nearby table. She poured two hefty portions. "Here's to us, Unk ... the both of us, which makes two of us."

"Hear, hear," he applauded and took a large pull at the drink and put it on the floor beside him. After a time it became warm so Bonnie lowered the flame in the heater and slipped out of her light tweed jacket and tossed it over the back of a chair. Her thin nylon blouse strained across her recalcitrant bust and Allen felt a little giddiness that had nothing to do with the liquor. She stood up and stretched her magnificent body like some lithe jungle animal, then flopped back on the couch beside him. He lit a cheroot and blew a ring at her finger.

They were silent in rapt consideration of each other.

He let his eyes wander from her head with its masses of copper-gold hair, following the soft line of her neck and shoulders to the gap in her blouse that could not come together. Through it he could see the tightly stretched web of her bra and he could follow it because she was turned sideways. He could see where the cup failed to contain its bounty and the creamy skin overflowed its rim in a slightly depressed line. Her eyes swept him also and she smiled. "From here you appear fair considering mileage and such."

"From here you blast the imagination," he returned. "And what I'm thinking would curl the pages of anything printed."

"Oh, Unk, this is so sudden." She stood up and replenished her drink and his as well.

"Sudden, my eye. Don't think for a moment my fine feathered niece—who is no kin to me—that I can't see through you."

"I always attempt to be very transparent so what you see is no credit to your acumen."

"With that cellophane waist on, you leave very little to the acumen."

"Why strain your imagination." She took a sip, chased it and with a single fluid movement that left him gasping, she slipped out of the waist and stood before him erect and proud.

He sat up with a sharp intake of his breath. "A man can stand just so much …"

"Which is exactly what I had counted on," she said, looking at him sideways through heavily lidded eyes, one of which was covered by a shimmering wave of hair that had slid forward over her bare shoulder like a silken cascade. She turned casually and with a deft twist of her fingers, the latch on the door clicked. She walked past him to the window and pulled the shade all the way down. Then she came back and sat on the couch, her long legs over the side facing him. She put her hands on his shoulders and her eyes were soft and moist.

"The fight's no good. It's right, Unk … I don't know how I know it, but I've known it for a long time."

Allen grinned and put out his arms. Her full petal-soft lips parted and she sank her mouth into his. He felt as though he had taken a fleeting grasp of a hot wire. A gush of passion swept over him like sheet lightning over a summer sky and his arms closed on her tightly. She forced him slowly backward and her body, moving sinuously, strove to match every outline in his. His fingers dug into her soft but firm back and moved downward to her slim waist kneading the fine skin with an excess of tender demand.

Suddenly she released him and stood up. Never had Allen seen a woman like this. Her body was aquiver with desire, she still controlled her movements making them so slow and provocative that he thought he'd go mad watching.

When she touched him, Allen went a little crazy. Her skin was a delight, and he tasted the shattering delight of her lips. His hand roved the length of her lovely legs. A moan escaped her lips and her body moved restlessly. He kissed her lips again, then abruptly sat up for a moment. There came the brassy tinkle of a belt buckle and the rustle of cloth ... silence, and a breath so sharply indrawn that it was almost a cry.

Time passed as time will and the moon probed vainly for entry through the shaded window.

She lay with her golden head cradled in the crook of his arm, her eyes closed, her breath easy and regular, and her face relaxed. He kissed the soft curve of her cheek and she smiled but didn't open her eyes.

"Sleep?" he asked in a whisper.

"No," she whispered in return. "Just so dead calm that it's a shame to move."

He was conscious of the contact of her quiescent body from his throat to his feet. He dozed a little and when he opened his eyes, she was looking directly in to them. Hers were pools of deep thoughtful gentleness, understanding and ... no, he could not be mistaken. Could it be that this twenty-four year old girl was in love with a man nearly twice her age. The thought filled him with a strange exhilaration and, before he knew it, his heart began to pump faster and his blood heated his skin anew.

"I can read your mind," she said, her voice low and incredibly soft and affectionate.

"In your position," he reminded her tartly, "any reading of minds that goes on is ridiculously superfluous."

A smile widened across her placid face like a ripple on a calm pool. "I might have fooled a younger man on that for a while maybe."

"Listen to who's talking. Woman, you're a hazard to mankind."

She smiled and bit his upper lip lightly.

She moved gently against him and his heart took up its wild cadence again. Her soft mouth melted against his and he could feel the straining against him. Freeing his left arm, upon which she had been resting, he returned the kiss with full fervor. She broke away and thrust her head back, breathing deeply. He followed her avidly.

The moon gave up its vain inquisitiveness and sank into the waiting arms of a gaunt lightning-blasted pine.

When Allen woke, Bonnie's left arm was looped about his neck, and the grayness of dawn crept through the translucent shade. He moved but her arm tightened about his neck and pulled him as close as she could. He shook her gently. "Wake up, you lovely thing, and face a frowning populace."

She moved over on her back and stretched tremendously, throwing all the delightful lines of her body into complete harmony, her legs close together and her arms stretched high above her head. He kissed her neck and the sweet pout of her curved lips.

She opened her eyes and smiled like a pleased child. "See what you've been missing."

"Holy smokes, let's don't go into that. I'll raise enough hell with myself as it is."

"And while you're at it, you might remember that I maneuvered the whole thing and was the aggressor all along."

"There'll be time for all that. Right now we'd better get out of here before Lucindy comes. That would look charming, us coming out of my office at five in the morning."

CHAPTER EIGHT

L UCINDY HAD MADE some coffee. She poured a cupful on top of two teaspoons full of sweet thick cream and whipped it vigorously to mingle it with two teaspoons full of sugar. She laid a tray with a white cloth and placed the coffee on it. She went upstairs, past the room shared by Bonnie and Jane to Allen's room. She was somewhat surprised to find the bed empty and not even mussed. She shrugged and turned about to return. As she passed the open door of Jane's room she stopped. Jane opened one eye and gazed owlishly at her. Lucindy grinned toothily. "You want this here coffee? Mr. Allen wasn't in his bed."

Jane sat up muzzily. "What an hour to wake up. What time is it, Lucindy?"

" 'Near 'bout six, I reckon, now."

"Yipe, and I didn't crawl in till one. Where's Bonnie?" she asked, glancing at the unspoiled other half of the bed.

"I don't know'm. I ain't seen her or the boss either."

Jane sat on the side of the bed and reached unsteadily for the cup of coffee.

"About two this afternoon I'll be as sleepy as Cooter Brown," she complained, holding the cup in one hand and rubbing her eye and cheek with the back of the other.

Lucindy started to leave. "You can fetch that cup down when you comes to breakfast."

Jane yawned widely and smacked her lips. "Sure, sure... I'll bring it along. Wonder where'n hell Unk and Bonnie went. Probably went some place and got drunk and ran off in the ditch."

Lucindy came down the stairs and started toward the kitchen just as the office door opened and Bonnie and Allen came out. Lucindy came to an abrupt halt. Their faces were calm and smooth with satiation, sleep and the absence of tension and conflict. Lucindy was a wise woman and a tactful one. Only a second did she hesitate. "Y'all come on in the kitchen. I took your coffee to your room, Mr. Allen, but you wasn't there."

He grinned easily and with a throb of her heart, Lucindy glimpsed a younger Allen Gordon. A headlong hell-for-leather boy who could be savage and yet as gentle as a woman. A bounding, indefatigable boy who adored his mother and father and whose rocketing laughter always rang through the halls of Loch Ness, lifting spirits and making it impossible not to laugh with him.

"That's right, Lucindy. I wasn't there."

"So I give it to Miss Jane. She was awake when I passed the door."

"And you saw that I hadn't been in bed either," Bonnie added.

Lucindy smiled broadly at them as they sat down at the table. "It ain't no business of mine, Miss Bonnie, if nobody don't sleep in their bed. Lots of people likes to get out on these cool nights and walk all night. Me and Amos done it many a time."

"I remember one night you and Amos stopped walking, Lucindy," Allen said teasingly. "I almost rode old Red over you."

Lucindy's yellow face turned a dusky red. She giggled like a school girl. "We was tired."

After breakfast he said to Amos. "How's to run over to your house in the Jeep and tell Honey to get her best looking dress on. Tell her I want her to look as slick as the slickest chick in the yard, and you bring her back here. As soon as you can, but tell her not to rush."

Lucindy looked over her shoulder at Allen and then back at the stove.

"Come into the hall, Unk … I want to ask you something."

He followed Bonnie out into the dim quiet hall. She faced him. "What's all this?"

He took her tenderly in his arms. "Bonnie, I want Honey there, do you mind?"

She sighed and rested her head on his chest. "No, Unk... I'd love to have her." She looked up again. "You sure you want to go through with this?"

His eyes were very serious. "I never wanted anything so badly in my life, Bonnie."

"It isn't because of last night?"

"Probably. I didn't wake up till last night."

"I mean you..."

"Shut up, you know as well as I do that all you're doing is fishing. Go get some glad rags on and hunt up Hank and Jane."

Hank and Jane were so completely dumbfounded that it took minutes to convince them a wedding was to take place.

"But holy smokes..." Hank scratched his head savagely as though to massage home the idea. "You and Unk... I mean..."

Jane sat suddenly on the bed. "This takes mature reflection and it's much too early to indulge in mature reflection. So all I can say is that I'll go along with anyone's joke just to be pleasant. Where is this momentous thing to occur?"

Bonnie snatched off her waist and let her skirt fall to the floor. "Unk hasn't told me yet and frankly, I don't give a damn. It's going to happen somewhere and that's all I care about."

Hank shook his head slowly. "You just can't doubt her, Jane... look at her. I've never seen her like that."

Jane gave her sister a careful searching look. She nodded. "The last person I saw who looked like that was me... in the mirror. As I recall Bonnie's exact words were... 'ooooo, what you did.' "

Bonnie smiled widely and stuck her tongue out at Jane and, whirling, dashed into the bathroom.

"What a time of day to take a bath," murmured Hank numbly, still in a daze from Bonnie's blunt declaration.

"Women who have been loved, son, do odd things at odd times."

"You mean women in love, don't you?" Hank was not his sharpest that morning.

"For the present, we'll let it stand like that," said Jane with a roguish smile. "Now git ... I've got to get pretty."

Hank got uncertainly to his feet. "Jane ... I'm sorta mixed up. Gee ... I'm pretty crazy about Unk and ... well, I think Bonnie is the best ever, but ..."

Jane walked over and placed her hands on Hank's broadened shoulders. "Henry, you're pretty young and this is a kind of shock but it isn't impossible. Unk is forty-one and Bonnie is twenty-four. It is pretty much a May and September affair, but ... well, he loves her and she loves him. That's what makes up the difference. They want to, Hank, and all in the world we can do is want it, too. If Unk suddenly decided to burn the barn down, all we could do is stand around and help. He's done too much for us to reap anything but good will and understanding. Personally, I think it's wonderful. I just don't believe he could have done any better ... do you?"

Suddenly Hank had all the lines straight in his hands. "No ... I guess not. Gosh, Jane, it is pretty swell, isn't it? Having her here all the time. It's ... it's kinda cozy."

Bonnie and Jane came down the stairs fully rigged and presenting a picture that made Hank leap from the sofa whistling a long low wolf call and make tracks for the long mirror to check himself for any faults in dress.

"I can see that this is gonna be a day," he said exultantly, turning away from the mirror.

They came in and also took a double check in front of the mirror, straightening stocking seams, giving hats and hair last minute touches.

"Hoooly mackerel, look at Unk," gasped Hank.

Allen stepped into the living room faultlessly dressed in a suit of powder blue flannel with a darker blue tie and black and white shoes. A blue handkerchief sprang carelessly from his breast pocket. His naturally ruddy face went darker under Hank's frank admiration.

"Gee, Unk, I wish I could dress that way."

"You can some day," said Bonnie, "when your shoulders get as wide as a door unless you let your stomach keep pace with them."

Allen grinned appreciation at Hank and turned to the girls. "May I suggest something?"

Bonnie shrugged and turned up her hands. "The whole idea is yours. Play whatever tune you like."

"Put the hats away. You've both got beautiful hair and I just don't like the hats on it. No harsh criticism of the hats intended."

Jane tossed hers on the top of the phonograph. "Good. I don't like them anyway."

Bonnie stepped over to her intended husband and kissed him tenderly. "I thought you were going to suggest something radical. I'm like Jane. I hate hats and it'll be a pleasure."

Some little incoherent noise from Hank made them turn around. Honey stood in the living room door. For a moment no one spoke. She wore a light grey tailored suit that fitted with such staggering perfection that it was unbelievable.

"Honey…" Bonnie's voice was a little squeaky. "That isn't the suit I bought you, is it?"

A small shy smile touched her lips as she stepped into the room. "Yes, that's it, Miss Bonnie. It does fit well, doesn't it?"

"Fit well," she said. "You wait till I get my hand on that woman at Behrman's. If she can do that with nothing but measurements to go by and I'm there body and all…"

"There is," Allen pointed out, "some slight difference between the bodies. With no darts at you, my dear, I think Honey's is a little more immature as yet and probably easier…"

JOHN B. THOMPSON & JACK WOODFORD

"Oh, shut up. You've said it now so don't try to cover it up."
She went over and kissed Honey on the cheek. "I don't think I
ever saw anything so sweet, Honey. You look darling and where
did you learn to put on make-up like that?"

The girl dimpled prettily. "I've practiced enough to learn
something. I never wear it much, but I've certainly used
plenty."

"Well, you did it just right. Just enough and not overdone
anyplace. Isn't she lovely, Hank?"

Hank gulped and said something in a muffled undertone.
His eyes kept darting away and back at the girl while she composed herself in a big chair with easy grace. Allen gave himself a
final pat before the mirror and turned to Honey.

"Come here, you beautiful hunk of woman and give your
pappy a hug around the neck."

With a delighted smile, she leaped to her feet and ran to him.
He kissed her softly and smoothed her jet hair. "Where did you
get that hair-do?" he asked. "It's the first time I ever saw it."

"I saw a girl in 'Vogue' who had very black hair that was very
straight like mine and she did it up like this." Her hair had been
parted in the middle extending all the way to the back of her
neck, and swept softly back to two wide flat buns that nestled
close behind each ear. The part had been so perfectly executed
that the even white line accented the pure classic cast of her face.
Her features had that wonderfully regular mould without lack-
ing sensitivity or mobility.

"What's all the dress up about, Mr. Allen?" asked Honey.
"Amos came in running and all out of breath, saying that you
wanted me over here all dressed up, but he didn't know why."

Allen beckoned to Bonnie who came over and stood beside
him. He placed an arm about her shoulders and together they
looked at Honey saying nothing. Her face went through a variety
of changes. First it questioned, then dawning comprehension,
finally ecstatic bursting happiness.

"Oh…" Her hands went up clasping the sides of her face in an adorable gesture. "Oh…Mr. Allen, Miss Bonnie…is it true…you and Mr. Allen…"

Bonnie, who beneath her crusty exterior, was as soft as dough, felt a lump in her chest. The child was overcome with joy because her god and the woman of his choice were about to be joined together. Her eyes misted over as she nodded. "Come here, Honey. You don't belong to Unk exclusively any more. You're mine, too, now."

Honey put her arms about both of them and wept a little. She dried her eyes and stood back to look them over. "Then…I do have a father and a mother, too?"

"You have a father and before the day is over you'll have a mother," said Allen, his voice warm and deep. "Well, what say we get going?"

Jane and Hank came woodenly to their feet. Hank looked miserable and happy at the same time.

"Where *are* we going?" asked Jane.

"Oh, it doesn't matter too much." Allen rubbed his chin pondering. "What say we go to Opelousas, then we can go to The Elms afterward and make a real day and night of it. We'll cross the river at St. Francisville and take our time. After all, it's not eight o'clock yet. Oh, yes, there's one thing I haven't done yet. I'll be back in ten minutes." He walked out of the room and they could hear his feet on the stairs.

He knocked on the door.

"Come in."

"Sorry to bust in like this, Millie, but I have something rather important to tell you."

"Certainly, Allen. Sit down." She sat on the edge of her bed, proudly smoothing the folds of the negligee that he had given her for Christmas.

"No, it won't take but a moment. Millie, this might come as a shock to you, but I'm not good at leading up to things. Bonnie and I are going to get married this morning."

The only thing that kept Millie from falling was the fact that she was already seated. She gasped whitely and her hand fingered her throat unconsciously. Allen waited impatiently and not a little fearfully for her to regain her composure. She relaxed a little and smiled. "This *is* sudden, Allen. I'm afraid I'm a little bowled over. When did it happen?"

"I guess it's been happening all along and I didn't know it. It appears that I was alone in my ignorance. Bonnie seems to have been pretty well posted all along. As she said, waiting for the psychological moment."

Millie came to her feet and walked to him, looking in his eyes. She caught him by both hands and pressed them. "God bless you both. I think she'll be good for you. I know you'll be good for her."

"Thank you, Millie." He was absurdly relieved. "I'm glad you feel that way about it. Frankly, I was afraid you wouldn't." He reached over suddenly and kissed her on both cheeks. "That's for being a good Joe, Millie."

He left her sitting rock-still on the bed, her eyes filled with wonderment and possibly relief.

The ceremony had been brief, so brief that Hank hardly had time to get himself oriented. One second they were niece and uncle, the next they were man and wife. Hank's reactions had doubled back on themselves in cross-current movement against his emotions so that he was in a floundering daze.

Honey stood beside him and sensing what he felt, caught his hand and squeezed it. Immediately, he felt better. He held on to the hand as though it was the one string attaching him to reality. His hand and arm tingled from the contact and he had to fight an overwhelming desire to kiss her. "I now pronounce you man and wife," said the grey little minister. "I believe it is the custom for the groom to kiss the bride," he added with a twinkle in his eyes. "Probably a relic from the days when people assumed it to be the first kiss."

As Allen bent to kiss his wife, a flickering pang knifed through Hank's breast and he turned suddenly to Honey. He didn't say anything but she needed only one glance at his eyes. He took her tenderly in his arms. He kissed her hard, feeling the sharp outlines of her teeth with his lips and he found the little opening between them so naturally that his conscious realization came some time afterward. The touch of her tongue lashed his skin with flickering fires and his world reeled drunkenly about him. Her body was soft and plaint against him and his boyish hunger fought against his ribs with piston-like blows.

"O.K.," came a voice, "break it up. After all, who's getting married around here?"

The voice came through his consciousness like the squeak of a whistle through a dense fog, but it was enough to straighten him up, gasping for breath. He didn't take his eyes from her face because he couldn't. On her lips was a little half smile and in her eyes was the world and all its love. He allowed himself to be led to the car in a kind of red, happy daze. Until now, he had never dared think or even hope that Honey might love him. This was a list in the right direction. Then, with true youthful pessimism, he began to invent reasons for her actions other than that of loving him, thereby working up a fine case of misery that left him white-lipped and suffering.

"Well, Honey," said Bonnie from the front seat. "You might be the youngest in the crowd, but if I packed the lethal punch that you do, I'd go about dropping them just to see 'em fall."

Honey smiled quietly and with her hand, checked a hot outburst from Hank. Just a light restraining touch on is hand, but he subsided with a growl.

"Some people are born with it," Jane said with a grin. "Me, for instance, I didn't have to learn."

Bonnie eyed her sister for a moment. "I'll think of something dirty to say to that when I get around to it."

That afternoon they drove to St. Martinville and visited the Evangeline Oak and its neat park. They drove about in the parish, admiring the great live oaks, the broad fields of rice just getting green and the old houses of the Acadian French.

"Didn't Albert's people come from somewhere down here?" asked Jane.

Allen nodded. "I don't remember just where. This country is full of Fontenots."

"St. Louis Parish will be full of them, too, one of these days," predicted Bonnie.

Jane was in no way put out. "We intend setting six as the first goal. Then we'll take a deep breath and decide where to go from there."

"Albert won't have a breath left by that time."

Jane laughed and looked at Allen. "Looks to me like Unk could use a couple of deep ones right now."

"I shall have to ask you two to cut it out. I refuse to be pulled to pieces by my two nieces ... er my niece and wife."

In the back seat, Honey and Hank listened but said nothing. When the talk turned to children, Honey turned her face away from Hank and wept softly. Hank looked desperately about. He glanced at the front seat and seeing that they were paying no attention to them, he placed an arm about her shoulders. "Honey," he whispered. "What's the matter?"

She shook her head angrily and dashed the tears from her eyes. "It's nothing," she whispered in return. "I ... just ... they were talking about children and I ... if I have children they'll all be bastards and won't have half a chance in the world ..."

Hank was stricken. Misery flooded his being so completely that it made him ill. She saw what her words had done and became tenderly repentant. She touched his face with her hand and shook her head slowly.

"You mustn't feel that way. Maybe there will be a way ..."

"There is no way," he whispered harshly. "The whole god-dam world is against us. A lousy rotten set-up that plays one way and acts another. A world that hides behind false faces, left hand clean and right dirty, so keep the right hand in the pocket where no one will see and all is well."

She drew his head down to her breast and smoothed his hair, breathing words of courage and hope into his ear.

By ten that night they arrived at The Elms and suddenly Hank jumped as if he had been stung. They got out of the car and started toward the entrance when Hank tugged at Allen's sleeve. "Wait a minute, Unk, I want to see you in private."

Allen chuckled. "If it's money you're worried about ..."

"No ... no. Come over here." They moved some yards away while the girls waited. "Unk, Honey can't go in there. They might be able to tell ..."

A broad smile leaped across Allen's face. "Good God. Have you been punishing yourself about that? Come on, let's go and just keep quiet and watch."

They passed the doorman, to whom Allen paid the cover charge, and were led to a table by a small dapper Frenchman with hair that seemed to have been sprayed with shellac. Allen punched Hank and nodded toward Honey and the waiter who was a little too solicitously assisting her to her chair. The rest of them were forgotten. He had eyes for Honey only.

Allen handed the boy a five dollar bill and said, "Keep an eye on us, son. We'll need a lot of service."

The boy said, "Yes, sir," but he said it to Honey.

"See what I mean?" said Allen under his breath as he shoved a chair under Bonnie.

"You mean he doesn't know the difference?"

"Not only that, she bowled him over like a runaway truck. I'll bet she'll have every eye in here before the night is over."

His prediction was true. After they had eaten he said to Hank, "Why don't you and Honey try it a lick? You can't learn any younger."

"Awww." Hank turned red. "I can't dance."

"Honey can't either, but I'll bet she'll try, won't you, Honey?"

"Yes, sir. That's good music and I can hardly sit still." She smiled apologetically as she spoke.

Allen stood up. "In my day, me proud beauty, it was said that Allen Gordon taught more lassies how to dance than any man in the Parish. Come and take a lesson."

They glided away on the floor, starting a little slow till Honey got the swing of it, then Allen really began to put her through the paces.

"Wow, look at that," breathed Bonnie. "It can't be true and yet I'm looking right at it."

"She follows like a veteran," said Jane. "And talk about light … hey, look at that leap."

Allen had swung her in a tight circle and instead of following him around in the normal fashion which would have necessitated her taking a number of short steps and running the risk of becoming confused, she merely leaped lightly in the air and he swung her around the turn clear of the floor.

"That's a trick it took me years to learn," admitted Bonnie grudgingly. "She did it the first time on the floor. She's the original Nature Girl. Everything comes easily to her."

Allen led Honey back to the table flushed with pleasure. "There … in one easy lesson and believe me, I put her over the jumps."

"Well, you have another candidate," said Jane crushing out her cigarette. "I can't cut a step."

"No you don't," snorted Bonnie. "Later, my girl. I didn't say anything about him dancing with his daughter before his wife, but I draw the line at you. Come, my dear and ancient. Rattle your bones."

"I'll rattle yours," he told her. "You just stay on the floor with the Gordon and you'll be the talk of the town."

"Don't you want to try, Hank?" asked Jane as Bonnie and Allen moved away.

"Naw," he said uncomfortably.

Jane fixed a baleful eye on him and began fixing a drink. She shoved it at him. "Take this and see if we can't change your mind. We'll kill Unk if this keeps up. Three to one is too much odds."

Hank took the drink morosely and downed half of it in one gulp.

"Easy," cautioned Jane. "I don't want to have to help you to the car."

He scowled at her, then at his perspiring uncle as they came back to the table. "What's so great about this dancing business?" he wanted to know.

A tall young man, beautifully dressed and perfectly groomed, walked over to the table. He addressed himself to Allen. "I beg your pardon, sir. My name is René Aldelarde. I know it is not the custom to barge in unasked, and I'm a little embarrassed to ask it, but if you would be so kind, I should like to ask the little lady to dance with me." He indicated Honey with a well-manicured hand.

Allen, stealing a glance at Hank's outraged face, grinned at the boy and introduced him the the rest of the table. "I think it would be all right if the lady feels up to it."

The boy bowed slightly, smiling. "If you would be so kind."

"You don't mind ... father." The word fell strangely from her lips, but somehow he felt he had heard it all his life.

"Certainly not. Go ahead."

She nodded sweetly to the young man and floated away in his arms. René proved to be a superb dancer and be fore they had taken ten steps there were a hundred eyes on them.

Hank sank deep in the well of misery and humiliation. Allen nudged him under the table and when Hank turned he saw that his uncle's eyes were hard and narrow.

"Now, damn you, take it like a man," he grated in an undertone. "You sit there and swell like a dead frog, but you wouldn't try it yourself. Be a knot on a log if it pleases you, but I don't go for dogs in a manger." Allen turned away and began chatting with the two girls.

To Hank's surprise the dressing down made him actually feel better. He hadn't thought of his action as resembling a dog in a manger. The parallel was not flattering, but that's the way it was. He finished his drink and thrust it to Jane for a refill. "Might even take a throw at it myself later," he said like a man upon whom the entire choice lay. Bonnie and Allen threw him a glance but went on with their conversation. Fresh drink in hand, Hank looked back at the dance floor. Honey and her partner wove in and out between the dancers with a practiced and almost professional ease. Hank marveled at the smooth effortless grace with which her slim flashing legs stepped out the rapid tempo. A little unsophisticated country girl. A Negro. Shame stung his face. What if she was a Negro? Why did he keep telling himself about it? His own heart had long ago overcome the barrier if there ever had been one.

The number finished with a smash of brass and immediately picked up again. This time the number was a sultry blood-quickening rhumba. For a moment, René stood away from her, explaining the basic steps, the movement of the feet as coordinated with the movement of the hips. She nodded and they started the dance. Allen looked about at a hiss from Bonnie. The lights dimmed and others came on that bathed the entire floor, walls and ceiling in a solid blanket of soft seductive crimson. Honey's hair shone with a sheen of polished metal reflecting the dull fire of the primordial glow. Her slim body seemed made for the dance. It was as pliant as a reed and responded to the savage rhythm like an atavistic return to some past age. Her eyes sparkled and her lips parted from the exultant blood coursing through her veins, awakened from some long sleep by the call of the primitive beat.

"That isn't just good," breathed Jane in awe. "It's out of this world."

"Everyone else seems to think so, too," said Bonnie who was watching every motion of the dancers. Allen looked about. The other dancers stopped and a wide circle formed. Now René was taking her through a series of tricky take offs. He'd whisper in her ear and they'd break, circling individually moving all the while to the muted thunder of the drums and the rasp of gourds and maracas.

With a tearing crash of brass, reed and piano the dance ended and the lights came back on. Allen leaned over Hank and said in his ear, "Look at her face, you dope, and if you can't feel glad she had the chance then you're an ass of the first magnitude."

"I know ... I'm a heel," admitted Hank. "But I'll get over it."

René brought her back to the table simply ablaze with happiness. Her face became something that was not merely beautiful but now wore the incandescent mantle of immortality. Her eyes sparkled like chips of crystal in the sun. "Oh ... Mr .... Father, wasn't it wonderful? Oh ... thank you so much, Mr. René. It was just ... beautiful."

René grinned attractively and turned to Honey. "I'd like to dance with you again if I may."

"Of course," she said. "Any time I'm not otherwise taken."

He bowed again and left the table.

"What a really nice boy," said Bonnie.

"Ummm, and good looking, too," amended Jane, cutting her eyes at Hank. Hank sat perfectly still looking at Honey with a look of smug satisfaction on his face. That's a change, thought Jane. He looked murderous a while ago.

The night then developed into an unceasing whirl for the girls. René brought friends and introduced them to Honey,

Bonnie and Jane. Every dance they would spare or could be cajoled into was taken.

Hank finally broke down and danced once with Bonnie. Later, and imbued with confidence, he danced with Honey. "I didn't want to dance with you first, Honey," he explained contritely as he swung her carefully to the strains of "Stardust." "I wanted to know a little something about it first."

She smiled tenderly up at him and squeezed him gently. "I know, Hank. I didn't mind."

The sedan rolled smoothly along the smooth macadam road at an easy sixty. Jane who occupied the front seat with Bonnie and Allen had gone to sleep.

Allen looked at his new wife with a soft light in his eyes. "Happy, Bonnie?"

She turned and raked her cool nose across his cheek. "You have no idea. Funny how people go in debt and hunt up strange surroundings calling it a honeymoon. All I want to do is go home."

He jumped guiltily. "Gosh, Sugar, I never once thought of it. I'm sorry, we can still ..."

"Oh, be quiet. I only thought of it for others. I never wanted to go on one. Where in the world can one find a place like Loch Ness or a cook like Lucindy? Besides, I don't think I'd like to be away from our daughter very long at a time."

He squeezed her hand. "If I never loved you for a single other thing, Bonnie, I'd go to my knees to you for that. I can't think of anything else that takes your measure so well. It's the difference between just a person and a wonderful gal. Believe me, I do appreciate it."

"I know, you great big savage sentimental pushover. I don't think I ever saw anyone with such a barnacled exterior that was so soft underneath."

He slowed the car and took a quick feast from her soft lips.

Allen stopped the car in front of the house and he and Bonnie began to wake the occupants. "Hank, you'll walk home with Honey, won't you?"

"Yes, sir," said Hank quickly.

Allen held Honey to him tightly and kissed her. "Good night … daughter."

"I … I just sort of had to do that tonight …"

"I know, and you did a good job. It's all right. You have a father *and* mother now, you know."

"And I had such a wonderful time. I've never had so much fun in my life."

"I'm glad you did … good night."

Hank walked by her side quietly. Finally he said bitterly, "I didn't help much with your good time."

She caught his hand and held it. "You were there to see me have a good time. I wouldn't even have been there if it wasn't for you."

"I mean the dancing. That René fellow and all the rest. They were the ones who really showed you a good time."

She was silent for a while. "If that had been you on the dance floor and I at the table, I would have been so glad for you. It would have been just like I was having the fun."

The boy moaned in anguish. "Jesus, the way you put it makes me feel worse than what Unk told me."

"What did he say?"

"He said, 'Look at her face, you dope, and if you can't feel glad she had the chance, you're an ass of the first magnitude.' I'll never forget those words." His voice was low and infinitely sad. So sad that Honey stopped him.

She was crying. "Please don't feel that way. You know that the dancing didn't mean all that. I just had never done it. I was right there in sight and I didn't do anything wrong. Please don't be hurt just because I had some fun."

"Holy smokes, Honey, it isn't that, it's just I'm a dog ... I know it, Unk knows it, and now you know it. I just can't seem to help myself. Please, Honey, all I want is ..." He stood stiff and white of face in the roadway.

"Hank."

"What?" He had to almost shout it to keep it from breaking.

"Look at me."

"No."

"*Look at me.*" He looked because he could not help himself.

She spoke slowly and distinctly. Her voice low and as soft as the crooning of a mother to a child. "I love you so much that to see you this way hurts worse than the time I was shot. I love you more than you'll ever be able to know or understand."

He crushed her to him with such force that she almost cried out. For a long time they remained in close embrace, her great love stimulating him and calming his hurt and confusion.

CHAPTER NINE

D<small>R. F</small>ONTENOT SAT on the broad V<small>E</small>randah at Loch Ness holding an outsize highball in both his hands. He considered Allen Gordon through whimsical eyes. "Who would have thought that the parish's most eligible bachelor would get himself snagged off in any such manner as this?"

"Fortunately for me," replied Allen, pulling a sliver of tobacco from his cheroot, "you don't know in just what manner I got snagged off, as you put it. I shall make a mental note to keep the mechanics of the matter a state secret. You know too blasted much about everyone as it is."

The doctor sipped his drink with great relish. "I think Albert has serious designs on your niece, Allen. Of course, he's young and hasn't lost enough sleep to be bothered but so far I'd say he's averaged two hours a night since he started in practice. The day will come when he'll start to figure that having her in the same house with him will save no end of travel and time."

"No comment," said Allen grinning. "And in the event of what you predict...no opposition. What I started, Albert has finished and the finished product is something any man would be proud of."

Dr. Fontenot smiled mysteriously. "Ethics. To him, she's something in the nature of a case."

Allen shrugged. "I think if she'd turned up with a psychotic appetite for the flesh, he'd have had to do more than just 'treat' her."

"Wonderful thing medicine."

"Rats. I've decided that he found she was a normal girl who had been squeezed too long into a boot that didn't fit. Naturally, she'd react differently from one who had been reared healthily."

"I don't think you really realize how luckily things have turned out for her. Frankly, I had noticed that queerly intent expression in her eyes, and unnatural tenseness, that is when they weren't frightened or looking at her mother in anticipation of disapproval. *Sacre nom,* what people will do for approval of others whose approval doesn't matter in ratio to the effort expended to get it."

"Unk, you look depressed." Bonnie sat at her dressing table and whipped a stiff brush through her shining hair with such vigor that it stood apart and crawled about as though each strand was endowed with a separate life.

"It isn't cricket to watch a man in the mirror. You catch him off his guard."

She stood up and threw her hair back with a single toss of her head. "No guards for Bonnie, Unk, please. Maybe I can't help you solve anything, but I can listen while you talk."

He looked at his wife and, as many times before, his heart picked up speed. She was dressed in a pair of pajamas that were little less revealing than cellophane. The points of her breasts moved about under the vapor of thin cloth as she walked, describing little figures that erased themselves instantly.

"Come here, Bonnie, and just love the old man a little. I do feel a little low. Dr. Fontenot and I talked about Hank and Honey this afternoon, and we got only to the point where we agreed that it was a hopeless situation."

She threw herself across the bed on her stomach and kissed the back of his big hand. "You deserve a little rest from problems, Unk. God knows you've had your share since we came here."

"Including a wench who deliberately made her uncle so she could marry him."

"That last was your own idea," she said, turning on her back like a cat and sticking her tongue out at him. "Naturally, with you nearly in your grave and me with my life before me, the deal was perfect. You'll die or be confined to a wheel chair and I'll deck myself out and find me a wholesome long-winded young man…"

He bent and kissed her, picking her up in the operation and dragging her across his lap. When he released her, she was out of breath and her skin was alive with delicious accelerated sensation.

"Think you can find one that good?" he challenged her.

She grinned. "It's a problem I had considered. I dare say it would be quite a hunt, but more fun hunting." She sat up close to him, and he could feel the warmth of her body through its thin covering. "Furthermore, I resent the implication that you're better than anyone else." She edged over against him very slowly with certain little motions that shook him deeply, then kissed him. The contact sent wave after wave of shuddering pulsations over him like a plague of small rigors.

His eyes were deep with feeling. "How easy are those things to come off?"

"They're a cinch," she replied and proceeded to prove her point.

CHAPTER TEN

T HE SUMMER PASSED hot and sticky like most Louisiana summers. Brilliant crashing thunderstorms made frequent lurid outbursts and Dogwood made many a rise and fall, changing drifts, washing up new sand bars and demolishing old ones.

Hank went to the University as did Emil, both with misgivings. Emil fought his studies tooth and toenail and managed to make a creditable grade. Hank made brilliant grades in everything except math and in that he failed ingloriously. He simply couldn't get it.

It was a clear, cool day just before Christmas. The sun shone warmly but frost had already laid its crispy fingers on most of the green vegetation, turning it a seared brown around the edges. It was just after the noonday meal and Dr. Fontenot parked his rusty coupe in front of the big house at Loch Ness. He bounded out and slammed the door. Allen met him at the steps.

"Hi there, you ex-sawbones. Had dinner?"

Dr. Fontenot shook hands and dropped panting into a chair. "Oh yes, at the abominable hour of eleven thirty. Maud had something on this afternoon and was in a sweat to get away. We had yesterday's remains of a fowl, fried rice, mustard greens, salad and com bread. Wonderful thing, com bread. Good intestinal abrasive."

"You haven't been here five minutes and you've already started indelicate talk," said Bonnie coming through the door with a huge highball in her hands. "I knew you could use this so when I saw you coming, I fixed it for you."

"You are a most perceptive female, Bonnie. Drink, as you will find out eventually, is the milk of the aged. I do not claim originality for that, but it's a clever remark anyway."

He took the drink and sipped it with relish.

Allen tossed away the butt of a cheroot and nodded. "Honey never seemed to be kiddish in the way you might expect. She would laugh and was always in a good humor, but I never saw her act giddy or silly."

"She makes me a little self-conscious even now," put in Bonnie. "I've still got a lot of the child in me and my antics seem to amuse her."

Lucindy and Honey had set cups and saucers on the little kitchen table, and they all gathered around and pulled up chairs.

Dr. Fontenot took one look at Honey and had to subdue a gasp. She had filled out and was a lot taller, and from her trim ankles to the crown of her smooth black hair she wore the touch of divinity. Her breasts were firm and full, sharply contoured by the fit of the green gabardine dress she was wearing. Her face had lost some of its carven planes and though none of the classic cut had been lost, there was a softer blending of lines. Her eyes sparkled with health and humor, and her smile made the old man's heart swell within him.

"Maybe it is my Gallic background," said the doctor to Allen in an undertone, "but that lovely child makes me sigh for my lost youth. I can't see how a man with red blood in his veins could possibly be such a dog as to consider whether she might or might not have some colored blood in her."

"They kicked prejudice out of you along with superstition and magic at Med school, but the rank and file that keeps them alive hasn't had that advantage."

Honey served coffee, hot, strong and fragrant, then drew up a chair and sat by Allen.

The doctor noticed the look she had in her eyes and suddenly had a pang for a daughter, a beautiful daughter who would love him like this waif did Allen.

CHAPTER ELEVEN

CHRISTMAS CAME, BRINGING Hank and Emil home for the holidays. Emil had lost his clumsy, fumble footed amble and now walked with his wits about him, his head up and quiet confidence in his mien. He was proud of the fact that he had battled his studies successfully, making creditable grades which surprised no one more than himself.

After the early morning distribution of gifts and wine to the colored people Millie sat beside Allen on the living room sofa.

"It was a year ago today, Allen."

"Er ... What say, Millie?"

"I said it was a year ago, today. It still angers me that something didn't show me the light. In a sense I was worse than Emil. You beat him unmercifully, or maybe I should say mercifully, and you had to beat me too, with a much worse whip. Now look at both of us. Who would recognize us?"

He smiled, "A year ago today I also told you we didn't allow useless recriminations in this house."

"I know, but one must cleanse oneself. Admitting it seems the best way I have available. I'm not a complete fool. I know what's going on between Jane and Albert, but ... just look at her. If it is so immoral and degrading why is it she flowers like a tropical plant? She's healthy, happy, and content. I'm afraid I've waited till I am an old woman to become confused. If morality as it is practiced is so wonderful and right, how can all this happiness, laughter, and health exist in the atmosphere of its opposite?"

"I'm glad you said morality as it's *practiced*, Millie, because as it's practiced, the main advantage seems in the talent for beating the rules they profess to revere. Justifying every one of their moves mind you. That's why all the lying, cheating, and treachery. As we treat things today, when you say morals you mean sex morals and you've already answered your own question about that."

Honey came over to them. "I'd like to thank you both for the lovely presents."

"I'm just glad you liked them, my dear," returned Millie warmly.

He pulled her down on a knee. "I hardly knew what to get you the way people are showering you with presents."

"I know how that is," she said. "I have so many clothes and I never wear them. You should see the lovely negligee Mr. Emil gave me. I never saw one so expensive."

Allen caught his breath. "Well I'll be damned!"

"Please tell him you like it," begged Millie. "He was in such a sweat over that gift. He didn't know how you'd take it."

"I certainly will." She stood up. "And I'll wait till no one's around because it would embarrass him." She walked over and joined the group where Bonnie was trying to work a nail puzzle.

"She didn't want to embarrass him, Allen. What deep consideration."

"I'm afraid we'll have to admit that she's a little more sensitive than we are, me at any rate. I would have thought of it too late, then I'd have been sorry. She anticipates things."

"No, I disagree. I think it is just Honey in operation. When we say, anticipation, there is a suggestion of conscious volition. She's just herself. She couldn't be any other way."

"I suppose you're right and that makes it even more odd. Where did she get all that sense of supreme fitness and unconscious talent for the right thing at the right time? It must be that thing Bonnie is always accusing her of—quality. Maybe she actually has in her what my family has been bragging about for two hundred years and has shown so little of."

He smiled tolerantly. "That must have been a shock, Millie, to have to come off that long occupied pedestal."

"You have no idea…no idea. If my children hadn't come back to me, I don't think I could have stood it, all coming at once that way."

Lucindy called them in for dinner and Emil, who was delayed trying on new boots, was left behind. Honey followed them to the door then turned back just as Emil got up from the floor. When he saw her, his face turned a flaming red.

Her lips formed a kindly smile. "Mr. Emil, I've never seen a robe as pretty as the one you gave me. I do thank you so much." She laid a gentle hand on his arm.

Emil gulped and looked miserable. "Aww…that was all right, Honey…I…Honey." He stopped and lowered his glance to the floor.

Her hand tightened a little. "What is it? You can talk to me."

He looked up encouraged. "Honey, I've just felt so bad about…about that day. I've felt bad for so long and I didn't have the nerve to come to you and tell you about it." His voice grew husky and dwindled almost to a whisper. "I'm so sorry." His eyes went to the rug again.

"I've forgiven you so long ago for that."

He looked at her for a long time. "Yes," he said slowly. "I wish I could have been born here. Maybe it wouldn't ever have happened."

"But you weren't and you can't help that. You didn't have anything to do with it. You can only make the best of it now that you're here, and you are making good."

"Honey," his voice was still husky. "I don't care what people might think…I mean I…couldn't you just call me Emil?"

One of her delightful slow smiles crept across her face. "Of course... Emil." She leaned forward, planted a soft kiss on his lips and turned about leaving him standing there.

He stood stock still for a while and a trembling finger touched the spot where she had kissed him, then he straightened up and seemed to grow. His big shoulders squared and his chin came up, his eyes were alive and serious. He walked toward the dining room with a quick sure step.

CHAPTER TWELVE

THAT SPRING HONEY was eighteen and Hank twenty. He had had to abandon his regular course due to his appalling weakness in mathematics and like Emil had to take a special course. When the school year was over, he was glad and looked forward to a summer of riding, roping and ... Honey. He was quieter now, his loud opinions no longer rang from the rafters, and his appetite was noticeably missing.

Bonnie had become concerned and one day she cornered him. "Why don't you tell me about it, Hank? You'll feel better."

His look was stupid. "What good will it do?" He rested his head on his hands. "I'm always sick, sort of. My head aches and I don't know when I've had a good night's sleep. What does a man do ... God!"

She stroked his hair. "It'll be all right in the end. I just know it will."

He uttered a foul word. "That's all I get, hope, faith and charity. I'm going crazy if I can't think of something." A kind of whining sob came from his throat and he wheeled and raced upstairs to his room. Bonnie went back to the kitchen and beckoned to Honey.

"Honey, your man's got the misery D.T.'s. I think he went to his room and I know he needs some comfort. Why don't you go to him and stroke his fevered brow or something."

A flash of pain crossed her face and without a word she turned and walked rapidly up the stairs.

The door stood open and she could see him stretched across the bed, his face buried in a pillow. She sat on the bed, and placed her hands on his shoulders.

"Hank, look at me."

His voice was thick with pain and shame. "You don't want to see a man that's been blubbering."

"Hank, please *look* at me."

He turned over and sat up, his eyes were red and a spasmodic sob wrenched him.

She put her hands to his face and said with compassionate gentleness. "Oh, Hank, you mustn't let it get you like this."

"Get me," his voice squeaked alarmingly. "Why shouldn't it get me? I want you so much, Honey, and I can't have you ... the way I want you." His head bent forward and hard dry sobs shook him.

She took him tenderly in her arms, her own eyes flooding. "Hank, you know I love you and I'll wait. We will be able to do something ... something ..."

He gripped her with a hysterical frenzy while the anguish in her heart tore him cruelly.

She made him lie on the bed and she stretched close beside him, cradling his head in her arms. "Just try to relax," she said soothingly. "Just relax and try not to think about anything."

"He's asleep, Miss Bonnie," she said thirty minutes later. "I quieted him and almost as soon as he laid down he went to sleep."

"He must have been telling the truth," said Bonnie thoughtfully, "when he said he couldn't sleep. Maybe Missy does know what she's doing, but do you think it's wise to let it go on like this?"

Honey bit her lip and pondered. "It does seem cruel but at least for the time being I'd rather let it go on like this. Miss Bonnie, he's still a boy or it wouldn't be getting him like this. I feel what he does ... rather I did till I knew that Mrs. Blumendahl convinced me, but I never lost hope."

"That's just another difference between a man and a woman, Honey. Men can be awfully spineless creatures sometimes."

That night after supper Allen told Hank, "Come out on the porch. I want a word with you."

Hank followed his uncle, feeling a chill of fear. Allen's voice had been hard and uncompromising.

"Now, just what the hell were you trying to do to your horse this afternoon that raised those big whelps on his hips and put those bloody rowel gouges under his belly?"

"He wouldn't jump a ditch."

"What ditch?"

"That one back of the feed house on the old Tailor place."

"A twenty-foot ditch and not a hundred yards from a crossing. Have you lost your mind?"

Hank said nothing, and Allen was silent for a while.

"How'd you like getting about on foot for a while?"

"Have I done anything to deserve to walk?"

Allen began to yank and tousel his thick hair. "Put yourself in the horse's place and answer your own question. What the hell has gotten into you lately?"

Bonnie stepped out on the porch. "Unk, he's all miserable about Honey. That's what's wrong."

He turned to Bonnie. "As much as I regret to tell you this, I'll have to point out that if I had wanted you in on this I'd have asked you when I asked him."

Bonnie, who knew that there was a time to fish and a time to dry nets quietly withdrew.

When he spoke again his voice was calmer but the worse for it.

"I've treated you as a man for some time now and maybe I've been premature. I noticed that streak of stupid jealousy you showed at Opelousas that night, but since it was your first experience I was willing to overlook it. After that you seemed to do all right, but for about six months now you've been going off the beam. I will not have my horses mistreated and as long as you're under this roof, you'll remember that. I'll not go into the details of just what sort of man it takes to man-handle a dumb brute. I leave that to your imagination. As for your reasons for your actions lately, it might interest you to know, since you obviously haven't the guts or the gumption to do your own thinking, there's another person in this. Several more, in fact. If Honey can take it, then one might expect you to show a little fortitude. Your misery while regrettable doesn't impress me to the point that it either explains or excuses your actions."

"Look..." The boy's eyes flared dangerously and he stepped closer to his uncle. "A man can stand just so much. Lay off the blisters or I'll lay one on you."

The door slammed and Honey stood before them. Her eyes blazed into Hank's face. "Unless I heard you with my own ears," she said with direct calmness, "I'd have never believed it."

Allen recoiled fully as vehemently as did Hank. Never had he heard her use such a tone of voice.

"You stand there," continued the voice, "snarling at Mr. Allen with your fist doubled up when all he's trying to do is to drive some sense through your thick self-centered head. What is it that you've had to stand that others aren't having to stand and had to a long time before you ever got here?" She looked him full in the eyes for a moment. Then with a deep breath that seemed laden with scorn and contempt, she turned and walked off the porch into the night.

The tenseness went out of Hank with a rush, his shoulders slumped and he dragged himself into the house and up the stairs.

"May I come out now?" asked Bonnie from the door.

Allen nodded and sat heavily in his chair. "Sure, come on out."

She went directly to him and sat on the arm of the chair. "I'm awfully sorry, Unk. All you said was the unvarnished truth, but even so I wish it hadn't happened."

"It had to happen," he answered harshly.

"Oh, yes, I know, I know. I mean I wish it hadn't had to happen."

"Sure, I do, too, but unfortunately we don't have everything to do with things like this. I don't blame the kid for getting sore because I think that's what I intended so as to make him put out an effort. I didn't intend that Honey hear it though. She couldn't have come out at a worse time."

"I tried to stop her, but suppose she hadn't come out, then maybe you two would have wound up in a fight."

"What happens now, Unk?"

"I don't know. I'm not going to mention it again unless he repeats himself some way or other."

Allen was something of a prophet, but he had no way of knowing this or maybe he could have prevented what happened the next morning.

Honey had gone to the store to get some parts for Amos who was getting his plowing gear ready for the spring breaking. At the store, Jesse King offered her a Coke and as he already had it opened, she accepted it just as Hank entered the store. His smouldering eyes flickered over them briefly as he walked on back to the office to talk to Tinker.

When Honey had gotten what she came for and finished her Coke, she left the store accompanied by Jesse who lived not too far from Amos' house. Jesse had known Honey since she was a child and he was a mature man with a wife and two children. His attention to Honey was no more than a passing neighborly gesture since she had been to his house innumerable times and loved his small twins who were as black as midnight in a hard rain.

Suddenly the rapid clatter of hoofs sounded behind them, and Honey, looking back, said in an urgent voice, "Look out, Jesse, I think Mr. Henry's mad at you."

Jesse looked quickly back and noting the boy's hard face and slitted eyes turned at right angles to run off the road, but he stumbled and fell. With pointed deliberation Hank guided the horse to run over the scrambling body of Jesse and one front foot struck him in the head with stunning force. Honey ran to his side and took one look at the ugly gash in the back of his head and started back to the store at a hard run.

Just before dinner that day Allen summoned Jake. "Jake, what are you doing this afternoon?"

"Nothin', sir. I washed the plane this morning and I got a horse to shoe, but I can finish that pretty fast. Just goin' to put on front shoes."

"That's good, I want you to take the Jeep and run Hank back to school."

Jake's eyes opened a little wider. "He got another week of vacation, ain't he?"

"Yes, he has, but he's going back anyway. He ran over Jesse King this morning and fractured his skull. I want to get him off the place before he kills someone or I kill him. I think he's losing his mind."

Jake scratched his head. "That sure ain't like Mr. Henry to hurt nobody."

"I'm afraid Jesse wouldn't think so right now if he was conscious."

Allen went back to the house and climbed the stairs to Hank's room. The boy was packing as he entered. "All right," he said before Allen could speak. "So you don't allow your horses and Negroes to be manhandled and you want to send me back to school. Well, I'm packing and I can do without your guff."

Allen eyed the boy in silence for a moment and his hand went unconsciously to his head and began to tug at his hair. "I'm trying to figure out what has gotten into you lately, Hank, before I give you a going over. I took a whip to Emil once because he was a dullard who couldn't understand anything else. I'm beginning to think the same thing about you."

"Any time you think you're good," snarled Hank belligerently. "Any time I catch anyone buying Cokes and walking down the road with Honey, he's likely to get run over."

Allen controlled his breathing carefully and sat down. "After last night I think any priority you assume over Honey is wishful thinking. And suppose it isn't. Jesse has a fractured skull. If he dies, I'll see to it that you are sent up for it."

Hank hesitated for a moment, his face white and tense. He seemed about to speak, but he clamped his lips shut and went back to his packing.

"Yesterday morning you had the world. Today you're a twisted bird-brained ass whose actions have earned him just what he deserves. If Honey now hates you the rest of her life, I should not be surprised."

"I told you I could do without your guff," exploded Hank, his face the color of cream cheese.

Allen rose to his feet. "Somewhere along the line you got an exalted opinion of yourself. You think you can walk over people. Somewhere Hank and his blithering personal problems which have been worked on a hell of a lot harder by others than by him have become all important. So important that he can bite the hand that feeds him and become frightfully independent and actually threatening. I don't know where it came from but I know where it's going."

"You mean I can't go back to school?"

"Oh, no. You're leaving for school in less than an hour. You'll probably remain there through the summer. In fact, when you see this place again it will be by my specific invitation. Jake will take you to Baton Rouge ... from this room."

"What do you mean from this room. I can walk."

"You can right now," said Allen ominously.

"Look, Unk, I ..."

"Shut up. You've done your talking. As of now it stops."

Allen's big right hand flashed out and cracked like a pistol shot against the boy's chest knocking him flat on his back on the bed. He was up with a rush, both fists swinging but again the rock-hard palm rang against the side of his face to be joined by the left on the other side.

Five minutes later Allen put his head out of the door.

"Jake!"

"Yes, sir."

"You can come on in. Clean him up or help him do whatever he has to do and take him back to L.S.U."

"He ain't had no dinner, Mr. Allen."

"Jesse hasn't had any dinner either."

Jake lowered his head. "Yes, sir."

Hank walked unsteadily down the steps and started down the walk. His face was swollen and his eyes were almost closed. He could see, but with difficulty. Jake trailed him, carrying two suitcases. Before they got to the front gate Honey came through it. Hank subdued an impulse to run and kept walking. She stopped and faced him as he came up to her.

"In case you'd like to run over someone else," she said, her voice clear and sterile, "I'd suggest Uncle Louis Lee. He's eighty-five and I doubt that he could get out of your way very easily."

Hank went white and gulped in a miserable voice, "I'm going back to school."

"That's a good idea. Why don't you stay there." With that, she scorched him with her hot eyes, walked swiftly up the walk and disappeared in the house.

For a moment he watched her retreating figure, then walked dejectedly toward the Jeep.

They disappeared in a swirl of dust and Honey clutched Allen's shirt and cried against his chest. "What could have happened to make him that way. Was it something I did?"

He caressed her soft hair and shook his head. "You know better than that. He's having a rough time, Honey, but let's hope he'll fight it out himself. That's the only thing that can do him any good."

She took a deep shuddering breath. "I know that. He's got to grow up and making it easy for him won't help."

"You're entirely right, Honey. He must mature before he can assume the responsibility of a wife. I know you'd be a big help to him, but he wouldn't be much to you."

"I've got to respect him," she said sadly. "I can't love anyone I don't respect and even if I did, it would be a terrible thing to marry someone feeling like that."

Ten days later Hank got a short note from Honey: "Jesse came home today. He'll be all right. Through no fault of yours, you're not a murderer." That was all. It wasn't even signed. He recognized her handwriting and felt immeasurably cheered because the likelihood of being hailed into court had kept him in a stew of fear ever since he had come back. Not a soul wrote him or sent him any news. Twice he had called up but each time the nurse gave him the same stock tale:"He's doing as well as could be expected."

Honey at least thought enough of him to write, even if it could hardly be called a letter.

He occasionally ran into Emil who would talk only if buttonholed. One day Hank stopped him.

"I haven't made up my mind about you," said Emil with blunt frankness before the other could get in a word. "I can't see how you could pull a stunt like that on Unk, trying to fight him. Why didn't you pick on Joe Louis or someone easy like that?"

"You pulled a knife on him once," Hank lashed back stung to the quick.

Emil nodded imperturbably. "That's right, but I ran like a son-of-a-bitch before he cut me down off that fence. You wanted to jump him that night on the porch just because he had told you a few things about yourself."

Hank boiled with rage and stepping in close said, "How'd you like a busted puss?"

Emil grinned slowly. "From you? Don't make me laugh, and get out of my way. I've got some meat to trim." He placed a huge hand over Hank's face and gave him a mighty shove that skidded him in the grass ten feet away.

"Grow up, sonny boy," jeered Emil as he walked away. "Else you might find another man in your way at a certain place we both know."

Sheer freezing terror gripped Hank as he raised himself slowly to his feet. He wanted to run after Emil and make him explain that last crack, but he knew that he couldn't hope to match Emil's great strength and he felt he had been laughed at enough for one day. He walked shakily back toward the dormitory, his brain in a racing turmoil.

That night Hank walked around on the campus trying to think. He climbed to the top of the Indian mound and sat under the starlight hearing but not hearing the breeze as it whispered through the long tendrils of moss above him. There were some things he should be doing but he knew that even if he tried to study, it would avail him nothing. He went back to his room and found Melvin Willis seated at the table buried in the clutches of calculus.

An hour and a half later Hank stopped the car he had borrowed from Melvin Willis in front of Amos' house.

"Who dat," called Amos.

"It's me, Amos, Henry. Is Honey there?"

"Yessuh, she here."

"Ask her if she'll step out here. I'd like to talk to her."

Honey came down the steps clad in a close fitting house coat of maroon pile that Allen had given her two Christmases ago. Hank's heart ached at the sight of her like a throbbing tooth. She came to the gate and stopped. Her eyes were cool and decidedly distant.

"You wanted to see me?"

"Yes, Honey. I'd like to talk to you please. I wouldn't have come, but, well, I had to. I either had to talk to you or leave school. I couldn't study or even think till I had seen you and gotten something straight."

"What is there to get straight?"

"Come sit in the car, Honey, it's cold out here and you're not too well dressed. I'll put the heater on." She hesitated a moment, then walked to the car and waited till he opened the door for her, then got in. Hank went around the car and got in. He closed the door and placing his back against it, faced her. He was calm now and knew what he would say.

"In a manner of speaking, Honey, I guess I'm sort of on trial, to you and Unk, I mean."

"Yes."

"Well, I know I was wrong, just like you both said. I did a pretty terrible thing. I know that. Today, though, something happened that raised a question that I'll have to have answered. If I can't get an answer, then I'd better just go off somewhere else and try to make a place for myself. I can't stay at school any longer the way it is now. If I can get some assurance, then I'll be better able to study and try to get back on my feet. What I'm trying to say is this. I've got to know one thing, Honey. If after whatever time is necessary, you feel that I've … I've done all right, will you be ready to let things be like they were before this all happened?"

She could see the pain in his face and she could tell that it was not the pettish disappointment of a spoiled child but deep harsh suffering. Suffering that had etched lines in the corners of the boy's eyes and made his lips continually tight and hard.

He continued without waiting for her to speak. "I … I've got to know if you've stopped loving me. If you still love me, I'll make it, but one way or another I've got to know. Today for the first time I saw I stood a chance of losing you, that maybe I had already lost you. Everything went black. I got sick and I found myself sort of walking around not knowing where I was going... not even caring. I'm not asking you to forgive me for what I did. I guess I'll have to earn that, but while I'm earning it, I've got to know, Honey... *I've got to know.*"

She wanted to scream at him to stop it, that he was tearing her heart out, killing her, but she sat calm and quiet, her face tranquil and showing nothing of what went on in her breast. They both sat silently for a while, then Hank said in a low voice:

"You can't answer me, Honey?"

"Yes," she said steadily. "I can answer you, but I'm wondering just how to put it."

The boy felt as though a cold wind had suddenly struck him. His head reeled and again that dreadful nausea swelled in his stomach making him grit his teeth against it. He gripped the steering wheel till his fingers ached. If she didn't know how to say it, then it must be just what he had been fearing, feeling all the while deep down that it would be all right... really.

"Hank, there's a lot you haven't understood and unless I can make you understand, then I will have only made matters worse. There is no way that I can make you see what Mr. Allen means to me. When you dared to raise your hand against him, something died in me. For a sudden awful second, I hated you. You, whom I have loved beyond all understanding. You brutally ran your horse over poor Jesse when all he did was give me a Coke and walk down the road with me in broad daylight. You resented that, even that little attention. At the club that night you hated the thought of another man dancing with me, not because he was infringing on your time because you wouldn't dance with me, but because he was using your property."

"*Oh, no!*"

"Don't interrupt me. I let you talk till you were through. I repeat, you did it because you looked on me as exslusively yours. The day you ran over Jesse you were a total stranger, not the handsome, shy, big-hearted boy I had known. You were a hard-eyed fiend bent on hurting and destroying a colored man who had done absolutely nothing to you. I can't love that in you. That's the way it is and I can't help it. Mr. Allen can be as savage as a tiger, but when he is there is a reason. What you did had no reason. It was just plain, mad jealousy which never reasons and it is something I can't stand. Some way, somehow, I had hoped we could be married and live a decent life and have fine children. I know that your rage and sorrow at not being able to marry me helped put you in the state you were in that day, but Hank, I'm in this, too. Mr. Allen hates the situation. He loves me the way I do him, and it hurts him so badly at the thought that I might not be happy. You always wanted me here. The only possible solution out of just living with me the way white men live with their colored women was to take me away from here to some place where we weren't known where I could pass for white and no one would question it. You never thought of that. You steamed yourself into those rages, you hurt people, you hurt me and you hurt your family, all because you couldn't have me the way you want me and yet you never once thought of taking me away. *You* don't want to leave, Hank, and God knows I don't blame you. It would break my heart to leave Loch Ness and all the people that are so dear to me, but I would have gone in a minute if it meant that we could be together in respect and honor, but you didn't consider it because *you* didn't want to leave here. You were very noble and fine wanting to do the right thing, but you turned about and placed the obstacle of your own desire to stay here directly in the path of it. I don't like to be harshly critical, but I have no choice. I won't marry you nor will I live with you until you can show me that you are a man, with a man's balance of mind, with a man's sense of justice, with a man's mature judgment in everyday things. I've loved you ever since you first came here and in order to live that love I was willing to give everything I have, endure any sort of ostracism from both white and black, some of which I have already tasted, shun my pride and shelve what we can call my honor just so I might have a little happiness with you. All I have asked of you is the amount of manhood that I think I have a right to expect. I love you deeply, deeply enough that I'm willing to see you curl up with misery in order that you discover your own strength. I'm running the risk that you'll turn to the first woman who'll listen to you in your pain, and men in pain often do strange and unaccountable things. I'm risking *you* in order that you may find yourself. I love you as you were before, happy, generous, amiable, kind and tender. Come back to me a man, Hank, and you may have me in any way we can manage. Come back a man and you will have all my love for all time." She placed a warm hand on his icy one and leaned forward, her eyes damp and starry. "And Hank," her voice almost broke; it was infinitely warm and sweet. "I have such an awful lot of love to give." She opened the door and stepped from the car. She came around to his side and placed a hand on his shoulder. "Come back to me ... soon." Swiftly she leaned in and kissed his cold white cheek and ran into the house.

The boy sat for a long time silent and motionless as a slab of marble, his face chill and bleak. He had seen his soul laid bare and flayed unmercifully by the one person in the world he loved above all things and still she loved him, she had said so. The realization flooded over him like a warm life-giving rain. Something seemed to snap and he bent forward on the wheel of the car and wept gently like a weary child.

CHAPTER THIRTEEN

SUMMER CAME WITH its humid scorching days and languorous nights, driving the Gordon household to the broad porch for relief from the heat.

Allen sat alone after supper and watched the blending of twilight with night. The silver sickle of a fairly new moon hung in the West near a star of unbelievable brilliance.

Albert and Jane raised a hubbub in the hall, making Allen frown slightly. It was too perfect a night for frivolity and he passively resented the disturbance. Bonnie preceded them to the porch and they all pulled up chairs and sat down.

"It's nights like this that have more to do with upping the population than rainy days," offered Albert.

"Looking for an argument," asked Bonnie as she stretched luxuriously in a colorful beach chair that she had recently bought.

"No, I was just making a statement. Smell the air. Feel it caress you, doesn't it make your blood race?"

"I take it as a good thing that such natural phenomena usually leave the speed of Bonnie's blood alone," said Allen. "If, of course, she was not born with a high blood speed affliction, which I more than suspect sometimes."

Bonnie gave a serpentine wriggle which made her lithe body undulate provocatively.

"I have what is known as control," she averred. "All I do is push a mental button and I have whatever mood I choose."

"I also note," he continued, "that with those rompers you're now wearing, you are a distinct hazard to the mood control of others."

"She'd better not uncontrol Albert here," said Jane. "The worst malady he ever studied would be as nothing compared to me mad."

"What the devil are you two waiting for anyway," said Allen. "You make Albert lose all this sleep that he needs and as far as I can see there isn't anything left now but a few magic words to mumble over you and there it'll be."

"I think, Albert, that we have just had a subtle hint."

"Very subtle," agreed Albert. "As a matter of fact, there isn't any reason actually. Pop had a little trouble getting material for the apartment, but that's been taken care of and the thing was finished a week ago."

"There are still curtains to be hung and a stove to be connected," supplied Jane.

"Yes, and a yard to smooth over and grass seeds to plant, but we could move in tonight if we ..." He stopped suddenly and looked at Jane. "Well ... want to?"

Whatever leaning Jane had ever possessed for fluttery demonstrations had effectively been refined out of her. She leaned back in her chair and waved a graceful hand. "Why not? That's the way to do things anyway, on the spur of the moment. Too much anticipation makes for disappointment. The mind can ever imagine more than the hand can produce ... Shakespeare."

Jane sat up, her eyes shining. "What do you think of it, Albert?"

"Well ... the devil, I only have on a sport shirt and slacks ..."

"So what," retorted Bonnie, getting to her feet with an acrobatic leap. "This is the best thing I've heard in a year. Unk, go to the corner of the porch and bray for your protégée and her entourage. I'll go call Doc and Mrs. Fontenot. Jane, you have on your play suit, so just go get the skirt and you'll be dressed just to fit Albert. What'll it be, clergyman or J.P.?"

"I want a clergyman," said Jane. "Justices are such commercial knot welders. I want all the sonorous phraseology and stuff. Tell Pop to bring Brother Baskin. He's a nice little man."

When the wedding plans started it was eight fifteen. Exactly fifteen minutes later the first guest arrived. It was Honey. She stepped up on the porch clad in a close-fitting skirt of white gabardine with a little blue sleeveless bolero jacket of the same material. Her hair was parted in the middle and drawn back done up in a simple bun at the nape of her neck. As she passed through the light of the open door, she seemed terribly young and at the same time delightfully mature. She was fresh and vital and gave off the fragrance of some fairy footed perfume, light and haunting.

Allen stood up as she came toward him. "Come to papa, sugar, and let me look at you. Gad, but you fairly take the breath away."

She came up and kissed him softly on the lips. "I can always depend on you to say something nice about me." She laid her shining head on his chest and hugged him around the waist. "Sit down, Pop, so I can perch on your knee. I've something to tell you."

She sat on his knee and looked seriously into his eyes. "I didn't tell you before, but a few weeks after Christmas Hank borrowed a car and came to see me. He was so terribly miserable and hurt that I could hardly stand it. He wanted to be assured that everything would be all right if he made the grade. I think he understood."

"If you told him, he understood," said Allen positively.

She sighed. "I told him that he'd have to prove his manhood and that if he did I'd be waiting for him."

"That's good. If it is made too easy then the lesson won't be effective. I want you to be happy, Honey, and I certainly didn't want him for a husband for you while he was still a child. Boys mature so slowly it seems. You know you're invited to a wedding tonight."

"Oh ... Jane and Mr. Albert?"

"That's right. We sat here on the porch and planned it in five minutes."

Honey's eyes shone with gladness. "I wish I could be married that way. Mr. Allen..."

"Wait, Honey. The time has come for a new deal. Think about it and find yourself a new name for me. Make it Unk or Pop or something else than Mr. Allen."

She hugged him hard around the neck. "I hope you won't mind, but over in Opelousas that night when I sort of had to call you Father, I'll never forget the warm feeling that came over me then. I guess I've called you Father a million times since then while thinking about you."

He kissed her warmly. "Then Father it is. Makes me feel kind of paternal or something."

She bit his ear playfully. "I think I'll go listen to the women chatter for a while. I'll be back."

He spanked her smartly. "O.K., if you must. Don't stay in there too long and leave me alone."

She smiled at him making his heart tingle. "I won't."

Honey had been gone some twenty minutes when Allen heard the thunder of hard hoofs muttering in the distance. The nearer they came the louder they grew.

"Whoaaa...Whoaaa...." Miss Maud Fontenot hauled her two nervous champing horses to a sliding dust covered halt in front of the gate.

"Wow! Boy was that ever a ride." Her voice drummed like distant artillery on the still night air. "Made it in thirty minutes."

"Missy," warned Allen, "you're going to get killed racing these animals like that."

"So what," she roared, "I had fun!" She smote clouds of dust from her jodhpurs with lusty blows.

"Unharness them, Jake," said Allen as Jake walked up, eying the animals enviously. "I'll tell you when she's ready to go."

They started for the house but Missy stopped and turned about. "Wait, Jake... Dammit, I forgot something." She went to the buckboard and rummaged in the back and shook the newspaper wrapping from three huge bottles of champagne. "Giggle water," she said, holding them up for inspection. "Chateau Imperial Valley, California, 1947. You ought to see 'em lap it up from those old *Mum's, Piper,* and *Braut* bottles I brought back from France. They never know the difference. Well!" Missy delivered a shattering welcome to the four women as she strode through the door. "How'n hell is everybody? Millie, damn if you ain't lookin' like a bride yourself these days. Bonnie, if I was Allen, I'd make you wear a chastity belt. Jane, ain't you the sudden one? Good grief, why all the rush? Miss a couple of weeks? ... don't mean a thing. I've done it time and again."

"She's just making it legal," said Bonnie, which made Millie blush in the midst of laughing.

"My sister," said Jane, whipping a brush through her hair, "tells on me, but wait till I get going on her."

"Well, Honey, I see you're looking sweet as usual," said Missy. "Why don't you females come to see me? Damn, but I've been lonesome the last few weeks."

"What, no parties?" asked Millie.

"If I could just get you to one of my parties, you wouldn't be asking any such questions. When is this fang dang coming off?"

"As soon as Pop gets here with the license, although I rather suspect my intended will hold up proceedings shaving and bathing, even though he started half an hour ago."

"Just like a man," said Missy. "My first husband was late. Said he couldn't find the ring, but from the smell of him he had stopped at a pub hard by and anointed his nerves with a little of what it takes." She looked intently at Honey for a moment. "Come here, child, I want a word with you." She led Honey into the hall. She fumbled with Honey's hand for a moment and said, "Now go back into the light." Honey walked back into the room and gasped.

"Ohhh ... Mrs. Fontenot ..." On her ring finger sparkled a magnificent diamond solitaire. It was set in a high old-fashioned

Tiffany mount and in the light gave off lances of blue white sparks. The girl seemed hypnotized by the ring, holding her finger at eye level drinking in the beauty of it. She turned, "You mean it's for me?"

"Hell, yes," exploded Missy. "You're wearing it, ain't you?"

"Ohhhh." Honey ran her fingers over its hard glistening surface, hardly breathing. "For me!"

"Oh come, child. It's only a ring. I've got dozens of 'em and if I'd have known what a splash they would make, I'd have given some of 'em before."

Honey faced her, a look of incredulous gratitude on her face. "Oh … how can anyone thank someone for a gift like this … for me." Her eyes went back to it and Missy looked at her critically.

"I must say your eyes make it look pretty sick when you hold it up like that. Never knew a diamond could be put to such shame."

Honey wheeled and threw her arms about the older woman's neck and kissed her heartily. Missy patted her shoulder with gruff impatience. "Oh, go some place and eat a peach. You'd think I'd given you the Bank of England."

Honey clasped her hands together and gazed raptly at the ring again. "There isn't anything like this in the Bank of England. Can I go show it to … Mr. Allen?"

"Show it to anyone you want to. It's yours, ain't it?"

"Come here, Honey, and let us see it," said Bonnie.

The girl was instantly contrite. "Oh, Miss Bonnie, I'm sorry. I didn't mean …" She looked very close to tears.

Bonnie smiled and squeezed her shoulders. "Of course, you didn't. You wanted to show Unk your present and you just didn't think."

"But I should have thought …"

"Oh, nonsense, Honey," said Jane, taking the ring from Bonnie. "What you did was perfectly natural."

It passed to Millie and they all admired it greatly and Honey shone with gratification. Then she rushed out into the hall and they could hear her feet clattering on the stairs.

"Missy, you have a certain dramatic flair for making people happy," said Bonnie squeezing her affectionately. "And I know just why you get a bang out of it. No one could have seen Honey's face and failed to understand."

Missy nodded. "There isn't a lot an old woman can do these days for the youngsters, but by God, I do what I can. What the hell good is that senseless piece of glass to me? I've got a quart of 'em. I don't have a damn thing that can match that child's happiness. When I do something like that, I get something you can't count in terms and dollars."

"You mean it really is glass," said Millie aghast.

Missy laughed. "Sure, it's glass. You can get another one just like it from De Beers for about four thousand smackers. Pretty good grade of glass, if you get what I mean."

"I'm sorry, Missy," said Millie repentantly. "I'm afraid I'm not up on the latest slang."

Missy waved it away with a careless hand and said, "Think I'll go down and make Allen give me a drink. That drive out whipped me. Boy, how did I ever make them Morgans step."

Honey came out on the porch and stood in front of Allen. "Father, guess what?"

He grinned. "I have no idea ... what?"

"Get out your lighter and make a light."

He did so and Honey thrust the diamond into the circle of light where it caught fire like a live coal sending out dancing sparks of red and blue flame.

"Good Lord," he burst out. "Where'd you get it?"

"Mrs. Fontenot gave it to me."

He looked at her closely in the glow of the lighter. "Stars in your eyes," he breathed. He took her in his arms. "Seeing you happy like this, Honey, makes me want to cry. I think you're the most beautiful woman in this world."

Honey did not make protests at this extravagant compliment, she merely cuddled a little closer to him and sighed. "I'm glad … Father, because if I'm beautiful, then it makes you happy. You love beauty so."

"How do you know that?"

"Oh, my, goodness. Haven't I seen you cup a gardenia in your hand and gaze at it like you were a doctor looking for a germ? Haven't I seen you sit out there on the bluff on Straw watching a sunset until it disappeared? Didn't you marry Miss Bonnie?"

"There's more billing and cooing going on around this house," yelled Missy coming through the door.

"Missy, that was a wonderful thing, giving that ring to Honey."

"Oh, nuts. I was glad to do it. She'll be needing an engagement ring anyhow. Think you can rustle me a drink, Honey? I'm perishing." Honey leaped up and disappeared through the hall door.

"I noticed one thing, Allen. She didn't open her mouth about, "Oh, you shouldn't have done it … I couldn't think of accepting it.' If she had, I'd have taken it back. That line irritates me beyond words."

"Honey is honest sometimes to a fault."

"I'll take honesty over faith, hope and charity any day," said Missy, fitting a cigarette to her long ivory holder.

The girl returned, bringing her drink.

"When're you going to get married, Honey?"

Honey was silent for a while, so Allen answered for her.

"Hank went off his base here at Christmas and we have him on trial now. He whipped one of my horses until he cut him up and ran over Jesse, one of my colored boys, bemit the boy was miserable and hurt because of this situation, but that was no reason to do what he did."

"The time to discover defective merchandise is before you buy it," said Missy throwing away the butt of a ciga-cause he was walking down the road with Honey. I'll adrette and fitting another into her holder. "The boy'll come through, though. I have no fear of that."

"It's hurting him so," said Honey in a small voice.

"Sure it is, baby, and that's just what he needs," said Missy puffing animatedly. "You are a tenderhearted little thing, but you've got to remember that a little hurt now may save him a great deal more later."

He chuckled. "Don't worry. He slipped up here one night and Honey gave him the works. I can just hear her right now telling him a few medium rare truths about himself."

"It was the hardest thing I ever did in my life." she admitted.

"That's what makes it good, baby. Something that's too easy to do never makes a demand on the person. Just like fear. A man that's not scared is called a brave man. One who is scared and runs away is called a coward. The man who is scared out of his pants and still does the job is the one who gets the nod from me."

Allen stood up and threw his cheroot away. "Well, there comes the wedding."

Dr. Fontenot and the Reverend Jonathan Baskin climbed from the doctor's elegant family sedan and came up the walk briskly.

"Isn't this just like 'em, Allen," piped the Doctor. "Here they've been waiting around for I don't know how long, then all of a sudden they want to get married."

They climbed the steps and Allen shook hands with them. Missy and Honey went into the house to start looking over preparations so the three men stayed on the porch.

"Build yourself a drink, Doc," said Allen. "Brother Baskin, I suppose you'll have a Coke or ginger ale."

Baskin nodded vigorously. He was chubby, bald and very pink of face, looking like an ecclesiastical cherub. "Yes, I'll have a Coke, and if Alcide will be so kind, about three fingers in the glass before he pours the Coke."

Both the doctor and Allen looked quickly at the minister. "You ... you mean whiskey?" asked Fontenot in mild amazement.

"But certainly. That's what's usually measured in fingers, isn't it?"

"He was a little dumped because he thought men of the cloth didn't drink," explained Allen laughing.

"No one mentioned that I was to be on my best behavior tonight," said Baskin easily. "I understood that I was called in to perform a wedding ceremony because of the sonorous verbiage employed by the clergy. The impression was even given that if I had not been available, Alvin Stewart might have done in a pinch. Consequently, I intend to be in on any celebrating that goes on."

"Bravo," said the doctor and smote Baskin between the shoulder blades with such force that he dislodged the little man's false teeth.

"Now, luff here Alcide ... kummpf ... fittt ... now. Blast you and your Gallic enthusiasm, you almost knocked my teeth out and that would have played hob with my sonorous delivery. Here, give me my drink and restrain yourself."

Allen helped himself to a big drink and said, "Doc feels that he has made a convert, that's why he is so enthusiastic. For a man reputedly with a foot in the grave he's pretty active, especially with his elbow bending."

"I retired before either foot reached the brink," said the doctor comfortably, "and will do fine as long as I don't get a bursa in that elbow." He leaned back in his rocker and considered his drink thirstily.

"He'll burn with very little extra fuel, Allen," said Baskin sipping his drink. "Just a touch of fire and he'll go up like a celluloid collar."

"Oh ... pouf to the both of you," said the doctor. "At the risk of repeating myself, Allen, Honey is especially lovely tonight. The child has filled out and as I predicted, she is now beyond description. The world is full of beautiful women taken physically, but take the best you can find and Honey'll top her by a mile and yet that isn't her most attractive point."

"If you are referring to Miss Anderson, I agree. The moment I looked at her I knew I was in a *presence*. If that sounds ambiguous, I'm sorry. I'm afraid I coudn't explain it very well."

"In this company you wouldn't have to," said Allen with a rush of warm parental pride. "We know just what you mean. By the way, Brother Baskin, did you know she's one that so much unfavorable gossip has been spread about? They say that I'm not helping the child because of pure motives but that I'm grooming her for a mistress."

Brother Baskin choked over his drink. "My God!" He wiped his mouth with a large handkerchief. "Do you mean to tell me she's a Negro?"

"We don't know," Allen told him. "She was reared by them and has passed for one. True, she doesn't look like one, but neither do thousands of borderline cases. Does that change what you just said?"

The chubby little man shook his head slowly. "Not in the least. I'll admit that the knowledge was something of a shock because in every case like this there's so much potential unhappiness and I detest unhappiness with all the vigor that I do sin."

"And can detect it ten times easier," said the doctor grinning.

"As to that, I'm going to have to agree with you, Alcide," said Baskin draining his glass.

"In fact," said the doctor, "I dare say you are not alone. Just a little more honest about it. However, Jonathan, should this get to your congregation, I'm afraid you'd be bounced for another with better concentrated hell-firing convictions."

"Without a doubt," said the other accepting another drink. He held it up. "This also would get me in hot water as though I don't enjoy an occasional, er, let's see, Sister McCallum has a name for it, oh yes, *drachm*. She delivers it not as a word but as an epithet."

Honey came out on the porch and approached the minister. "They are ready, sir."

He looked her over carefully and she returned the gaze with calm unruffled dignity. He drained his drink and said, "Tell them I'll be right there. Come, gentlemen, and let us place the seal of legality upon this happy couple. I'd feel a lot better about it if God were to manifest some unmistakable sign of approval." A tremendous flare of heat lightning in the East lit up the horizon from North to South, flickering fitfully for a few seconds, then dying.

Dr. Fontenot chuckled. "Heat lightning is a very kindly type of electrical discharge. It makes ozone. God appears to sanction your thoughts, anyway."

"I'll thank you not to be blasphemous, Alcide," said the minister with mock severity.

Half an hour later the company, with the exception of Albert and Jane, were assembled on the porch making inroads into Missy's champagne. "Drink it up," she roared. "I ain't takin' it back. Lovely ceremony, Brother Baskin. I thought it was beautiful."

"Thank you, Mrs. Fontenot," he said heartily. "I'm afraid that for the first time in my life I kissed a bride with an alcoholic breath."

"Well, maybe you set a good precedent," she said with a bellow of laughter. "Where'd they go all of a sudden?"

"You of all people ask that, Missy?" said Bonnie.

"Oh, hell, I know that, but they seemed in an awful hurry. Well, maybe they *were* in a hurry."

"I think," said Honey comfortably, "that something was said about making up beds or some such domestic activity."

"I think I'd call that a useless gesture," said Bonnie at-taking a fresh magnum of champagne.

"Here, Honey, why don't you try some of this giggle water. It's mild."

"Thank you," said Honey, "I've had two glasses already and it's making my stomach feel sort of hot."

"Heat 'er up, kid," said Missy loudly. "Nothin' like it I always say…for other people. Give me bourbon for regular serious drinking."

Honey accepted another glass of champagne and sipped it slowly looking at Allen a trifle guiltily. He smiled and patted her hand.

"You're one person in the world for whom I have no fear as regards drinking. Alcoholics are mentally confused, eh Doc?"

He shrugged. "Dipsomania is now regarded as a psychological problem all right. Remove the problem, of course, if you can find it and the drinking can be controlled. Finding the trouble is often the hardest thing."

It was nearly one when the party broke up. "Now all of you people come to see me sometime," brayed Missy, but as I have said, don't make it on one of my party nights. Make 'em bring you along, Millie, and you, too, Honey. Might as well make this a real fang dang."

"Honey…what is it?" He took her hands from her face and saw in the dim light that it was wet with tears. "Honey, baby, what's the matter?"

"Oh, I'm just unhappy, I guess, Father." She put her head on his broad chest and wept softly but seriously. Bonnie threw an arm over the girl's shoulder and squeezed it.

"Tell us about it, baby," she said gently.

"Oh…I don't know. Maybe it was the champagne, but the wedding helped I guess. I suppose I just want Hank."

"Do you think he'd had enough time, Honey?" asked allen.

"I don't know. I hope so. He must be miserable down there wanting to come home so badly."

He raised her wet face. "If you say the word, Honey, we'll get him home tomorrow."

She nodded. "Please, even if it's just for a day. I've had to be strong and I *have* been strong, but I feel like it's going out of me. I don't believe I can stand it any more."

"You poor child," said Bonnie chokingly. "God knows you've taken beatings from every imaginable angle. I certainly don't blame you. Why don't you go call him up now?"

"Would they let me talk to him now?"

"He's not on the campus this summer, Honey, he moved out just a little ways. He's staying with a Mrs. Powell. Just ask exchange for Mrs. Powell's residence on Chimes Street. She'll be furious, but tell her it's very important."

"Hello," the voice was thick with sleep.

"Hello, Hank, this is Honey."

"Honey?" The boy woke with a snap. "*Oh, hello, Honey. God, you don't know how good your voice sounds.*"

"Oh, darling," tears almost choked her voice. "Come home tomorrow."

"WOW!" he screamed. "Did Unk say it was all right?"

"Yes, Hank, he said to come."

"Oh, Lord, now I gotta wait till morning, there's no bus 'til eight."

"Get on it, Hank, please, and don't stop for anything."

A series of strangling noises came over the phone. "If I thought I could make it any sooner, I'd walk, Honey...wait, I can get a taxi and be there in an hour. Will you wait up for me?"

"Even if it takes you all night, darling. I'll be right here on the porch waiting."

Hank let out a war whoop. "Just give me a little time. Just a little and I'll be there before you know it."

Honey cradled the phone and turning her face to the wall wept from happiness and relief. Hank had sounded like her boy should sound and all was going to be well.

It was a few minutes under an hour when the taxi came racing up the long curving drive. Honey ran to the front gate and opened it just as Hank threw his valise into the grass and leaped for her. For along time under the cover of the star-studded sky they remained as close to each other as they could strain.

Very slowly they came up the walk, not speaking, just looking at each other. They sat on the top step of the porch and held hands, sitting as close as they could.

The boy ran a caressing hand over her face as though etching its outline in his mind for all eternity. "It hurts, doesn't it, Honey? Funny about that ... love hurts."

"Not always, Hank," she said with incredible tenderness. The boy took her in his arms cradled across his lap, holding her as though she were the most precious thing in the world, and kissed her first with almost religious gentleness, then demandingly, hungrily. His hand pressed against her slim waist and savored the soft resiliency of her flesh.

A pain sprang up beneath his heart and he broke away and turned his head. "I'm so happy I could die," he said in a trembling voice, "and what do I think of but who you are and what this damn country would do to us if we married. There's only one thing to do, just like you said, and that's to get out of it. We'll go some place, it doesn't matter much where. They'd love you because you are beautiful and good and would never ask any questions, just like that night at Opelousas. They couldn't tell the difference."

"No," said Honey, pouting. "I won't go."

"But, Honey," he cried in amazement. "The idea was yours. You beat me over the head with it that night I slipped up here."

She shook her head adamantly. "Just flat ain't goin'."

The tone of her voice made him look sharply at her. "Say, what's going on here?"

Honey sat up and put her arms about his neck. "Hank, you thought you were happy here; and you were. But you won't be happy if you run away. This is your home, and mine; and our friends are here. This is where we're going to have to stay, whether we like it or not. And with the friends we have, I think we're going to like it."

Hank was stricken into silence. For along time he sat like a stone. He passed a trembling hand over his face as though mildly surprised to find it there. "Honey … are … you … sure?"

"I was never more sure of anything in my life, darling. I just know we can do it."

He was still not convinced. "But I don't see how …" He shook his head. "I wish I could believe it."

She took his face in her hands and kissed him sweetly. "Hank, I believe it."

He pulled her over against him and held her close. "You poor kid, just think what you've had to go through with. You wanted me even if you couldn't marry me, didn't you?"

"Yes, and I wouldn't have missed getting you either."

He shook his head. "I wouldn't have had you that way, Honey."

"Then those few words that'll be spoken over us make all that difference to you?"

"No, it isn't that. It's the system I hate."

She smiled tenderly and kissed him. "Hank, I love your nobility but you don't see that if we can't have what we want then we must take what we can get."

"That's reasonable, of course, but I never had any reason about me where you are concerned. I love you so much I'm half crazy most of the time. You'll never know the hell I've gone through these last six months."

He sighed. "Yes, I suppose you were all right. I feel like I'm a hundred years old now. What an insufferable idiot I must have been. The first thing I must do tomorrow is to go see Jesse."

"Jesse has no grudge, Hank. He has already forgiven you. Actually, I believe he enjoyed his stay in the hospital."

He shook his head. "Maybe he's forgiven me, but I won't forgive myself till I've told him so. My manhood is at stake like it was when I called you that terrible name and had to come and admit it. That was the hardest job I ever tackled, I believe."

He looked suddenly at her. "Do you realize that we'll he married, Honey, and live like people really should?" He leaped to his feet almost spilling her to the floor.

"YEEEEOW!" he screamed at the top of his lungs, the echoes ringing back at them from the hills.

"Hank, you'll wake everybody."

"Who the hell cares? I'm sittin' on top of the world…YEEEEEEEEOW! Come on and let's wake Bonnie and Unk." He caught her by the wrist and against her protests dragged her into the hall. Hand in hand they raced up the stairs and down the hall, bursting nosily into the room.

"What the hell's going on here?" growled Allen sleepily as he turned on the bed light.

Bonnie rolled over and opened a sleepy eye. "Holy mackerel, don't you two ever sleep?"

Hank bounced on the bed and hugged his uncle ecstatically. "Boyoboy, she told me, Unk. I think I'll go crazy."

"That would be a short trip," said Bonnie, sitting up and pulling her pajama tops together.

Hank suddenly sobered and sat straight. "Golly, Unk, I've caused everybody a lot of trouble and now this…I guess I don't deserve it."

"You don't," said Allen stifling a yawn, "but as long as you realize it, you're doing O.K."

"Emil's got Jane's room, Hank," said Bonnie stretching. "You can sleep with mother or on the couch in Unk's office."

"Yeah," said Allen. "You two get out of here and let hardworking people sleep. We'll listen to your enthusiasms in the morning…Honey, what are you smiling at?"

"Was I? I didn't notice."

"Ummm, well, it was one of those cat et the canary smiles."

"Yes," agreed Bonnie, "I was wondering what you were thinking about."

Honey blushed prettily but said nothing.

"I'll take a blanket from the chest in the hall," said Hank. "That'll be all I need. I won't bother Mom at this time of night."

"Well," said Bonnie as they left the room. "That's the first time I ever saw Honey blush. I wonder what she was thinking about?"

"Probably her wedding night," said Allen rolling over and pounding his pillow.

"Yes... probably."

"I worked up a sweat in my hurry tonight," said Hank. "Want to wait till I shower and ... oh, I'll walk you home, Honey. I forgot."

She picked up his pajamas and placed them in his arms. A big bath towel followed. "Now go on and take your bath. I've walked across that pasture a thousand times by myself. It's silly to walk all the way over there."

"But, Honey ..."

She came close and kissed him like the touch of a kind breeze. "Hank, do what I said."

He grinned. "O.K., I'll be back in a few minutes." Hank went into the room behind the office and on through to the shower which was just off the room. Honey spread the blanket on the couch and smoothed it out carefully. Then she stood back and gazed at it for a moment. Her lips tightened with decision and she sat down.

Hank was back in ten minutes, clad in his best silk pajamas, mopping at his thick taffy hair which was damp and touseled. He glanced at Honey. "Well, you look comfortable."

She lay on the couch with the blanket pulled up under her chin, looking very demure and lovely.

"I'll let you stay there for six or seven kisses," he said banteringly, "then out you go, else people might talk. In fact," he pulled the shade down, "it wouldn't do for anyone to see even this innocent joke."

"Who do you think is out there at this time of the night?" she asked. "It's after three."

"The night has a thousand eyes," quoted Hank, sitting on the edge of the couch and kicking off his slippers. "Now, move over, here I come." He ducked under the blanket and grabbed her playfully in his arms. His eyes grew wide in astonishment and his body went as taut as steel.

"Oh, Honey."

"Oh, Hank, take me close and love me ... love me."

A wave of unendurable passion swept over him like a tide and he held her close murmuring her name over and over. "Honey ... Honey ... Honey." Her body had the ecstatic flawlessness of a fresh ripe peach. His pajama coat came open and the touch of her breasts was almost more than he could stand. His lips roved searchingly over her face, lips, her ears and throat. Just the touch of her fine skin against his lips, his chest, made his heart throb in his ears like dull distant thunder. His own skin seemed terribly hypersensitive and a sound came from his lips as though he were in pain. He drew her close again, kissing her closed eyes, her lips, and caressing the silken denseness of her hair that had come down in a smothering cloud. "Oh, Honey, why did you do it?"

She snuggled closer and kissed him with intense demand and hunger. Her arms seemed to have the power of ten. They hurt his shoulder blades and all but crushed the breath from him.

Her eyes were closed and her breath came easily and sweetly. He tenderly brushed away a tendril of hair that was making her nose twitch. "Honey ..."

"Don't talk," she whispered. "Just hold me."

Hank held her close and ran his hand from one smooth tanned shoulder to the gentle rise below her waist. She shuddered a little and gasped. He desisted and lay his face close to hers feeling the slippery touch of her hair as it lay spread out on the pillow. His nostrils drew in the warm clean sweetness of her body that emanated from beneath the blanket like some enchanting perfume. In her hair there was a lingering fragrance that could scarcely be detected. Her face was calm and lovely in the half light and Hank's throat contracted and his eyes stung wetly. He closed them with something like humility and threw his arms protectively across her shoulder. He slept.

Day was dawning when they awakened. Honey easily, Hank with a start. He sat up.

"Gosh, Honey, what'll we do?"

"Nothing," she said smiling. "Didn't you know that Father and Miss Bonnie were seen coming from this very room the morning of the day they married?"

She pulled him back and kissed him with maternal tenderness.

Hank frowned and bit his lips. "Honey, why'd you do it?"

"For several reasons. One, because you said you'd never do it. Two, because I wanted to show you that there were stronger things than what people call propriety. Three, because I wanted to be loved, Hank. Loved by you, not next week or next month, but last night. I wanted to see if I was bigger than your convictions and whether they were stronger than the real Hank. Most of all, I guess was because last night was something special to me. Getting you back after all that time was just more than I could stand and love was hurting me, too. Last night it didn't hurt, did it? ... afterward?"

Hank looked at her fixedly for some time, thinking hard. "Honey, I can hardly believe that anyone your age could possibly be so wise. You've always seemed grown up to me. I guess that's why I've always been a little afraid of you." His face changed subtly. "You know I thought about it last night ... what you just said. Love didn't hurt ... afterward. It mellowed down to something warm and wonderful. The pain was gone and in its place was a sweet dreamy peace. And you knew it all the time."

She nodded. "Yes, Hank, I knew. That's another reason why I cornered you last night. I had hurt until I couldn't stand it any longer."

He scooped her up, blanket and all, and held her close. "I'll spend my life being grateful for all you've meant to me, Honey. I guess I'll have to live another life to make up for all you'll be in the future." He brushed her hair back with his fingers and hooked it over her small perfect ears. "How much can a man love a woman?"

She snuggled her face close to his. "Just love me as much as I do you, Hank, and you'll never hear a word of complaint from me."

CHAPTER FOURTEEN

THE MOON GLEAMED down on the broad, tree-dotted meadow in front of the big house at Loch Ness.

On the big verandah sat Doctor and Missy Fontenot, Bonnie and Allen. They were relaxed and happy after Brother Baskin's simple ceremony had made Hank and Honey man and wife.

"With the qualities Honey has," said Bonnie positively, "I can't get it out of my head that she must spring from some very noble line and when I say that, I am not talking in terms of money or social position."

"Applesauce," said Missy draining her glass. "As for what social position means in this country, let me be the first to cheer that statement. It has about as much relation to nobility as some of those moth-eaten royal houses in Europe, where a man's nobility didn't prevent him from committing the most heinous crimes in the book. In fact, they took advantage of their 'nobility' to commit them." Missy accepted another drink from Bonnie and leaned back in her rocker. "I wonder what the kids are doing right now."

"If you knew," said Bonnie, "it might embarrass you."

"Haw," exploded Missy violently, "it might fill me with a sense of lost powers but not embarrass me, dearie. Embarrassment is the brand of small souls. Once Jane got straight with herself and got all the kinks out, she stopped getting embarrassed, didn't she?"

Bonnie nodded.

"Well, there you are. People who live in the open are not likely to bother if the house burns down."

"Whose idea was the camp for a honeymoon spot?" asked the doctor.

"Mine, of course," said Missy. "I knew damn well they didn't care about tearing off to some stinkin' city in the summer time to swelter and steam. The honeymoon is another great American custom that is overdone. They are now only ten miles away and only a mile from Old Ben who watches the place for us. Ben's wife cooks for them and the whole thing is cozy and real. The woods, a beautiful stream at their front door and all the solitude they want."

Allen raised his glass. "Here's to two of the finest kids in the world. May their pains in the past portend comfort in the future."

"*Skol*," said the doctor.

"*Gesundheit*," said Missy, "or is it *Prosit?*"

"Down the hatch," said Bonnie.

Without another word, and with complete understanding, the Doctor and his wonderful wife walked off the verandah to the family car and drove slowly off, the Doctor at the wheel.

"On Balafalaya River, Unk, the moon is shining just like this and the frogs are croaking and the lightning bugs are lightning."

He pulled her across his lap and kissed her hard. "You love the kids, don't you?"

She nodded. "Probably as much as the one I'm gonna have."

He almost dumped her to the floor. "What?"

She kissed him lightly on the lips. "You heard what the woman said."

Allen relaxed and let go a gusty sigh. "Well, you never can tell about these forty year old men."

"That's right, you can't," said Bonnie. "If you're slipping, then I'm glad I didn't get you when you were about twenty-five."

He hugged her tight and nibbled an ear. "What a night, what a gal, what a moon…" He chuckled. "I'm like Missy. I wonder what the kids are doing."

On a twenty-foot bluff overlooking the river, there stood two lithe bodies shining whitely in the moonlight. They glowed like marble in the pure light. The girl was a dream of classic sculpture, her hair flowing in soft jet masses over her shoulders. On her left hand blazed a great diamond sending off splinters of coldly beautiful sparks. The man was slender yet muscular, his golden hair gleaming like a helmet of metal. She turned and smiled at him.

"Race you to the other side." Simultaneously, they struck the water, cleaving it like white spears. They came up and raced toward the beach which gleamed just ahead of them. He helped her from the water with tender solicitousness. They pulled a blanket from a nearby branch, spread it on the sand, and lay down side by side.

He stripped the water from her face with a gentle hand and looked into her eyes with open honest adoration. "If it was any better, Honey, I couldn't stand it."

She smiled and nodded. "I know, I'm here, too."

The touch of her water-sleek skin sent a shiver over his body. "Cold, Hank?"

"No, just ecstatic. Honey?…" He pulled her very close so that their bodies fitted line for line. Her dark eyes were luminous, warm and hungry. "What, Hank?"

"My love is hurting me again."

Her teeth gleamed as her lips parted. "We learned what to do about that, didn't we?"

He nodded and pulled her even closer. Their lips met and mingled, and about them in the cool woods peace and silence settled down for the night.

END

LOVE IN LOUISIANA

CHAPTER ONE

Antoinette de Lage Salton stared into the cold merciless gullet of the pistol with numb fascination. Her palms were dank with sweat from the hysterical force with which she gripped the weapon. The muzzle leered at her, every tiny detail appearing to her staring eyes in etched clarity. Her pulses hammered thunderously in her ears and a tight suffocating weight lay heavy in her chest. She gazed at the shining serpentine bands as they wound their way from the depths of the barrel, stopping at the muzzle like long deformed teeth through which death would spit when she pressed the trigger. "Everything will be over … everything will be settled … everything will be all right…." It seemed as though the gun was speaking to her but she knew it to be the thudding of her own thoughts.

Suddenly, with a spasm of revulsion, she hurled the gun from her with a frenzied motion, backing away as though from a poisonous reptile. The gun almost struck Granny Rosa who came through the door as Antoinette threw the weapon. Granny was about as wide as she was tall, her face smooth and virtually devoid of wrinkles, with eyes keen and wise.

She halted, favored Antoinette with the briefest of glances, then waddled over to the bed and dropped the load of sheets she was carrying. She turned and faced the girl.

"Whut you doin' chunkin' dat gun 'roun' like a tater? You might nigh struck me."

The girl might not have heard her and she continued to stare with a trance-like fixation at the gun as it lay on the floor. With a powerful sweep of her arms Granny hurled a chair behind Antoinette, striking her at the knees and precipitating her roughly into a sitting position. Granny pulled up another chair and sat.

"Now, den, Sugar, you can tell you Granny bout it. Ain't I riz you frum a li'l bitsy ole baby, all the way...."

Antoinette broke the chains of her fear with an almost audible sound and fell against the old woman's breast with a sobbing cry of relief. She cried long and stormily, gradually subsiding into jerking sobs. She could smell the clean starched odor of the old woman's clothes, shot through with the friendly pungent aroma of plug cut tobacco and a well seasoned stone pipe.

"Come on, now," prompted Granny, "and tell me all about it."

A cry came from the girl's throat that made Granny wince. "Why... why... why did it have to happen to me?"

Granny rubbed the back of her hand against her nose. "How come *whut* happen?"

The girl sat up straight and dashed the tears from her eyes. "Granny Rosa, I'm way over time...!"

Granny chuckled. "Shucks, you had me mos' skeered t' death. Lotsa gals yo' age had dat happen, 'specially if you been playing 'roun...."

Antoinette grasped the old woman by the arms with such strength that Granny gasped. "I haven't, I haven't, I tell you! I didn't play around, Granny. I was... *forced!*" Another hard sob shook her and her head sank in abject misery. Her voice was the wail of a lost child. "Oh, God, Granny! What am I going to *do?*"

"Rat, now," snarled Granny, bouncing to her feet, "us goin' tell de Boss and us goin' have a lynchin' roun' hyar... after you tells me who done it."

Antoinette's silence stung the old woman into action. She lifted her from the chair by main force and said, "You tells me, or I slaps hit outen you." Her voice was hard and uncompromising, reflecting the iron discipline which was Granny's toward both black and white who were in her charge.

The girl began to weep bitterly. "That's the trouble. I don't know. It was at night and I never saw him. I just waited and hoped I'd never have to tell...."

Granny sat suddenly. "Jesus," she breathed faintly. "Us is in a fix." She sat and thought for a minute, then she motioned with her hand. "Set down," she commanded, "and you can tell me all 'bout it frum start to finish."

The girl closed her eyes tightly and struggled against nausea for a moment, then nodded, "I'll tell you...."

The night was humid and muggy. Not a breath of air moved the leaves of the giant magnolia outside her upstairs window but the heavy perfume of the blossoms weighted her down like thick strangling webs. In the east, across Big Buff Creek, lightning flared and flickered along the horizon, showing the serrated teeth of tall pines. She lay in bed and tossed, partly because of the heat and partly because she had been getting a lot of sleep lately and her young pliant body was demanding activity. Thunder, muted and ominous in timbre, muttered fitfully in the distance between periods of heavy silence. Insects and frogs were silently awaiting the onslaught of the storm.

She got out of bed and stood in an open window, trying to catch a bit of air, but it was as tepid as that around the big bed, so she just stood watching the play of electricity, wishing the wind and rain would come.

She went to the bathroom and found a towel that would reach from her chin to the floor and mopped her face and neck. On an impulse, she ran water over it and wrung it out, and slipping her thin gown over her head, sponged her body, gasping delightedly at the cool rough touch, prickles of pure sensual ecstasy coursing over her. She scrubbed her back and thighs thoroughly, then her stomach and sharply erect breasts, touching them with careful pride, smiling to herself as their pink tips became taut and hard.

She sat on the window sill and draped the towel over her from chin to knees, tucking it close to afford the maximum benefit. Soon it was warm and she shook it out to cool, the air seeming hotter than ever. Again she ran the towel over her body, wishing it were not so much trouble to wet it again. She decided against it and draped it across her stomach, chest and shoulders.

The thunder had risen from a low growl to the sharp crackling explosions of field guns and a lone bolt of lightning tore a sprawling jagged crack across the sky. Immediately there was a rolling cannonade which almost split her eardrums—that one had been close. She fancied she could smell the sharp odor of ozone, where the bolt had seared the atmosphere, and her nose wrinkled appreciatively. Another bolt blazed across her vision like the forked tongue of some giant serpent, and again the window-rattling explosion and the long echoing roll. A little breeze sprang up and got stronger gust by gust.

Toni loved storms with all their prodigal waste of wind, water and electricity. Everything seemed cleaner and refreshed when they were done and the extravagant splendor of their displays delighted her. She pulled herself up in the window, a slim but marvelously curved silhouette in the violet spasms of light, her misty blond hair waving softly in the wind which now had mounted to gusty violence. She touched the cool skin on the under side of her thighs and on her arms, then thrust her hands under the mass of her hair, shaking it out to the full force of the wind. It whipped about, stinging her back and cheeks as the gusts played toss with it.

The first drop of rain was as big as a twenty-five cent piece and struck her slightly rounded stomach near the navel depression. She flinched and shuddered a little. Another followed, striking the valley between her breasts and trickled down to join the other. Then with a roar, the deluge came down. Toni stood on the roof outside her window and, holding her head inside, let the chill water sting her shoulders, back and legs. Like an acrobat, she arched her body, let her stomach catch its share then with a serpentine twist leaped back into the room and punished her tingling skin with a rough dry bath towel.

Invigorated and relaxed, she climbed naked in bed and lay spread-eagled on top of the cover, cool and comfortable. Outside, the storm fretted itself out in a final burst of rain and colorful electric display. The wind settled down to a cool steady zephyr, covering the girl's naked body with soothing caresses. She slept with the distorted flexibility of a kitten, her fine hair tousled and wild over her pillow, one arm across the smooth expanse of her stomach, the other outstretched toward the edge of the bed. One leg was extended straight out in front of her, the other drawn up, making a figure four. The lightning had ceased and the thunder was out of breath. Only the drip, drip from the eaves of the house and the ecstatic glee club efforts of thousands of toads disturbed the purple silence.

Toni slept on in the untroubled relaxation of youth and perfect health, her breath regular and calm. Her door opened slowly. In the inky blackness she would not have been able to see the intruder, even if she had been awake. The shadowy figure crept closer on carefully placed feet and stood above her. There was the sound of the rasp of cloth like the belt of a bathrobe being carefully untied, followed by a slithery gasp as though a bathrobe was being dropped to the floor.

Toni slept peacefully on and not until a heavy body landed upon her, did she awaken, her scream stopped by the palm of a hard hand. Her legs snapped instinctively together, but it was too late. Her strong young body arched and writhed with all the mad strength of terror, but the weight was too much. The cold sweat of numb freezing horror stood out in droplets and her partially pinioned hands gripped and clawed at the arms and shoulders above her, trying to reach his face and eyes but falling short by some inches.

Her legs strained and clenched with despairing strength but the efforts only weakened her further. She tried to bite the hand that was crushed over her mouth with such brutal force, but her teeth slipped off the tough palmar hide without being able to get purchase. Suddenly a sensation shot through her, and with another attempt to scream, she fought with renewed vigor but her strength was gone and it was only a brief hysterical spasm. The sensation went from a mere impression into a blinding wave of red raw agony which shot through her stomach and upward like a wave of wet fire and she fainted.

"You see," she screamed, "I told you ... I don't know ... I never will know ... I ... oh, God!" A hard convulsive shudder shook her body, and her breath straining through set teeth bore droplets of froth.

Granny Rosa, pain and helplessness cutting a relief map of ridges in her face, slapped the girl a sharp blow across the face. Toni's cries became silent and sobs, hard and shaking, took their place.

Lavender Salton was taking her beauty nap. One might have said, without being too unkind, that she needed it. When taking the nap it resembled no skin ever seen in its natural state reposing beneath layers of various unguents designed to feed starved tissue and to strengthen sagging muscles. She wore, in addition to the creams, a device which was supposed to avoid "gobbler's neck" or the wattle that comes with middle age, and which her husband had crudely termed a halter.

Her figure was slight and delicate like the lines and skin of her face. There were no bovine traits in the Patterstall line she would say at the slightest or no provocation. She considered her skinniness sylph-like, and her starveling breasts as further evidence that there hadn't been a bull or cow on her family tree for three thousand years.

For her figure, for her aura of culture, and for the generally nebulous background which she made the most of she was an envied member of the Literary Club, The Daughters for the Preservation of Southern Culture and other such.

Lavender was not Southern, she was Boston, and she always contrived to picture Boston as suffering considerably by virtue of her absence from its august environs. Her sighs for Beacon Hill and Back Bay were echoed by the culturally undernourished, one and all, save those who had been there and had come away callously unimpressed just as some people can visit Richmond, Virginia, without suffering from anything save the inhabitants' stuffiness. With those who had visited Boston Lavender was delightfully vague as to just where she had lived or how long. This was because she had been there only twice in her life, once at the age of three.

She sat up in bed, after having been awakened, with a vigor that was both uncomfortable and unnecessary. "Rosa, how many times do I have to tell you not to awaken me when I'm taking my nap? If I've told you once I've told you a thousand times that when ...."

"I come to ax you weh de Boss is," said Granny breaking in on what she had learned might be a marathon of complaint.

"I'm certain I don't know. There are things which I have striven might and main to place on something like routine around here, and to date I seem to have reaped a veritable bumper crop in exactly the opposite direction. What has happened that should make his presence so terribly important as to ...." She stopped. Not even Lavender enjoyed talking to a closed door.

Jefferson Salton's face twitched alarmingly and he rubbed it hard with his long sensitive fingers. "Now come over that again, Granny, and do it slowly. I'm afraid you lost me somewhere ...."

"I sed she done got bigged. Dat otta be plain enuff fer you. Some low bastud done ravished her in her bed and hit was dahk and she couldn't see who hit was. Now she in a fambly way, and whut us gon' do 'bout it?"

He sat suddenly in a handy chair and held his face with both hands. He had had a certain trying scene with Lavender last evening and today his usual quart had disappeared immediately after dinner. Since then another quart had gone the way of its predecessor. He wasn't drunk but he had trouble focusing his mind.

"Where is she now?"

"She in her room sleepin'. Dat's weh I lef' her bout a hour ago."

"Who do you think it could have been, Granny?"

"I ain't got no ideer. All I know is, my Sugar Baby is in a passel o' trouble and up till now, she done allus come to me and I been able to do somethin'. Dis here thaing done got me and I can't think o' nothing." The old woman began to sob, tears trickling down her fat cheeks.

Jeff sat silent for a while, his gaze flitting aimlessly across the broad, tree-dotted lawn. Tremendous columns narrowing the view, making him unconsciously frame the landscape between them, blocked his vision on either side.

Granny Rosa sat on the porch steps and wiped her eyes on her apron. "Fust time she ever come to me fer sumpn' and I couldn't tell her whut to do. I operated on a white gal onct a long time ago and she likened to died. I ain't never tetched another one since and I ain't gon' touch my Sugar Baby neither. Peoples can set back and make all sortsa rules fer other peoples but I ain't never seen *dem* ackin' so sweet. Now mah Baby done hadda mislick and us can't do nuthin'."

A slim blue convertible flashed around the driveway on the east side of the house and disappeared in a swirl of dust. Salton shook his head. "There she goes," he said sadly, "I wonder what she intends to do?"

"Well," rasped Granny, standing and glaring at him, "I come in her room rat after dinner jes' in time to stop her frum killing herself wid yo' pistol." With that, she left him still sunk in his chair, trying to make his sulky brain function.

Lavender came out on the porch and sat near him. "I can't tell you how sorry I am," she said softly. "What a terrible thing to happen to you! What a blow it must be! I am awfully sorry, but I must say, I'm not terribly surprised."

He faced her slowly. His usually mild brown eyes were flaming and held mad glints. "A terrible thing to happen to *me?*" The muscles controlling the corners of his sensitive mouth were leaping spasmodically unnoticed. "What do you think it is to her—or don't you give a good God damn? You're sorry?" His snort of derision left little to say. "That is the lie of the year!"

He leaped to his feet and strode over to her, his six feet two inches giving him now the stature of a colossus. "One blessed word out of you to her and I make you this promise. You'll want to pull your tongue out by the roots when I'm through with you!" Leaving her shocked and shaken, he strode out to his car and drove off in a billowing cloud of yellow dust.

After a fruitless evening of searching, Jeff came wearily home and dropped exhausted and dispirited into a chair on the verandah. His daughter was in trouble. She had tried to kill herself, and her father, miserable and stricken, could do nothing…. The pipestem snapped between his teeth. He took it out of his mouth and stared at the jagged ends.

CHAPTER TWO

DR. ALCIDE FONTENOT smoothed his black spade beard with long sensitive fingers and swallowed a sudden spurt of saliva initiated by a gust of air that had previously flowed over Maud's roast as she took it from the oven for basting. Maud could do wonderful things to a roast. He faced the man seated across the office from him and nodded vigorously. "Yes, I treated her because I had no choice in the matter. God knows how she managed it, but it is certain that some sharp instrument had been employed either by her or some clumsy abortionist. It was providential that she or they didn't go through the vaginal wall and into the peritoneal space. Death, then, would have been almost certain unless she had received immediate attention."

Jefferson Salton squirmed a little in his chair and gripped the bit of his pipe with a bulldog hold. His lean powerful jaw, strutted with hard muscle, showed a quivering nerve near the corner of his mouth. He ran his hand over his iron gray hair and tried to relax by slumping in his chair.

Dr. Fontenot eyed him keenly. "She's all right now, isn't she?"

"Perfectly," said Salton, removing his pipe and massaging the St. Vitic nerve. "In body, that is. It's her mind I fear for. I tried to get her to tell me who it was but she began to show signs of hysteria so naturally I let the matter drop. I was hoping that maybe she had told you."

The doctor shook his head. "Not a word did she tell me. Maybe I'd better tell you the whole thing as I know it."

"Yes, I'd like to know."

Dr. Fontenot, semi-retired physician, whistled merrily as he gave the finishing touches to a dry fly. Bits of hair and feathers littered the carpet and a bottle of metaphen stood nearby attesting, as did spots of the antiseptic adorning his fingers, to the doctor's not infrequent slips with both hook and knife.

Cars did not interest him overmuch as they passed on the street, but when he heard the crash of his fence and saw the coupe charging across Maud's roses, to come to a grinding sudden stop against his concrete steps, he was both pained and angry. He leaped to his feet and strode out on the porch. His furious speech died on his lips when he looked at the girl's face. It was deathly white and as he looked, she collapsed over the steering wheel, sending the horn into a fury of noise. As Maud came placidly out on the porch, he leaped youthfully to the ground and opened the door of the car.

He gasped, "*Sacré nom du petit cochon.*" He called to Maud, "Come help me, Maud. The child is bleeding to death!"

They pulled her from the car and a great pool of blood was clotted on the leather of the seat. Her dress was soaked from waist to hem. Together they carried her into the doctor's office and minor surgery.

"She ought to go to the hospital," said Maud coolly. "I'll call the ambulance."

"You will do no such thing," said the little man rapidly. "There's something queer here." He raised the girl's dress and stripped off her blood-soaked panties. "See—what did I tell you. This is Jeff Salton's daughter and I'm sure he won't want this bruited about. Call Jane and tell her to locate Albert if she can and have him come home immediately. Now, if you'll get my instruments from the autoclave there—they've been run, haven't they?"

She nodded, "Yes, I ran them this morning."

"Good, I'll try to locate this bleeder and—Oh, yes, I'll want some triple zero silk suture and a small needle. For goodness sake, throw those little needle forceps away and get mine!"

"Albert likes the little ones," said Maud, placidly.

"Albert is a fool," he retorted testily, scrubbing his hands hard. After the prescribed seven minutes, he dried them on a sterile towel.

Maud opened a pair of sterile gloves and powdered his hands heavily.

"I'll manage now," he said. "Go see if you can locate Albert. No, put Jane on it and come on back. I may need help."

Antoinette Salton lay quiet and still in a deep drugged sleep and Dr. Fontenot watched her with bright black eyes. Her hair lay spread on the pillow like a shimmering blond veil and he could see the faint veins in her smooth lids. Her face was too strong to be pretty and her full firm jaw with its deeply cleft Salton chin dissipated the suggestion of weakness displayed by her full, somewhat petulant lips. The forehead was broad and high and the ridges of the brow were almost prominent. A decidedly striking face but more for its strength than its beauty. The little man moved the tiny goatee on his nether lip up and down in perplexity and vexation.

Albert, his son, came quietly in. "Mom says you did a good job on her."

"I always do a good job!" snapped his father. "You needn't talk so blasted low. She had morphine and luminal. Thunder wouldn't wake her. She'll be all right unless Jane's blood kills her."

"Did you get anything from her about ... ?"

"Not a word. She was in no condition to talk. It has me worried though. I'll have to tell Jeff about it because he'll be looking for her."

"He's a right guy," said Albert. "If it was ninety nine out of a hundred fathers, make something up I'd say, but not to him."

"Yes, that's true but ... well, dammit! I like Jeff and ... but he's got to be told so I'd better phone him." Dr. Fontenot left the room with a brisk stride and Albert looked at her for a while, frowning.

Dr. Fontenot sipped at his highball. "Well Jeff, there you are. That's all I know. During the week I had her here. I tried every way I could to get something out of her without actually pinning her down. I even tried that once and all I got was a shake of the head."

Salton gripped the arms of his chair and his teeth gritted on his pipestem. "Give me that bottle, Alcide," he ground out. Fontenot shrugged lightly and handed him the bottle. Salton placed it to his mouth and lowered the contents noticeably. He wiped his mouth delicately with a white handkerchief and handed the bottle back.

"Will that help?" asked the doctor.

Salton shrugged and renewed his grip on the dead pipe. "Answer your own question, you're the doctor."

"How much do you drink, Jeff?"

"Possibly a quart a day ... a little more some days."

"And yet I've never seen you drunk."

Jeff smiled, showing his strong white teeth. "I've never been drunk in that sense and I've never had a hangover. I guess it'll kill me some day."

"I doubt," said the doctor, "that whiskey ever killed anyone *per se.* Hopeless dipsomaniacs often let their diet go to pot, or the same condition which caused the drinking likely produced a freshet of ulcers. By the way, Jeff, you're an intelligent man. What do you think makes you drink?"

Jeff spread his long-fingered hands out on the chair arms and considered them for a while before he spoke. "No single thing, Alcide. Dozens—hundreds—of things all gathered about my head and started buzzing. I can only still them with the bottle. My first mistake was marrying the second time or maybe it was the first time. I don't know. I do know that after a wife like Antoinette, I was a fool to expect the same stroke of fate which sent her to me to repeat. There never was a woman like her for me, at any rate, and she spoiled me utterly. When I married Lavender, a stupid name for a thistle, I apparently suffered from a complete mental blackout. Never, in all my drinking life, have I ever displayed so dull a wit."

"What," asked the doctor, puffing a flame into the end of a thin cheroot, "exactly is the matter with Lavender other than her appallingly stupid sense of values?"

"She is like many another, Alcide. Her stupidity might begin there, but that doesn't end it. She lives in the questionable sunlight of past ancestry. Some peasant grandfather who allegedly came over on the *Mayflower,* some malcontent or criminal or other miserable expatriate possibly has now been elevated to the stature of Charlemagne's brother-in-law or some such preposterous thing. As if that made any difference. A little reading in anthropology or genetics would dissipate all this ancestor worship."

Fontenot shook his head. "I doubt it. You are going on the assumption that they would be amenable to reason, which they are not. Wiggam pointed out that a few healthy near relatives are a lot more important than any number of interred and consequently sainted ancestors."

"Well you have made my point for me though I digressed in speculation. There is nothing in the world that will change such people's attitudes and Lavender, the thistle, has more than her share."

"Snobbery," put in Dr. Fontenot, "is probably one of the most drastic self-indictments ever seen. I say self-indictment because that is actually what it is. Not intentional, naturally, but true, none the less. It is one of the more pitiable methods of self-inflation detectable a mile off, and worse by far than streptococcus which, if left to its own devices kills with relative dispatch; whereas snobbery is slow death and invisible to all but a few of those very rare people who at long last make some serious effort at self-evaluation."

"Alcide, I curse myself that I haven't talked to you more in the past. You are an intellectual tonic."

"That is a high compliment, Jeff. I'll try to deserve it." The tone was ordinary but had a certain steelly quality that jerked Salton away from an inspection of the whiskey bottle.

"You meant something then which you didn't put into words?"

The doctor poured out a generous portion of whiskey and added Coca Cola and ice. He faced Salton with characteristic suddenness. "Yes! I know I'm beginning to sound like Missy Blumendahl but I doubt that I could find a better one to emulate. She always dove headlong into a problem and vowed to solve it without having the remotest idea as to how she would accomplish it, but she always did. There are ways out of everything, Jeff, because problems are posed by the human brain. *Ergo,* no miracle will solve them, only the human mind can."

Jeff bit down on the stem of his pipe. "Before you put me down as schizoid, I'll admit that with a little more strength I might be able to do more. Drink is the milk of the weak and the aged. I'm not yet in the latter category so I come under the former. In other words, my problem as you have pointed out is my own fault in the essence. For instance, if I had had enough sense to steer clear of Lavender in the first place, I wouldn't have a problem to my name, unless I slipped up in some other fashion."

"Prescience," said Dr. Fontenot, "has been denied us. One has to accept the responsibility of his actions without being technically responsible for their birth."

"Then you don't believe in free will?"

The little man uttered an oath. "Man is an animal, Jeff, and a good half of his troubles would evaporate if he'd embrace the full array of implications and truths that fact projects. Free will, like everything else that the finite mind of man can grasp, has its limitations. You are free to choose between cold and hot, soft and hard, sweet and bitter, practically anything that has to do with animal reaction and creature comfort but when you go against the animal self, then it is when the individual capacity comes to the fore. We do, under the pressure of social codes, about what we can and from there on in, it is a matter of avoiding discovery, avoiding punishment and scorn and justifying to ourselves such off-the-path exploration. The church rests its entire case on the absoluteness of free will because even in his somewhat childish mind a God who punished man for what he could not help would be a tyrant, indeed, therefore he is saddled with it from sheer necessity. Science and evidence, no matter how conclusive because in such a hierarchy the edifice must endure no matter what the cost to the flock, will ever make an impression, I'm afraid."

Salton sighed and brutalized his pipe stem. "Living in Louisiana has I suppose taken a lot of the original whalebone from the Salton line. Here we live and let live. We are somewhat slothful and addicted to easy living. Some would call it degenerative processes at work."

"Speaking of that I'm reminded of that poor girl, Feathers Maidstone, sprung from a long line of eccentric aristocrats with money."

Jeff grimaced. "I need no reminding of that. As neighbors they are in my hair more than I would like to admit. Aristocrats who are so totally blind that Old Obadiah Maidstone and Jessica pretend to be in flat ignorance of their daughter's gluttonous sex cravings. Every Negro on the plantation flees into hiding the first glimpse he gets of her. It is a wonder she hasn't caused some poor Negro to be lynched. I can imagine the ire of the countryside should such a thing get about in the right circles. It is sad and distressing."

The doctor nodded. "I think that her utter lack of pretense is her only virtue. She is quite open except in company and I've seen her absolutely tortured by some circumstance that kept her on good behavior for a space—say some social function of sorts."

"Yes," said Jeff, whimsically. "Like one of Lavender's teas. I'm tortured by them too because they sometimes cut me off from my room or office and I either have to barge through and get tripped into a lot of stupid guff or I stay and wait till they've had their fill of deploring the generally poor breeding of the world as a whole and guessing whose wife has managed to perform a perfect assignation."

"It has been talked about," said the doctor, tossing his cheroot away, "that poor Feathers will submit to the attentions of anyone if she is tortured too much."

"Entirely possible," said Jeff. "I recall once she caught me down by Big Buff Creek. To say she was mad would be mild. I had just taken a swim when she came tearing up on that big red horse. She had evidently seen me and made preparations. Before I knew it she had practically assaulted me right there on the creek bank."

"Did she?"

Jeff smiled ruefully. "Well, I can tell you it was an experience I'm not likely to forget soon."

"I'm sure you won't," agreed the doctor. "Only a medical man who has had a number of women on his list of patients could thoroughly sympathize with you."

Jeff mauled his pipe ruminatively. "I guess you could say that a great deal of my present condition is because of a certain moral cowardice, the shrinking away from unpleasantness and the eternal hope that somehow things would work themselves out."

The doctor shook his head. "As to that I refuse to go on record. What I should like is the omniscience necessary to envision you as a savage on a tiny Pacific isle without a single spot of civilized taint. It is a mortal impossibility to say what is heredity and what is environment as regards the whimsies of human conduct."

Jeff nodded in agreement. "My father and I are good examples of that. Same environment and close blood ties and yet his principal morality seemed that of observing good taste. I am, on the other hand, beset by all sort of fears of social indictment. That is certainly not like him."

"Recalling your father with some clarity, I should say it is a pity," commented Fontenot dryly.

"Granny Rosa intimated the same thing the other night. In fact, in a few words, she told me a number of things I hadn't known, or admitted, which is much the same thing."

Dr. Fontenot built himself a highball and handed the bottle to Jefferson.

Jeff shook his head. "I think I'll let it slide for a while. That's what talking to you does for me."

The doctor tasted his drink and lighted a cheroot. "Now, Jeff, allow me to point out the ramifications of that single difference between you and your father—but first let me ask you a few questions. What was your sex life before marriage?"

Jeff flushed. "If anyone else had asked me that...."

"No one else did," snapped the old man, "answer the question!"

"Well, as I recall, there was a great deal of experimentation and clumsy fumbling which stood me in poor stead when I finally married."

The other nodded with satisfaction. "A normal thing, in spite of those who are convinced that at the age of twenty one they are suave artistic wolves. Now, what about your marriage to Antoinette?"

There was a sad but delighted gleam in Jeff's eyes. "Like nothing ever seen in this world," he breathed, looking backward through the happy years. "At tea, at dinner, at a dance, Antoinette was as fine a lady as ever walked but in the bedroom she was the most accomplished savage that mind can imagine. I'll never forget how she took my breath away. The only thing that kept her activities from shocking me was her absolute genius in lighting the fire in me. Never once during our entire life together did sex acquire the routine habitualness that I'm sure happens often. Never once did she invade a contrary mood, or place me in the position of performing to please her."

The doctor sighed. "One of the more stellar accomplishments of the clever woman who suffers, doubtlessly, from the lack of equal cleverness in the male. Now, tell me what your sex life has been with Lavender?"

Jeff shuddered. "That is one I was hoping you would miss. In short, it has been nothing. She was frightened half out of her mind at first, then when after the expenditure of much careful effort I quelled her fears, she was about as attractive in bed as a corpse. She freely admitted that the whole idea revolted her and made it plain that since it was her duty she would suffer bravely."

Dr. Fontenot grimaced. "Such women should be spayed at birth if there was some way to detect them. Then they'd grow hair on their faces and at least be detectable. But that's another matter. Last question, how long have you and she had separate rooms?"

Again Jeff flushed. "Three years ago, after a particularly repugnant scene I suggested it. It had gotten to the point that had she lighted a cigarette or read a book during the act, it would have been no less obvious that the whole proceeding was a rattling bore."

"And since that time?"

Jeff took fresh purchase on his pipe and picked up the whiskey bottle. "Nothing... no one. This drink I'm about to take, in no way reflects on the turn of your conversation. It is merely," he shook the bottle, "the introduction to my mistress. She never fails me." He drank deeply. "Nor does she ever come up wanting. She performs too well if anything."

"And that," said the doctor sharply, "is the exact point of my questions. You drank like any gay blade before marriage. Married to Antoinette, you probably drank socially. Since Lavender has been on the scene you have been pouring it down. I ask you what would your father have done under like circumstances?"

Jeff tamped rough tobacco in his pipe and lighted it. "First off, he wouldn't have had Lavender on a horse trade. If he had, just on a supposition, he'd have left her to her ways and taken on some sharp female to provide what she couldn't."

Dr. Fontenot sighed. "Well, there you are. He lived for himself and with other people. You're living for other people and raising hell with yourself. Society would, of course, have another set of terms for that and go their merry way doing as they wished and hiding it. The difference there is that they haven't the guts to dredge up a bit of fundamental honesty. That's why the matter drives so many of them bats. One has to get along, I'll admit that, but it need not creep into one's conversation with one's self and so distort things that it becomes a virtual impossibility to have any self-honesty, the lack of which mental deterioration is made of."

Jeff rose to his feet. "Alcide, I want you to promise to let me come again. I'll have to be getting along now because I don't want to work Granny Rosa to death. She hasn't hardly left the room since Toni came home. I certainly don't want Lavender to find her alone and have a chance to get in some of her kind of sympathy."

"By all means, Jeff," said the little man bounding to his feet, "and some day when I haven't anything to do, I'll visit you and we'll blot up a few highballs. I'll want to see Toni in a couple of days anyhow."

Jeff grasped the older man by the hand. "You've made me feel better than I have in years. You have done my daughter and me a great favor and I assure you that neither of us will forget it."

Fontenot wriggled. "I do what I can for my fellow man, Jeff. I have no religion of the usual sort but I love my fellow man for all his faults and I hold out a hand whenever I can."

CHAPTER THREE

ONI LAY VERY still on her back and stared at the ceiling. The sheets were clean and cool, smelling of the ancient wooden drawers where they had been stored. Granny Rosa sat nearby and nodded in her chair, having found that her Sugar Baby either had nothing to say or was not in the mood for conversation. A discrete knock sounded on the door.

Granny awoke with a start, "Who dat?"

"It's me, Granny," came Jeff's voice. "Is Toni asleep?"

"Nawssuh, you can come in."

Jeff opened the door and walked swiftly to the bed. "Feel O.K. Kitten?"

Toni managed a smile and nodded. "I feel sort of dead, Pop, that's all."

"I saw Dr. Fontenot today. He says you'll be all right."

"Yes sir."

Jeff felt helpless. Toni agreed with no enthusiasm whatever, and things had been like this for days. He turned to Granny Rosa. "You can go, Granny. I'll stay with her now."

Granny stood up. "I could manage with some res' myself. I ain't ever got Monday's ironin' done yet, neither."

"Why don't you make Odele help you?"

"Cause Odele ain't got nuff sense to feed herself, let alone momuckin' up my linens."

After the old woman had gone, Jeff took a chair and lighted his pipe. "I'm your father, Kitten," he began, "but I guess somewhere I've failed you."

She shook her head slowly. "No, Pop."

"Yet when you got in trouble, I was the last to know about it. I should have moulded things so that I would have been the first."

"It's not that simple."

"Then let's talk about it. You're not in the right frame of mind and you know it."

"What sort of mind should a person have that has done what I have?" Her pale face was set and her mouth a white slash in her face.

Jeff gnawed savagely at his pipe stem. "Doesn't the fact that you had nothing to do with what happened make any difference?"

"The thing which has me flat on my back and sick to death of me, hating me for a murderer is of my own doing." Her voice tottered and almost fell into a break.

The muscles across his shoulders grew so taut they ached. He clasped his hands tightly and tried to keep his mind from knotting up into flickers of confused thought.

It wasn't the whiskey today, he told himself, because he hadn't had that much. He turned tired eyes on her. "Kitten, I want to help you. Dr. Fontenot wants to help you and Granny wants to help you. None of us can if you won't let us. You'll have to help."

She turned her face away and remained silent. For a long time there was silence, then she faced him again. "Pop, will you come sit by me?"

He sat on the edge of the bed and held her hands.

"Pop, you know I love you, don't you?"

His voice was husky. "Yes, Kitten, I know you do."

Tears came to her eyes. "Something terrible has happened, Pop. I can't control it … I just know something's gone. That awful night—that terrible old woman, her instruments—the pain …" She broke into uncontrollable weeping and Jeff lifted her against his chest and held her close while she cried herself out, then he laid her back against the pillow and sang to her in a rich low baritone. He sang her an old lullaby at which she smiled tenderly at first, then her face relaxed comfortably and she slept. He watched her for some time, then tiptoed from the room.

He sat by the old crank phone in the dim cool hall and asked to be connected with Dr. Alcide Fontenot in Kenton. The sleepy Port Hull operator yawned and said, "Thangkew."

"Alcide, this is Jeff. It pains me to call you this soon even though you said you wanted to help with...." A burst of angry French at the other end of the line made him smile.

"All right, all right! Talk English, won't you? From here you sound like a flock of blackbirds gabbling."

"Never mind your blasted Anglo-Saxon insults," the little man shot back. "What's the trouble?"

"It's Toni. She is overcome by the enormity of her act and I can't get to her. She has erected a wall of resistance that I can't get through. I can't make her talk."

"Well, goddammit, let the girl alone!" snapped the doctor. "She isn't well yet and has your youth been so long ago that you have entirely forgotten that everything seemed twice as bad then as when you grew up? Use your head, man. Let the matter lie and give her time."

Jeff bowed his head. "I wish you'd come to see her," he begged humbly. "I'm afraid she'll try to do away with herself."

"I doubt that, but I'll come if it will make you feel any better."

"Please do. You have no idea how much better it will make me feel."

"I warn you, Jeff, I'll look at her but unless she's a lot better, I'm not going to try to talk to her."

"That, of course, is up to you but please come. Try to make it for supper."

"Very well, Jeff. See you then."

Lemuel Patterstall slouched across the front yard toward the house. He had been drinking as usual and as usual he had a noticeable list.

Jeff's snort of disgust reached the ears of Lavender who sat on the porch twenty feet away. She looked around. "You say one word to my brother and I'll...."

"You'll do what?" he snarled.

She sat back with a hurt look on her face. As a face it was singularly unattractive this afternoon. It had been too hot for her nap and Lavender was one of those people whose routine must go through unbroken or it upset her whole day. Her hair was done up behind her head in an unattractive knot accentuating the poverty of her facial structure and slightly receding chin.

Jeff shuddered and looked at Lemuel as he came up the steps. He was rather large but his shoulders were narrow and his hips wide. He had a peculiar sour-bitter smell that hung about him at all times like cheap perfume. His face was the counterpart of his sister's and his gross body gave the eerie impression that it had once belonged to someone else. His eyes were piggy and furtive and as far as Jeff knew, he had never shed a drop of honest sweat. As he reached the top step, his feet became intangled with each other, causing him to fall heavily and roll in a wild flurry of arms and legs to the bottom of the steps.

Jeff fell back in his chair and roared with mirth, not noticing the look of murderous hatred cast in his direction by his brother-in-law. Lavender leaped to her feet. "Come into the office, Jefferson. I want to talk to you."

Inside the office, she said, "Are you deliberately trying to get rid of us?"

Jeff looked her over coolly. "It wouldn't be a half bad idea."

"It can be accomplished," she retorted furiously, "for a price. Just one more scene like that last one and you'll find out what the price is."

"If I had had a higher set of steps, I think half the problem would have solved itself," said Jeff grinning furiously. "Why don't both of you fall off the roof and break your necks?"

She stared at him a long time. "Neither of us will be that easy to get rid of. Have no illusions about that, Jeff dear."

"Any illusions I had about you and Lem, and there must have been a power of them at one time, have long since gone by the board. If I had the guts of a fly I'd kick both of you off Fomalhaut and be rid of you."

"But you won't do that, will you, Dear? If you did, it might get circulated about that your daughter was raped and had an abortion performed."

Jeff's long fingers drove nails into the palms of his hands like spikes into soft wood. Stark murder gleamed in his usually mild eyes. "I doubt, Lavvy," he said, using a nickname which she loathed, "that you'll ever *fall* from anything!" He stopped to readjust his breathing which was threatening to drive the blood through his skin. "But it would be just as effective to *throw you off the top of the house!*" He leaned forward and delivered the last words with such vitriolic malignance that she recoiled a couple of paces. Breath whistled through his distended nostrils and he took a step toward her. "Think that over, my dear. Just let me get the barest suggestion of any such thing and that'll be the day you putrid, crawling, yellow bitch snake!"

Jeff stalked from the office and back to his seat on the porch. He was weak and trembling and needed a drink but refused to take one.

Lemuel walked up and down in his sister's room massaging his damp hands. "You should be more careful, learn to control yourself. Suppose he would run us off? What would we do then? I doubt that you'd interest the chorus boys any more."

She strode forward and slapped him with all her strength. "Say that again and I'll kill you."

He sat down rubbing his face with a curious avidity, and seemed neither hurt nor angry. She watched him for a moment and her face underwent a subtle change. Quickly she closed the blinds, effectively darkening the room, went to a closet and came back with a short many-tailed whip. There was a short whispered conversation, a rustling sound, then the swishing crack of the whip, groans, and from the woman's mouth a stream of obscenities, vicious, revolting, and delivered with a weird crooning gusto.

"Well, as I told you over the phone, Jeff, she's not ready for your blundering psychotherapy, yet."

Jeff nodded numbly. "You're right, I suppose, but this thing is killing me. I'm afraid for her mind."

"Oh, pish!" scoffed the doctor. "Her mind's probably a lot more stable than yours. However, I'll see what I can do."

As they walked down the big upstairs hall to Toni's room Fontenot stopped him. "I'll go the rest of the way, alone, thank you. I don't want any fathers in my way when I talk to my patients."

Jeff nodded and stopped. He watched the doctor open the door and close it, then he turned slowly and walked down the long winding stairway through the downstairs hall, on to the broad verandah where he slumped into a chair.

Dr. Fontenot breezed into the room. "Well, how's my patient this evening?"

She looked at him but didn't speak immediately. When she did, her voice was small and disembodied. "I want to thank you, Doctor, for what you did. I'm really very grateful."

He frowned. "Nonsense. Right in my own front yard—front steps to be exact. What else could I do?"

She smiled slightly as he sat on the bed. "Be self-effacing, then."

"I'm tickled pink that I could help, my dear. Self-effacement is a gesture. I'm really flattered." He pulled the covers down and palpated her abdomen. "Any pain, there?"

"No sir. It's still a little sore but it doesn't hurt." He nodded and felt gently of a firm breast. She gasped a little and flinched.

"How long, my dear ... how long was it ... ?"

"Six weeks, I think—thereabouts."

"Ummm, hummm, too soon for any noticeable lactation." He pulled the covers up again and let his glance wander over her.

"You seem to be in good shape now, physically. Why are you trying to freeze your father out?"

Tears sprang into her eyes. "I'm awful, I'm a murderer."

His breath hissed in sharply. "Every woman is a murderer and every man also every time birth control is used successfully."

"Oh, no ...."

"And pray why not?" He placed a gentle hand over hers as it lay flaccid on the coverlet. "You see, Toni, such things are unfortunate and wholly undesirable, but just the same they happen. I brought up an extreme, but it contains some element of truth as certain sects have long maintained for reasons of their own. I mentioned an extreme to show you that you are trying to be an extremist. The only difference is one of degree.

"In your case you were driven to your deed by the consciousness of what society would think, knowing that as long as they are kept in the dark you may enjoy all the privileges of and be called the nicest of girls, no matter what you do out of their sight."

Dr. Fontenot continued talking to her in his soft kind voice drawing out her opinions, exposing them and attacking them with furious barrages of crystal logic.

She listened fascinated, uplifted, and at times frightened. "I don't think I ever heard things explained quite like that before," she said at length.

"A great pity," he shot back. "Had you been reared to know these things you would have taken your trouble in stride and it wouldn't have thrown you like this and you would have managed things better. Had I not been on the scene, luckily, you might now be dead. Be thankful that you're not."

"The way you put it, it makes sense but ...."

"I know. You were given the facts as viewed from a rational angle. If you cannot fit them into your own mind, it is certain that no one can do it for you. What I'm concerned about is what effect it has had on you in your man-woman relationship."

She turned her head away from him and for a long time did not speak. When she did there was hatred in her voice. "I never want another man to touch me as long as I live. I think I'd kill him if he touched me like that." She rose to a sitting position, her eyes blazing and her face white and twitching. A hard convulsive shudder shook her and she bit her lips to keep back a cry. Dr. Fontenot put his face close to hers.

"Stop that!" His voice had the hard explosive command of a gun shot. It frightened her a little and she breathed better. "Now lie back and relax." It was a soothing order which he accompanied with firm hands on her shoulders that shoved her back to the pillow.

"Now, young woman, I forbid you to think about this thing any more for the present. Get out of that bed and recover physically. Then I promise to beat you to death with that unnatural attitude." If he had hoped to win a smile from her, he was disappointed. She only retreated deeper into the cover, her eyes still taut with anguish and revulsion.

Dr. Fontenot found Salton on the porch sunk deep in reverie. "Have a chair, Alcide, and what about a highball?"

"Never ask me that," said the little man. "Just bring it along and I'd advise you to have a long snort, yourself."

"You would?"

"I would, indeed. You've been off it ever since Toni's trouble and it's tying you in knots. Save that will power for some worthy cause or, better still, to temper your quantity."

Jeff raised his voice, "Odele?"

A voice answered him from the direction of the kitchen.

"Come here a minute."

A tall colored girl came gracefully along the porch from the west side of the house.

"Did you call, sir?"

Jeff stared. "Where's Odele? Who're you?"

"I'm Granny Rosa's granddaughter, sir. Odele is ... going to have a family. I took her place."

"You're Archie's daughter?"

"Yes sir."

"When did you arrive?"

"A week ago, sir. Father died not long ago, you know?"

Jeff nodded. "Yes, I was sorry to hear that, but I .... Well, anyway, you seem capable and you speak well. Did you attend school?"

"Yes sir, I finished high school and went to business college."

"Hope you like it here," Jeff finished lamely, realizing that he had been conducting an inquiry. "Will you bring a bridge table, some Coca Cola, ice and a bottle of whiskey? There should be a bottle on the sideboard in the dining room."

She nodded respectfully. "Yes, sir."

Dr. Fontenot fixed a pair of bright blue eyes on Jeff, till the other began to feel hot and uncomfortable.

"Er hummm," began the doctor, "holding out on me, eh?"

"Really, Alcide, that's the first time I ever saw her."

"Likely story," scoffed the doctor. "But no matter, I don't know who Archie is but I will say that he did well by the girl. Her skin is amber, gold and honey, and my God! What a figure! Generosity certainly missing in no place."

Jeff became acutely uncomfortable. The sight of the girl had shaken him sorely and wakened things he had thought dead. He tried to be casual. "Oh, sure ..." and failed.

The other cackled delightedly. "Just what you need, and don't try to get cagy with me. I've seen more than any hundred men and have experienced more than any ten you can name. I think she's beautiful, don't you?"

Jeff suffered, but nodded. "Yes, I guess she is at that, but...."

Fontenot snorted. "But what? Just because she has colored blood in her? Phooey! I thought you were a man of the world. Trouble with you good old Anglo-Saxons is that you still have that lodge meeting attitude about everything. Any fool could see that she shook you where you live, and yet you want to pretend it is nothing really. Thank God I'm a Frenchman with the ability to get outside myself. I'd burst if I didn't."

"Yes," agreed Jeff, "I believe you would."

"So will you if you don't watch out," said the doctor, accepting his highball and tasting it.

Jeff tossed down half a gill and cleared his throat. "What about Toni?"

The old man put his highball down carefully and lighted a cheroot before answering. "I don't like it."

Jeff didn't have to question that statement and for a while they were silent, gazing past the mighty shadowy columns onto the moon splashed lawn. The night was a good deal cooler than the day had been and the atmosphere had some motion. Miles away, a tugboat towing a long string of barges swept the sky with the misty finger of a searchlight. The mournful hoot-hoot of its whistle came to them faintly.

Jeff loaded his pipe and lit it. "What, exactly, don't you like?"

Dr. Fontenot sat his drink on the floor and sighed. "Principally her attitude toward sex. The shock and horror of that night will wear off but the first time some lad wants to do a little mild necking, she's going to bust him one in the puss and he's going to be mildly surprised to say the least."

"She *should* slap the hell out of him," said Jeff frowning. "I don't want my daughter...."

Dr. Fontenot smote the arm of the chair vehemently. "Jefferson, you may poison me with your liquor or shoot me with your gun but pray do not bore me."

Jeff grinned weakly, "O.K., I take it all back."

Fontenot sniffed. "Do, for Christ's sake, then go bury it far away."

"I guess it's just hard to grow out of."

"Probably, but just remember that to ever grow into it, you had to bruise every natural impulse you ever had. How old were you, Jeff, when you had your first necking session?"

Jeff flushed, grateful for the dark. "Twenty. I had pecked about before then, but the first real one was twenty. I'm afraid both of us got sort of carried away in the rush...."

"Naturally, naturally. You were lucky that her father didn't come searching for you with a shotgun."

Jeff leaned back and savaged the stem of his pipe. "I seem to recall wondering afterward why anything so wonderful could be wrong. I was too young to see what the dangers were."

"Many a similar wonder has wended its way heavenward," said the doctor.

"And you think Toni is going to have trouble along those lines?"

The other nodded. "She is, and it is a national pity, a horrible waste of good woman flesh, the like of which is seldom found. The thought of her being ruined like that makes me ill. You still have no idea who it could have been?"

"Not the slightest. The storm had Lavender and me both stranded. She at. the MacAllisters' and I in Port Hilton. She was alone, except for..." Jeff came upright in his chair, his eyes gleaming hellishly. "Lemuel was here," he ground out, breathing heavily.

Fontenot waved his hands madly. "Let's not go rushing to conclusions and acting foolishly. Remember, it was pitch dark. So far, we haven't got a word from her. If she knows, she isn't talking and any move made now would be without information, therefore, foolish. Right now, there is nothing to do but to wait. Time has a way of taking care of such things." He finished his drink and got up. "Have to go now, Jeff. Maud'll be wondering whether I've had a wreck. Just stick tight and let the girl alone. In fact, I forbid that you even hint at the subject."

Dr. Fontenot turned out his lights before he reached the cabin and with a deft twitch of the wheel, tooled the drab little coupe off the road and stopped beneath a big spreading china tree. It was in full bloom and its flowers had draped a cloak of heavy perfume over the immediate area. He stepped from the car and undid the chain latch on the picket gate. A cur set up a terrific clamor effectively halting the doctor till a bellow from the house drove the dog scampering under the house to peer out with suspicion but silent. Granny Rosa's discipline was as effective with animals as with people. She waddled to the door and stood silhouetted by the weak rays of the oil lamp. "Who dat?"

"Call off your dogs, Granny. It's Dr. Fontenot."

"Do Jesus," she bellowed. "Come in, Doctuh, come on in. I ain't seen you since de time us tuck dat 'flicted thaing from Josie Tillis wid a plow line."

"Quiet," said the doctor as he mounted the porch, grinning. "Don't advertise our methods. People might talk."

"Let 'em talk. Dey does ennyhow. Set down and…. Coppercawn! Git some o' dat jewberry wine outa de loft and pour de doctuh a glassful. Hit's three years old, Doctor, and strong as a deck o' fawties."

"Coppercorn?"

"Yassuh, dat's Archie's chile. Archie was mah fus' boy. Died las' month wid de high blood and hart trubble."

A little tingle went over the doctor. He'd welcome a chance to see the girl under a better light. His first impression had been distinctly delightful.

She came out presently and he could tell she wore only a single cotton garment. The effect was nothing short of electric. Her long powerful legs showed plainly through the thin garment, her breasts seemed about to burst through the straining cloth and her waist was slim and long. "Dis Dr. Fontenot, Coppercawn," said Granny proudly.

The little man rose and took her strong shapely hand. "How are you, Coppercorn. Sounds like one of Granny's names."

"How do you do, Sir—yes it is. I was named for the tropic."

"Oh—Capricorn!"

"Yes sir." He accepted the drink and sat down.

"Fine looking girl, Granny. She's awfully light, though."

Granny laughed. "Sho she is. Might nigh white. Couldn't tell de differunce on a night like dis here one. 'Tain't no wonder, though. Her mammy was a bright gal, too and ... well, you ought t' know. Me and you brung both of 'em." She motioned with her head and the girl obediently went back in the house.

"We did what?"

"Me'n you. Us d'livered both dem chillun ... oh way back in sebenteen. Member, I sont fer you cause I knowed dey wuz twins and I wuz skeered I wasn't smaht nuff t' d'liver em by mahself."

He smote his leg. "Well, I'll be damned. What do you know ... ?" A crafty look came over his face. He glanced back in the house and seeing that Capricorn was not in hearing, he said in a low voice, "Remember what she told us that night before she died?"

Granny nodded soberly. "Sho do but dey don't know it. I ain't never told 'em."

"Did you ever tell Archie?"

"No suh, I ain't tole him neither. I don't see no sense telling sompn' whut ain't gonna do no good and kin do a lota' harm."

He nodded vigorously. "A sentiment which could be allowed to spread."

"A which?"

"Good idea, I mean. Let's see some wise man put it this way. 'A truth that harms one without helping another loses its virtue.' No need for Archie to know that they were a white man's children."

"Yassuh," agreed Granny hazily. "I reckon so ...."

"Where's the other one ... she stay in New Orleans?"

"Nawsuh, you didn't see her at de house?"

He drank the rest of the wine and smacked his lips. "This has been a night of surprises, Granny. Twins, and I thought it was the same one. Then it turns out that you and I delivered them. I came by here to ask you something."

"Ax it," she said with a chuckle. "Gawd knows, I owes you a few favors. You done me plenty."

"When I saw that girl at the house I began to think. She said Odele was about to have a family. When I saw Odele two weeks ago, she couldn't have been over two months. Now what goes on here?"

Granny grinned mysteriously. "Oh—leetle idee o' mine. I handles things at de house. Dat Yankee woman ain't got nuff sense to po' water on a fiah and she don't care. De boss glad to have me 'round and so's mah Sugar Baby. So I 'ranged thaings t' suit myself."

He flicked his beady eyes over the old woman's placid face. "That's what I'm getting at. Odele could have worked another three or four months."

"Not'n git her chile brung free she couldn't."

He grinned delightedly. "Now we're getting closer to pay dirt. *Why* did you want to replace Odele?"

Granny grinned widely."I axt you once how you knowed sumpn' and you said, 'Granny, ah knows everything.' You figger hit out fo' youself."

CHAPTER FOUR

BULL FALLON WALKED along the woodsy path with a light and springy step in spite of his work-hardened two hundred pounds of bone and muscle. He had "breshed up" against Marthy Petersen at the supper and things had begun to happen. Marthy was lush and sultry and high brown and tonight she was being left severely alone, due to the razor wielding proclivities of her escort who was temporarily absent getting some pink lemonade for himself and his girl.

Marthy glanced at him coquettishly out of veiled eyes and whispered, "What's the matter, Bull, you fraid of a razor too?"

Bull stiffened. *"Who?"*

"You!"

Bull glanced about and saw Prince Jones buying two glasses of lemonade at the makeshift counter against the wall of Phillydelfy Washington's house.

"I ain't no trouble maker," he announced loftily, and leaned back against the house. Marthy turned her back to him and leaned back. The hot soft pressure of her buttocks sent blood leaping through his veins and his left hand crept around her waist and downward.

"Oooowee," she moaned softly and pressed harder against him. They were somewhat protected by the insufficiency of the lights which were kerosene-filled wine bottles with old twists of quilts for wicks. Prince had to do a little searching before he found her and when he did, the sight did not amuse him. He dropped the lemonade to the ground and said, "Come out hyer."

"She can't come," said Bull, whose previous resolution not to start trouble had departed.

"How come she can't come?"

"Cause I got her."

"Den you turn her loose."

"Go git lost, nigger," said Bull, contemptuously, recalling a line he had heard in a mystery play on the boss's radio.

"One nigger in de hospittle now, cause he played 'roun wid mah wimmen," pointed out Prince, his right hand sliding into his back pocket with a significance that was not lost to either Marthy or Bull. With a sweep of his hand Bull tossed her aside and as the razor came from Prince's pocket it continued on its way out of the circle of light as though he had thrown it. Bull's mighty hand had closed over the smaller man's wrist and flicked it with such irresistible power that the fingers lost their grip on the weapon. Then with a contemptuous twist, Bull broke the arm and hurled Prince into a moaning heap. The other Negroes looked on with interest.

"Hit don' pay to muck up wid dat Bull," said Uncle Rafe Lee, "razor or no razor."

"You sed whut Gawd love," agreed Uncle Alvin Mack, maneuvering lemonade deftly around the quid of Days Work which swelled one side of his cadaverous face. "Ole pappy of his'n wuz de same way."

"Sho wuz," piped Si Witherspoon, a weazened little dwarf of a man who had always wanted to be big and brash. "I mind de time he tuck'n bet de Boss's daddy he could butt de head outen a po'k ba'l. He done it too."

Bull, after a glance at Prince, whirled and walked away from the house. A hundred feet down the path, Marthy caught up with him. "Bull, wait."

"Whut fer," he rasped. "You ain't good for nuthin' but stahtin' trouble. Go home."

She caught him by the arm and pulled him close to her. "You don't want me to go, does you?"

He placed his hands on her smooth shoulders and strained her to him, then they turned and walked down the road, arms about each other, Bull's gigantic shoulders swinging proudly.

She lay on the soft grass, her breathing gradually coming back to normal, sweat beading her upper lip and forehead. Bull sat up and lit a cigarette.

"You going back to the supper, Bull?"

"Unh unh," he blew smoke toward the mounting bank of clouds that marched sullenly from the eastern horizon.

"How come?

"Causen I don't want to. I was leavin' when you cot me."

"You ain't skeerd of Prince, is you Bull?"

He grunted disdainfully and refused to answer. She rolled closer to him, passing an arm about his waist and squeezing him. He ignored her completely, watching the dark cloud with its flickering play of white and blue lightning.

"Hit's gonna rain," he offered. Her arm tightened about him but still he paid no attention. Her hand began to grope and fumble, making Bull turn his attention to her, kneading her strong back with his fingers. He rolled over and crushed her to the ground. A bit of stubble hurt her head but the sensation was one of delight. Her head went back hard and she grasped handfuls of grass. She bit back her moans and the stubble pricked her harder. Her mouth came open and the cries came out unheeded as thunder shook mightily in the near distance.

As Bull walked along the path through the woods, he wondered if he'd reach John Harrel's old house before the rain came. He hoped so. He already had grass stains on his new blue slacks and the Boss was sure to have to kid him about them. He wondered if he dared try to remove the stains with soap and water. The first drop plopped in the dust ahead of him with an audible sound and in the distance he could hear the drumming roar of the rain. He broke into an easy long striding run.

He leaped nimbly up on the crumbling porch as the first of the rain thundered on the dry, warped, shingled roof like hail. Lightning ripped a blinding burst of blue flame which might have showed him the big red horse tied to a fig tree in the yard but Bull wasn't looking for horses.

He flung the door open and closed it with a bang almost fainting from fright the next instant. In the flare of the bolt, he saw that the house was already occupied. His gin went out of him so suddenly that it left a strange empty buzzing in his head. Standing now between him and the door was Feathers Maidstone. The lightning was almost continuous now, showing her taut angular face, the hard ruggedness of her not unlovely body and the strained intentness of her green eyes. She was dressed in a polo shirt and blue jeans when he first saw her, and seconds later, it seemed she was a beautiful and terrifying vision.

Bull, his teeth chattering with terror, whirled with every intention of hurling himself bodily through the window but a rattling snarl stopped him. Between him and the only means of escape stood a great Belgian police dog, his fangs gleaming in the flickering light. Feathers caught Bull about the waist and with surprising strength threw his palsied body to the floor, half stunning him. He could feel her hands roving over him, her voice and her words babbling and hardly coherent. "Be good, Bull. Be good. I won't hurt you Bull, be good." He shivered and lay still because he was too frightened to do otherwise. She caught his hands and passed them around her body, panting hard. Bull sent a short prayer to his maker and gave up.

It was an hour later. Twice he had tried to move from her embrace and twice she had said something to the great dog who growled a gutteral answer. Both times the movement sent her into fresh spasms of demand and now Bull was bathed in the sweat of a multitude of warring emotions. He could see his body tied to a green pine tree soaked with kerosene and the grim-faced men who stood back trying to strike matches in the rain. He shivered and lay still.

Her hands began to rove over his broad chest where his shirt hung open and then his stomach and then ....

It was nearly dawn when Bull opened the door of his house. His sister was just getting up to cook breakfast and he smelled the strong odor of coffee parching in the little wood stove. He mounted the porch steps and staggered as he reached the top. He felt sick and feverish and he was so weak he could hardly stand.

"Whut the matter, Bull? Wheh you been all night?"

"Shet up," he said shortly, "and bring me some coffee."

She went back to the kitchen and brought him coffee. His hand jerked so that the cup chattered against his teeth before he could steady it with his lips.

"You sho looks terrible," offered Alice. "You looks sick."

"I done tole you t' shet up," he snarled. "Ain't nuthin' wrong wid me. Hit's Sunday and I'm gonna git me some sleep. I ain't had no sleep." He beamed inwardly at his facile excuse. "Dat whut wrong wid me. I ain't had no sleep."

Alice looked him over critically taking in his ruined and stained slacks.

"Dem pants needs more'n sleep," she averred, turning away from him and entering the kitchen. He looked at his slacks. She had spoken the truth. They would be good for nothing except field work from now on, even if he had the nerve to wear them to work which he doubted. The Boss would have the laugh of his life if he could see those pants now.

Feathers rode her horse slowly toward the big old house. It was one of those relics of past days which were so plentiful in St. Joseph's Parish as well as St. Louis and other nearby parishes. The big horse stepped lightly through the water that rushed nois-ily in the ditches. Rain still fell in tiny misty drops cooling her hot face. She swayed dreamily in the saddle and throbbed with satiety, caressing her bruises with a tender hand. Never had she been so roughly used yet so completely satisfied but she knew it wouldn't be for long.

At the crumbling old barn she unsaddled the horse and turned him into a stable where she fed and rubbed him down. She leaned against his warm back leg and rubbed her body against it. The sting of his sweat burned a skinned place on her arm and she deliberately rubbed it on him, savoring the astringent bite of the salt. King, the great dog, whined and nuzzled her hand. She left the stable and led the dog to the hallway of the barn. She stroked his flank and he whined expectantly. At one end of the barn there was a room filled with cotton seed. She led him to the door, opened it, and he went in.

CHAPTER FIVE

ALBERT FONTENOT SAT with his father in the living room complaining bitterly because the backwoods women would only come in when they were having trouble with childbirth. "At least they could come in and get an occasional check. Now I might lose both mother and child out of this caesarean this morning.

Dr. Fontenot lighted a cheroot. "You have your troubles and I have mine."

"You mean at the Saltons'?"

"Yes. Trouble of the sort I'd like to see wiped out once and for all."

Albert grinned tiredly. "All right, wipe it out."

"Don't be any bigger fool than you have to. How would I go about that?"

Albert shrugged. "I'm sure I don't know. I'll bet she now has a full blown revulsion toward anything sexual since that bad time she had!"

Jane came into the living room and handed the older Fontenot a highball. "You want one?" she asked Albert.

"No ... can't. Have an operation at one o'clock."

"Yes," barked his father suddenly.

"Yes what?"

"You're right. She is revolted at the mere idea of a man."

"Well since you're the happiness doctor why don't you vaccinate her?"

The little man's beard danced angrily. "Albert, I'm tempted to beat you over the head with a blunt instrument. Happiness, that is to say the contentment most people think of, is nothing but sloth and in sloth there can be no progress. Suppose Columbus had been satisfied to sit in Genoa and drink wine? Suppose men like Charcot had been happy, contented, and non-productive? In contemporary times suppose men like Fermi, Bush, Einstein, Oppenheimer, and others had been content to make deodorants, tooth paste, and fruit salts?"

"We wouldn't have had the atom bomb," said Albert triumphantly.

"Right," shot back his father, "and Germany would. Where would we be now?"

"I give up," said Albert grinning.

The older doctor was pulling his beard victoriously when Maud came into the living room. "Missy Blumendahl is on the phone."

Dr. Fontenot frowned. "Now what does she want?"

Missy Blumendahl was St. Louis Parish's undisputed social empress. She gave parties at which practically everyone could be found basking in her reflected light. She was rich and eccentric, admitting privately that her parties were conceived that she might laugh at the antics of those who came.

"Hello," she bellowed over the phone. "That you, Alcide?"

"Yes, Missy, what's the trouble?"

"A pain in the gut, and, by God, I want you out here on the double!"

"I've retired," he told her shortly. "I'll send Albert out."

"Albert can't come," she retorted. "He has a caesarean this evening. Anyhow, I dont want any young jackanapes jooging me in the belly."

"The last time you had a pain in the gut," he reminded her, "I found you eating onion and sardine sandwiches, chasing them with beer."

"Look, you clabberheaded superannuated rake! I said I have a pain in the gut and I do. Get out here or you'll have a corpse on your hands." She hung up with a crash.

When Dr. Fontenot arrived at Fahenstock, Missy's ancestral pile of brick, columns, and pink plaster, the mistress was reclining in her bedroom clad in innumerable yards of lavender chiffon, emitting a smell which suggested Bradsher's Special Age Bourbon.

She rose to her feet, noticeably favoring her right leg. "Come in," she brayed loudly. "Sit down."

Dr. Fontenot felt driven bodily into his chair. "Now," he began, as she was seated again, "what's your trouble?"

She made a face. "Pain in my right side, Alcide, I believe I have appendicitis."

He rose and gestured toward the bed. "Spill yourself on the bed."

She did so and the big four poster creaked alarmingly because Missy weighed in the neighborhood of two hundred pounds. She laid her head carefully on the pillow so as not to disturb her tightly waved yellow hair.

"Ow...dammit!" As the doctor touched a sore spot. "That's where it hurts."

"What are you drawing your right leg up like that for?" he asked.

"Because it feels better that way. If it'd help I'd sit like a Yogi worshiper."

"Appendicitis, all right," he said. "Get Lula to fix you an ice bag and we'll run you in to the hospital this afternoon about six. We'll put you through the lab tonight and, if indicated, operate in the morning."

"You'll do it, won't you? Albert may be all right, but I don't want any spriggins probing around in my guts."

"Yes...if you insist. I must tell you though, when I come out of retirement my fees are stiff."

"The hell with it," she said casually as she sat up grimacing when a twinge struck her. "I could buy you three times over and sell you at a loss … in fact if I did sell you it would be at a loss." She guffawed loudly and pushed a button on the table near her couch.

A plump yellow Negro girl came to the door. "Yassum?"

"Fix me an ice bag, Lula and don't be all day about it … I'm dying. Bring another bottle of Coca Cola. This old bastard will want a highball I know." Lula bowed and departed grinning behind her hand.

"Do you have to revile me before the help?" reproved the doctor mildly.

He made an undignified, unprofessional face at her and ducked through the door to escape a bedroom slipper thrown with deadly accuracy. As he went down the spiral steps he caught a glimpse of Lula as she dashed across the hall into the servants' quarters in the rear. She had been bathing and was only about half clothed.

His beard moved up and down rapidly. "Not bad," he murmured to himself.

Jeff Salton sat with Toni on the broad verandah and watched the tree tops change color as the sun sank lower over the Mississippi. The world seemed touched with a light crimson dust and the atmosphere was warm and quiet. From the living room there came the hum of conversation telling of one of Lavender's teas.

"Your stepmother is in her glory," said Jeff, saltily. "One can concentrate and hear that raspy voice which she keeps down to a minimum when there's company."

Toni, pale and subdued, nodded abstractedly but did not answer.

"She hasn't been bothering you, has she?"

"No—she has spoken very little to me. I'm glad."

"She's on orders," Jeff said. "I told her if she so much as opened her mouth to you about it, I'd make her wish she hadn't."

Toni compressed her lips and looked away and Jeff sighed heavily. She faced him suddenly.

"This has been very bad for you, Dad. I ...."

"Nonsense. It has been bad, of course, because I hate to see you unhappy, but you're the one who has had to take it. Don't worry about me."

"But I do. You don't like to be looked at as the father of a loose woman."

"You couldn't help what happened, Kitten, and it has been kept very quiet."

"Who'll ever believe I didn't just get caught like many another girl?" she said bitterly, "And I'll bet you it has been talked about, this very afternoon in there." She indicated the living room with a limp hand.

"It better not be," Jeff scowled and gripped the stem of his pipe harder.

In the living room Lavender was indeed giving her friend Agatha Silvers an earful.

"It is such a warm thing to have a friend like you, Agatha. We don't see enough of each other ... really."

Agatha flushed with pleasure. "That's sweet of you. We'll have to do better. Now, my dear, I've been just simply bursting to ask you about Toni. I've been hearing all sorts of things ...."

Lavender turned up her palms and sighed off a ton of weight from her chest. Her eyes were tragic and dismal. "Please ... too, too terrible. I couldn't talk about it. Really, to think that a Patterstall should ever ... but I can't go on, I simply can't!" She dabbed at her eyes with a wisp of a handkerchief.

"Oh, my dear," sympathized Agatha, leading her to a chair. "I didn't mean to make you sad ... how terrible it must be for you." She snorted and looked toward the verandah. "The Saltons always so high and mighty, too. Well, you never can tell. The girl's mother was one of those … French … or Creoles or something … like mother like daughter, I always say."

Lavender nodded silently and turned her face away, the more effectively to suffer without any strain.

"Why Lavender! Whatever put that stripe on your leg?"

Lavender jerked about and snatched her dress down where it had crept a little high disclosing a long livid mark. "Nothing at all," she said so sharply that Agatha started involuntarily. "Nothing really," said Lavender with greater calm. "I'm so tender, you know … an old Patterstall trait. I scraped my leg on a projection on that old cherry wood bed of mine. Now tell me, Agatha, what is the news? I haven't heard anything for a week."

Agatha's eyes gleamed and she lowered her voice confidentially. "Well, did you know that old man Chester's colored mistress had another boy … that makes eleven boys and they are all the image of their father."

"I can't understand it," said Lavender. "The Chesters are some of the best people in the South."

"Humph, if you think that's bad, let me tell you! One of the Bell boys is right now living in the flats with a nigger girl … living with her, I tell you. They never come out unless a flood runs them out, or they need groceries or something. I'll tell *you* if any kin of *mine* ever pulled such a stunt, they'd rue the day. I've asked Henry and he says he can't understand this weakness so many white men have for Negro girls. It's terrible!"

Lavender almost laughed. Henry might not be able to explain the anomaly but he had experienced it and Agatha was too dumb to know it or pretended it wasn't so. Lavender had it from the best sources that Henry and Charlie Chester had almost come to blows because Henry was paying too much attention to Charlie's oldest daughter by his dusky mistress. Henry had threatened to shoot Chester if he interfered and Chester being an arrant coward had retired in bad grace to growl and threaten.

Agatha chattered on for half an hour and exhausting her store of dirt, left.

Lavender sat in the dim light of the living room and stared unseeingly at the wall. The sun had set and the old house was as quiet as a tomb. Occasionally she could hear the faint clatter of a pan as Granny Rosa and the new girl cooked supper.

She stroked the welt on her leg with a curious avidity. What if Jeff had a colored woman that he was sleeping with? The thought struck her and rage foamed up. She had no proof but she was suspicious. If she ever caught him .... She got to her feet and stalked out into the wide hall and back to the kitchen. Inticing smells wafted through the open door to meet her as she approached.

"Rosa?"

"Yassum."

"Come out here on the porch for a minute. I want to talk to you."

Granny came through the door wiping shreds of biscuit dough from her hands with a dish towel. She took her pipe from her mouth and beat the ashes out on the heel of her hand.

"Rosa, who's the new girl?"

"She mah grandotter. Name Ge'aldine Cancer Jones."

"Good gracious, what a ridiculous name!"

"Yassum. She got a twin livin' wid me. She name Hilda Coppercawn. I give dem gals all dem names. Got 'em outa geography."

"Oh ... Capricorn and Cancer ... the tropics ...."

"Yassum, dat's whut I sed."

"Well, what's the matter with Odele?"

"She in a fambly way."

"Yes, I seem to remember ... however, it seems that a handsome girl like ... er ... Geraldine would get married."

"She ain't ready yit."

"Hummm. To tell you the truth, Rosa, I don't know that I like having such a girl as that about the house. You know men,"

Lavender tried to smile, but Granny's gimleteyed stare made it difficult. "Might make a man like Mr. Jeff get ideas...you see what I mean."

Granny eyed her steadily. "Ef a man git whut he want in his own bed, he don't go pirootin' roun' lookin' fer nuthin' else."

Lavender flushed scarlet. "Why...Well, I never.... Do you mean to say that *I'm* at fault if he goes hunting on his own?"

"No'm," said Granny calmly. "Dat ain't whut I *sed*."

"But you meant that."

"How come you thinkin' bout de boss. Whut bout Mr. Lem?"

She flushed again and her breathing became labored. "Lemuel can take care of himself and he isn't married. I must say, Rosa, that for a servant you take great liberties."

"You stahted de tawk," Granny pointed out with caustic logic. "An' enny time you wants to git yo' own cook in dat kitchen, you kin do it...leastways long's she keeps outen mah way when I'm cookin' vittles fer de boss an' mah Sugar Baby." With that, Granny turned and waddled back in the kitchen, picked up a bell and rang it lustily to announce that supper was ready.

"I think," said Lavender, at the supper table, "that we should get another girl."

"What's the matter with Geraldine?" asked Jeff, ladling out heavy cane syrup on his hot buttered biscuit.

"Well, she's sort of quiet..." Lavender realized immediately that she must sound silly.

Jeff chuckled. "That, in my book, is a virtue of no mean caliber. I'd keep her for that reason if for no other."

"Well, I don't want her here."

Jeff was nettled. "Indeed, and what are your reasons? Certainly you aren't silly enough to want to get rid of a girl just because she's quiet."

Lavender lost her temper. "Isn't the fact that it is my desire enough? Haven't I, your wife, some say in the running of the house?"

"I seem to remember that you turned that chore over to Granny soon after you came here with cheers."

Lavender seemed to choke. "Then you won't send her away?"

Jeff shook his head. "That'll make Granny mad and I wouldn't want to do that."

Lavender leaped to her feet. "Then it *is* true…you *are* in love with her." She flinched as she realized that she had said the wrong thing and the blood receded from her face leaving it an ugly white.

Jeff slowly placed his knife and fork on his plate and folded his hands in his lap. His hard eyes almost beat her back into her chair and she started weeping into her handkerchief. "So," his voice was silky soft, "it finally came out."

"Really Jefferson, I …."

"Oh, my God!" Toni rose to her feet. "You make me positively ill. What if he is in love with her? What have you done to prevent it?"

Jeff's heart leaped within him. At least Toni's revulsion toward things physical hadn't gone too deeply. "Sit down, Toni."

She put down her knife and fork. "No thank you."

"Henceforth," he told Lavender, who sat white and stricken in her chair, "scenes like this will be confined to some other part of the house. You've ruined Toni's supper and you've given me indigestion. This particular scene will not be repeated *anywhere*. I'm not in love with Geraldine and she stays."

Lavender got up slowly and went dispiritedly out into the darkness of the hall. He could hear her feet on the stairs. Lem came into the dining room with a muttered greeting and sat down and began to wolf food. He wasn't drunk as he usually was at this time of the evening and Jeff looked him over. "Where've you been, Lem?" he asked conversationally.

The other gave him a quick furtive glance and lowered his eyes again. "Oh…looking around, walking around…nothing."

Jeff grunted and began to pack his pipe. Geraldine came in quietly and her soft liquid brown eyes sought his with calm contemplation and held them for a moment. Instantly he knew she had heard what had been said at supper. It gave him an odd feeling of exultance and his own eyes remained steady. She turned away and began to stack the dishes. Lemuel watched her as she moved about, not missing anything. His heavy tongue licked thick sensuous lips and Jeff saw green glints deep in his eyes. When Geraldine went out with a load of dishes, Jeff said, "See something you like?"

The other started gultily, muttered something unintelligible beneath his breath and attacked his supper again.

Jeff eyed him for a long time, then rose to his feet. "You," he said, transfixing Lemuel with a stiff forefinger, "had better be a good boy. I promise you, you'll be sorry if you don't." He walked out on the verandah where Toni sat curled up like a ball on the glider.

He sat beside her and she sat up to lean on his chest and hug him around the neck. "I'm sorry about that, Dad. She's a bitch … horrid."

He held her close and stroked her smooth back. "It's all right, Kitten. She won't do it again."

"But it was so snide—so uncalled for."

He nodded gravely. "Uncalled for, certainly, but understandable. Alcide could probably put it better, but here's what initiated it. She realizes, as you pointed out at the table, that she has done little to—well, she hasn't been much of a wife, physically speaking. Apparently, she can't. It's just not in her. She was an old maid too long, or I wasn't the swain I should have been. She resents that fact even though she can't do anything about it. She realizes the possibility that I might go in search of what she hasn't been able to provide. She won't provide nor would she allow me to attend to my biological needs elsewhere."

Toni looked him in the eyes. "You go right ahead and attend to your biological needs. Don't let that dried-up bud stop you, the vinegary old bitch!"

"Here, here. Let's not be disrespectful. She is your step-mother, you know ...."

Toni flounced about on the glider. "I could kill her. She's no mother of mine." She stopped suddenly, her breast rising and falling rapidly to the spur of some emotion. She collapsed on his chest. "Oh, God, Pop, *I want my mother!*"

The pressure in Jeff's chest was almost unendurable. Quick hot tears stung his eyes and his throat worked as he tried to swallow the lump. Tears dripped on Toni's hands, making her look up, instantly contrite. "Oh ... I'm so sorry. I shouldn't have said that."

"You do need your mother, Kitten ... and I need her, too." Father and daughter held each other close and wept. Shedding tears for the dead but still revered Antoinette, the kind, the understanding, the beautiful.

CHAPTER SIX

B ULL FALLON WALKED proudly along the road toward Granny Rosa's house. There was a lithe swagger to his stride and he whistled a tune that finally broke into a song.

Gon' tell mah Mammuh ... uh ... uh Bulldog done broke his chain—

His heavy bass voice broke sharply in the approved blues ending and echoed from the tall pines flanking the woods road. He had seen Hilda Capricorn the day before on the way to the store and Hilda had openly admired him. "Hi ya gal," he had greeted her.

"Good evening," she had replied quietly.

"Wheh you been?" She had an armload of groceries which made it obvious, but Bull was making talk.

"I've been to the store."

"You talks like a gal whuts been to school!"

"I have."

"I ain't never went no futher'n de third grade."

"That's a shame. Everybody ought to finish high school at least."

"Couldn't. I had t' wek in de fiel'. I gits along, though," he added proudly.

"You're big and strong. I'll bet you could really do some work."

Bull swelled mightily. "Ain't a nigger in dis pa'ish whut kin keep up wid me."

"Well, I got to be going," she said. "These packages are getting awfully heavy."

"I got to be going too," he said regretfully. "Got to git dese fo' plow pints shahpened down to de blacksmith shop. Wisht I wuz goin' back. I'd tote dem rations fer you."

Hilda Capricorn smiled showing strong white teeth. "Glad I saw you. Maybe I'll see you again sometime."

Bull bellowed with laughter and swung his shoulders. "Ain't no way you kin keep frum it."

They both laughed and went their respective ways. Bull was now keeping his promise. The tune had changed. The whistle again gave way to full throated words delivered with a deep blue refrain.

"Ummm…ummmmm, ain't got no mama now.
Told me late las' nigh…ite
Didn' need no mamma no how."

"Shet up singin' dat reel in frunt o' mah house, you deh, Bull. Gwine straight t' hell when you dies if you don' straighten yo' ways."

Bull laughed keep in his cavernous chest. "Tek mo'n dat t' sen' a man t' hell, Sis Rose. Wheh dat sharp lookin' chicken gran'dotter o' yourn?"

"Come on in, boy," said Granny Rosa in a kinder voice. "She in de back somewhere. How's all?"

"All's well…how's all wid you?"

"Tollable…tollable. Nuthin' t' squall 'bout. Wheh you been keepin' yo' self."

"Wekin'. I'se a hard wekuh, Sis Rose."

"Nacherly, you is. Yo' paw wuz a worker befo' you and yo' mammy. I hyeerd de Boss say ef he hadda place full o' niggers like you, he'd set on de gall'ry and tek root."

Bull began to swell. "Ef ever'body weks, den ever'body gits along. Us gits mo' and de Boss gits mo'.'"

"Dat's de gospel," said Granny, smiting her meaty thigh. She turned in her chair. "Coppercawn, git sumpn' on an' come out hyer. You got cump'ny."

In a few moments, Hilda came out on the porch. She was dressed in cool white sharkskin and Bull's pulse hammered heavily. She was the most beautiful thing he had ever seen in the female form.

"Whooie," he sang. "Well done Jesus, Sis Rose. Dat gal fitten."

"Sho she is," said Granny, pleased immeasurably. "You oughta seed me when I wuz a shoat."

Bull gallantly pulled up a chair for Hilda and assisted her to sit. "Thank you, Mr. Fallon," she said formally.

"You is twict dat welcome," he said, not to be outdone in matters of form. "Hit wuz a stomp down pleasuh."

"Thank you, Mr. Fallon, you're very nice."

"Jools to de queen and candy to de kids," he shot back instantly. "Things whut come easy ain't no pain. Anything you wishes, you can have."

"Oh, y'all shet up all dat 'lasses tawk," growled Granny. "Soun' like a coupla white folks."

"Mr. Fallon is a very gallant gentleman, Granny."

Granny snorted and fingered a pinch of tobacco from a package of Red Tag and stuffed it in her pipe. "Well, I'se goin' t' bed," she announced. "Den, y' all kin play all de highfalootin' you wants to. Be keerful wid dat big nigger," she told Hilda with a sharp glance. "His pappy wuz a demon wid de wimmen and I hear tell … well, I ain't one to pack tales but you be keerful."

"I'll treat her like de fines' Dusbin china, Sis Rose," said Bull gallantly.

Granny snorted and stalked into the house.

"You mean Dresden China, don't you, Mr. Fallon?"

He waved a deprecatory hand. "I reckon so. I never could git dem Affykin names."

"But Dresden isn't in Africa, Mr. Fallon."

"Wheh it at?"

Hilda doubled up with laughter. "You really are priceless, Bull, no foolin'."

Seeing that she wasn't laughing at him too critically he joined in the laughter.

An hour later, they were seated in the swing in the full glare of a brilliant moon. Bull found himself examining her repeatedly from her trim ankles encased in white strap sandals upward past her fine husky calves to the shape of her round firm thighs outlined under the soft material of her dress. Her legs and hips blended smoothly and flowed gently, curving toward her small waist where the dress was secured by a green sash. Her breasts were high and full and they surged against the tight cloth in a manner which made Bull's mouth flush with a sudden freshet of saliva. The dress was cut low and the creamy valley, thus revealed, made him want to kiss her throat and work gradually downward. He placed an arm against the back of the swing and said huskily, "I ain't never seen a woman whut gits next t' me like you does."

She smiled gently and rubbed a cheek against his bulky shoulder. "You're kind of nice, too, Bull."

He sat up and making a half turn in the swing, faced her. "I c'n be a lot nicuh."

She put her head back against the swing and looked at him through deep slumbrous eyes. She smiled slowly and wrinkled her nose at him.

"Gawd," he breathed as he sank toward her. He found her lips expertly and proceeded to live up to the reputation he had inherited from his father. When he released her, she was starry eyed and breathless. She ran a red tongue over her bruised lips, her body shuddering slightly at some powerful emotion.

"Bull ..." her arms became bands of steel and dragged him back into her embrace. This time it was Bull who was left gasping and dizzy.

He gazed cautiously at the open door. "If Sis Rose wuz to come through dat door rat now, I'd tek dat fence like a rabbit."

Hilda got up and flounced to the edge of the porch where she gazed upward at the moon and stretched. Bull followed her, stretching also. The dress rose, showing several inches of sturdy thigh and Bull squeezed his eyes shut and shook himself. This was maddening. She turned to him and reaching up, kissed him softly and quickly on the mouth. "If you really think I'm all that nice and if you're scared of Granny, it looks like you could think of something."

She had thrown the gauntlet down and Bull was on test. His mind moved like lightning. Alice was away at a quilting party and would be gone half the night. His house! That was the answer. He pulled her close and ran his hands lightly over her resilient back. He closed them about her waist and lifted her easily and kissed her. "You ax de questions, I got de answers.... Le's go."

When they arrived at the house the windows were dark and sightless. They mounted the porch and opened the door. For several seconds, the only sound was a slither of cloth then Hilda hurled herself at Bull with such force that it almost knocked him down. Gone was her educated veneer and to the ascendent came the hot blood of her savage forebears. Bull's nostrils dilated and his breath whistled as he, too, answered the call. Their writhing bodies came together in one mighty collision.

"How's Missy?" asked Maud, as Dr. Fontenot sat down to eat breakfast. He tasted his coffee before answering and smacked his lips appreciatively. "Fine. We operated last night because her white blood count was out of sight. She was bellowing like a bull this morning. Wanted to know if we intended to starve her to death and said if that was the case, why hadn't we let her die under the ether and save her the torment. She has all the nurses in stitches half the time and I had to take the other patient out of the room. Missy would have killed her in another day. The poor woman had had a cholecystectomy and Missy was about to kill her with ribaldries that'd make a statue die of mirth. That woman!"

"When'll she be able to go home?"

"Oh, in a week or so, I guess."

Dr. Fontenot attacked his eggs with avidity and soon had his breakfast where it would do the most good. "Think I'll run over to see Toni Salton today. Might come back by Allen Gordon's and cast awhile for bass. Don't expect me till late. Oh.... er.... you wouldn't be one of Missy Blumendahl's stooges, would you?"

Maud eyed him woodenly and said nothing.

"Ummm, well just thought I'd ask. You women...." He stalked from his house and got in his car.

Dr. Fontenot accepted a highball from Geraldine and as he did so, he gave her a quick searching glance. As far as he could tell, Cancer was as like Capricorn as the lines on the map indicated. "Where's Toni, Jeff?"

Jeff removed his pipe from his mouth. "She's still resting. I have insisted that she not get up until she has to."

"Good idea. Anything happen I ought to know?"

"No...oh, yes. She has picked up quite a lot of animation and she accused Lavender last night of dereliction as regards my biological needs. I think this revulsion of hers is merely a condition connected with that night. I don't think it runs too deep."

"That would be a break all right. Time and the right man will do the trick as I have said ... or did I say that?"

Jeff grinned, "You said part of it. It is grand of you to take all this interest, Alcide."

The other shrugged. "I am interested, Jeff. If I may be a little harsh on your parental propriety, I'm doing it because the girl is a delightful morsel and should not go to waste. Some deserving man must get her and in the proper shape for a happy life. To be married to your daughter in the present frame of mind would be probably the most exquisite torture you could imagine."

Jeff nodded. "A lot of the prudery has leaked out of me lately. I'm not offended. I think I'm just beginning to see just how many tentacles this business of sex has. It drove me to think, it drove some low bastard to attack my daughter, it drove Lavender to accuse me of being in love with a colored girl, it drives poor Feathers to chasing everything that might provide a moment's gratification. I've wondered if there is anything more powerful in the whole tapestry of our existence."

"If there is I haven't found it," said the doctor tasting his drink. "For every one you mentioned there are a hundred others."

Toni came out on the verandah and shook hands with the old man. "You should have seen that breakfast I just put away."

"I'm glad to hear it, my dear. You're looking very well. Jeff, take a powder. I want to talk privately with my patient."

Jeff's eyes slitted, he clenched his pipe between his teeth and walked through the house toward the kitchen.

"Now my dear," said the doctor in a kindly voice, "is there anything you want to tell me?"

She met his gaze calmly. "No, I guess not. Nothing's changed ... nothing ... I still can't stand the idea of ... She bent her head over and held it up with a hand while a sob welled up in her throat.

CHAPTER SEVEN

ULL FALLON SPOKE sharply but absently to Laura, his big red mule. "Haw! You deh, you fas' steppin' red bastud. Wheh you think you goin'?" Laura obediently hawed and stepped faster. The ground was in good shape and the sharp plowpoint made little subdued thudding noises as it sheared through grass roots. The furrow tumbled cleanly against the one previously plowed and Bull, one hand on a handle, maneuvered the point deftly past a small stump which he had been laying off to "grabble" out. "One o' dese days," he muttered, "Ah'm gonna ketch a plow pint in dat stump and bust a beam er sumpn. Recon I'll grabble it out some day when it's too wet to plow."

Laura put her head down as they struck a spot which had been but recently converted from turf. Bermuda grass grew thickly here and plowing was harder. Her ears flapped forward and back in time with her strides and the point made a steady tearing sound in the tough roots.

"Woah," Bull pulled the plow backward and scuffed damp dirt from the point. "G'up." Again Laura took up her swift pace and Bull broke into exuberant song.

"You got to treat yo' baby right
Treat 'er eve'ry night,
Er she won't be home when you calls."

Bull ceased his song and stopped his mule. He had seen a furtive movement at the headland where plum trees grew thickly.

He had the usual amount of suspicion of things half seen so he peered steadily at the spot. Hilda stepped around the edge of the plum thicket and walked toward him. Bull's big face split wide open in a mighty grin, his white teeth gleaming in the sun.

"Seen you, but I thought you wuz somebody tryin' to play shahp wid me."

Hilda walked up and handed him an earthenware jug full of fresh cool water. "I thought you might want a drink, Bull."

"I sho wuz. Alice oughta been hyer wid mah wateh fo' now." He threw the jug across his thick forearm and let the water gurgle into his mouth. He handed it back to her and wiped his mouth with his wrist. "Dat wuz jes' right. Much obliged."

She smiled at him with such brilliance that he felt his skin go all prickly. "Come hyer, gal," he said huskily. She came to him obediently and he dropped his plowlines over the handles to have both hands free. He pulled her close with a jerk. His hands kneaded the firmness of her back muscles and looked into her eyes.

"Day time is a bad time," he said breathing heavily.

She smiled and nodded happily. He could feel the warmth of her stomach against his own and the hard pressure of her breasts. He stepped back and shook himself.

"Dis ain't breakin' no ground," he said harshly. "Much obliged f' de wateh."

"Will I see you tonight, Bull?'

He laughed deep in his throat. "You bettuh not be seein' nobuddy else."

He slipped the loops of his lines over his wrists and hurled a hook into Laura's flank with the plowline that made her jerk. She leaped ahead with the trace chains crashing and the hames on her leather collar creaking. As they turned at the headland, Bull again thought he saw the figure near the plum trees. He frowned as he heeled the caked dirt from the plowpoint. He could see Hilda walking with her free long-legged stride along the terrace of the opposite hill. It couldn't be her. Bull made a decision. He'd investigate the next time he neared the plum thicket. People didn't play sharp with Bull Fallon.

As they drew abreast of the thick growth of plum and blackberry briar, he pulled Laura to a halt and strode belligerently toward the thicket. "Whoeveh you is, come on out fo' I comes in deh and gits you." There was no sound so Bull ducked low to avoid the thorny low limbs and went in. Children picking plums had worn the ground smooth within the enclosure and the leafy walls made a pavilion of the growth. Bull straightened up and pulled a yellow plum from a low branch and popped it into his mouth. He spat out the seed and hull and reached for another but his hand never touched the fruit. There, sitting on his haunches not twenty feet away sat a great police dog which he recognized all too well. He whirled about with every intention of crashing to safety through the leafy wall that so effectively screened the tableau from the outside but there, as he had expected, stood Feathers. Her oblique green eyes burned with a restless fire and her face was cut with lines of intense desire.

"If you try to run, King will cut you to pieces," she told him. His great shoulders slumped dejectedly. He was beaten and he knew it.

When Alice arrived at eleven thirty with Bull's dinner, she found Laura unhitched, standing in the shade eating her corn. Bull lay stretched out on the ground nearby, drenched with sweat.

"You fell in de bayou?" asked Alice innocently.

"No ... I ain't fell in no bayou 'cause deh ain't no bayou t' fall in," snarled Bull rudely sitting up and mopping his face with a trembling bandanna.

"How come you so je'ky? You looks like sumbuddy run you fer ten miles."

Bull eyed his sister with smouldering hostility. "You," he said with slow distinct accents, "kin set dat vittles rat deh under dat gum tree. Den you kin turn roun' and go home jes' as strate as you feets kin go."

Alice eyed him for a space, then put the food down. "You sho is gittin' tetchy dese las' few days. Eveh time I opens mah mouf to you, you spews up like a bottle o' sour sorgum lasses."

Bull sighed heavily. His sister was something of a gossip and a trial. At such times as this, she was well nigh endurable. He picked up his dinner pail but his hand was shaking so badly that he set it down again quickly. Alice, seeing that Bull was likely to get violent in his efforts to get rid of her, turned about and started for home. "Don't you fergit n' leave dat bucket in de fiel'. Hit's de las' one us got."

Bull grunted and watched her out of sight. He glanced at the plum thicket and wondered if Feathers had gone. He fervently hoped so. Something would have to be done about her but though he pondered and scratched his head, he could think of nothing. Should he tell the Boss.... He quailed at the thought. The Boss was a good man, he knew, but white people were a little crazy where their women were concerned. What would the Boss's reaction be if he knew.

Bull shuddered and yanked the top off the pail. Alice hadn't punched holes in the top and the hot rice and biscuits had sweated against the sides of the pail. The biscuits were soggy and the rice was wet. There were three huge slices of sowbelly there that looked good so Bull shoved a bite into his mouth and crunched down on it. Taking up his spoon he shoveled rice and gravy behind it and took a bite from a big red tomato. The cornbread was soggy too, but it went well with the collards. He finished the rice and gravy, collards and the sowbelly, then broke his last six biscuits and a square of cornbread into the bottom of the pail and poured on a half pint of thick cane syrup. He mixed it all together with his spoon and soon had the pail clean. As he finished, he looked up and there was the Boss astride Big Red, looking down at him and grinning.

Jeff had a way of catfooting about and sneaking up when least expected. He had seen a lot by just such tactics that he never would have otherwise. Bull grinned guiltily as it was just twelve o'clock and he was supposed to work till twelve. He could hear the plantation bell ringing in the distance.

"Get hot, today, Bull?"

The big man glanced self-consciously at his drenched clothing. "Yassuh." This should be a good excuse for stopping early. "Sho is hot today. Hottes' day ...."

"That's funny," Jeff interrupted. "Laura don't seem to mind it too much."

Bull hung his head. He was caught. Laura was not a heavy sweating mule to begin with and today she had her usual wet ring around her neck where she had sweated under the collar and a streak along her belly. He felt a sudden urge to confide in the Boss but his blood turned to water and he remained silent.

Jeff dismounted and let Big Red crop the grass that grew thickly in the shade of the tree. "What was Feathers doing around here this morning?"

He darted a quick glance at Jeff. "You seed her?"

Jeff nodded, careful not to seem too interested. "I thought maybe she was looking for me." Out of the corner of his eye, Jeff saw the hurried but searching glance Bull cast in the direction of the plum thicket.

"Better tell me about it," said Jeff quietly.

Bull's chin touched his breastbone in an agony of indecision and consternation. Finally he sat straight and looked Jeff full in the eyes. "Boss, you got to help me."

"What's wrong?"

"Hit's .... Miss Feathers." Bull spat on a forefinger and held it to Heaven. "Hope Gawd strack me daid rat hyer in front o' you, Mistuh Jeff.... I'se a nigger and I don' mess roun' wid no white peoples. But one night I run into John Harrel's ole house t' git outa de rain and she wuz deh. I tried to jemp outa de winduh but she put dat big dawg on me. Ever'time I'd tried to git out dat dawg 'ud growell at me. I couldn't git loose, Mistuh Jeff, Gawd knows I couldn't." Bull's face screwed up dismally and great hot tears rolled from his eyes. "I hope Gawd'll strack me dead in mah tracks ef I ain't tellin' de Gospel."

Jeff placed a sympathetic hand on Bull's knee. "I know, Bull. She got me once."

A sob of relief welled from deep within him. If she had got the Boss, then he knew what it was like. "Sho nuff?"

"She sure did. I know just what you went through with ... but my God, she must have handled you rough."

Bull shrugged and rolled his eyes. "She might nigh kilt me bofe times. I ain't never seen a woman like her in mah bawn days."

Jeff swung up on Big Red. "Keep your eyes open and if you see her trying to get at you, come to me."

"Yassuh, I sho will but dat woman too smaht. Bofe times she had me fo' I knowed she was around."

"Well, do the best you can and I'll try to think of something."

"Yassuh," he broke out in a cool sweet sweat of unutterable relief. He had known all the time that the Boss would understand ... and *he* had been caught too. There was something comical about that and Bull let a rumble of laughter seep from the depths of his chest. It was easy to laugh now because the world had taken a definite turn for the better.

He stood up and stretched. It was interrupted at the peak of satisfaction and he almost broke into a run when he heard a noise behind him. He whirled about and was immeasurably relieved to see the fat shapeless form of Lemuel standing there.

Bull grinned amiably. "Mawnin' Mr. Lemuel."

Lem hiccoughed and lurched nearer. "I saw that fine looking girl here that brought you water this morning." His grin grew wider.

"Fine as a fawty dollar cow, ain't she?"

Lemuel looked up slyly, "Sure she is, and I want her." Bull stood stock still while icy waves flickered through his muscles. His fingers twitched as he swallowed a flare of raw fury. For a second, Lemuel was not a white man or a black but just a man who had evidenced a desire for Bull's woman. "Want and be goddamned!" hissed the Negro through his teeth. He paused appalled at his temerity while Lemuel grinned crookedly.

"Talk big, don't you?"

"I begs yo' podners, Mr. Lemuel," he said quietly, "I forgot who I was tawkin' to."

"Well, see that you don't forget again. I repeat I want that girl and you're going to get her for me."

Bull strove manfully to hold his temper, his black eyes turned bloodshot from the effort. "Don't tawk like dat t' me, Mistuh Lemuel."

Lemuel sneered, "I'll talk to you any way I want to. Now listen to me. You know John Harrel's old house? Well, I want her there tonight and you'll talk her into it."

The man's teeth showed whitely against the black skin and his great hands clenched murderously as he took an ominous step forward. Lemuel backed up rapidly. "Or I'll tell them what I saw in the plum thicket this morning.... I was right there and when I tell them about it in town, you know what'll happen to you. I'll expect her tonight." Lemuel turned and shuffled rapidly away.

Bull sank on the ground and shuddered with black despair. He was ruined and that was all there was to it. The Boss...that was it. He held his head up. The Boss...he'd know what to do. Bull leaped to his feet and with a swift motion he wrapped his lines about the hames and leaped on Laura. She took off toward the plantation house with a fast mincing pace.

He rapped her a sharp blow under the belly with a plowline and Laura, unaccustomed to this rough treatment, promptly kicked backward with enough force to burst the planking on the barn.

He patted her apologetically on the neck and by the time they came through the lot gate, Laura with an eye on another feed was loping rapidly along, trace chains jingling like sleigh-bells. Jeff seated on the verandah with Lavender and Toni, leaped to his feet and growled out an oath.

"What's the matter, dear," asked Lavender in her usually sac-charine voice.

"Nothing," answered Jeff shortly as he gripped the pipe tighter in his teeth and leaped down the steps.

"I do wish your father would mend his ways of speaking to people," she complained. "It is so rude and boorish."

Toni let her violet eyes rest on her stepmother for a time, then looked toward the barn again. She said nothing.

Bull slid from Laura's back and when Jeff walked into the barn, he had the gear off the mule and was turning her into a stable.

Jeff walked up. "Not already, Bull." The man's stricken eyes told the story. "What's the matter?"

Bull sat down abruptly on a feed basket. "Ever'thing's de matter, Boss." Then he told his story. Jeff sat very still and lis-tened. "I been a good man, Boss. You knows dat. You had to pay de lawyer dat time Sis Tilly Bryant put de law on me dat time bout Sissy. But Boss, Hilda is plumb differunt. Dat gal done got me and when Mr. Lemuel tole me to fetch her to dat ole house, I might nigh fergot I wuz a nigger."

"Filthy son of a bitch," Jeff ground out, leaping to his feet. "Where is he?"

No answer was needed because at that moment, Lemuel loped into sight on a little pinto, the only horse on the place he'd ride. He rode into the barn, but coming into the dark building from the bright sunlight, he didn't see them till he had dismounted.

"Come over here, Lemuel," said Jeff in an ominous voice.

Lemuel shrank back against a stable door. "Now look, Jefferson … I …."

With a bound Jeff covered the space between them and fastened his hand in Lemuel's shirt collar. He forced him back hard against the door and began to beat him about the face with hard bruising open-handed slaps. Lemuel screamed and struggled but in Jeff's mighty grasp, he was helpless. Jeff wore a huge graduation ring, a heavy hunk of metal that was cutting Lemuel's face to ribbons. With a surge of power Jeff pulled him away from the door and hooked a terrific right to the other's ear. It cracked suddenly and Lemuel crumpled to the straw and dung covered floor of the barn. Jeff breathed hard, looking at the prone figure. He took out the handkerchief and wiped the blood and saliva from his hands.

Bull sat riveted to the feed basket, numb with satisfaction. That's what happened to people that got sharp with the Boss's Negroes.

Jeff turned to him. "Take the rest of the day off. You need it. You want to marry Hilda?"

Bull got slowly to his feet. "More'n I want to live. I'da never done what Mr. Lemuel said."

Jeff nodded. "Of course you wouldn't. You can go to town tomorrow and tell Sol Lehven to let you have what furniture you need. That stuff in your house is about to fall to pieces. You wouldn't want to bring a good girl like Hilda into a house like that. Tell Sid Wright I said to go over the house and put it in top shape. If you want a coat of paint on it, you can do it yourself. I'll give you the paint."

The Negro swallowed something that had risen in his throat. "Boss, I can't say it."

Jeff smiled and struck him on a hard shoulder with his fist. "Don't say it, then. We're grown men. We understand each other."

Lemuel had to be taken to the doctor. His face was cut deeply in a dozen places and was bruised to a wonderful shade of blue. Lavender immediately launched into a fit of hysterics and Granny Rosa had to put her to bed. Jeff refused to get into an argument about what had happened and there was nothing left to do but have hysterics. Toni strode off and left her so Granny dragged, rather than carried her to her room and left her.

When Lemuel was led into the room two hours later, she was composed and immediately jumped on him.

"Well…so now *you're* running after Negro women. You nearly got yourself killed for your trouble. What'll it be, next?"

Lemuel lay on the bed and sobbed into his bandages. "You made me like this," he was sobbing pitifully. "I was a normal man and you made me into one of those…those…creatures. I never wanted to be anything but what I was…you made me…made me." He sat up in bed and pointed an accusing finger at her.

"Shut up!" she blazed. "You were always as twisted as you could be. It was born in you like it was born in me. I don't know where you got this normalcy thing. You never did before we came here."

"I never wanted to, before we came here," he sobbed. "You never gave me a chance. You always made me do what you wanted and I never went against you, never. You shouldn't want me to not ever have any…any…anything of my own."

"I don't care what you have," she said harshly. "What I do care is that you are a fool. Look at what you just did. Have you no sense at all? Don't you know that Jeff Salton is quite capable of killing you? You and your threats! All they'll do is cause trouble for us. I hope you see that now."

Lemuel's sobs quieted a little and he did not speak.

The week following, Lemuel so effectively kept out of sight that Jeff could almost feel that he had gone. If some stroke of divine providence could have taken Lavender along too, everything would have been fine. He wondered if she would make good her threat to blacken Toni's name? What would he do if she did start poisonous whisperings?

Lavender had no such intention. If she could have by innuendo said something to let it out, she'd have done it already, but on that score she was more than satisfied. Her talk with Agatha Silvers had shown that the knowledge was abroad and she had, without saying anything directly, given support to the rumor. Agatha would now tell it as first hand information. Lavender was not a fool. She could see that beneath the good natured and easy going surface of Jefferson Salton, there was a streak of finely tempered steel.

At Fomalhaut she had a good thing of it. She was looked up to, socially, being a parishwide leader in all cultural and social affairs, and she enjoyed her position. She was not going to jeopardize it by any stupid obvious act. Whatever she did, she'd do it under cover.

It was three o'clock in the afternoon and Jeff rose from his afternoon nap feeling logy. The weather was abominably hot and his head ached slightly, a dull full feeling that resembled a hangover. He thought of a drink and put the thought from him. It was too hot to drink. Iced tea … that was the thing.

He walked through the hall and back to the kitchen. Granny Rosa sat in a big rocker in the shade of a column and slept, her lips popping occasionally as she breathed.

In the kitchen, Geraldine was tending a big pot full of dish cloths which were undergoing their weekly boiling in strong lye water.

"Good evening, Sir. Can I get you something?"

"Er—yes, Geraldine. I'd like some iced tea. Why don't you wait till dark to boil these things? It's too hot now."

She smiled. "I don't mind the heat, Sir. It's the cold that gets me. I'll get the tea."

He sat on the little kitchen porch that was away from the sun and shaded by the branches of a live oak. It was cool and there was a little breeze.

Geraldine came back quickly with a tall frosted glass of tea and handed it to him. She hesitated for a moment and Jeff looked up. "You've worked in that kitchen long enough," he said with a smile. "Get yourself a coke from the ice box and come back here and rest awhile in the cool."

She came back with a glass full of coke and ice and sat on the steps at his feet. He could see where the sweat had wet her simple gingham dress down the deep cleft of her strong back. Her hair was damp around the temples and extremely soft. Being conscious of her hair and proud of it, she had always paid it a great deal of attention. It was shoulder length and fell orderly in deep soft waves. Usually she had the bulk of it tied with a bit of colorful ribbon making it fit her face closely. This afternoon, being hot, she had it pulled closely back and above her ears. Jeff noticed that they were well formed and small, nestling close to her head.

"Mr. Jeff, you won't let them do anything to Bull, will you?"

"Not if I can help it, Geraldine. What Bull did was not his fault. Everyone knows that who knows anything about it. Bull wants to get married, I think."

"Yes sir. My sister Hilda is so crazy about him, I think it would kill her if a mob got him."

"I think Lemuel is cured," said Jeff, his voice getting hard and angry lines showing on his forehead.

Geraldine shuddered at the mention of the name. "It gives me goose bumps when he looks at me."

Jeff was shaken by such a blast of rage that he nearly dropped his glass. "He hasn't done … made any moves toward you, has he?"

"Oh, no, Sir," she said quickly. "I just don't like the way he looks at me."

"I don't blame you. I wonder why he picks on Hilda. You're here every day and anyone can see he has an eye for you, and you look just like her."

Jeff could see her fine tawny skin go dark under the wave of blood that mounted to her face. She remained silent. Suddenly he became curious. She knew something or she wouldn't have blushed.

"Geraldine…."

"Yes, Sir?"

"What were you thinking about, just then?"

She turned her face away and a strange feeling came over Jeff. Suddenly it seemed important that she should know that she could tell him anything without reservation. He didn't want her to feel stiff and uncomfortable around him. Although the feeling startled him somewhat, he was too honest at heart to deny it or pretend it hadn't happened.

"Geraldine."

"Yes Sir."

"Why don't you tell me?" His voice was deep and gentle.

She faced him and he could see the effort she was making. "Please Sir, can … you won't be mad at me if I tell you?"

He smiled his assurance and managed to look almost boyish. His clear eyes sparkled and goodfellowship shone from them. "I'm not an ogre. You've been here long enough to know that."

She swallowed and looked out across the green stretch of the lawn toward the bluff. "I don't really know why Mr. Lemuel hasn't … you know … but Granny says it's because …." she stopped and hung her head.

Jeff leaned over and placing one hand on her firm shoulder made her face him. "Yes?"

She looked him full in the eyes. "Granny said she told Mr. Lemuel that I was yours and that if he bothered me, you'd kill him."

Jeff sat back, his strength suddenly snatched from him. His head whirled and maddening half thoughts fought for coherence. Honesty made him admit that this strange girl attracted him greatly but four thousand years of prejudice and white supremacy prevented him from making the final admission. As a result the effect was one of great confusion.

"You're not mad, Mr. Jeff?" she asked fearfully, anxiously.

He grinned weakly. "No, Geraldine. I'm knocked over, that's all."

He could see the thread of tension break within her and relief take its place. She put her hands up to her face and held them there for a long time. Jeff said softly, "It took a lot of courage to say that to me, didn't it?"

"Yes sir, it took more than courage, Mr. Jeff."

He did not ask her what she meant by that, for the simple reason that he was afraid to.

"How did you feel when Granny told you she had told Lemuel that?"

She was silent for a while and Jeff began to wish he hadn't asked the question. "Mr. Jeff, I can't talk about that."

"Why, Geraldine?"

"Because it's too close to me ... it's ... ."

He made an attempt at lightness, feeling as he did so that he was getting close to dangerous grounds. "Well, it's pretty close to me, too." Oh, Lord, he thought, I've done it now.

He had. She faced him quickly, her mouth slightly opened and her breath coming swiftly. "How is it close to you, Sir?"

Again he attempted to be gay. He smiled widely. "Because I'm in it, too. I'm the one she scared him with."

"Oh ... ." Her voice was very small and far away. He felt that he had hurt her and he was afraid to analyze the extreme distaste which rose in him at the thought. White men did not bother to wonder or even care whether they hurt their colored retainers. Often they hurt them and never knew it because they never thought about the matter at all. His next remark showed how thoroughly he had been thrown off his course.

"I thought ... the reason I asked you. ... I thought maybe when Granny said that, you wouldn't have liked the idea of ... being mine." He raged inwardly at his traitorous tongue.

She stood up, her dark mysterious eyes resting on his with upsetting directness. "Mr. Jeff, you haven't asked me to be yours. Whenever you do, I'll be ready to answer you." She turned swiftly away and disappeared into the kitchen.

CHAPTER EIGHT

B ULL FALLON LAY on his corn shuck mattress and tossed fitfully. He seemed nervous and fretful, which was something
entirely foreign to his nature. Usually he was asleep by the time
he had arranged himself comfortably but tonight he could not
sleep. He quit flouncing and lay very still so as to not arouse
the dry protest of the shucks which always made a great deal of
noise when he moved. Suppose Mr. Lemuel did tell off on him
like he had threatened. He sighed heavily. Between Feathers and
Lemuel he was in the hottest of water. He shivered thinking of
the plum thicket episode. Never in all his varied experience had
he encountered such a woman as Feathers. There had been several lynchings in the state during his lifetime and he had a vivid
recollection of each one. The night outside was quiet and very
dark. There'd be a moon but not till after midnight. Insects by
the thousands gave out their cheepings and raspings. A sleepy
mockingbird let fall occasional trickles of melody and a great
horned owl, up from the flats on a raid, chuttered nastily a quarter of a mile away. A stick snapped outside the house and Bull
started nervously and sat up in bed. His nerves quivered and all
his senses seemed to become abnormally sharp. He heard a muttered word and another stick cracked. With scarcely a sound, he
slid from the bed and drew on his trousers.

Hilda and Geraldine lay on their bed clad in colorful pajamas. Geraldine was asleep but Hilda lay on her back and thought
about her man. Her body wriggled with the sensuous trend of
her thoughts and her breath came a little faster. Outside the

JOHN B. THOMPSON & JACK WOODFORD

house on the main road, she heard the crunch of gravel. At first, she thought nothing of it until it seemed unduly prolonged, then she became curious. She slipped from her bed and crept to the front door, cracked the portal and peered out. A number of men were passing and most of them walked on the shoulder of the path to avoid the noisy gravel. Others didn't seem to mind and she heard a smothered chuckle which was echoed by a drunken laugh.

A sharp voice spoke and the noise subsided. A match flared and she saw a sharp featured white man apply the flame to a cigarette. She saw something else too. The man walking beside him carried a double barreled shotgun. Cold sweat broke out on the girl's amber skin and a sob caught in her throat. Scurrying back to their room she swiftly slipped from her pajamas and into a pair of Levi's and into sneakers. She slipped a black pullover sweater over her head and silently crept out of the house. She followed the band of men until she was sure that they had gone to Bull's house, then she stopped to consider. What should she do? The same doubt assailed her that had caused Bull's hesitation on another occasion. Should she tell the Boss?

In what way was he different from most white men except that all his hands seemed to think that he was the best boss in the parish? Hilda stood and squirmed in an agony of indecision. If she ran to the Boss and he turned out to be of the same mind as the mob, she had made matters worse; if she didn't go to him, Bull hadn't a chance. She heard the mutter of hooves behind her and leaped to the cover of a thicket of blackberry briars just in time to avoid a horse being ridden at a rapid pace. She couldn't tell who it was but as soon as it had passed, she came out into the little side road again. Suddenly she made up her mind. She'd tell the Boss. Bull was certainly lost if she didn't, so she started toward the big house at a rapid dogtrot. She hadn't gone a hundred steps when a shotgun exploded ahead of her. She was cut off from the house and they were shooting at Bull now. She clutched her head in a frenzy of despair and moaned loudly, "Jesus, God...do something... *do* something."

Feathers took off her clothes and ran under a cold shower in her rooms on the second floor of the old gray Maidstone house. Finishing her bath, she scoured her skin with a rough bath towel, savoring the bite of its rough nap on her back and stomach. Then she hurled herself across the bed still nude and lay supinely for a while. She sat up and gazed abstractedly out into the star-studded night. She thought of the dark night of the thunderstorm when she had caught Bull in John Harrel's old house. She lay slowly back and rolled sinuously on her stomach. Her eyes stared at the ceiling and in her mind she could feel again the strutted crush of his great muscles and the savage abandon of his thrusts, the strong masculine scent of his magnificent body. A light sweat broke out on her upper lip and forehead.

Some time later, Feathers came from the shower again and stood in the window allowing a cool wind to touch her damp skin. On the porch below, she could see the dim forms of her mother and father as they sat and rocked silently. A man came up from the black shadows and addressed her father. She could hear snatches of the conversation.

"...and we think you oughta come along."

"Ah ain't never been with a mob in mah born days," she heard the rumbling drawl of her father retort, "and Ah don't aim to now."

"I don't believe you know," said the man in wonderment.

"Know what?" asked Maidstone.

For a moment the man stood silently, then walked away into the shadows. A wave of horror swept over Feathers as the import of the last remark struck her. If her father had been sought to join a mob and the man thought it odd that he didn't know what for, then it could mean but one thing. They had found out about Bull in some manner. With a pantherish spring, she leaped away from the window and slipped into her jeans. Dressed, she went to a closet and pulled out a slim automatic shotgun and breaking open a fresh box of shells began to cram them into her pockets.

King preceeded her through the door and together, with the utmost caution, they descended the long winding stairs and went out the back door of the big house. Ten minutes later she mounted her red horse and trotted silently away, the heavy turf muffling the hoof beats.

Two earsplitting explosions from a shotgun fired close to the house snatched Jefferson Salton from his bed with a jerk and before he was half awake, he had his pants and slippers on. The dull roar of many voices rose in the distance and he heard the sound of pounding feet coming nearer. With a bitter oath, he went to his dresser, took out two heavy Colt automatics and checked the clips. He worked cartridges into the chambers and thrusting them into the waistband of his pants, ran out of his room and down the stairs. As he came out on the verandah, Bull coming in a dead run, almost knocked him down.

"Boss, dey comin' fer me," he panted raggedly. With a flip of his hand, Jeff turned on three powerful floodlights that turned the lawn into day. Some forty men in a straggling group came trotting across the lawn.

"Get back into the house, Bull," Jeff ordered. "Did they hit you?"

"Nawsuh—not bad. Jes' some birdshot under mah skin."

Jeff closed the door on him and walked to the edge of the porch to face the men.

"Good evenin', Mr. Salton," said Jasper Mutlock, evidently the leader of the group. His eyes were bleary and red. A quick glance showed Jeff that the whole group was more or less drunk.

"What do you want, Jasper?"

"We wants that big nigger what just run in here."

Jeff hefted the two big Colts in his capable fists and looked the group over with unfriendly eyes. "You have two minutes to get off this place."

A murmur ran over the crowd but they made a noticeable mass retreat.

"We don't aim to have no trouble, Mr. Salton," said Jasper, careful not to get too far from the mass of his followers, "but we want that nigger."

"And I say you don't get him," said Jeff, his voice hissing between his set teeth.

"Jefferson, you come in the house this instant," shrilled Lavender from behind the door. "If they want the Negro, let them have him."

"Half your time is up," said Jeff, ignoring his wife. "You are trespassing on private property and…." The gun in his right hand thundered and Thad Berry screamed, grabbed his knee and sank to the ground. He had tried to take a bead on Jeff with a twenty-two rifle.

"Take him and get going," said Jeff. "The next one will get it through the head."

The men were silent for a moment, the only sounds being the whines of Thad begging someone to help him. A revolver cracked in the rear of the mob. Jeff swayed like a stricken pine and fell full length down the front steps, both guns going off as he fell. One bullet ricochetted off the live oak, a few yards away and went whining into the night. The other struck the stone flagging of the walk, ricochetted and nearly tore Thad Berry's head from his body. A deep silence fell that was broken by a roar from Bull as he leaped from the house to help his master.

Long and well did the mighty Negro strive and many were the bones that snapped under the awful drive of his mighty arms and his powerful legs, but gun butts are too hard and the men were too many and ten minutes after he had leaped among them, Bull was a bruised bloody hulk securely bound with insulated telephone wire and strapped like a gutted deer to a long pole by his hands and feet.

As the mob trooped away from the house bearing their dead and cripples, Hilda Capricorn sank to her knees and terrible sobs tore themselves like lacerating grapples from her heaving chest. Again she heard horses' hooves, but this time they were rapid and staccato. She didn't care about horses now and Red Mack's agility saved her as he carried over her with a tremendous bound and snort. Feathers pulled the champing animal to a sliding halt and turned him around.

"What are you doing there," she asked

"They got Bull," said Hilda numbly staring up at the straight figure of the girl on the horse. "You got him in this … why don't you get him out?"

Feathers looked at her for a moment. "I will," she rapped out and wheeling Red Mack on his haunches, she cut him under the stomach with her quirt and was gone. Hilda seeing the shotgun in her hands sobbed with relief and took out after her as fast as she could run.

Bull was tied to a young pine. He was only half conscious and his eyes were nearly closed from the terrific beating he had received. He could smell kerosene and felt its warm dry bite as Jim Hardt splashed it on his chest and legs. A droplet went in one eye and it began to smart but he was only slightly conscious of this last extra bit of pain. He breathed deeply and straightened his body against the tree. Thirty feet away, a huge fire roared redly. "I'll burn like that," he thought, "but I won't last as long."

Bull prayed that in some manner death would come quickly but he knew of these things. They didn't want it to come quickly. He looked the group over. Most of them he knew and all he knew were *buckrahs* … po' white trash … the kind you steered clear of in town on Saturday night … the kind to whom the nebulous tenets of white supremacy were the only thing they had with which to feed their pride. The good white people, he remembered looked down on the *buckrahs,* while the trash had no one to look down on but the Negroes. The bottle passed freely and Jasper Mutlock addressed his men in a thick voice.

"If we all 'lows niggers t' carry on with our women, what's this here country coming to? Somebuddy answer me that." No one answered him but a mutter of approval went through the crowd.

"This here is a white man's country," continued Jasper, "and if the niggers are gonna take it over and rape our women, then we all had better move out."

"What we need," said another voice, "is the kluxers to come back."

"That's 'zactly right," said Jasper with heat, "and till they gits back we's the ones to take care of rapers."

"Who got raped?" asked Will Hadley as he sat some feet away watching the men through narrow lids. Will had talked against the lynching and Jasper wheeled on him.

"Miss Feathers, that's who, and if you don't like it here, why don't you gwan home?"

Will looked at Jasper for awhile. "That's a goddamned good idea."

He rose and walked away through the woods. He had hardly passed from sight when a shotgun thundered nearby and the whiskey bottle disappeared from Tom Sturgun's hands and most of it entered Zack Ellier's face, leaving it red and raw as a piece of beef. Zack screamed and fell backwards away from the fire, holding his face with both hands. Four more shots rang out and the man, bitten hard by bird shot, ran pellmell through the woods, followed by the hard hoofbeats of a running horse. Other shots rang out and other screams sounded through the tangled underbrush. Hilda rushed from cover and tore frantically at the wires binding Bull to the tree.

Finally he was free but he couldn't walk. He sank to the soft pine needles and began massaging his feet with hands that were little more than sticks, dead from lack of circulation.

Zack was crawling aimlessly in circles whimpering for some one to help him, that his eyes were put out. Bull glared at him and picking up a pine knot bounced it expertly off his head. Zack yelled and lurched to his feet and finding that he was not as blind as he had supposed took off under forced draught through the woods.

By the time Bull had rubbed sufficient circulation into his legs to stand, Feathers was sitting on her horse on the other side of the clearing, watching them silently. Hilda looked at her with dumb gratitude notwithstanding the fact that it was primarily Feathers' fault that the trouble had occurred. Bull staggered a little as he tried to walk. "I sho thanks you, Miss," he said, "I sho does."

Feathers looked steadily but said nothing. Finally she pulled Red Mack's head around and disappeared in the darkness.

"Got t' git back to de house. Dey shot de Boss."

"Sure, Honey, but take it easy. You can't walk good yet."

"Sho I kin walk," he said crossly and set out at a fairly good pace. He found himself tiring before long, however, and had to slow down.

"Honey, you don't have to show off before me. I know you're good when you're well but you have been beaten up something terrible. It's only good sense to take it easy."

He grinned a crooked self-conscious grin. "You's too smaht fer a woman. You reads people's minds."

She hugged him and made him slow down. They skirted the bluff and just before they came out into the open, Bull had to sit down.

"Mah head goin' round like a 'lasses mill," he complained holding the offending member with both hands. Hilda sat beside him.

"It'll be all right if you'll rest awhile."

But it grew worse and finally Bull passed out cold. Hilda then became frightened and started to go for help. She hadn't gone thirty feet into the clipped area of the lawn when she heard a noise. Turning with a gasp, she saw Lemuel leering at her. "So Bull wouldn't help me out eh? Well, now, isn't that tough. Look where he is now?"

Hilda said nothing but stood still watching his slow approach. "I won't need Bull now," he continued. "I can get along without him. You and I can be good friends."

"Don't put your hands on me, Mr. Lemuel."

His lips curled, "I'm not asking, Hilda. I'm taking!"

He grasped her roughly about the waist and pulled her to him. With a serpentine twist, Hilda tore away and slapped him a resounding blow in the face. Lemuel lost his temper, lunged at and threw her roughly to the ground. Even then, she might have been a match for him but Lemuel had no intention of losing this battle. When he saw that the struggle might go against him, he scrambled to his feet and as she came up, he struck her twice in the face almost knocking her over the edge of the bluff. He pulled her back, half conscious, and calling for Bull in a weak voice.

"No damn good…to call him…he won't…come." He deliberately struck her again on the point of her chin and she sagged limply, unconscious. A cackle of laughter came from him as he fondled her breasts and tore at her clothing. So rapt was he in his own intentions that he went high in the air and over the edge of the bluff without ever knowing what agency caused his soaring flight. At the bottom of the bluff some seventy feet down was the body of an old car with two windshield uprights pointing drunkenly at the sky. Falling the entire distance, Lemuel was spitted like a roasting fowl on one of those uprights with eighteen inches of it protruding through his fat belly. Bull was bending over Hilda and scarcely heard the tinny crash that came faintly from below.

When they reached the house, it was ablaze with lights. Geraldine and Granny Rosa darted hither and thither at Toni's orders, her first having been to banish Lavender from her father's room.

Bull and Hilda dragged their weary feet up the steps to the back porch near the kitchen.

"De Boss ... he hurt bad?" he asked Granny as she bustled up.

"Don't know. Dr. Fontenot and dat boy doctor o' hisn on their way hyer now. How you got 'way frum dem peoples?"

"Miss Feathers saved him, Granny. She shot men as long as there was any to shoot."

"She sho did dat," agreed Bull nodding.

"Gawd bless de Fillystines," squeaked Granny in stunned amazement. "Whut goin' happen round hyer nex'?"

"Us gon' git ma"ied," said Bull proudly.

Granny sniffed and disappeared into the kitchen. Her voice floated back to them, "Better! Else funny thaings gon' be comin' round hyer ... if y'all don' watch out."

Bull and Hilda stole a cautious glance at each other and Bull shook his head, grinning, "Dat ole 'oman ...."

Dr. Fontenot placed a tender hand on Toni's shoulder. "Nothing to worry about, child. The bullet was small ... a thirty-two, I think. Just grazed the skull a few inches and knocked him silly. What is that other pool of blood near where he was shot?"

Toni shuddered. "When he fell his guns went off and one bullet hit a man in the head and ...."

"Never mind," interposed the little man. "I saw the place ... I know. Too bad he didn't have a Tommy gun in each fist and could have got the whole crowd. Poor Bull. He was a fine fellow to have around."

"I'se still here, too," said Bull, putting his grinning face through the door.

Toni spun around and gasped.

"*Sacré nom du mort.* He's still alive. Well, devil my liver!" whistled the doctor.

"Sho is," said Bull, sidling into the room. "Kin I see de Boss, please suh?"

Dr. Fontenot waved his hand. "There he is, in good shape. I've got him asleep now, but he'll be all right…. Albert, don't take all night with that dressing. We've got to get back some time tonight."

Albert put on two more strips of tape and stood up. "Excellent job, even if I do say so myself."

"Nuts," said his father rudely. "I could have done better in half the time."

Toni caught them by the arms as they went out. "I don't know how to thank you two. I called you sort of automatically even though there were other doctors nearer."

"A natural desire for the best," said Albert laughing. "We understand and when you get our bill, you might want to take back them kind words."

Toni sat on the verandah and watched Dr. Fontenot and Albert disappear around the curve of the long driveway. It was late but Toni did not feel like sleep, rather like a deer that had escaped the hunters after a long hard chase. She smiled grimly at the thought. Bull was the one who should feel like the escapee. He and Hilda had disappeared arm in arm after Dr. Fontenot had examined him and found no serious injuries.

Toni sighed. Bull and Hilda seemed as carefree as though the attempted lynching hadn't occurred. She wished she could shake herself loose from the strangling fingers of her own trouble. She was intelligent enough to know that her chances for happiness with her present fixation were nothing to speak of. She recalled the night, the animal like relish she had felt with the cold rain pelting down on her bare skin and the abrasive joy of the rough bath towel. Abruptly she changed the thought because it would progress to where she had awakened and felt the heavy body on her … the heavy body with the sour smell.

She heard a quiet step behind her and turned around. It was Geraldine.

"Is there anything else I can do, Miss Toni?"

"No thank you, Geraldine. I guess that's all. Pop's resting easily and I'll just sit here till I get sleepy."

"Why don't you let me fix you a stiff drink? It might make you sleep better."

Toni considered, then nodded. "That might be a good idea."

Geraldine disappeared and came back quietly with a highball. Toni took it and smiled her thanks.

"You might as well go on home, Geraldine. There isn't anything else … and thanks a lot."

"That's all right, Miss Toni, I was glad I could help." She stood uncertainly for a moment and Toni looked at her keenly. "Is there anything … ?"

"Yes'm. I don't think Mr. Jeff should stay in that room all alone. He might wake up and be out of his head or something."

"That's right. I'll …"

"No, please mam … let me stay. Mr. Jeff is always anxious for you to get all the sleep you can. You've had a bad night and I … well … I'm a lot stronger than you. I'll be glad to stay."

The tense urgency of Geraldine's voice penetrated, but Toni couldn't account for it. She searched the calm face as shown by the dying rays of the moon but there was only a certain breathless tension about the eyes. She wanted to stay … wanted very much to stay.

"Certainly Geraldine. I'd appreciate it if you'd stay."

Geraldine ducked her head in a quick bow and turned away. For a long time Toni sat and sipped her drink, thinking. She put the empty glass on the floor and stood up. She was a little dizzy from the drink but she felt relaxed and sleepy. She took one last look out across the dimly lighted lawn where even the katydids had ceased their rasping songs, turned and walked into the house, still thinking about Geraldine. Why had she been so anxious to stay? Probably taking cue from the loyalty of her grandmother.

Toni undressed and slipped into a sleeping garment fashioned after a play suit. It was thin and cool and she now had a frightful aversion to sleeping nude. Previous to her experience, she had preferred to sleep in the raw but now she couldn't bring herself to do it. She also paid meticulous attention to the door which she locked every night.

She leaped into bed, flouncing like a fish on dry land, landing spreadeagled in her favorite position, her head half buried in a soft pillow and her limbs pointing to all points of the compass.

Involuntarily her mind wandered back to Geraldine. She *had* been very anxious to stay…she had been the first to find Jeff sprawled at the foot of the steps since Toni had unaccountably slept through the whole thing only half awakening when the shots went off, taking some ten minutes to fight her way to full wakefulness. The shotgun blasts had wakened Granny and Geraldine and they had gotten to the house before Toni was fully awake. She'd never forget that Geraldine had carried her father from the stone walk to the living room couch without help…alone she had carried him and Jeff was no small man.

A tiny bright light suddenly glowed in Toni's brain. Could she be in love with Jeff? The thought was such an edged one that Toni sat upright in her bed. Well, what was there to prevent the emotion if the ingredients were present? She remembered Jeff's flustered look as he had come from the rear of the house the other day. Had he been to the kitchen? Was it an attraction to Geraldine that had made him flush so redly and say he had been thinking about a girl?

Toni thought of her acidulous stepmother and her lip curled only to smile with a certain devilish crinkling of her eyes. Given a choice between Lavender and Geraldine, what man could be blamed if he leaned toward the latter? A little ripple of laughter trickled from deep in Toni's chest and she slipped lithely from the bed and rammed her feet into a pair of bedroom slippers. Jeff's room was down the hall and to the left, just opposite Lavender's and Toni made for it with cautious soundless strides. There was a small table lamp on which sent a feeble fan of light through the door that stood several inches ajar.

When Geraldine came upstairs, she walked to the room and slid through the small opening in the door leaving it as it was, because it had a tendency to squeak and she didn't want to disturb the patient. She lifted a chair and placed it carefully near the head of the bed and sat down. She hitched it a few inches closer till she could peer directly into the face on the pillow. For a long time, she looked at him devouring every line in the placid face and conquered a desire to smooth the little laugh wrinkles at the corners of his eyes. She sat back and settled herself for the vigil.

Geraldine must have dropped off to sleep because Jeff's voice coming out of the night startled her and her eyes snapped open. He was looking at her with a queer fixed expression in his eyes.

"Antoinette, why aren't you in bed?"

Geraldine swallowed and felt a wave of cold flicker over her body. He thought she was his dead wife … he was living in the past. Bravely, she mustered her will. "I didn't feel sleepy," she said softly. "Go back to sleep."

He tried to sit up but she placed her hands on his shoulders. "Don't try to get up …."

"My head hurts," he said simply, laying back on the pillow. "I've been having a bad dream too. I dreamed that you were dead. Why does my head hurt and why is it bandaged?"

"You fell and cut your head on a stone," she said, hoping it would be the right thing to say.

He seemed satisfied with the explanation but tried to sit up again. She restrained him. "The doctor said you'd have to stay in bed for awhile. You'll be up in a few days."

He looked at her a long time. "You used to rub my head when it hurt," he said accusingly, childishly.

She pulled her chair closer and began to massage that part of his head that was not bandaged. He sighed and relaxed, soothed by the methodical movements of her strong fingers. The touch of his skin under her hand made her chest ache and a tear collected in each eye, and her breath became labored. He smiled and caught her hands in his.

"I think if you'll kiss me, I can go to sleep now." His words stabbed her like a poniard ... she'd have to ... she couldn't even think it out ... hesitate ... nothing ... go through with it. She bent over him and kissed his lips with infinite tenderness. His hand went behind her head pulling her close. When he let her go, he smiled and lay back on the pillow. "Don't stay up too late ...." He was asleep.

Geraldine sank back in the chair exhausted, her breast almost bursting from the charging emotions it housed. In the morning it would all be gone. For a few brief moments she had been loved dearly ... mistaken for some one who was dead. In the morning he would remember nothing ... nothing. In the morning he'd be the Boss again and she'd be a colored maid who worked in the house. Geraldine bent forward and buried her face in her hands weeping bitterly but silently.

Toni backed suddenly away from the door, her eyes burning from a hot surge of tears. She had witnessed the entire tableau and had watched every emotion that passed over Geraldine's face. She felt suddenly ashamed that she had been watching and yet she was conscious of a curious exultance. She glanced at Lavender's door and smiled victoriously through her tears. "You haven't been a wife to him," she thought, "but in the end the laugh will be on you." With a long shuddering sigh, Toni turned and made her way back to her room.

CHAPTER NINE

TWO DAYS AFTER he was shot, jeff sat on his verandah with a tall glass of iced tea in his hand. Toni sat beside him and watched him from the corner of her eyes. He seemed wrestling with some problem. His brows would knit up from time to time and he'd gnaw pensively at his lips.

"Something on your mind, Dad?"

Jeff started guiltily. "Er ... no ... yes. I feel fine, the headache is gone, but do you know I had some strange things happen to me when I was cracked out from the bullet."

"Like what?"

He frowned again and stared for a while out across the lawn. "It's hard to tell just how it felt but I had the strangest feeling that I was with your mother." He grinned. "Maybe I died and we met again in spirit."

Toni did not join his attempt at lightness. "That could not have been," she said with deadly seriousness. "You were not hurt that bad."

"Oh, I know that," he said deprecatingly. "I was just kidding but it was the most graphic thing I ever had in a dream. It was plain as day and yet I ...." He hesitated.

"What, Pop?"

He frowned again. "As plain as it was, there's a tiny feeling that it wasn't her at all. Oh, hell ... the whole thing is silly."

Toni said nothing but she could see that he was under tension by the little muscle that twitched like a tortured caterpillar

280

at the corner of his mouth. He savaged the bit of his pipe and tried several times to light it.

"It was her and yet it wasn't her," he said half to himself.

"Could you explain that a little better, Dad?"

He shook his head. "No, I couldn't. I know how foolish it sounds but there it is. I saw her as plainly as I see you and yet I have an equally certain knowledge that it wasn't her."

"You probably had fever," she said. "People have strange dreams at times like that."

"Sure, sure. I know. I've had nightmares and dreams before, but nothing like this. It was entirely too plain for a dream and it was a pretty shoddy thing for fate to do, too." His lips closed hard and stiff over his pipestem. Toni turned her head so he wouldn't see the tears in her eyes. She blinked rapidly and caught them surreptitiously in her handkerchief as they emerged from her eyes.

"What did the sheriff have to say?"

He took his pipe from his mouth and smiled. "It's great to be a figure in the parish. Alex assured me that I'd be put to no inconvenience. I'll have to appear before the grand jury probably but it'll be just a form. Alex knows."

"Has an eye on the November elections, eh?"

"Right. I'll bet a dollar Jasper and the rest of that rabble won't be molested either. Their vote counts as much as the next one."

"Someone should talk to Feathers."

Jeff nodded. "Someone should, but who would you nominate for the job?"

"I'm sure I don't know. I don't think I'd be up to it."

"Exactly. I've done some thinking on the subject and as I see it the only one, now this might sound a trifle silly but think it over, the only one to make the appeal is Bull himself."

"Say," Toni sat bolt upright, "it doesn't sound silly at all. It makes good sense. If Bull could be persuaded to see it... I'll bet he could make a good one too, after having run through that mill."

"That's the way it seems to me. I'd die of mortification if I had to tell her and since neither her father and mother chooses to realize what's going on, then you may be sure that any appeal to them would be asking for a row. I can see their looks of affronted dignity right now but you are sure they're bound to know."

"Of course they know. They are like a lot of parents … shut both eyes and pretend it isn't so. Just like Philip Wylie said … that a lot of people are sleeping with a lot of others but we just go along pretending it's all a lie invented by the communists or someone."

"I'd like to know what the initiating element was in Feather's case."

"It'll probably never be known. There's a lot that isn't known about the malady."

Geraldine came silently out on the porch and Toni watched her carefully. Her face was set but her eyes caressed Jeff as she stopped before him. "Can I get you some more tea, Mr. Jeff?"

"No thanks, Geraldine. I've been wanting to thank you for helping Toni the night I got hurt. She's been telling me how much help you were."

"That's all right, Mr. Jeff. I'm glad I could help. You got hurt trying to help Bull. There aren't many white people who would have done it."

Jeff smiled. "Well, Bull is worth helping. I could say I did it because it would have cost me a lot of money if they would have lynched him."

Geraldine took the empty glass from his hands. "You could say that, Mr. Jeff, but you won't." She turned and disappeared in the house.

"I guess that'll hold you for a while," jibed Toni. "You self-effacing people."

"It always makes me uncomfortable," he complained, "...Geraldine's directness. It takes away one's defenses."

"Those things can be an awful drag sometimes."

He looked at her quickly, but her eyes were wandering. "Yes," he agreed, "I can see where they would."

Toni's smooth brow furrowed slightly. "You know, so much has happened lately but I've been wondering. I haven't seen Lemuel in some time."

"Probably sulking somewhere after the beating I gave him. I wonder if he told on Bull." A sudden rage struck him. "I'm glad I thought of that...that you reminded me I mean. I got a few things to talk over with him."

"Not now," she protested. "You're not well and a bout of anger won't help any."

That night at supper, Lavender who had been as quiet as a mouse since Toni, in a storm of rage, ordered her away from Jeff the night he was shot, cleared her throat several times then asked, "Jefferson, have you seen Lemuel lately? I haven't seen him for days."

"No, I haven't," said Jeff shortly, "and if I find out that he set that mob on Bull, he'll wish he had kept going."

Lavender stopped eating and sniffled into her napkin. "You are not at all charitable, Jefferson. Lemuel is not a normal boy. He...."

"If he isn't, then the place for him is at Jackson," he said viciously. His temper was none of the best at the present and he was not feeling at all charitable. "He chases the colored women and if it keeps up, that's where he will be put. I've had enough of him and his trouble making."

"That *woman*," she put a wealth of disgust and poison in the phrase. "She's the one who made the trouble. She's the one that should be put in Jackson."

"Probably," agreed Jeff, "but she is not my daughter and it isn't my place to put her there. At least she keeps her mouth shut and doesn't go around shrieking that she's been raped. Whatever she does, she does in as much secrecy as people like Lemuel will let her."

Lavender buried her face in her napkin and ran from the room.

"Now," said Toni balefully, "we can enjoy our supper."

The next morning after breakfast, Jeff wandered to the barn where the music of trace chains told of work animals being readied for the day's work.

Overhead came the whistling whoosh of a buzzard coming in on a bombing run at dizzy speed. He watched it out of sight beyond the lip of the bluff, then turned to Limm, the cattle wrangler.

"Limm, jump on your horse and run over there and see what those buzzards are after. Some old cow must have fallen over the bluff."

Limm, long and cadaverous, nodded and leaped on his unsaddled horse and cantered toward the bluff.

Jeff walked on to the barn where he stood about making suggestions and giving orders until gradually the Negroes had gone to their respective fields riding their mules sideways.

Having a slight headache, he walked back toward the house. He heard a clatter of hooves and turned to see Limm riding hard across the pasture. He had a handful of the horse's mane and was leaning low over its neck slapping it under the belly with the reins at every jump. Now what, thought Jeff, as he stopped. Limm slid off the horse and almost fell.

"What's the matter with you?" asked Jeff with irritation. "You look like you've seen a ghost."

Limm passed a quivering hand over his face and gulped noisily. "I done seen wusser'n dat."

"What is it?"

Limm swallowed again and clenched his teeth to keep them from chattering. "Hh-h-hit's Mr. Lem."

Jeff cursed beneath his breath. "Where?"

"Oo-o-over dey...stuck up on dat...dat ole car body by dat big 'simmon tree...musta fell frum de bluff...blow flies...Lawd...Lawd...."

Jeff leaped on the horse. "Get up behind me." Limm did as he was ordered and together they struck out toward the persimmon tree that stood on the edge of the bluff where the pasture joined the woods.

Jeff was not normally a squeamish man but the sight which met his eyes as he rode up to the old car body nearly threw him. Lemuel was impaled as neatly as an olive on a toothpick, the windshield support having entered his back in the mid thoracic region and come out just below the sternum. The torrid summer weather had turned him black and he was swollen almost beyond recognition. His jaws were spread wide open, his tongue, black and distended, protruded between his teeth in a leering grimace. A shred of flesh torn off by the blunt metal shearing through his body had clung to the end of the support and dried curling like a drake's tail.

His body had bent to a horrible angle, the feet in the front seat and the head resting on the rusty motor; his back broken and skull flattened from the impact. Swarms of blue bottle flies covered the body, their gauzy wings seeming to fan the tearing stench out, making Jeff clench his teeth against nausea. In the trees surrounding the area black vultures gasped and coughed asthmatic opinions back and forth among themselves waiting till the men should leave so they could resume their feast. So far, they had managed to do little damage.

Jeff picked up a branch and hurled it at the nearest tree and the birds launched themselves heavily into the air scampering upward, into the sky. "I'd better stay here with him, Limm, in case those buzzards come back. You go back to the barn and get one of those old haystack tarps. Don't get a good one because it'll have to be burnt. Tell … no just bring the tarp back and tell no one. I'll have to call Preston Varden to come out. He's the only one who can do Lem any good, now."

Limm took a look at the body and shuddered. "I wouldn't tetch 'im rat now fer a cahload o' 'possums. Mr. Varden sho weks fer his money." Limm leaped on the horse and cantered off. Jeff watched him as he threaded the narrow trail to the top of the bluff, disappeared, he looked back at the mortal remains of Lemuel and tried to feel sorry for the man. How had he fallen? Jeff looked back to the lip of the bluff. It was not humanly possible for Lemuel to have fallen from the edge of the bluff and struck the old car. Some other than natural agency had done the job because Lemuel would have had to leap at least twelve feet outward in order to strike where he did. Could he have committed suicide … ?

No, Jeff shook his head in answer to the question. Lemuel wasn't the type, to begin with, and no one with more brains than a grasshopper would leap from the bluff as a means of self-destruction. If it had not been for the old wreck of a car Lemuel *might* have been killed but more likely he would have only gotten badly broken up. No suicide. How then and why? Could he have been thrown or pushed? Pushed probably, but he would have struck the base of the bluff some fifteen feet from the bottom because it began to slope outwards at that point.

Thrown? Jeff shook his head. Lem was no giant but he weighed all of one hundred seventy pounds. Being short, he looked heavier but even so what man could have simply picked him up and tossed him over the bluff like a sack of hay? Jeff pondered, listening for Limm, hoping he'd hurry. The stench seemed to follow him where he went, pulling big drops of sweat from him and his breakfast seemed very restless.

With an effort, Jeff tried to concentrate. Who, in the entire parish was strong enough to pick a grown man up and throw him bodily over the edge? Bull Fallon! Bull Fallon could do it with a bigger man than Lem and who had a better reason than Bull for doing it? Jeff's eyes narrowed. It was no certainty but it sounded reasonable enough to send him into a frenzy of action. Like a goat he ran up the side of the bluff holding on to vines and myrtle bushes. Twenty feet from the bottom he looked down. Five or six feet below him was a bump of red clay which was just right for his purpose, being lined up with the car.

Jeff leaped out and down, landing rump first on the hard ground. It jarred him horribly, making his recent injury send jagged knives of pain through his brain. He continued to fall and almost did the job too well. Headed straight for the old car, he had to perform an acrobatic twist that would have done credit to a circus performer and getting his legs under him for a second, made a terrific leap outward, barely managing to clear the car. He got up, walked over to a young gum tree, leaned against it and breathed heavily, holding his palms tightly against the gripping pains in his head. Sweat poured down his face and a fresh burst of odor from the corpse turned his stomach over so suddenly that he had no time to get set and had to let his breakfast do what it would.

Feeling relieved, he broke the top from a small pine and proceeded to beat the red clay dust from his khakis then he walked back to the fly feast and looked over the trail he had made in the dirt and grass. Eight feet above the body of the car, the trail ended making it appear that Lem had fallen from above and struck the ground to bound up and strike the car which was the only way it could have happened had the man actually fallen. Satisfied, Jeff walked away and sat beneath a tree. He brought out pipe and pouch and began to fill the bowl of the much used briar.

By the time he had it going, he saw Limm come over the lip of the bluff with a mouldy tarpaulin across old Dapp's haunches.

As Limm rode up, his eyes were showing that amount of white about the irises which indicate great fright.

"Now what?" asked Jeff, prepared for anything.

"De law ... at de house," gasped Limm. "Stopped me and axt me wheh you wuz ...."

"Well, why didn't you tell him?"

Limm's jaw grew slack with amazement. Telling the law *anything* was something Limm viewed with considerable alarm even during normal times. With a corpse on their hands things were distinctly abnormal ... so Limm reasoned.

"You means you want him *hyer*?"

"Of course. We'll have to get him some time, so why not?"

Limm shook his head vehemently. "I don' b'lieve in having no truck wid de law notime."

Jeff took the tarp from the horse and with one hearty swing covered the body and most of the car. "Now trot right back to the house and try to lie out of whatever lie you told in the first place. Tell Alex to get down here right now, but don't tell another soul ... got that?"

"Yassuh."

"O.K. Get going."

Limm got, showing by his very reluctance that he could get along very well without any truck with the law.

Twenty minutes later, Alex Touchstone, followed by Avery Garder, his number one deputy, came to the edge of the bluff. "What you got down there, Jeff," called the sheriff.

"Something pretty ugly, Alex. Come on down and see for yourself. Turn down the bluff to your left and take that cattle path down when you hit the woods. You can make it all right."

It took them ten minutes to travel the path and as they came up, Avery put his hand over his nose. "You got a corpse. Don't nuthin' else in the world smell like that."

Jeff nodded and together they walked to the old wreck. Jeff whipped the tarp from the body and stood back.

"Arrragh," croaked Alex, backing hastily away holding his nose and fanning at the flies that had been aroused.

"Jesus," mumbled Avery, under his hand backing away also. "Who is it?"

"It's Lemuel, my brother-in-law."

Alex took out a big pocket handkerchief and held it over his florid nose. "How'd it happen, Jeff?"

Jeff shrugged. "You got me. We've missed him for the last couple of days and since I had to beat the hell out of him the other day, I didn't think it strange. He was an odd one, anyhow. Furtive and sort of creepy. Stayed drunk most of the time."

"You say him and you had trouble, Jeff?" asked Avery, raising his eyebrows.

"Yes."

"What about?"

"He was chasing one of the Negro women and one of my men didn't like it, especially when he tried to get him to play pimp."

Alex shook his head. "Some niggers don't like that."

"Who was the nigger, Jeff?"

"Bull Fallon."

"Uh oh…" Alex flushed at the memory of the dilemma in which the attempted lynching and its repercussions had placed him. "That's the nigger they tried to lynch, ain't it?"

Jeff nodded. "Yes it is." He didn't care to go into the matter, and neither did Alex Touchstone, who proved it by letting that facet of it drop.

"I doubt," said Jeff, thinking he'd better get in a word now, "that Bull would have done it. He had too much else on his mind and I know for a fact that Lemuel was alive at supper the same night. The mob caught Bull in bed and when he heard them, he took out for the house. After he had been freed, he was too beat up to do anything."

Alex nodded, obviously glad to agree in order to stop the conversation. Avery began to circle the wrecked car, looking for evidence. He stopped by one rear fender and looked up. "What'd he do, fly?"

"Looks like it," agreed Jeff. "Unless he jumped or was thrown."

"He'd be damn fool to jump," said Avery. "He couldn'ta knowed he'd light on that there old buggy and if he didn't he wouldn'ta done nothin' but get broke up."

Jeff nodded but said nothing and Alex pulled a stem of green bull grass and chewed it absentmindedly. "Nobody throwed him either," averred Avery looking up again. "They'da had to chuck him a good ten feet out before he'da lit on …. Hey, look up there." Avery scrambled up the side of the bluff, taking the same course that Jeff had taken, climbing it the first time. Avery stopped opposite the little ledge and pointed. "That's where the body landed. You can see where it rolled on down and hit that there bump and bounced. That's why it hit the car … bounced there and left the ground and stuck that upright through his belly."

"Never mind all the details," growled the sheriff. "We can see where it went through. I guess that's what happened. Avery, you go back and get the coroner. He'll have to see him before he's moved."

Jeff said, "Would you mind telling Pres Varden to come out … better tell him what sort of shape the body's in so he'll come prepared."

Avery nodded and started to leave. He turned to the sheriff. "Look's like to me that's what happened. He either fell or was pushed off the bluff. He lit up there and bounced onto the car." He looked at Jeff. "You can bet he wasn't throwed, Mr. Jeff. Ain't nobody in the world coulda throwed a man that size that far out." Jeff nodded slowly as though reluctant to believe it, at the same time heaving a silent sigh of relief.

Alex walked away and finding himself a tree, sat and prepared to wait. "Do your folks know about it, Jeff?"

"They know he's missing but they don't know that he's dead."

"You might as well go on and tell 'em. I'll wait here till Avery gets back…. You go ahead and I'll take care of everything here."

"That's nice of you, Alex."

Alex jumped to his feet. "Not at all," he said heartily in his best campaign manner. "You go ahead and let me earn my money for a change…. Oh, by the way, I came out to tell you that you'll have to appear before a grand jury just so they can find a no true bill and make everything right. Nothing but a form."

"Thanks, Alex," Jeff turned away. He was moved to vote for Alex not because he was a good man but because the ones running against him would probably be worse. Alex wasn't the sort to ruin his chances at the polls, and as a peace officer, he was good enough as long as things went well. Other politicians with a great deal more at stake acted no different than he, so why hold that against the man.

When Jeff reached the house, he saw Lavender and Toni standing on the porch looking his way. It was a little too much to suppose that they had not suspected something to be amiss, what with all the odd activity, but he wished there was some way out of having to talk about it. Lavender, he knew, would throw a fit and he didn't feel up to enduring one of them. His head ached and he was still nauseated. He felt he could still smell the stench and had an overpowering desire to take a bath in spite of having taken one before breakfast.

Before he reached the steps, Lavender started. "What on earth is going on, Jefferson? Limm wouldn't talk except for whispers to the sheriff and…."

"You'd better brace yourself, Lavender."

Her hand went to her throat. "Oh … not … Lemuel?"

He nodded. He felt that if he had to be sympathetic, he'd vomit again, realizing suddenly how much in his life was gesture at which his instinct rebelled and how brutally he had beaten it down to conform.

Lavender swayed and leaned against a column for support then she stiffened. "Tell me … ."

Jeff mounted the steps and sank into a chair, noting as he did so a queer gleam of triumphant malice in Toni's eyes. Wondering passively at this phenomenon, he said, "He was either pushed, jumped, or fell over the bluff. He was killed instantly."

Now she'll faint, he told himself, and I'll have to catch her, but she didn't. Instead she sighed sadly and dropped her hands. "Poor boy," she said. "Too bad he had to come to such an end. He was a brilliant boy at one time."

Jeff sat up in surprise. "Lemuel?"

She nodded slowly. "Yes. When he was going to the University of Connecticut. He had a wonderful future … brilliant marks … ."

"What happened?"

She turned on him like a tigress. "None of your goddam business," she screamed, her face distorted and burning with hatred and malice. For a few seconds she faced him, her eyes wild and flaming, then she turned and fled through the door into the hall and up the stairs.

"Well," said Toni, letting her breath go gustily. "What do you make of that?"

Jeff tried to quiet the leaping nerve in his face with a hard hand and shook his head. "You got me there, Kitten. She sure blew up didn't she?"

Toni sat beside him on the arm of the chair. "Why don't you go to bed, Dad. You're not well enough for all this. It'll make you sick again."

He rubbed his face. "Kitten, get on the phone and call Alcide. Tell him to come over here if he can possibly make it. I feel the need of a good talking to."

She got up quickly. "That's just what you need."

Jeff watched her slim curved figure disappear into the hallway and sighed. Everything was topsy turvy at Fomalhaut. A woman who had placed one of his Negroes at the mercy of a mob, then had rescued him. A daughter who had been raped in her own bed. A wife who was no wife at all. A brother-in-law who wanted Negro women but who was now dead. His own dream that was so graphic but untrue. The devastation wrought by Geraldine every time she was in his presence.

Dr. Fontenot was not in and couldn't be reached but Maud promised Toni she'd have him call as soon as he could be contacted.

"I'm going to have a cup of coffee, Dad. Care to join me?"

He nodded slowly. "Yes… I'll have one… anything to be doing something."

Toni left the verandah and sneaking into her father's room took two capsules from a box on his bed table.

Downstairs again she found Geraldine. "In about five minutes," she instructed, "will you bring a couple of cups of coffee to the porch and empty these two capsules into this deep blue cup. That'll be for Pop. I'll take the yellow one. It's that sedative Dr. Fontenot left. He's got to calm down or something'll happen."

Geraldine's eyes were softly understanding. "Yes, Miss Toni. I'll be there after a while. You go on back."

Toni walked back to the porch, feeling relieved. "Geraldine'll be here in a minute with the coffee, Pop," she said as she sat down. "Why don't you lie down for a while, after you drink your coffee?"

He sighed. "I'll try it if you say so, but I doubt that I could lie down and stay there very long."

Geraldine gave coffee to Toni first, so there'd be no possibility of a mistake and Toni, who had envisioned putting the cup near his hand so he'd take it, silently applauded the colored girl's cleverness. Jeff drank his coffee without gusto but with a certain grim determination. Fifteen minutes later he began to feel quieter and half an hour later felt a little drowsy.

"You know I might be able to sleep a little if I'd lie down."

"Go to bed, Dad. I'll take care of everything."

"Nothing to take care of, Kitten. I've sent for Varden already. He'll remove the corpse after the coroner has taken a look. I guess they'll bring men out for the inquest. Tell 'em I can't be disturbed. Tell 'em I'm a sick man."

"Don't you worry," she said grimly. "They won't bother you."

CHAPTER TEN

A MONTH AFTER LEMUEL'S burial, Lavender left for Connecticut to visit relatives and Toni and Jeff on orders from Dr. Fontenot left for a trip to the West Indies.

Lavender returned and finding them still away, promptly left again. In mid September Jeff and Toni returned and three weeks later, Lavender, for the second time.

Toni and Jeff were darkly tanned and looking very fit, as did the young man they brought back with them. When he was introduced to Dr. Fontenot, the doctor felt a quick twinge of interest because it was obvious that his presence made Toni ill at ease. It was also obvious that he was badly smitten with her, following her every move with his eyes and hanging on her every word.

Albert Fontenot walked into his father's study-surgery-office one afternoon and flopped in a handy chair. "Guess who I saw catching the plane at Harding Field this morning?"

"I'm not at all good at guessing games as you should know by now," said the father acidly, putting down his reel and oil can. "Who was it?"

"Tall, broad, and bronzesome … Toni's new fellow. Devall's his name, isn't it?"

The old man cast a malignant eye at his drink which melting ice had weakened beyond repair. "I glean from that hodgepodge of words that it was Toni's fellow you saw board the plane?"

"That's right and he didn't look happy. I tried to engage him in conversation and got an unintelligible mumble. All, I take it, is not well with the romance."

"Ummm… well, I'm glad you told me. I think I'll be paying them a visit." He put his reel away and put on a battered felt hat.

Jeff met the doctor at the steps with outstretched hand. "You must have heard my mental radar signal."

"Why? Something wrong?"

"Everything's wrong. Toni blew her top last night and I had to give her some of those pills you left me when I got that crease. She hasn't left her room all day and I can think of no good reason to go in. In fact I'm afraid to."

"I'll go up. A doctor has a ticket to every room."

In thirty minutes he was back, his face grave and still. He sat down heavily. "I had hoped for a lot from that trip. Too much maybe. She's right back where she was in the summer. We haven't gained an inch."

Jeff paled. "Is it that bad?"

"It's that bad. Devall stood it as long as he could then he seized her and kissed her … forcibly, the idiot."

Jeff brutalized the stem of his pipe. "I thought something like that had happened but I didn't dare ask. Just how bad do you think it is, Alcide?"

"It couldn't be any worse," he said without animation. "It's terrible. If I thought it would do any good, I'd recommend Askins. He's in Bainsville and the best psychiatrist I know and he'd come here but I don't think it would do any good."

Jeff shook his head slowly. "Well, that's that. If I had been able to do anything I'd say I've now given up, but I never did anything. I'm beat."

They were silent for a long time, each submerged in thought. Finally the doctor said, "Had any more raids by Feathers?"

"No, not a one. I made Bull go talk to her. It was a job and he was frightened to death but he managed it someway. He says that she didn't answer him yea or nay but I do know she hasn't been on the place since that night. Maybe she has other outlets."

"Let's hope so. Nothing ever came out about Lemuel's push or fall."

"There are two people … no three that know the truth of it," said Jeff in a low voice. "Bull, Hilda, and me. He told me but I had about figured it out … considered it at least. Lemuel attacked Hilda when she went for help. Bull had passed out from his beating, and Lemuel was about to succeed when Bull came to and heard the sounds of the fight. He came on the scene just in time, picked Lemuel up like a three weeks' old puppy and threw him over the edge of the bluff. He didn't realize at the time what he had done and it was not till Lemuel's body was found that he knew. They kept it to themselves till just before we went on the trip. It was the night before they married that they came to me and told me."

Fontenot smiled and tugged at his beard. "And you told them to keep their mouths shut."

"I did just that," said Jeff challengingly.

"I'm glad to know that," said a voice behind them. They turned to see the spare figure of Lavender standing in the doorway. They had been so interested in their conversation they hadn't heard her approach. She gave them a scathing look and disappeared in the house.

Jeff gripped his face hard with both hands. "Last spring it began to rain on this plantation. It has poured ever since. I wonder, Alcide, just how much a man can stand."

Dr. Fontenot's goatee bobbed up and down rapidly. "It is at times like this that I consider murder to be a very salutary solution. Don't let that remark make you do anything foolish, Jeff. If you kill her off be sure to burn the body and scatter the ashes. I'll say I took her to the train on the first leg on a twenty year trip around the world."

Jeff grinned a little. "I doubt that I'd have the nerve to murder anyone, now, Alcide."

The doctor took his leave a little while later and Jeff sat in the gathering darkness staring out across the quiet lawn, his mind as much of a void as he could make it. When Lavender hurried past him wrapped in a short coat against the gathering chill, it didn't occur to him to ask her where she was going at this odd hour, until ten minutes later. Toni came quietly through the door and sat on the glider.

"Feel better, Kitten?"

"A little. Where was Lavender going?"

"I don't know. What say we slink off to town and see a Tarzan picture? I need some diversion."

"Why not?" She went into the house and got a coat, bringing him a leather jacket. "It's getting cold nights."

It was Limm Washington complaining loudly and bitterly that everything happened to him, who found Lavender the next morning. Trembling and ashen faced, he told Jeff about it. Immediately, even before calling the sheriff, Jeff called the doctor and they arrived almost together. Again, Alex Touchstone and Avery Garder went over the same ground, finding not a single clue. Dr. Fontenot, pleading age and infirmity, stood on the edge of the bluff and looked down ... when he wasn't looking about. Then he sat down very suddenly, eased something into his pocket, then stood up immediately, unnoticed by anyone below.

Two hours later, the coroner's jury, remembering a similar "accident" was more cagey but scarcely more helpful in rendering a verdict of "death at the hands of person or persons unknown."

Toni, Jeff and the doctor were seated on the verandah. "I feel numb and stupid like I had been on a bender," said Jeff mechanically. "I didn't do it, Alcide."

"Hah," the doctor snorted. "I knew that. In your recent state of mind you wouldn't have done such an excellent job. Any prime suspects?"

"None, not a single one. I'm not up to any keen thinking lately anyway."

"Why not me as a suspect?" asked Toni. "I can't think when I've ever been so pleased over anything."

Jeff smiled weakly. "Mainly because you were with me at a moving picture at the time of her death as guessed by the coroner and we both saw her leave the house as did Geraldine."

Something clicked in the doctor's mind and he closed his eyes quickly to avoid letting the light through. He felt the steady pressure of a hard object in his pants' pocket. He rose to go. "I'll have to be moving, folks. I'll be back tomorrow … going to have services here, Jeff?"

"No, I'm shipping the body back to Connecticut. I'm sending Lem's along at the same time. Nice gesture, you know. He wouldn't like to be down here all alone."

The doctor's eyes twinkled. "Indubitably … indubitably. I'll see you soon then … probably before the end of the week."

When the doctor arrived home, he routed Albert out of a textbook where he was looking up some strange malady. "I'd make him eat that book, Jane," snapped the old man. "Reading up on something that a soda mint will cure."

"He either reads or sleeps, Pop. There's nothing I can do about it. He claims I keep him awake a lot so he has to catch naps."

"He'd claim that as a defensive measure. Come on offspring. I have work for you to do."

Albert groaned and put his book down. "I like Cecil better than I do you."

"Never mind your impertinence … come on."

In the little laboratory back of the office, the old man took an object from his pocket and handed it to Albert. "Take a look."

Albert did. "What is it?"

"Dummy, it's the heel of a shoe."

"Am I to turn cobbler after a day's work as belly seamstress?"

"No, tell me what that heel walked around in. I'll be in the office having a drink with my lovely daughter-in-law. I hope it takes you all night."

Thirty minutes later, Albert called his father. When he entered the laboratory, his son wore a look of tired triumph. "There you are, my dear Holmes." He held out a sheet of paper on which he had jotted his findings.

His father scanned it. "Hummmm … traces of food particles, namely protein, starch, vegetable matter. Saponified matter … in plain English, soap. Well, it would appear that the heel had been in a kitchen. Scrubbing same probably. Wouldn't you say that?"

Albert nodded. "I'd say that. From these clues, I'd say the murderer is a famous chef who put too much red pepper in the chili thereby murdering the victim who had a passion for chili."

"And," said the doctor tartly, "if you did, I'd say you are the ass I have long suspected you to be. Now, Merlin, take that heel and that sheet of paper, plus your memory of the last forty-five minutes and burn them very thoroughly in that little furnace there. I do not ever wish to hear the subject mentioned again either in jest or otherwise."

Albert folded his hands in front of him and bowed respectfully. "It shall be done, my father, even as you say."

"You're dang tootin' it'll be done," said the little man taking a pull at his drink.

It was one of those sweltering September days that can at times outdo August. The sky was an inverted brass bowl that seemed to reflect the burnished disc of the sun and concentrate it all to earth. Not a breath of air stirred. Cattle, horses, chickens and man had sought the shade and relief, each in his own way. Trees were beginning to turn faintly yellow, brown and red, but as yet only the pecan trees and sycamores had lost an appreciable amount of leaves. It hadn't rained in a month and a fine coating of gritty dust covered all low growing vegetation.

Toni was in the lowest mood of her life. The future looked as black as had the recent past. She could still feel the quaking revulsion that had covered her when Phil Devall confronted her suddenly in the dark hall and kissed her again and again. She grew nauseated at the thought and sucked on a piece of ice which she fished from her coke. Phil was a fine man with a good future. He was clean cut and handsome and in every way desirable and eligible. With Phil went her last hope of shoving into the mists of the past her revulsion at the touch of a man. She thought of Lemuel and Lavender. At least they were past all feeling. If they did not enjoy or thrill to life, at least they did not harbor hopelessness and despair.

Drawn by an almost hypnotic desire to see the spot of the other two deaths she dropped her house jacket to the floor at her feet and donned shorts and a halter. There was an automatic numbness to her movements, like a sleep walker.

She stood on the edge of the bluff and looked at the old car that had been Lemuel's death. Lavender, they said had been unlucky. If she hadn't broken her neck, she would have hardly been scratched. Unlucky... how did they know that? Had anyone ever come back to tell a story? She recalled a Jack London story about a coolie that was to be beheaded and the jailer tried to comfort him by saying the guillotine might even tickle.... no one knew just what it felt like. The coolie's last conscious thought had been that the jailer was wrong... it didn't tickle.

Maybe they were better off... maybe *she* would be better off. A shudder shook her but she took a step nearer the edge.

"That's the trouble with this country," said a voice. "No mountains. A little tumble like that would only sprain your ankle."

Toni gasped and whirled about. Sitting only thirty feet away, his feet hanging over the edge of the bluff was a young man. A man with humorous eyes that also had a certain look of cynical wisdom. His face was a little too craggy to be handsome but it was a good face with a very sensitive, slightly curved nose. His mouth betrayed his eyes because it was mobile, wide and she could tell it laughed easily and it had a certain tender quirk at the corners.

"Two people died on this spot," she said a little nettled.

"Wrong," he corrected easily and pointed. "Down there, and they were just unlucky... or lucky, depending on the point of view."

"I had no intention of jumping," she said, anger making her voice slip a little at the corners.

He shrugged. "I didn't say you did. You were considering it in the abstract, let us say. I'm sure that you were not standing at the site of two deaths wondering what you'd wear to South of the Border tonight."

"I don't think I like you," she said angrily for lack of something better.

"You haven't had a chance to think on the matter at all. I'd advise against any hasty opinions. It is much easier to defer than to change them."

"Oh, you know everything, don't you?" she cried, stamping her foot.

"Practically," he said with infuriating coolness. "I will admit that women have me stumped. The more I learn the less I believe."

"Now, isn't that just too bad? The womanhood of the nation should go into mourning."

"If I should die, there'd be a wave of suicides that'd make the country weep from one end to the other."

"*Oh...*" Toni was totally without words this time. He got to his feet and approached her, grinning like an adolescent. "Let's cut out all this nonsense, Toni. I'm Ike Blumendahl."

He held out his hand and for some reason, which she half resented, her anger drained out of her leaving her feeling very young, young and foolish. She took the hand almost shyly and they both burst out laughing. It was such a relief to laugh, that Toni went in over her head and she couldn't stop. Tears came to her eyes and she started crying. He caught her by the shoulders and shook her, but she only laughed and cried the harder. Regretfully, he released her left shoulder and slapped her a stinging blow on the cheek. She gasped, touched the spot and started crying, just crying. He drew her to his chest and smoothed her soft tousled hair and said kind things to her.

"There now," he said, as her crying slackened. "Take hanky and blow nose." She giggled shakily and blew loudly on his handkerchief, folding it neatly and sanitarily and handing it back to him.

"Feel better?"

"Much better, thanks. You … you woman beater!"

"The old cave man stuff gets 'em every time. Nothing like it."

"Won't you come to the house? I'll build you a drink or something."

"I'll take the drink. I'm just out of school and I'm an inveterate gong kicker."

Geraldine served them the drinks on the verandah and as Toni arranged herself comfortably on the glider, Ike took swift inventory. Her legs were long and slender, but he could tell that they were not the soft spongy legs of the sedentary woman. They were hard and tan and muscular, straight and made to walk and run with. Her waist, where the halter exposed it, was smooth and narrow and he noticed the fine luminous quality of her skin. Her breasts were full, erect and excitingly pointed beneath their covering which all but failed at its task. He let a little silent quake of a laugh shake him from within. His mother had put this thing up to him as a task, which due to her unwise boasting had to be done to save the family honor. He could see that it would probably be the most delightful task he had ever undertaken. He recalled his paternal caresses while she was crying and decided that her revulsion wasn't as deeply rooted as was supposed. Her hysterics, the slap, plus confusion and anger had been stronger than the revulsion. He also sensed an unutterable relief, like the breaking of a long tension. Her face was placid and relaxed and her eyes were laughing and full of mischief.

"I guess," she said, stroking the moisture from the glass, "that I was pretty much of a baby."

"Men and women," he said, frowning at her, "have long placed the therapeutic value of tears second to a certain stupid loyalty to a calm exterior. The straight face under all stresses. There are things more foolish but offhand, I can't think of any."

She looked at him with wide eyes. "You know, you sound just like Dr. Fontenot."

"Then," he said, his eyes twinkling with good humor, "your Dr. Fontenot must be a very wise man. My mother said he's a devil that reads people's minds."

Toni sat up suddenly. "Oh ... you must be Missy Blumendahl's son. I didn't know she had any children."

"She had one. That one took all the time she had to spare."

"I'm ... I'm amazed. What on earth were you doing on the bluff?"

"Two things. I was looking at the river ... the view is superb and I was hoping you'd come out."

"Why that's silly. Why didn't you come to the house? I'd have been glad to show you the view."

He shook his head vigorously. "Uh uh, I like it my way. I like to do strange things at unexpected times. Like for instance, as soon as I finish this drink, I'm going home and bathe and dress. I'm coming back to supper and then we're going to South of the Border for some dancing and possibly get a little tiddily."

She made a face at him. "How do you know I'll go with you?"

"I didn't ask, did I? There's just one thing. You mustn't expect any necking. I detest it and I never saw the girl I'd kiss." He didn't look at her but the angle of his vision showed the look of relief that passed over her face.

"I think I'll be able to bear up," she said with a chuckle.

"See there, you've agreed to go already. No trouble for the great Ike. Technique is what does it."

"I could refuse, just to burst that egotistical bubble."

"Then it would show that you were doing it out of vindictiveness which is a sop for small souls. I have every reason to believe that the dimensions of yours are positively cyclopean."

Toni burst into a gurgle of mirth. "You are the most abandoned nut I ever met."

He bent her an arch look. "Careful, squirrel. I have a thin shell but the meat is excellent. See you about five thirty."

He leaped from the porch and was gone. Ten minutes later she heard a car start just within the fringe of woods bordering the bluff. She sighed and laughed aloud. It felt good to be able to do that. She got up and went inside singing at the top of her voice. She was young, much too young to interrupt a happy mood with analytical thought.

As Ike escorted Toni to the car, he glanced appreciatively at the white dress she wore. He paid a great deal of attention to the exquisite fit and the delightful slide of her thighs beneath its softly draping folds.

"What do you call that material?"

"What? Oh … the material. I don't know. It's some sort of synthetic stuff I got in St. Thomas. A native woman made it and I don't think I ever had a dress that fit better."

"It is certain," he said with laughter just beneath the surface of his voice, "that a dress never had a better torso to fit."

Toni laughed easily, and felt a little surprised. Laughter hadn't been easy this past summer.

At the club they found an excellent colored orchestra and after the first round of drinks and a few games of bingo, at which Ike won a gigantic doll and fifty dollars, they took to the almost deserted dance floor. Toni was light as a feather on her feet, yet she was weighty enough to make Ike know he had an armful of delightful woman. Ike was tall and lithe and together they made people notice them. They both had perfect time and a flair for the exotic and spectacular. Ike bribed a rhumba from the band with Toni's recent trip in mind and they wriggled swiftly into the first steps. Toni suddenly tore away and walked quickly to the table. Ike followed, his eyes narrowed, not in question, but in intense concentration. As she sat down, they opened... he understood.

"I'm sorry, Ike, I...."

He waved a hand to indicate that it was nothing. "Never mind, squirrel. I was sort of weary, anyhow. Waiter?"

"Yassuh."

"Another round of drinks, only this time, make them double." The waiter nodded respectfully. He moved away.

"Who'd expect to find a nice place like this way out in the country? I heard about it from some tourists up in Maryland and I made a mighty vow to visit it."

"Does it equal your expectations?" she asked reluctantly following his lead.

"Surpassed 'em. I'm a clubber by nature. My mother was one before me."

Toni felt a warm rush of affection for Ike. The little unpleasantness, he had ignored so totally that it might not have happened. She wondered what had turned him against necking.

"How does it happen that you are so averse to necking," she said in a bantering tone.

"You won't change my mind on that. It ain't sanitary."

"A bacteriophobe, I take it?"

"Dyed in the wool."

"Well, I wasn't about to twist your arm. I just wondered about it. Unusual to say the least."

"You have known me only a short time," said Ike with a grin. "Just wait a while. You haven't scratched the surface."

"I'll bet I haven't."

"You will allow me to hang around, won't you?"

Her face darkened. "I'm sort of contaminated, Ike. Maybe you hadn't better."

He was silent for a moment and when in curiosity, she finally mustered up enough courage to look, he had a grin on his face that showed what a sound set of sparkling white teeth he had.

"Is it that funny?" she said, sparking a little.

"It's twice that funny." He sobered. "What made you pick me for such a thorough-going dunce as to be moved by any mass reaction? I know all about it. My mother has an espionage system that'd make the F. B. I. look like Junior Red Ryders. She knows everything and she doesn't mis-value much." He stopped and looked at her seriously. "What say we whip this goddam thing, Toni?"

The waiter brought the drinks and Toni seized hers avidly and tossed it down. She tried to see Ike again but tears made him an indistinct blur.

"No one can help me," she said through tight suffering lips.

"That's right," agreed Ike. "*You've* got to do it. All I can do is to try to keep you occupied, kid you along, and come around once in a while, since it seems that the manhood of this country is such that you're lucky to find out about it so soon. Think what it would be like married to one of them."

Toni reached over and seized Ike's drink.

"*Put it down, Toni!*" His voice lashed her across the face like a whip and she almost dropped the drink in her haste to obey the blazing command. Ike, then smiled at her so winsomely that she weakened, the rage died like a guttering flame and she held her face in her hands and wept from sheer nervous relief.

"That's the ticket, squirrel. Snort and slobber to your heart's content, then we'll blow hard and dance."

Her head came up and she wiped her eyes. "I could *kill* you."

"Faith and bejasus, and whoi would ye be after murtherin' me, now?"

"Because you make me so mad I could scream and before I can even open my mouth, you've done some silly thing to make me all...."

"It's that weird mixture of Hebrew and Deutsch … a sort of composite magnetism which mows down all opposition. We can't have you funnelling drinks and getting top-ply. Not here. Some night we'll go out on Big Buff Creek and get stinko but you're in the public eye right now. That's all they'd want, you know. You'd not only be a loose woman but a loose drunken woman. I'm sorry I barked at you but you are so fast with the flagon."

"You may be good for me if I don't wind up hating you."

"No danger of that. I have too much respect for that excellent if somewhat underdeveloped mind of yours. You're young and maturity will come in time. In fact, you had rather a rush of it, this past summer. You'll hate me a dozen times but I won't hate you and you'll recover."

Toni clenched her hands and her eyes supplicated. "Promise you won't ever hate me."

"That's a promise. You couldn't make me hate you. I can be a pretty hateful person at times …. Let's dance."

CHAPTER ELEVEN

Mɪssʏ Bʟᴜᴍᴇɴᴅᴀʜʟ ᴄʀᴏssᴇᴅ her thick legs, shut one eye and gazed at the sunset through her glass of Bradsher's Special Age. "And so you feel that Alcide's pessimism is unwarranted?"

Ike Blumendahl shoved his hands deep into his pockets and after much searching brought forth a battered lighter with which he proceeded to set a cigarette afire. "Didn't say that. I said that things are not impossible. From necessity, Dr. Fontenot had to view the situation from the angle of a retired but entirely capable practitioner. He couldn't be expected to effect the sort of transference that I could."

Missy shoved a cigarette into one end of her long mellowed ivory holder. "What do you know about transference, you impertinent pup, and you not dry behind the ears yet?"

Ike eyed his mother severely. "Madame, I shall have to require that you speak of my father's most outstanding son in a manner befitting his station. Did you think it took me all that time just to finish medical school and my internship? You are speaking to a most brilliant psychiatrist."

"Cats and dogs," moaned Missy, "and here I expected you to make a name for yourself in the South with your wonderful practice and you turn out to be one of those things."

"My dear and revered mother, how much money have we?"

"Plenty," said Missy easily. "Don't let that bother you."

"It doesn't. I might point out, though, that there aren't enough good psychiatrists in Louisiana to play a set of tennis doubles and I'm intending to supply a long-felt need. I'm to be the much sought after consultant. I'll lend my services at certain times on certain special cases. Say a couple of days a week at Jackson, a day in New Orleans every now and then, one in Baton Rouge, and all that sort of delightfully slothful rot."

"You're no son of your father's, if you can be slothful."

"I think," said Ike putting down his glass and lighting a cigarette, "that an inquiry about supper is the most harmless thing I can think of right now. What are we having?"

"Chicken pie a la Mandy, green salad, steamed cauliflower with Roquefort sauce, rice and gravy and blackberry cobbler with thick cream."

Ike let the breath steam from him slowly. "Ahhhhh … let's to the festive board Mater. I have worked up an appetite."

Some time later Ike moved away from the table a few inches.

"I shall have to invent an entirely new term. To call this a meal is leaving so much unsaid. Look what's left over."

"It won't be when Lula, Mandy and Louis get through with it. By the way when does your next treatment of Toni come up?"

"Tomorrow. We will agalloping go over hill and dale and in some cool spot we shall dismount, pluck violets and sniff geraniums. In short we shall commune with nature."

"Better leave your personal natures out of it. She isn't that much improved is she?"

"Unfortunately, no. Even the rhumba is too fundamental for her tastes at the present but strides are being made. Last night she almost licked my hands when I let her little act of revulsion go unnoticed and regaled her with my inimitable brand of chatter."

"Suppose you fall in love with her?"

"Well … suppose I do? It's a fairly common phenomenon and I must say it holds no fears for me. She's just my type and never in all my searching have I located a more breathtaking collection of structural divinity. She is a bit of all right."

"Right overhead," said Missy reminiscently, "in my room I saw something once that I never thought I'd see. I made a girl disrobe and take off her underthings because her wedding dress wouldn't fit them. It had been cut to fit her and it refused to accept her lingerie. Her body was the most utterly beautiful thing I have ever seen. It just wasn't real."

"Oh, yes, that big Fourth of July wedding you had that time. You wrote a book-length letter about it. I wished at the time that I could have been here. She must have been a dream."

Missy nodded. "She was and that's about all one can say."

As Ike prepared for bed that night after having been warned again by Missy that the servants' quarters were out of bounds, he heard a light tap on the door.

"Come in."

Lula came into the room, her usually bright face dulled with thick embarrassed blood. Her eyes strayed to the floor in front of her and stayed there. "You want some hot chocolate or sumpn', Mr. Ike, befo' you goes to bed?"

"Er...no thank you, Lula." He let a glance crawl over her a little slower than he had previously and more completely. She had changed to a simple well fitting blue dress which was cut low at the neck revealing a delightful crease which began high and disappeared downward. "I don't believe I want any chocolate."

"Yes, Sir." She turned reluctantly to go and threw a glance over her shoulder.

"Er...Lula." She stopped and faced about.

"Yes, Sir."

"Where is your room?"

"It's de fust one you comes to on de left side of de hall." Her eagerness was manifest.

"Who else stays down there?"

"Mandy sleeps 'cross de hall frum me."

"Mandy's sort of nosey, isn't she?"

"Yes, sir."

Ike, his eyes lit with a devilish light stood up and walked over to where she stood. Leaning over he whispered in her ear. She giggled and nodded vigorously and, turning about, left the room.

Ike showered and donned a soft silk robe. Walking to the window he looked out on the broad moon-splashed lawn where sheep and cattle grazed quietly. He tied his robe loosely at the middle and lit a cigarette, tossing the match out on the verandah just outside the window. It rattled softly on the old cypress flooring. Ike listened to the raucous clamor of the silence and smiled. He had only been to this place a few times but he loved it with a passion that he found hard to explain. He wondered how city people ever got so accustomed to their brawling smelly existence that they could prefer it to the peace and sweet cleanliness of the country, where the air was fresh and you had room to move about. He had been reared in New York and had hated it with gusto ever since he could remember. When he graduated from high school Missy had moved back to the old place and Ike visited her at intervals. Now he was here to stay and . . . .

He heard the door creak open and since the light had been turned off he waited for some signal. He heard a low whisper calling his name. He turned around and walked across the room seeing only the dim shadow of a woman by the door. With a quick twist of his wrist he jerked the knot of his robe loose and it hung open. He came up to her and touched her shoulder. It was bare and still damp from her bath. Its fine texture sent an electric shock up his arm. He reached up and slipped her robe off the other shoulder and with both hands stripped it down the back. He embraced her and felt the excitement that filled them both.

"Mr. Ike . . . oooo . . . Mr. Ike . . . ."

CHAPTER TWELVE

JEFFERSON SALTON SAT on the verandah and had three large drinks in rapid succession. Granny Rosa watched from the hallway and shook her head. Jeff tried hard to think but he couldn't. His body and mind demanded and his past revolted. It started a football game in his head and he squeezed it between his palms. The vision of Geraldine floated before his eyes and a tremendous ache came up in his chest. He saw the vision of Antoinette immediately following and cringed but to his surprise she did not seem angry. Then he remembered her last words before she died. "Don't grieve for me, Jeff. Live! Live like we have lived. Love life ... love living." He had thought she was sleeping and she was ... the long, long sleep. Tears came to his eyes and a hard sob jerked him from chest to knee. He drank again and again until his thoughts were a group of shrill children shrieking in a cave of resonant walls, their voices beating back and forth till his skull shuddered to the impact of a thousand impulses, orders, and the screeching voices grew louder and louder. He held his head hard and whimpered like a wounded animal, the sound bringing Geraldine out on the porch.

"Are you sick, Mr. Jeff?"

He raised his head. What was she doing out here ... laughing at him when it was all her fault, all her fault? He leaped to his feet, swaying dangerously.

"Get out of this house," he yelled.

"But Mr. Jeff..." Tears came to her eyes making Jeff sick with self-disgust. He took the refuge which has been the outlet for distracted men since the world began. He completely lost his temper.

"I said get out!" He swung his open hand which cracked sharply against her cheek. Geraldine didn't flinch, she didn't move. She just looked at him for a few seconds, then turned and walked slowly down the steps. Jeff attempted to make it to his room but only got as far as the sofa of the living-room.

Dr. Fontenot found him there four hours later. He looked down at the prone figure and tugged angrily at his beard. "What happened, Granny?"

"He drunk too much."

"That's obvious all right but why did you call me?"

Granny sighed. "Come back in de kitchen and I'll fix you a cuppa cawffee."

Over coffee Granny told him all that had occurred. "He hauled off and slapped her in de face. Dey wusn't nuthin' she could do but go."

"He was out of his mind," muttered the doctor grimly. "He's getting to be more of a problem than Toni."

"She young," opined Granny succinctly.

"That's right. Youth has a lot more bounce. How does Geraldine feel about it?"

"I don't know suh. If I know her she ain't gon' git on no high hoss."

"Sensible woman."

"She a nigger too," said Granny pulling fiercely on her pipe. "Mah ole man uster beat me onct er twict a mont'. I likened t' cut his throat wid a lamp globe onct, too. Us uster fight ever now'n den."

Dr. Fontenot smiled a little. "Is that the reason Geraldine doesn't mind?"

"Sho. I knowed mah ole man didn't mean t' be bad, and she knowed de boss wus drunk and all tore up in de head. Dat gal ain't no fool."

"Who's that talking back there?"

"Don't tell 'im I called you," whispered Granny. The doctor nodded and went back into the living room. "Well, you decided to wake up, huh?"

Jeff sat up and swayed. "Wow, what a head!"

"Granny, bring three aspirins and a cup of hot coffee," called Fontenot.

After three cups of coffee Jeff began to feel better. "Nearly dark outside. You haven't seen mine and Missy's offsprouts, have you?"

The doctor nodded. "Yep. When I passed the swimming hole coming out here they were apparently leaving the water. They'll be in in a moment."

"Mustn't let them see me like this."

"Right. I'm going to give you a pill and send you to bed. I hear you ran Geraldine off."

"Yes." Jeff's jaw hardened and his lips grew thin. "I couldn't stand to have her about."

"Was it necessary to slap her?"

"Give me the pill, Alcide. I'm in no condition to match wits with you."

"You never were," retorted the doctor. "Take this with a little water and hit the sack. I'll see you tomorrow on something important."

Jeff went upstairs to take a bath and tumble into bed. He was asleep almost instantly. Granny, seeing that he had left the light on tiptoed upstairs and turned it off. She stood watching him for a while then shaking her head she turned and waddled out closing the door softly behind her.

The next afternoon at four the doctor showed up again, his face serious and his step rapid and purposeful. "Good afternoon, Jeff," he said as he bounced up the steps. "You look a little shaky."

Jeff smiled ruefully. "I'm shaky as a groom on the way down the aisle. Have a chair and a drink."

"You been hitting it again?"

"No, just put it out for you."

"Why don't you have one?"

The other shuddered. "No thanks. I can't gauge it anymore."

"Then I'll gauge it for you." Dr. Fontenot poured. "There, now, dump that small one and in fifteen minutes I'll give you another."

Jeff drank and grimaced. "If I had that other one right now I think I could make it thirty minutes."

"Yes...probably." The doctor poured again and handed it to him.

"Now, let's get down to business and to start it off I'm going to tell you a story of some people I know because they remind me of you. The man of the family had a shrew of a wife who couldn't see a thing but social life and parties and ancestor worship and the like. Her husband couldn't see it at all but he let her go her way. This woman was an odd sort who seemed to have no sex response at all and before long they were sleeping separately. The man in confusion and frustration took to drink. After so long a time a servant came into the house who was quiet and dignified and ... well, beautiful. She obviously loved the master and he found a strange attraction in her, but there was the wife, and there were his inhibitions engendered by years of white supremacy. It started a war within the man that threatened to upend him. Then one night his wife fell from a precipice and was killed ...."

"This story is a little *too* much like me." Jeff's face was gray and tense, the nerve leaping uncontrollably in the corner of his mouth.

"Shut up and don't interrupt. As I was saying, everyone thought the wife fell from the bluff but she didn't fall."

Jeff leaned forward, his hands clenched into steel hand balls. "What makes you say that?"

"Several things. First, the man had told a doctor friend of his a secret which his wife overheard and knowing his wife he had a strong suspicion that she'd make trouble. It is reasonable to suppose that others overheard also and knew that the wife had overheard and that she'd make trouble. Later that evening the wife left the house. The reason will probably never be known but she did leave. The next morning she was found dead just a few feet from where her brother had also been found impaled on a piece of steel on an old car body. The doctor friend went to look at the scene staying on the bluff and while there discovered a shoe heel which looked new. He took it home with him and analyzed it, finding that the wearer had been employed in a kitchen. It was not hard to test the heel and find that out. He burned the heel and up till today has never mentioned it to a soul and from this day on never will. He told it today to try to prevent the man from making any bigger ass of himself." The doctor sat back, his beard bobbing furiously, and quaffed his drink.

Jeff sat in his chair like someone who had been slugged with a sandbag. His hand wandered absently to his face and massaged the lean jaw. For a long time he looked sightlessly at the floor. "Looks like we won't have any rain before Christmas, Alcide. Things certainly are dry."

"That's right. I'm having to water my fall garden every afternoon and Maud is complaining about the quality of the beans. Here, Jeff, have a drink." The doctor poured him a stiff slug and handed it to him. He drank it gratefully and sighed with something like relief.

"You're the only doctor I know who prescribes whiskey for his dipso patients," said Jeff with a stiff grin.

"I'm the only doctor you know who knows which patients to prescribe drink for. I'm not afraid of your drinking, Jeff, once you get straightened out."

Jeff fell silent for a while, taking a little longer to down the last drink. He seemed to be able to think a little clearer, and the first sting of the shock was clearing away. "She did it for me," he half whispered.

Dr. Fontenot said nothing but drained his glass and refilled it. Out to the northeast of the house he could see Toni and Ike galloping across the broad pasture on their way to the Big Bluff Creek swimming hole. He nodded to himself and smiled as he watched their horses come close together and the mock fight that ensued. Ike pulled her from her horse then led the horse rapidly away forcing her to follow and beg. Fontenot could hear their laughter and shrill banter and felt a sense of complete comfort and well being. "Look yonder, Jeff," pointing a finger.

Jeff looked and nodded. "The boy'll have her straight in no time if he knows what he's doing."

"And I'll bet my hat he knows what he's doing. Cuss that Missy. I wanted to do this job myself but she had to horn in. She had the right sort of man available and I had married mine off a year ago to Allen Gordon's niece. I doubt that I could have done it alone."

Jeff got to his feet and walked to the edge of the porch. "Let's walk over by the bluff, Alcide."

The doctor nodded agreeably and leaped to his feet. Together they walked across the broad grassy meadow toward the river. In the distance an old stern wheeler fought upstream, white puffs coming from her exhaust stack. A spurt of steam squirted away from the whistle but it was minutes before the rasping hoot came to their ears. The grass was dry and dusty and as they walked along their shoes raised clouds of the powdered clay making their shoes pink. High overhead a flock of egrets winged along in perfect formation.

"It was right here," said the doctor pointing at the ground. "I saw it and sat down and slipped it in my pocket. I didn't say anything because I wanted to know more about it before I did. I'm glad now."

Jeff gnawed nervously at his pipe and nodded. "She did it for me," he said again his voice soft and wondering.

"And for herself … that is to say, Bull and Hilda. I dare say she ran quite some risk and maybe someone else saw something but after this long it would have come out if it was coming out."

"My God, I hope no one else saw her," said Jeff fervently. "That would be the last straw."

"When are you going to fall off your bluff, Jeff? You've been teetering around for some time. What is it going to take?"

Jeff massaged the back of his head like it was aching. "I don't know, Alcide … I don't know."

"She has loved you since she was sixteen, you know," said the doctor casually. "She has never had anything to do with another man."

Jeff stopped dead in his tracks and turned around. "Say that again."

The doctor obliged. "You should have known, you ass. She did everything but write it out."

A great light burst on Jeff and he understood clearly what his background had been trying to confuse for him. Everything had a steel etching clarity now. "Let's go back to the house, Alcide, I want another drink … if I can have one."

"Sure, have one … have two if you make them small."

All the way back to the house his step had a curious spring. "Things begin to look better, Alcide," he confided with a certain bubbling exultance. "About Toni, I mean, you know, coming along like she is."

"I know exactly what you mean," puffed the doctor almost trotting to keep up. "And what's all the hurry?"

Jeff grinned like a schoolboy and fell into a shorter stride and as they reached the verandah he dropped behind and grasping the doctor under the armpits tossed him easily to the porch. The old man squealed and beat at the hands as they released him. "Goddammit, turn … let … but hell you've done it now." He brushed off his clothes and adjusted his tie. "Sit down and calm yourself," complained the doctor, "and drink your drink. I take it that you have come to some monumental conclusion?"

Jeff downed his drink in a gulp. "Precisely, as you would say." He reached over and placed an affectionate hand on the older man's spare thigh. "Missy didn't have anything to do with this, Alcide. You did it all yourself. I'll never be able to thank you enough. You have been the saving of both Toni and me even though Missy might have supplied the means for Toni's deliverance."

"Oh, do shut up, Jefferson Salton and fix me a drink. You have unnerved me."

Dark came early as it was nearing winter. Dr. Fontenot refused the invitation to stay to supper and left.

Jeff lighted his pipe and sank back on the glider. He felt content yet he was taut and nervous. Must be that binge he went on yesterday, and yet he had had enough tonight to calm his nerves. He wasn't nervous exactly. It was …. He decided he didn't know what it was. He bit down on his pipe stem and sighed. He hoped Geraldine wouldn't be too sore at him. He deserved it for striking her but he hadn't meant to. It was a sort of hysterical impulse that came on him before he could head it off. He finished his pipe and stoked it again. He didn't feel at all sleepy. Fontenot's pill, no doubt. Too much sleep last night.

Two pipes later he began to feel a slight chill in the air but he was so comfortable that he was reluctant to move. He saw something moving toward the house coming up the driveway. Whoever it was had on light colored clothing and he could see the figure long before it got to the porch. Thirty feet away he could see from the free and easy stride that it was Geraldine and his stomach knotted up and a freezing fear came upon him. Hastily he grabbed the whiskey bottle and took a terrific drink which seared him from gulp to gullet. She came slowly up the porch steps and stood before him. The moon was just coming up and he could make out her calm face in the dim glow.

"Hello, Geraldine...I...er...did Granny tell you what I said?"

"Yes, sir."

"Well, I'll repeat it. Yesterday I was miserable and confused and unhappy and drunk. I'm really sorry for what I said and for slapping you. I don't know why I did that."

"I think I know why, Mr. Jeff, but it doesn't matter." She stood there looking at him with her soft steady eyes which were making him decidedly uncomfortable.

"Come," he said in a strange voice. "Sit here a while."

She sat with her usual grace and lack of embarrassment and the small size of the glider made her quite close to him. She had evidently bathed recently and he could smell the lingering fragrance of her toilet soap. It was a good clean smell. The last drink of whiskey was making him feel exultant and transcendent. "It was good of you to come back, Geraldine, but you needn't have come till morning. That is...I mean, I'm glad you came but I..."

"Yes, sir. I know what you mean. I came because I wanted to, Mr. Jeff."

"You wanted to?"

"Yes, sir."

"Why?"

"Mr. Jeff, you don't know?"

Again that agonizing knot in his stomach, the feeling that he was about to break out in cold sweat. He sat back and relaxed, forced himself to relax. "Yes, Geraldine, I guess I do know."

"I knew you didn't mean anything when you slapped me. You were all upset and everything."

"I'm glad you feel that way. Some people wouldn't."

"I'm not some people, Mr. Jeff. I'm only Geraldine."

The moon came over the fang-topped pines and shone brightly on them, revealing Geraldine's tear-wet eyes but her face was still composed.

Jeff sat up with a start. "Why are you crying?"

"I don't know, sir. It looks like I've wanted to cry for so long. I don't think I can hold it back much longer."

Jeff was stung to the quick. "Was it as bad as that?" He didn't recognize his own voice.

"It's been bad but not till lately has it been almost more than I could stand."

She caught her face in her hands and her smooth shoulders heaved with deep sobs that hurt him every time they shook her. He placed his hand on the nearest shoulder.

"Geraldine...I, what can I do? I haven't intended to hurt you...I...."

She straightened up and made a magnificent effort to control herself. She seized his hand in both of hers and looked at him through her tears. "I know that, Mr. Jeff. I know you haven't meant any of it but please, sir, have you ever been...been..." A shudder ran over her and her head drooped again.

"You mean in love, Geraldine?" His voice was gentle and full of understanding.

She looked at him gratefully through her tears. "Yes, sir... For nine years and only *see* the person. Never able to speak a word...that's what I mean. I guess I'll never be able to tell you, tell you that. No matter how much I ..."

Jeff's head began to reel. The poignancy of the situation was a knife deep in his vitals twisting, twisting.... Suddenly he could see Geraldine on the brink of the bluff looking over. Lavender had already taken the plunge. He could almost hear her say, "You wouldn't, so step aside and let one who can and will." He slid over very close to her and took her wet face in his hands.

"Geraldine, would it help if I said that I know just what you have gone through with and that I know what you've done for me … us, Toni and I, and that I …."

She grabbed his arms in a grip so hard that it hurt. "Please, sir, don't say it … even if you mean it. Not now. I have hoped all these years that I could just be your woman. I know you better now. You wouldn't just take any woman. It means more to you than that. It does me, too." She couldn't go on. She rested her forehead on his forearm and wept bitterly. Jeff was cut to the very depths, the drink was confusing his thoughts again, Geraldine's nearness making his blood course faster and faster. Then it struck him. His mind flashed back to the night of his dream. It was Antoinette and the conviction that it wasn't her at all. Now he knew. It had been Geraldine. Something in her nearness, her touch … something, made the light burst upon him with dazzling brilliance.

A strange calm came to Jeff and in some way her head came to rest on his shoulder. He put an arm about her and drew her close. She looked up wonderingly and as she did he kissed her, softly at first with respect and gentleness, then nature's demands, long dammed in both of them, broke and flooded. Minutes later they parted and looked with wonder and awe at each other. For a long time neither spoke, just looked.

Geraldine took a long shuddering sigh. "I've waited so long for that, Mr. Jeff … so long."

Jeff breathed deeply and his face took on a ruddy hue. "I guess I have, too." Then he backed away. "Geraldine, this … this thing isn't fair to you. You stand to gain nothing but …."

"That's all I want, Mr. Jeff. Don't think I haven't thought about it through and through a thousand times. It can't be any other way so that's the way it'll have to be. We can't make over the world so we'll have to beat it. We'll take what we can and get whatever happiness we can without their vows and rituals and their good will. I'll be the house girl and I'll be near you to serve you and see that you're comfortable. And at night, whenever you wish…. What more could a wife do except bear you children? I'll even do that if you want me to but I don't think it would be fair to them."

"Geraldine, you're an immensely intelligent person, a much better integrated person than I am."

She shook her head and smiled showing ivory white teeth, even and regular.

When they parted this time they said no word but got up and started for the North side of the house. They found a stairway there and climbed it to the second story verandah and entered Jeff's room.

An hour later the moon crept slantingly through a window and threw a golden saber across the bed. Jeff had not gone to sleep but she apparently had. Her face reposed in utter peace, her breath coming in the regular rhythm of perfect health. The beam of moonlight struck her across the stomach at a sharp angle and reached to her forehead, caressing the smoothly flowing rise toward her firm erect breasts, touching them and sending tent shaped shadows against the amber perfection of her skin.

He sighed and laid a caressing hand on her velvety expanse. Her eyes opened and she smiled softly.

"I thought you were asleep," he said half accusingly.

"Not asleep, just relaxing." She caught him in her arms and strained him to her with tender yet demanding pressure. His breath came sharply through his nostrils and they shifted. She cut short a sibilant gasp, his muscles tensed and a wave of shattering passion engulfed them.

Jeff waked the next morning with a sense of well-being that he hadn't felt for years. He glanced guiltily at the empty space beside him then smiled and relaxed. A tap came on the door and Geraldine entered. "Good morning, Mr. Jeff." Her face wore the same placid reposed look it always had. She put the tray with coffee, cream and sugar on the little bed table.

"Good morning, Geraldine, did you sleep well last night?"

Her smile sent dimples deep in her cheeks. "When I slept I did very well."

He caught her arm and pulled her over on the bed.

"Be careful," she whispered. "Miss Toni is awake."

He held her close for a moment then let her go.

Geraldine gathered up the coffee utensils she needed and stood up. "I'll go now and take Miss Toni's coffee."

Jeff sat upright in bed. "Can you come again tonight?"

She didn't answer immediately but studied him intently for a moment. "Mr. Jeff, I'll come any time you say ... any time."

He felt a knot in his throat and tried unsuccessfully to swallow it. "Yes," he said huskily, "I know you will."

She turned and left the room.

"Here," said Geraldine to Toni, "don't try to drink that lying down. You'll scald yourself." Her voice had an authoritative ring and she punctuated it by knotting up a pillow and placing it behind the girl's shoulders. Toni laughed inside. Geraldine sounded just like a mother and she remembered what Dr. Fontenot had said.

"Geraldine, this is very nice of you to bring me coffee. You haven't done it before."

Geraldine smoothed the girl's hair gently as she moved away. "I don't think I've ever felt toward you, Miss Toni, like I have the last few days."

"You've been acting very maternal and possessive," said Toni with a smile.

"That's the way .... *Oh, Miss Toni, please try to understand.*" Her eyes were aswim with tears of supplication.

Toni felt a sudden pain in her chest. This woman, whatever her color and origin, had feelings, emotions, fears, hopes and a heart. She suddenly felt proud of her position as she remembered what Dr. Fontenot had said, "It's a wonderful thing to be loved. Never question it." Toni's voice was low and vibrant. "Come and sit by me, Geraldine. There now. You love me because you love Dad ... isn't that right?"

Geraldine nodded. "You know then?"

"Yes, Geraldine, I watched through the door that night when he thought you were mother. You've sort of felt that way ever since, haven't you?"

The other nodded, tears dripping from her eyes. "I can't help it. I'm just hoping you'll understand, not hold it against me, not hate me, not ..."

"Geraldine!" It was a cry of pain, of pity, of gratitude and understanding. A cry that held all the loneliness of a spirit that had long been starved for the affection and gentleness of a mother and who at long last saw it in a woman of another race. They wept tears of relief on each other's shoulders and Anglo-Saxon pride fell vanquished by another nobler and closer emotion, the need of one another in personal harmony.

.

CHAPTER THIRTEEN

M ISSY BLEW INTO Ike's room the next morning wrapped in only a few dozen yards of chiffon housecoat that billowed out behind her like a barrage balloon.

"Well... gad, look at that bed! Who slept there, a litter of pigs?"

Ike put down his coffee cup and looked saddened. "I am not a pig, Mater."

"You're worse than that. What gives at the Saltons?"

He shrugged. "You mean beyond her attachment to the way I spray words around...."

"You know what I mean, you bent-nosed mongrel."

"Please, Mater ... my sensitive...."

"To hell with your sensitivities. You know what I mean—the way you met her, for instance. What was that for?" "Multifold purposes," said Ike eyeing himself in the long mirrored door of the armoire. "People who meet formally must spend precious moments going through a ritual which is worse than that used by the Chinese because it is fatuous, purposeless and unlovely. It took Toni and me about forty-five seconds to become bosom buddies. My justly famous charm played quite a large part I am reluctantly forced to admit."

"My, but I have a smart son! I know just how reluctant you are to admit it."

"What are we eating this morning?" he asked, switching the subject.

"Food," she barked and swept from the bedroom.

Ike lay on a colorful beach robe, his eyes closed against the fierce rays of the sun. By his side, on her stomach and elbows, making figures in the sand with a slim finger lay Toni. She was wearing a sky blue bathing suit which gave the demoralizing impression that it had been painted on with a spray gun. For some time neither had spoken and the only sound was the lazy gurgle of Big Buff as it wound its slow way to the Mississippi, and the rurppp rurppp of the horses grazing on the bluff above them.

"Ike!"

"Yeah!"

"What are you thinking?"

"That question brands you as a female female."

"Double, huh?"

"Double with a vengeance. I'm quiet, therefore I'm thinking, therefore I might conceivably be thinking of you, therefore you want to know what it is. Plucking a phrase from the middle of that sentence upon which to comment I might say that at this particular time, even though I have my eyes closed, if I were thinking of anyone but you I should be bled dry and my veins filled with vinegar and red pepper."

"That would embalm you."

"Yes, I could be eaten without seasoning. The pepper would lend piquancy and the vinegar would tenderize …"

"Oh, Ike, shut up. You make me ill."

"Very well, then entertain me with a fast commentary on man, morals and society."

"I'm afraid I couldn't do that very well."

"Why? You can talk, can't you? That's all that's necessary. If you spoke stupidly it's a lead pipe certainty that you wouldn't speak with nearly the amount of stupidity which characterizes ninety percent of the gabble on the subject."

"That's not much encouragement."

"I guess not. Yet I find that some of the less informed people speak very well about it if they have a fair amount of intelligence and some theological superstition hasn't amputated the part of their brain usually used for free thought. I had a very devout Baptist landlady once who had more sense per cubic centimeter of cranial space than any ten of the men she listened to every Sunday. She thought! Therefore, it was inevitable that she should come to some very sound skepticism. A great deal of it would have caused the elders to give her the old heave ho had she spoken it about too freely. As is often the case she looked upon me as damned anyway so I was the recipient of many a long discussion. What she really wanted was some support on certain rather abrupt departures from doctrine. Naturally I gave her the desired support because she was a pretty keen-minded old lady and her ideas had snap and aim."

"Ike, how good are you at projecting yourself away from your surroundings?"

"The best. Once I projected myself right out of jail where I had been incarcerated for pinching the deacon's bottle while prayer was in progress and got pickled before the collection plate was passed. I dipped thereinto and ..."

"Oh, Ike, be serious. I mean it."

Ike rolled over very close to her and his dark soft eyes looked squarely into hers. She felt their impact like a physical blow. These sudden transformations of his were disconcerting but this time she didn't avert her eyes or move. "Squirt, squirrel," he said smiling, taking some of the sting out of his abrupt act.

"What I mean is ... you're a psychiatrist. What's wrong with me and how am I doing? I feel that I'm improving but the fear is still there. Will I ever lose it?"

Ike rolled over on his back and closed his eyes. "No spik english."

Toni sighed. "That's why I wanted you to take a distant and detached view of the thing and tell me. I knew you wouldn't do it if I didn't … why won't you tell me?"

"Because, squirrel, there's no point to it. Naturally you are anxious to know and naturally I'd like to tell you but you must forget the psychiatric angle entirely. As you have seen I'm not practicing on you."

"That's what I mean," she cried sitting up. "Why aren't you? You're here every day nearly and it looks like the opportunity would be too much for you to resist."

"Smatter, ain't my company enough?"

She was hurt and when she spoke she was near to tears. "I didn't mean that, Ike … you know I didn't."

"I'm sorry, squirrel, but can't you just leave it like it is?"

She was silent so long that Ike opened his eyes and sat up. She was looking down the creek at nothing. "I'm going to say something and if it sounds silly then I'm sorry, but speaking in cold detached terms surely you must have thought that I might fall in love with you, or you with me?"

"The eventuality has occurred to me, yes, as has marriage, a cottage with roses, vines and children. What's wrong with the picture?"

"You're deliberately making me draw a map," she said angrily. "Do you think that's quite fair? You must know that you're only making it hard for me."

"Squirrel, you're being thick."

"In what way, pray tell?"

"Well, let's take one of your possibilities. Suppose you fell in love with me?"

"Well?"

"Wouldn't that mean you were cured?"

Toni looked at him with miserable eyes. "I didn't know," she said finally, "that I was that thick."

Ike grinned engagingly. "You'll survive." He sobered instantly. "Let's you and me make a bargain."

"Like what?"

"Like this. Just let things go on as they are. Let me come over as often as I can. We'll play and fight and kid and in general disport ourselves as two adolescents should. We'll swim till it gets too cold. We'll ride and when fall gets here we'll hunt quail and go to see the L.S.U. football games and maybe to New Orleans to see Tulane when they have an especially good game. At any time during that period if I think you're cured I'll tell you so. Bargain?" He stuck out his square hand with its long sensitive fingers.

She nodded and gripped his hand. "Bargain, Ike. You're a very nice man."

"'Fer sho,' as Mandy would say. How could you have ever doubted?"

She leaped to her feet. "Race you to the water."

He scrambled up and after a short chase caught her at the water's edge. He stuck out a foot and tripped her and she tumbled into the shallows. She sat up coughing. "That ... was a d-d-dirty trick."

"Natch. I'm full of 'em. Wait till I pull your pigtails."

At South of the Border that night Toni was beautiful. The weather was still warm and she wore a light blue dress that was almost in two pieces. The short sleeved jacket reached the skirt in the back but the front showed an expanse of tan skin that made Ike's mouth water. Her hair had dried riding back to the house and she had brushed it till it shone like burnished gold. Her eyes sparkled and laughter bubbled easily to her lips. They ate all the pizza they could hold and after the proper waiting period had several drinks which made Toni's eyes sparkle all the more. Ike excused himself and went to the men's room and on the way back noted that Toni had taken similar refuge in the ladies' lounge. With a quick lunge he swerved and walked quickly to the bandstand.

Flipping a folded dollar bill to the big yellow Negro who led the band he said, "A rhumba, Jackson. The most savage and abandoned thing you can think of. Do it well and there'll be another buck coming up."

The Negro grinned, showing two rows of shining gold teeth. "Yassuh! She comin' up aftuh dissun us playin' rat now."

"Jackson, you're a positive jewel," said Ike elegantly. "I shall remember you in my will."

Ike arrived at the table some three minutes before Toni came back. He had ordered another round of drinks and was busy readying his glass for more.

"If I felt any better, Ikey," said Toni as she waltzed toward her seat, "I'd be ill."

"Maybe you will be before the night's over."

"Crepe hanger."

"Want to finish this dance, squirrel? The rhythm sends me."

She was on her feet almost before he finished speaking. "I feel especially lightfooted tonight."

"Mademoiselle," he said bowing low, "if you are any lighter than you have been previously I shall be forced to squeeze you mightily to hold you on the floor."

"Sir Ike," she said bowing in return, "your kind but flagrantly fallacious fabrications fill me to the full with gratitude."

"I shall have to remind you," grated Ike in her ear, as they moved smoothly across the floor, "that snappy speeches are my exclusive province and I shall resent any further intrusions... Damn!"

The music stopped and swung immediately into a slow primeval rhumba. The lights went dim and the walls and floor turned a dull red from the special lighting effects. He could feel the muscles in her smooth back go taut. Her lips compressed into a hard line. "Let's dance, Ike." Her words were as brittle as thin ice and her eyes were tight with determination.

Ike caught her by the arm and started back toward the table. "As I was saying, there is nothing so irritating as to be able to do some one thing well, not that I can't do innumerable things well; to do something well, then have that position usurped by a mere fluff of a female."

Toni was subdued and quiet when she sat down. Ike rattled on as though they had sat down only because they had tired of dancing. A slim, red-headed boy of about twenty-three detached himself from the crowd at the bar and came toward the table.

He had a clean, well-scrubbed face and a generally wholesome appearance. He was neatly dressed in a chocolate brown double breasted suit with brown and white shoes. A white handkerchief hung casually from his breast pocket.

"Hi, Toni," he greeted her as he came up to the table.

"Hello, Frank," she said without enthusiasm. "May I present Mr. Blumendahl, Mr. Holliday?"

Ike stood up and shook hands allowing that he was positively overjoyed to meet any friend of Toni's and managing to say it in a tone that made her throw him a quick glance. If Frank thought the greeting a shade too flossy he didn't show it.

"Haven't seen you lately, Toni. Where've you been keeping yourself?"

"The same place," she said coolly. "I don't move around much."

Frank was momentarily flustered and was more so a moment later.

"Why haven't you been out?" she asked.

Frank turned scarlet. "Well, you see we've been rounding up for the fall branding and ...."

"I meant during the summer. Unless my memory is playing tricks on me you were pretty well underfoot for some time. Then I didn't see you any more."

Ike kicked her under the table but she ignored him. Frank was suffering and looked about for rescue.

"I also recall you making the remark once, Frank, that what you did was your own business and Vanetta didn't have any control over your actions. Did she draw a gun on you?"

"You've got it all wrong, Toni. You see ... I ... that is ...."

"That's what I thought all along, Frank," she said smiling with acid sweetness. "Now you can run along. We have things to discuss."

Frank gulped twice and beat a hasty retreat. The back of his neck glowed like a tail light.

"That was just a shade unkind," said Ike mildly.

"Are you going to suggest that I turn the other cheek? He happens to have been one of the most attentive and persistent of my swains till my little accident and from then till now I have neither seen him nor heard a word from him."

Ike's planed face grew hard and bleak. "One of these, eh? I didn't know."

"Furthermore, he came to me. I didn't go out of my way to be ugly but I'm afraid I'm not noble enough to put on a show now that Missy Blumendahl's son is seeing me, thereby making me socially okay."

Ike was pale with anger. "Is that true?"

"Oh, very. He and several of his cronies wouldn't miss one of her parties for anything. They are among the faithful who think that anything she does or even implies ... as we have seen, is simply the voice from Olympus."

Ike rubbed the back of his head and blew out his breath with a gusty whoosh. "I am a man of peace," he said with soft deadliness. "I think public brawling is both vulgar and ridiculous. However ...." He looked toward the bar, his eyes burning hotly. Suddenly he was on his feet, and before Toni could stop him he was several strides in the direction of the bar.

Toni started to her feet, arrested the motion, then decided to continue. With great deliberation she walked toward the bar.

Ike tapped Frank on the shoulder. "A word with you, my turkey-necked friend."

Frank turned around and proceeded to live up to Ike's description. "What is it?" he choked.

"Miss Salton asked you a question but you didn't answer it. Your pressing business has no doubt been taken care of by now and I'd like to hear what it is."

Frank as have many before him took refuge in anger because he was not equal to the question.

"What's it to you?"

Ike quirked an eyebrow amusedly. "You still haven't answered the question."

"Think you can make me?"

"I hadn't entertained the notion but now that you mention it...." He slapped Frank so hard across the face that he almost went down. Immediately there was an uproar. Men backed away and Frank came back with a roundhouse that was tagged with stars but Ike stopped inside it, let it whistle harmlessly by his ear and dug his left into Frank's unprotected midriff with a curious hitch of his shoulder. An involuntary sound came from Frank's throat that was neither a cry nor a gasp, having qualities of both, generously decorated with bits of breakfast, dinner, supper, and whiskey. Ike stepped nimbly out of the way of the debris and backed a few feet away. Several strong looking men came from nowhere.

"No trouble in here, buddy," said one, catching Ike by the arm.

Ike looked the fellow full in the eyes. "You will take your hand from me," he said softly. The man having dealt with men some years of his life stepped back without feeling that he had been abandoned by his courage. Toni touched the man on the arm. "There won't be any trouble, Jake."

Jake grinned. "O.K. if you say so, Miss Salton."

"Thanks, Jake. Ike, let's sit down."

Ike allowed himself to be led docilely back to the table.

"You were wonderful, Ike, and I'll have to admit that I very deliberately came to the bar to watch it well done."

He smiled and shrugged. "Frank's outdoor life has not hardened his stomach. It was as soft as the udder of a cow. Interesting collection of regurgitory jetsam. He evidently likes to put on the feed bag."

"Let's go home, Ike."

"After a decent interval," he said calmly lighting a cigarette. "I should not like to have it said that I struck a stout blow then took to my heels."

"That," she said grinning roguishly, "should indicate something."

He nodded. "A remnant of my little, little, complex. I'll never be free of it I suppose because there will always be people who think Jews won't fight, what happened in the near East recently notwithstanding."

They had several more drinks and seeing no belligerent signs, left. The top of Ike's convertible was down and the moon flooded it with silver light as they rode slowly along, headed south. They both sat deep in the cushions, relaxed and comfortable. Ike had noticed that Toni sat nearer him when she entered the car, something she had been careful not to do on all other occasions when they rode together. Somehow their hands touched and Ike closed his long fingers over her soft cool ones. She didn't try to disengage them and he sensed rather than felt a kind of watchful tautness in her. He held her hand for several miles then put his hand to his head where he proceeded to tousle his thick black hair.

"I'm that kind of a sensualist," he said, "who likes to have his head massaged. I go to sleep in the barber chair and lie down grunting when my back is scratched."

"Shall I scratch your back?" she asked with a chuckle.

"Not now…can't lie down and grunt. Other times, other places. I shall issue a rain check."

The cool night air whipped softly about them, laden with scents of all sorts from the pungency of pine needles to the sere smell of dying leaves, and the ever present subtle perfume of ripening wild plum. Overhead the pines seemed to arch thir lofty heads while gum and oak squatted majestically at their feet. A night bird, his jewelled eyes shining in the glare of the headlights, waited till the last moment before springing into graceful flight to avoid the car.

"What are you thinking, Ike?"

"Not again?"

"Whenever you're silent I seem to feel mighty grinding thoughts giving off rays like some invisible lamp or X-ray or something."

"With such an instrument I could study your skeleton perfection which I freely predict without any previous information is the equal in every way of what the eye can see."

She pinched him in the side. "There, I asked you a sensible question and you darted off at a tangent as you so often do."

"I have a mind that leaps about like a phrenetic kangaroo. Some of my thoughts are the distillate of nobility, others are the distillate of dark seething evility."

"Yap, yap, yap, how you do talk on and on like the rent and taxes."

"Pure chaff, my dear, to obscure what I was really thinking."

"Now you are mean and I insist on knowing."

"Well, you asked for it. I was thinking that I have been in the big cities all my life and, having the eye for lovely, desirable women, I have seen what I thought was the best. Yet, here I come into what I thought would be a rather backwoodsy place and I find a gal whom the best I've ever seen before can't touch with a ten-foot pole. It's not only amazing, it's uncanny."

Toni was silent a long time. He let her think without interruption, feeling that she needed the time. Finally she spoke. "Ike, that was very sweet."

"In just what way I fail to see. I spoke what I believe to be the truth. If I can be complimentary and tell the truth at the same time the effectiveness is doubled and I suffer no twinges of conscience."

"Do you ever feel twinges?"

Ike grinned and lighted a cigarette. "Rarely. I'm a man of no morals but I afford sustenance for several rock bound principles. The principles are necessary for my self-esteem to see that I wrong no person. Morals in a sense are hats hung on a rack from which they fall ever and anon upon the proper pretext."

They were silent for several more miles.

"What are you thinking, Toni?"

She started a little and remained silent.

"I asked you a question, squirrel, or do you think it's cricket to ask then deny me the same privilege?"

"I'm ashamed to tell you what I was thinking."

"Then you pay me little credit. Don't you know you could tell me anything in this wide world and it would be perfectly all right?"

"Yes, I do feel that way. Well, to be frank I was thinking about what if you fell in love with me. It would be sort of terrible … me like I am and all …"

She could see the muscles knot in Ike's clean-cut jaw. "And I think," he said in a voice that was soft but trilling with feeling, "that it would probably be the most wonderful feeling in the world."

A pain tugged at her throat. "But, Ike, you know how I am …" She was very close to tears.

"If I'm willing to consider it, knowing how you are, why are you yelling?" He was rough and a little loud.

"I'm not yelling," she said in a strange voice. "I wouldn't want to hurt you."

"If you didn't want to hurt me badly enough you wouldn't do it."

It took her some time to digest that and by the time she had, Ike stopped the car in front of the house. They sat still for a moment, Toni watching him and Ike looking out past the bluff.

"Good night, Toni."

He seemed distant and cool and Toni felt the reaching fingers of hurt, knowing that she had no reason for feeling as she did.

"Won't you come in for a while?" She sounded like a small child begging.

In one of his flashing transitions Ike whirled on her and smiled broadly, his white teeth gleaming in the moonlight. "Not tonight, squirrel. It's getting late and for some lousy reason my belly is trying to act up on me. I'd better be getting home." He could see the flooding relief surge through her and felt light and happy deep inside. Her face brightened as he opened the car door.

"I always forget that you have twenty or so miles to go when you leave me. Good night, Ike."

"Good night, Toni."

"Ike!"

"Yes?"

"I had the most wonderful time. I really did."

"Thanks, squirrel." He reached over and squeezed her hand. "I'm glad you did because I did, too."

CHAPTER FOURTEEN

"WHERE'S IKE," ASKED Jeff casually one morning as they sat on the front verandah.

Toni compressed her lips. "He's been sick. Some sort of stomach trouble." She didn't add that it shouldn't have kept him from calling nor that he hadn't seemed too sick when she last saw him.

"I had about gotten used to him about the place," said Jeff gnawing the stem of his pipe. "Seems to be a very likable lad. He sure can talk up a storm."

"He can that," agreed Toni shortly, then she straightened up. A buckboard had just turned into the drive and the two red morgans pulling it broke into a mad racing run toward the house. They skirted the live oak directly in front of the house and were pulled to a sliding halt a few feet from the steps. "Whoa, you hard-mouthed bastards," roared Missy as she sawed them to a stop.

"If," declared Ike, brushing gravel and spots of debris from his clothes, "I ever get rooked into another ride like this I'm going to have my head examined by the most competent man in the business who, of course, is me and having already made the examination I know in advance what the verdict will be...dementia paralytica."

"Ah, hell...git outa the buggy and let's sample some of Jeff's bourbon. It'll beat that jabber of yours a mile." Missy leaped out of the buggy to be followed slowly by a protesting Ike.

"Did I but care to I could produce reams of documentary evidence to refute...."

"Hiya, Jeff," boomed Missy as she mounted the steps.

Jeff gasping from laughter held out his hand to her. "Come on in, Missy, Geraldine will have the drinks out in no time. Where've you been keeping yourself?"

"This sissy offspring of mine has been having a noble dose of the trots and what with this and that he's been a problem, laying in bed all hours complaining that he is unto the death or some such maudlin moaning... say, you're looking up. Last time I saw you you looked like hell."

Jeff glanced at Ike and Toni who had walked to the other end of the verandah.

"Things have changed here somewhat for the better. Toni has improved to a remarkable degree and I guess I have you to thank for that... indirectly, at least."

Missy dismissed it with a wave of her plump hand. "Don't waste it on me, Jeff. I get a bang out of it. Now, what has happened to you?"

Jeff flushed and looked away. "What makes you think something has happened to me?"

"Oh, for Christ's sake, don't get coy with me... well, I'm glad to hear it. It makes a difference, doesn't it?"

It was an effort for him to face her but he made it and even managed to be bold about it. "Yes, it does," he said challengingly. "I had no idea how much difference it would make. Love, Missy, crosses many rivers and barriers."

She nodded vigorously. "I oughta know. I tried it twice and both times people said I was a fool because one was a Dago and the other was a Jew. I must say that I haven't a single word to utter about them except the best. They were as fine a pair of men as ever was. Of course, I had my troubles with them. Tony was sucked out of his stride by any skirt that passed and Ike thought about business too much but I'm glad to say that I dealt with each in my own way and everything turned out all right."

At the end of the verandah Toni leaned back against the corner column and faced Ike. Her dress was of green gaberdine and it fitted with that breath-taking exactitude which is calculated to produce disturbing emotions. Ike was properly impressed, eyed her boldly and noted that she took it in stride. "Allow me to say, squirrel, that you present a picture which for sheer feminine elegance has no peer."

She curtsied and her face shone with pleasure. "I never tire of such talk. Tell me more."

He noticed that she had unconsciously drawn her shoulders back and her stomach slightly in which resulted in her breasts sprouting upward against their restraint. The effect was dizzying.

"Sorry I didn't get over the last few days. I …" He stopped on the verge of telling a lie.

"Yes, I've wondered why. You didn't seem too sick when I saw you last."

Ike clamped his lips shut in a tight line and mustered his courage. "I wasn't sick."

Her eyes opened a little wider. "Then …." She stopped not knowing what else to say.

An inspiration struck Ike then which almost blinded him. That was the answer and although it was no less dangerous it at least gave what he might use as a valid excuse.

"Let's go for a ride. I can't talk here and I've got to talk. Can we use your car?"

"Of course. It's around the side of the house."

They got in the convertible and drove off. Toni whipped the car suddenly from the road and plunged into the woods on what seemed to be little but a trail winding between the trees. They rode along through the fall woods with its brilliant leaves and baring branches for a mile, then stopped in a little natural clearing, showing that they had made a half circle and come to the bluff again.

"This used to be a favorite smooching place," she said lightly as she braked the car to a stop. She spun on the seat and faced him. "What's the trouble, Ike?"

He deliberately allowed some time to pass before speaking. "Toni, this association is getting the best of me."

"I was afraid of that. I could see it, so what now?"

He shook his head. "I don't know. To tell you the truth I don't want to fall in love."

"But why? You said ...."

"I know what I said," he retorted roughly. "I just said too much I guess." He propped his jaw in his left hand and looked at the bottom of the car.

She slipped over near him and took his hand away. "Ike, look at me."

He looked and the sight cut him so deeply that he felt a physical pain. If ever there had been a portrait of love painted on a face Toni was now that canvas. It was aglow, surpassingly lovely in spite of its strong cast, her eyes wells of tenderness and desire. Ike took her in his arm and drew her close, sliding past her parted supplicating lips, buried his face in her soft fragrant hair. For a time he held her then as he drew away he miscalculated and her damp warm mouth encompassed his. For the space of a moment he felt as though some blunt instrument had slugged him a mighty blow back of the head and his senses spun, darted, and floundered crazily. Then with a mighty effort of will he tore away and sprang from the car. "I never neck," he said in a foreign voice.

"Ike, tell me what's wrong." Her voice was deep with feeling which held an agonized note.

"Nothing's wrong. I'm afraid I'll fall in love with you and I can't, that's all."

"What would be so bad about it?"

"You'll just have to take my word for it. I can't explain it." He came to the driver's side and got in making her move over. Then they drove home in total silence.

Toni and Jeff stood on the porch and watched the flashing departure of Missy's team.

"I don't understand Ike at all," said Toni in a sobbing voice. Jeff looked at her but couldn't think of anything to say.

"Er ... Alcide called up. Wanted to know how you were."

Toni gave a startled exclamation and leaped into the hallway where the phone was.

Dr. Fontenot helped Toni from the car. "Come in, my dear. I called because I was afraid of something like that and I wanted you to have someone to talk to if you wished."

"But I don't understand him at all, doctor," she said very close to tears as they walked up the strip of concrete from the street to the house.

In the office he helped her into a chair and sat down opposit her. "Now, tell me what happened."

She told him everything. "And all of a sudden when I ... well, I guess it crystallized when I saw that he was holding back. Something came up in me stronger than any emotion I ever had. I knew I was going to kill that reticence. A woman only has herself to accomplish that with and before I knew it I was in his arms ... the old feeling gone and a bright new possessive feeling like the old me in its place. I knew then that I had whipped it, that I was a woman reacting like a woman should and I don't suppose I ever kissed a man like I did him. It simply laid him out, doctor, I know it did. I can't have been wrong about that. For a short moment Ike loved me with all his heart and soul then he tore away and I couldn't get through his defenses again. We went home then and I'm about crazy. What *can* be the matter? Do you suppose it has something to do with what he told me about never caressing women? He said that the first night I went out with him and at the time I was glad but later on I thought he must have been kidding me because in every other way he seemed normal. He said it again this afternoon."

Dr. Fontenot pulled at his beard and gazed at the ceiling. "Just sit here a while my dear. I must make a phone call."

He came back in ten minutes and his face looked pleased. A half smile toyed with the corners of his mouth. "Toni, I … er, that is, *we* have a plan."

The sun went down on Fahenstock that afternoon in a sea of blood. A mighty roiling fire blazed and tumbled about the horizon in a perfect frenzy of extravagant color. Ike looked at it and caught his breath. "If ever man could reproduce something like that then I'd believe in art. As it is his puerile scrabblings have to be 'explained' in his own esoteric and abstruse terminology all amounting to a lot of pooh bah."

Missy sat, her glass on the concrete floor, and said, "I'm glad to know you can talk. You've been a perfect bear ever since we came back from Fomalhaut. Of course I'm sure Toni Salton had nothing.…"

"Then you advertise the total imperfection of your knowledge," he assured her testily. "She had everything to do with it."

"The honesty of the younger generation never ceases to be a marvel to me," said Missy crossing her legs with panting difficulty. "I was certain you'd give me an argument about it."

"I'd then have been a fool," he snapped, "and I've already come too near to it to suit me."

"In what way?"

"I almost succeeded in falling in love with Toni. At least I succeeded in curing her and making her think that I am in a sense as badly off now as she. I made her think I couldn't abide the amorous clutch."

Missy barked out a short laugh. "Any woman who has enough sense to spit out an olive stone would know what a stupendous lie that is. Ike, you are probably the world's best liar as was your father but the moment you step out of character you become the worst. Any announcement from you that the touch of a beautiful woman revolts you would have the ring of a lead coin on a glass counter. You may be the world's best psychiatrist since Strecker but you'd better listen to your mater on this."

Ike eyed his mother in morose silence. "You think it fell flat?"

"You kissed her, didn't you?"

"No, she kissed me."

"And you sat there like a log and didn't return it, I suppose?"

Ike looked a little crestfallen. "Any time I get kissed by a woman like Toni and sit there like a Sphinx and take it unmoved then I'm going to order thirty gallons of testosterone and drink it all at one sitting."

"O.K., then you spavined maverick, you think she didn't know that? Where'n hell are your brains?"

"Then it appears that I did make an ass out of myself?"

"You have been an ass for years," said his mother brutally. "Just my maternal affection has kept me from telling you."

Ike rubbed a day's growth of chin whiskers. "You sound as if you meant that."

"I do," she barked. "You're just like your father. You are brilliant but you have spells of thinking you're God. Neither of you ever recognized anything as being too tough to tackle."

Ike sat back in the big cane-bottomed rocker and pressed his fingertips to his forehead. For a long time he sat and thought, the only interruptions being Missy's strong teeth crunching ice, a habit which irritated him to shrieks. The more he thought the more confused he became, and all of a sudden the thought struck him that if he persisted in his attitude he'd likely lose Toni and the pain thus induced was sickening. He pictured her flying across a pasture on her big gray gelding, blond hair flying in luscious disarray, her flashing smile, the ready friendliness of her handshake and the wholesomeness of her comradeship. He pictured her long glorious body with the skintight blue bathing suit slipping through the water with the ineffable grace of a naiad.

"Mother, I'm miserable," he said in a rather small boyish voice.

It stung her with a quick deep pain and her big heart was filled to bursting but she fought the feeling down. "Well," she said with a lightness that surprised her, "when engaged in making a bed the possibility of having to occupy said couch should always be considered. You going to be at the party tonight?"

"Oh, for ... no! Not just plain vanilla no, but *hell* no!"

"I'd like you to be. It will be a diversion and you'll meet some odd characters."

Ike considered. Anything was better than sitting alone in his bedroom all alone with his thoughts. "Oh ... maybe you're right. Shall I dress?"

"By all means. Remember that this is the house parliament for society in these parts, and I'm the Queen Empress."

Ike attended the party and tried to get drunk to escape females ranging in age from twenty to grandma, all seemingly intent on the same thing, but something had happened to his inebriative quotient. He continued to drink but seemed to achieve no success at getting drunk so he lost his temper and with a wink at Lula went up the stairs to bed. She followed after a decent interval and remained an indecent one considering where she went.

The next morning Dr. Fontenot called Missy on the phone. "What happened?"

"Nothing," she fumed. "He drank like a fish, stayed upright as a Billikin, got propositioned half a dozen times and I more than suspect he went off with Lula."

"I compliment his taste," said Dr. Fontenot raffishly.

"Nuts. We're just going to have to try something else. Getting him drunk and working on him that way will first have to wait till he gets drunk and it seems that he never does. Is Toni there?"

"Yes," he said cautiously, looking back quickly to see if anyone was listening.

"O.K., then, just hold on for a while. He's out on the verandah pacing up and down like a caged lion and it's ten to one it'll work tonight. I'll call you if it does."

"What happened last night?"

"I made him attend a party and he ran into some girl who needed attention, medical attention, I think it was. He's been obscure about it. I intended for him to get drunk and he didn't."

"Very well … do the best you can." Dr. Fontenot thoughtfully hung up the phone and returned to the living room where Jane and Toni were playing gin rummy. They quit as he came in and answered their questioning looks with a shrug. "Still no soap."

Toni bit her lip and her eyes filled with tears. "It's no use. After all, he certainly didn't come into this thing with the idea that he'd be snapped up into …."

"You stop that," barked the doctor, his eyes sparking. "You must stand by and give this thing a fair trial. If you don't fight for your man then you don't deserve him."

Another night passed and still no word from Missy. About ten o'clock in the morning Dr. Fontenot answered the phone. "Alcide, I give up," came her strident voice.

"Give up? Have you lost your mind?"

"I'm well on the way," she said wearily. "I can't even get him to talk anymore. He drinks but stays as sober as a judge. He paces the floor and has a vacant look in his eyes. He says he's not sure he's fit to marry anyone. I didn't mention anything. He offered that right out of a clear sky."

Dr. Fontenot's brow knitted in thought. "And what do you suppose he meant by that?"

"I'm sure I don't know but I do know I'm beat."

"Very well. I don't suppose there's anything ... ahh-h-h—"

"What?"

"I don't know yet but I just had a flash of inspiration. I'll call you when I get it straight in my mind."

The sun was two hours high and though it was shining bright the atmosphere had a definite chill. The grass had been touched with frost the night before, leaving the edges brown. Leaves cascaded from pecan and gum trees in a brown yellow flood, the breeze catching them and stringing them out over the meadow like an army in frantic retreat. Ike Blumendahl sat on the verandah gripping the arms of his chair. He had been doing this for some time and finally the ache of his forearms filtered through his chaotic mind and he relaxed. Instantly his thoughts lined up in some semblance of order and charged down on him with a shock that brought him upright and gasping in his chair. Point one ... you're losing Toni. His weak rebuttal that he hadn't wanted her anyway was stormed under in a twinkling. Point two ... what if she does become really suicidal and? ... that left his brow beaded with sweat. Point three ... why did you go into this thing if you're going to let it wind up on this note? I didn't know it was going to wind up on ... Didn't you, then why not? You're supposed to be clever and consider all the possibilities. You started off with a bang and now you've fouled up like a stumbling amateur. And while you're turning it over in your mind think this over: *Why are you sitting here in your own house battling yourself like a man sentenced to the death chair?* A sob of relief escaped him as he saw Dr. Fontenot's battered little coupe turn the last curve approaching the house. Ike bounded to his feet and went to meet the little man.

"Allah be praised ... am I glad to see you!"

Fontenot stepped slowly from his car, his face set and etched in lines of pain. "Maybe you won't be when you hear what I have to say."

Ike stopped dead in his tracks. The breath froze in his nostrils and a cruel icy hand clutched his throat. "What....."

"I had a call from Jeff a few minutes ago ... half an hour probably. Toni has disappeared and she left a note that Jeff couldn't read to me so it must have been terrible."

Ike swayed in his tracks and every moment in his association with Toni flashed before his eyes like a speed mad movie. "She ... they didn't find her around the house?"

"Not a sign."

Ike passed a trembling hand over his eyes. A groan of sheer agony forced its way through his pallid lips. "Not in the house. Not in the ...." His head came up in a flash. *"Not in the house.* He wheeled about and sprinted around the near corner of the house. Seconds later his big convertible roared around the other side of the house like a runaway train. It made the first turn by the verandah and skidded madly, throwing gravel thirty feet out across the lawn. He yelled something at the doctor who stood slump shouldered, the picture of grief and dejection where Ike had left him. All he could understand of the shouted sentence was "... the bluff ..." and Ike disappeared in a cloud of dust.

"If you weren't so blasted old," yelled Missy coming out on the porch, a drink in each hand, "the loss of Barrymore might be remedied. You can straighten up and come on in and toast your victory."

Grinning satanically the old man walked rapidly up the steps and accepted the highball from Missy. "You see," he said with amused spitefulness, "you couldn't quite bring it off without the delightfully delicate touch of the Great Fontenot. Oh, well, I shall be charitable. You did a fairly good job yourself."

Missy eyed him sourly. "Thank you, you gloating Franco-American bastard. Your charity astounds me."

When Ike skidded to a stop in front of the Fomalhaut plantation house he leaped from the car and shouted but not a sound could he hear in return. "All out hunting, I suppose," and broke for the edge of the bluff in a mad run. He reached it and stopped, his heart pounding his ears with audible blows. Wheeling he raced along the rim for several hundred yards traversing the whole distance back of the house. He came to a fence and clambering over ran until brush and vines began to impede his progress. He looked swiftly about. No one could have gone through this without leaving some signs and there appeared to be none. He turned about, raced back to the fence and clambered over. Back in the pasture he made better time and soon came to the woods. He dove headlong into the wooded area, carefully keeping to the rim of the bluff, ran as swiftly as he could, stopping momentarily to peer over the edge cringing, each time expecting to see the girl's body at the bottom. Then he stopped short. Why wouldn't this same thing have occurred to the other searchers?

Ike felt somewhat foolish so he slowed down but did not abandon his search. Then he saw her. She was standing out on a little promontory made by the roots of a hickory tree that had held on despite torrential rains and wind storms. She was leaning against the tree looking out at the river three miles away across the flats. A wave of relief passed over him and he felt like crying. His stomach lurched and for a moment he felt as though he would be ill. His hands trembled violently as he dashed the sweat away. He must not frighten her—he'd have to be very casual and matter of fact about .... She turned and saw him.

"Oh, Ike, you've come back!"

She rushed to him and he took her in his arms cursing her in a low voice vibrant with emotion and relief. "Goddammit, Toni, what do you mean scaring the hell out of people, running off this way ...."

She buried her face in the curve of his neck. "Nothing mattered, you don't love me ... Oh, Ike, why couldn't you have stayed away a few minutes longer ...."

He shoved her back and looked into her eyes. "All right, so I'm a heel. It took me a long time and something like this to make me see. I'm not a very good choice for a husband either."

"Why, Ike?" Her eyes were damp but humor lurked in their depths.

"Because I'm just a natural pushover for women. I don't have any backbone where a skirt is concerned."

"Is that supposed to set you apart?"

"No, that is, I suppose a lot.... No! I'm not hiding behind the masses of males who seem to be like me or I like them."

She kissed him and he immediately proved his weakness by promptly forgetting what he was talking about.

Realizing what her kiss had done, Toni pressed her advantage, kissing him again and holding him tightly. This time she felt the dam break and knew that he was hers when his arms tightened about her in a grip of steel. Their lips mingled in passionate longing and as they lost consciousness of all else besides themselves, they fell to the ground together, still holding to each other. The deaths that had come about at this spot had wrought great changes in many lives; but what was happening here now had greater and more earth-shaking consequences....

Hours later, Ike wordlessly lifted Toni to her feet and they started to walk. When they were nearly back to the house, Toni said, "Ike, you were saying about your weakness. I know about such things." She stood back from him and poised on her tiptoes, her arms held high showing even more of her smooth tan stomach than the Tahitian print playsuit did normally. The skirt was unbuttoned to her waist showing the elastic legs of the romper shorts beneath, and the delightful length of perfect leg from ankle to thigh. Her breasts, unconfined save for the thickness of the halter, jutted proudly, and Ike's senses swam giddily. "I think I can keep your mind off the rest of them," she said and made a face at him.

He caught her roughly in his arms. "Are you deliberately trying to run me crazy?"

She kissed him again and when she finally let him go he was breathless and not at all steady on his feet. He grasped her roughly by the arm. "Come on and let's do something legal about this before I attempt something illegal."

Missy Blumendahl, Jeff Salton and Dr. Fontenot sat in the big living room at Fomalhaut and watched the flames of the fire dancing up the chimney. The weather had turned suddenly too chilly for the verandah to be comfortable.

"Well, Alcide," said Missy in a surprisingly mild voice, "we dood it again."

The little man nodded, sipped his drink and fumbled for a cheroot. "God bless youth," he said fervently, "even if they do cause us oldsters to outdo ourselves once in a while. I was beginning to think that Ike would prove too tough for us."

"That was something of an inspiration you had Alcide," said Jeff laughing. "I'll never forget the look on the boy's face when he raced up to the house and called out. We were watching through the windows. For a moment I thought he had taken the wrong direction but he turned back. He came in so fast that Toni was almost caught in the house. She had just gotten to the woods when he jumped from the car."

The doctor puffed contentedly on his cheroot while Missy fitted a cigarette in her long holder.

"I think, Missy," he said, "that we'd better make a pact to operate jointly from now on. It appears that however we do it we eventually have to join forces."

She nodded somewhat suspiciously. "I make no commitments although the idea has its points. Whatever gave you the idea that Ike'd think about the bluff?"

Fontenot shrugged. "Ike's young but he's smart as hell. When I said she was nowhere around the house then I knew he'd think about the bluff. He thinks she was considering the leap the first day he met her."

Geraldine came in and replenished drinks around. She moved silently and obsequiously and left when she had accomplished the task.

Missy glanced at Jeff as did Dr. Fontenot, then they glanced at each other and back to Jeff who by this time was a healthy tomato red. A storm of laughter arose and Jeff said, "That's right, go ahead and laugh but I can always point to the shoves I got from you." He lit his pipe and puffed out a cloud of fragrant smoke. "And by the way … thanks a lot."

Dr. Fontenot waved a hand and wiped his eyes. "Nothing but the best for a friend," he said. "By the way, Missy, the McKammon girl came back yesterday."

"McKammon … who's she?"

"The girl Ike sent to Albert. She had an operation in New Orleans and it looks like a cure."

Missy nodded her head. "I'm glad," she said softly. "Now, if he could work the same thing on Feathers?"

"Bull would be glad," put in Jeff. "She hasn't bothered him any since she almost got him lynched but he's afraid she'll break loose again."

Missy sighed comfortably. "Looks like we're sort of gathering a nucleus, Alcide, from which to operate. You, me, Albert, Ike. Let's say we're the brains … no reflections, Jeff." Jeff nodded and smiled.

"Then, let's say that we can count on Jeff, Toni, Allen Gordon, and Bonnie. Hank and Honey if they're not too taken up with their twins will be a good pair to help. Oh, yes, I think this gathering could whip almost anything we cared to."

"Please count on me in anything this side of murder to help any unfortunate person you run on, Missy," said Jeff earnestly. "If it hadn't been for you and Alcide I shudder to think what would have happened to us. As it is …."

"This is undoubtedly the most delicious food I have ever tasted," said Toni.

"For which the Ming House is justly famed," mumbled Ike through a mouthful of fried rice and candied oxtail. "We are on the first leg of a trip which I confidently predict will draw gasps from you of all sorts. Here you gasp with delight as you will in Tutuila, Samoa when you eat pig, fish, and chicken that have slowly been steamed in the earth for eight hours with yams, onions and red pepper. The pineapples are big as nail kegs and the bananas—you've never tasted anything like 'em. Papayas as big as street lights for breakfast and mangoes that taste like peaches that grew on cedar trees. You'll see!"

Toni's eyes shone. "And all free?"

Ike frowned. "Chief Leato, Vaa's, Fui, Tui and Masoliga would die of mortification if they heard you ask such a thing. We'll be guests. Of course we'll go armed with wrist watches and such things but that'll be gifts from us to them. Tapa cloth, shell beads, tava bowls and all that good chow will be their gifts to us."

Ike merely raised his eyes to a waiter and in a flash the man was at the table as silently as a shadow. "More tea, please." The waiter bowed soundlessly and departed to return with a steaming pot of fragrant tea. "You may tell the management," said Ike, his eyes twinkling, "that as an old chopsticks fencer I boldly announce this to be the best Chinese food in the country."

The man smiled, showing twin rows of ivory white teeth. "I will tell him, sir, thank you."

"And now, squirrel," he said as Toni drained the last of her tea. "What say we dissect a Persian rug at the Top o' the Mark or some such plush hostelry."

She smiled, her eyes caressing him gently. "Lead on, globe trotter, and start me on my first tottering steps. Do we still board the clipper in the morn?"

"We do unless my lovely wife desires otherwise. The Matsonia, the Lurline, the Clipper or shall we purchase a yacht and take our time?"

"Let's do it the Clipper way first. Then next time we can go leisurely."

Ike leaned over and kissed her.

She blushed. "Not here, Ike."

He grinned. "Look about you." She did and she found the impassive faces of the waiters gazing fixedly at distant objects or nothing at all. The other diners were intent on their food.

"See? Wonderful people the Chinese."

Hilda Capricorn Fallon sat in a plain straight chair by a flickering fire. Bull sprawled in another chair near her and gazed into the dancing flames. Hilda flinched slightly and unbuttoned her dress. Her stomach bulged in a sizable arc and the skin over it was as smooth as peach down. The flickering rays of the fire played on its amber perfection and Bull laid a rough hand gently on its surface. His eyes opened wide as he put gentle pressure on her. "Well… cuss mah cats… feel dat li'l sap sucker kickin'?" Hilda smiled and put her hand on top of his. "He's been doing that for a couple of days now."

Bull shook his head in amazement. "Whut you kno 'bout dat. Sho it gittin active quick like."

"They all do that, Bull."

"Sho, I know dey does but I bet you ain't never hear tell o' one rampin' 'round dis early."

Hilda smiled and kissed him on an inky cheek. "It's kinda cool. Will you close the window?"

Bull rose to his feet and pulled the swinging window shut. He opened it again and peered into the darkness. "Thought sho I seed somepn." He shrugged and closed the window. "Musta been mah 'magination."

Outside there stood a great red horse with a shadowy rider. At his heels was a Belgian shepherd dog who watched the lighted square of the house with somber yellow eyes. On the horse's back the girl sat as still as carved stone. Her face was cut with lines of… who could tell? Calipers were around the mouth and the eyes had lines radiating out toward the hairline. The forehead was cut sharply, too, and one might say that the lines represented pain. She sat a while longer, motionless as the animals with her. Two tears started from her eyes and coursed down, finally running into the corners of her mouth. Her shoulders slumped and her head bent till she only had to raise her wrist a little ways to wipe the tears from her face. Then she silently turned the red horse and they slowly walked away from the house where the closed window only showed faintly lighted cracks. She shuddered against the chill of the night and a desperate loneliness which the closing of the window seemed to exemplify. Shut out. Shut out of the warmth of other lives. Shut out of the close comradeship of her fellow man. Her shoulders slumped ever lower and the girl, the horse, and the dog passed on down the hill to be swallowed up in the gloom of night.

THE END

www.ingramcontent.com/pod-product-compliance
Lightning Source LLC
Chambersburg PA
CBHW020421030726
47495CB00006B/1609